PIANO

Jean Echenoz

PIANO

*Translated from the French
by Mark Polizzotti*

THE HARVILL PRESS
LONDON

First published with the title *Au piano* by Les Éditions de Minuit, 2003

2 4 6 8 10 9 8 7 5 3 1

This book is supported by the French Ministry for Foreign Affairs,
as part of the Burgess programme headed for the French Embassy
in London by the Institut Français du Royaume-Uni.

Liberté • Égalité • Fraternité
RÉPUBLIQUE FRANÇAISE

Published by The Harvill Press 2004

First published in Great Britain in 2004 by
The Harvill Press
Random House, 20 Vauxhall Bridge Road,
London SW1V 2SA

Random House Australia (Pty) Limited
20 Alfred Street, Milsons Point, Sydney,
New South Wales 2061, Australia

Random House New Zealand Limited
18 Poland Road, Glenfield,
Auckland 10, New Zealand

Random House South Africa (Pty) Limited
Endulini, 5A Jubilee Road, Parktown 2193, South Africa

The Random House Group Limited Reg. No. 954009
www.randomhouse.co.uk/harvill

A CIP catalogue record for this book
is available from the British Library

ISBN 1843431807

Papers used by Random House are natural, recyclable products made from
wood grown in sustainable forests; the manufacturing processes conform
to the environmental regulations of the country of origin

Printed and bound in Great Britain by
William Clowes Ltd, Beccles, Suffolk

I

ONE

TWO MEN APPEAR at the end of Boulevard de Courcelles, coming from the direction of Rue de Rome.

One, slightly taller than average, says nothing. Under a large, light-coloured raincoat buttoned to the neck, he is wearing a black suit with a black bow tie. Small cufflinks set in onyx-quartz punctuate his immaculate wrists. He is, in short, very well dressed, though his pallid face and gaping eyes suggest a worried frame of mind. His white hair is brushed back. He is afraid. He is going to die a violent death in twenty-two days' time but—as he is yet unaware of this—that is not what he is afraid of.

The man accompanying him is the complete opposite in appearance: younger, considerably shorter, small, garrulous, and smiling too much; wearing a small brown-and-tan checked hat, a pair of trousers faded in patches, and a formless sweater with nothing underneath. His feet are clad in moccasins marbled with damp spots.

"Nice hat," the well-dressed man finally observes as they are about to reach the gates of Parc Monceau. These are the first words he has spoken in an hour.

"Really?" worries the other. "It's useful, in any case, that's a fact, but aesthetically speaking I'm not quite sure what to make of it. It's salvage, you understand. I wouldn't have bought it myself."

"No, no," the elegant one protests. "It's nice."

"My stepson found it on the train," the other replies. "Someone must have forgotten it. But it was too small for him, you see, my stepson has an extremely large skull, not to mention an enormous IQ. But it's just my size, which doesn't mean that I'm not any more foolish—I mean, that I'm any more foolish—than the next man. How about a walk in the park?"

On either side of the rotunda where the park's watchmen were on guard, the monumental gilded cast-iron portals stood open. The two men passed through them and entered the park and, for a moment, the younger one seemed to hesitate as to which direction to take. He masked his hesitation by talking nonstop, as if his sole reason for being there was to distract his companion, to try to make him forget his fear. And this was indeed his role. But although he performed it conscientiously, he didn't always seem to enjoy complete success. Before arriving at the park, he had explored various topics of a political, cultural, or sexual nature, without his monologue triggering the slightest exchange, without any of it blossoming into conversation. From the park entrance, he cast a distrustful gaze all around, from the

Virginia tulips to the Japanese loquat trees: waterfall, rocks, lawns. The other man seemed to look at nothing but his own internal terror.

The other man, whose name was Max Delmarc, was some fifty years of age. Although his income was quite respectable, and although he was famous in the eyes of a good million or so people and had for the past twenty years undergone all sorts of psychological and chemical treatments, he was, as we said, dying of fright. When the feeling enveloped him to this extent, he would normally fall completely silent. But now here he was, opening his mouth.

"I'm thirsty, Bernie," said Max. "I feel a bit thirsty. Supposing we stop by your place?"

Bernie looked at him gravely. "I think it would be better if we didn't, Monsieur Max," he said. "Monsieur Parisy wouldn't be very happy. And you remember what happened last time."

"Come on," Max insisted, "you're two minutes away from here. Just one little drink."

"No," Bernie said, "no, but I can call Monsieur Parisy if you like. We can ask him."

"Fine," Max surrendered. "Forget it."

Then, noticing a kiosk to the left selling waffles, cold drinks, and skipping ropes, he walked briskly in its direction. Bernie, having followed, passed, and preceded him towards the menu displayed near the cash register, quickly glanced over the list before Max could catch up—no alcohol, all's well.

"Would you like some coffee, Monsieur Max?"

"No," answered Max, disappointed by his own perusal of the menu, "that's O.K."

They started walking again. They passed in front of the bust of Guy de Maupassant hovering over a girl, then, on the other side of the lawn, a statue of Ambroise Thomas accompanied by another girl and, farther to the east, Edouard Pailleron towering above still another girl in a fainting fit. In this park, apparently, the statues of great men feared being alone, for each of them had a young woman at his feet. And better still, just after the waterfall, no fewer than three female companions—one of whom had lost both her arms—surrounded Charles Gounod. But Bernie preferred that they avoid passing the composer's memorial. Worse than that, from farther away he spotted, close by the children's play area, the monument to Frédéric Chopin: good God almighty, Bernie said to himself, Chopin. Especially not Chopin. He changed course abruptly, forcing Max to make an about-turn and diverting his attention by praising the variety, abundance, and polychromy of the flora, pointing out the great age of the sycamore maple and the substantial circumference of the Oriental plane tree.

"Look, just look at them, Monsieur Max, look how beautiful it is," his voice filled with emotion. "The world is beautiful. The world is beautiful, don't you think so?" Neither slowing his step nor answering the question, Max pretended to grant this world a look and lightly shrugged his shoulders. "All right," Bernie conceded sheepishly, "fine. But at least agree that it's very well lit."

After dragging Max through every corner of the park, other than the area around Chopin; after trying to make him admire the oval basin, the pyramid with its pyramidion; and after secretly glancing at his watch, Bernie inflected their path towards a park exit, taking Allée de la Comtesse de Ségur, along which sat Alfred de Musset. No problem with Musset, except that the right arm was also missing from the young creature who, leaning over him, rested her left hand on Alfred's left shoulder.

It was seven thirty-five p.m., a hesitant late spring, but the sun was still present. Their faces directed towards its imminent setting, heading west on Avenue Van Dyck, the two men left the park. Since his attempt to procure a drink, Max had not unclenched his teeth, while Bernie, playing his part diligently, did not stop talking or watching him. Max had not left his side except for two or three minutes, just long enough to discreetly go and vomit from fear behind a Hungarian oak. As he had already vomited twice that afternoon, all that came up was bile in a series of highly painful heaves. Now, outside the park, they walked up a service road of Avenue Hoche, taking the first turn on the right—at the corner of which stood a bar, where Max tried once more to entice Bernie in and Bernie silently refused—then a few more yards and there it was, number 252. They were here.

They went in. Stairways, hallways, passageways, doorways that they opened and shut until they reached a dark space littered with cables, pulleys, large open cases, and displaced furniture. In the air floated the noise of a swell or a crowd. It was now eight-thirty on the dot. Max had just removed his overcoat and suddenly, just when he least expected it, Bernie shoved him from behind through a curtain, the swell was immediately transformed into a tempest, and there it was—the piano.

There it was, the terrible Steinway with its wide white keyboard ready to devour you, those monstrous teeth that would chew you up with the full width of its ivories and all its enamel, waiting to mash you into a pulp. Almost stumbling from Bernie's push, Max just managed to keep his balance. Drowning in the torrent of applause from the packed auditorium that had stood to welcome him, he lurched, short of breath, towards the fifty-two teeth. He sat before them, the conductor brandished his baton, silence immediately fell, and they were off. I really can't take this any more. This is no kind of life. Although, let's face it, I could have been born in Manila and ended up selling loose cigarettes, or a shoe-shine boy in Bogotá, a diver in Decazeville. Might as well get on with it, then, since we're here. First movement, *maestoso*, of the Second Concerto in F-minor, Op. 21, by Frédéric Chopin.

TWO

FROM THE AUDIENCE, even from the front row, no-one can imagine how hard it is. It seems to happen all by itself.

And in fact, for Max, things do begin moving by themselves. Once the orchestra has embarked on the long overture, he starts to calm down. Then, on cue, as soon as he enters into the movement, everything seems better. His fears subside after a few bars, then fade away with the first wrong note—a good wrong note, in a rapid passage. The kind of mistake that passes by overlooked. At this point, Max becomes liberated. Now he has the situation in hand, he can stroll around, he is in his element. Every half-tone speaks to him, every pause is right, the series of chords touch down like dancing birds, he would like it never to stop, but already it's the end of the first movement. Pause. Everyone has his little cough while waiting for the next one to begin, you rake your throat, you expel the mucus from your polluted lungs, everyone clears his windpipe as best he can and then up starts the second movement, *larghetto:* slow, meditative, extremely exposed, no room for mistakes, and Max doesn't make any; it comes off as easy as pie. You cough some more, then it's the third, an elegant *allegro vivace*, just watch me hand you this one on a platter—ouch, a second false note at around bar 200. I always slip at the same place in the finale, but there again it's lost in the rush. They haven't noticed a thing. We're getting there, we're almost through, chromatic descent and rise, then four punctuations by the orchestra, two concluding chords, and there you go, it's in the bag, bravo, goodnight, bravo, curtain, bravo, no encores, end of story.

Tingling with fatigue but having forgotten all about his stage fright, Max went up to his dressing room, which was flooded in bouquets. "What is it with all these flowers?" he groused. "You know damn well I can't deal with them, chuck them out for me."

"Right away," said Bernie, who gathered up the offending bouquets *presto agitato* and slipped out, loaded down like a hearse. Max fell on to a chair in front of an untidy console-table dominated by a mirror, in the depths of which, in shadow, Parisy was mopping his neck with a rolled-up ball of Kleenex.

"Ah," Max said without turning around, preparing to unbutton his shirt, "there you are."

"That was excellent," beamed the impresario.

"I know," said Max, "I thought so too. But I don't really feel like playing that thing again, I know it too well. And besides, the orchestra part's pretty weak when you get down to it, you can tell Chopin wasn't too good at that. Anyway, I'm rather fed up with orchestras in general." As he undid his top button, it jumped off his shirt and took refuge in the mess on the console-table.

"Anyway," Parisy said, approaching, "you don't have anything but recitals until summer. You know—Berlin."

Still not turning around, searching for the fugitive button, Max watched the mirror amplify Parisy's massive and balding silhouette, the physique of retractive Turkish delight with thick glasses, check-patterned suit, chronic perspiration, and voice of a light tenor. "Remind me what the programme is," said Max.

"O.K., so you've got Nantes at the end of the week," Parisy warbled. "You have the recital at Salle Gaveau on the nineteenth, then nothing until that business on TV. And then Japan called again, they want to know when you can get back to recording the complete Chausson, they need a date so they can book Cerumen."

"I need time," said Max. "I'm not ready."

"What I mean is, they need to know very soon," Parisy emphasised, "they have to plan their schedule."

"I need time," Max repeated. "I'm dying of thirst. Where's the kid?"

The kid had returned, minus the flowers. He was standing by the door, waiting for someone to give him something to do.

"I wouldn't mind a drink, Bernie," Max indicated, still without turning around, while finally snaring the errant button between two empty vases. Bernie opened a cabinet and pulled out a glass and a bottle. After clearing off a corner of the console-table, he set them on a tray in front of Max.

"I'll be back," said Bernie. "I'm going to Janine's to get some ice."

Without waiting for its arrival, Max filled his glass four-fifths full under the reticent eye of his manager, still framed close-up in the mirror. "Don't go on at me, Parisy, if you don't mind. We agreed that I'm allowed after a concert. Beforehand, fine, no problem, but afterwards I'm allowed."

"That's not really it," Parisy qualified, "it's just that you haven't left much room for the ice."

"Right you are," said Max, emptying half his glass in one gulp. "See? Now there's room."

Parisy shook his head, searching his pocket for a new Kleenex, and grimaced when he noticed it was the last. He crumpled the packet and tossed it towards a wastepaper-basket as Bernie re-emerged, carrying an insulated yellow-and-white ice bucket. "Thanks, Bernie, no, no, I don't need the tongs. On the contrary." Max plunged two ice cubes into his glass before running a third cube over his forehead, temples, and neck; then, continuing to address Parisy in the mirror: "Where would I be without Bernie?"

"Good, good," the impresario approved vaguely.

"While we're on the subject," Bernie timidly intervened.

"What?" said Parisy.

"Well, the thing is," said Bernie. "I'm afraid I'm forced to ask you, if it's possible, of course, for a small rise."

"Absolutely out of the question," Parisy said stiffly.

"It's just that I have expenses," Bernie elaborated. "For instance, I have a stepson who's very intelligent, I have to help finance his studies. He has a very high IQ, you see, I have to send him to the top schools, which means private lessons, which are very expensive."

"Crap," decreed Parisy.

"Moreover, keep in mind," stressed Bernie, "that my role is very delicate. I have to assist Monsieur Max in all kinds of situations, watch over his diet," (Max smiled at these words) "buck him up when he doesn't feel like playing. That all makes for a heavy responsibility. And besides," he impressed upon them, "pushing him on-stage every evening isn't always easy. Sometimes he fights back. Monsieur Max is an artist," Bernie concluded. "He owes himself to his public, and please understand that in a certain way all of this happens through me."

"You must be joking," said Parisy.

"Pardon me," Max broke in, "but I completely support the kid's request. He's indispensable to me and I won't take responsibility if I don't have him."

A soaked Parisy squeezed out his Kleenex, looked for another one before remembering that there weren't any, then used his sleeve to dry his forehead. "I'll have to think about it," he said. "We'll have to talk about it."

"Why don't we talk about it now?" asked Bernie.

"Absolutely," Max instigated, "why put it off?"

"Let's have a seat, then," sighed Parisy, pulling from his pocket a small rectangular object, like a mobile phone or electric razor.

"With pleasure," said Bernie as Max emptied his glass and stood up.

"Well," he said, "I'll let the two of you work it out."

When he left the dressing room, Parisy had just pushed a button located at the end of the rectangular object, which turned out to be a small, battery-operated portable fan, whose rattling click Max could hear all the way to the end of the hall.

THREE

WHEN MAX GOT HOME from Salle Pleyel, Alice displayed little reaction, which was not surprising given that she was already asleep. She and Max occupied two large floors in the eighteenth *arrondissement*, near Château-Rouge—large enough so that each of them could live and work there in complete independence, she upstairs and he downstairs, without seeing each other from one day's end to the next if they didn't want to.

Max closed the entrance door softly before going into his studio: a grand piano; a small desk; a very small fridge, the kind you find in hotel rooms; shelves full of musical scores; and a divan. That was where he spent most of his time, linked to the upper floor of the maisonette by an intercom, protected from the bustle of the street by two double-glazed windows. As everything was well insulated for sound, Max could make as much noise as he wanted without the danger of waking Alice and, once he had taken something to drink from the refrigerator, he lifted the fall board of the piano. Setting his glass on the instrument, he stared at the keyboard. It wouldn't have been a bad idea to revisit the evening's two blunders, to isolate those passages, study them, take them apart like little watches, two little mechanisms that you could then piece back together after identifying the damage, repairing the defective gear for next time. But then again, I've really had enough of this concerto. And besides, I'm tired.

So he might as well take a shower, then go back into the studio, pick up his glass, and carry it into the bedroom. Once in bed, Max nonetheless thought some more about his two wrong notes, at the beginning of the first movement and in the second third of the third. It wasn't serious; they weren't bad wrong notes. To muff a note, or even a chord, is inconsequential when it's buried in a huge cascade. In those cases it passes all by itself in the flood, and no-one notices. It would have been more troublesome to have erred on a passage in the second movement, which is less dense, more fragile and more naked; everyone might have heard it. But anyway, enough of that. Instead, think about Rose for a moment, as you do every night. And besides, you've had enough to drink as it is; nobody's forcing you to empty that glass. It's late, let's turn off the light. Good. O.K., now go to sleep. What, it's not working? O.K., fine, take the pill. With a glass of water. I said water. There.

The pill took effect after twenty minutes, and twenty more minutes later sleep became paradoxical: for a handful of seconds, an inconsequential dream agitated Max's brain while his eyes also fidgeted rapidly beneath his lids. Then he woke up earlier than he would have liked and tried to fall back asleep, but in vain: keeping his eyelids shut without managing to reach a true state of wakefulness, he was beset by absurd ideas, shaky reasonings, pointless lists, and endless calculations, with brief dips back into sleep, but all too brief.

Right, now get up, it's after ten. Come on now. Fine, all right, not just yet, but certainly no later than ten-thirty. Sure, go ahead, then, think about Rose all you want. Doubt it'll do you any good, but that's your business.

FOUR

THE STORY OF ROSE goes back to his days at the conservatory in Toulouse, something like thirty years ago. In her final year of cello classes and endowed with supernatural beauty, Rose owned a white Fiat that was a little too large for her. Every day she emerged from it at the same time in front of the same café where, always at the same terrace table, she spoke only with the same bearded and rather fierce-looking individual who (to cut to the chase) didn't appear to be her boyfriend. Every day she was more incredibly beautiful, even if one could perhaps object to a single detail, her nose, which was slightly too hooked. On the other hand, that only made her more attractive: it was the nose of an Egyptian empress, a Spanish aristocrat, or a bird of prey—in short, a real nose. For that entire year, Max had contrived to be seated every day at the same time and at the same café as she, but at another table, neither too far nor too near, from which he watched Rose without daring to speak to her—too good for me too good for me, what in God's name can they be talking about?

Only once had Max taken the plunge and sat at a table next to hers. She asked him for a light, which might be considered an advance, perhaps even an encouragement, but that's just it: it was such a predictable advance, so conventional an encouragement that it wasn't worthy of such a supernatural beauty. It was disrespectful even to have entertained such a hypothesis, forget all that forget all that. So Max handed her his lighter with a detached gesture, painstakingly indifferent, without the spark from the lighter igniting the least speck of powder, and that's where they left it. After that he continued to look at her as she looked elsewhere, without letting himself be too noticed by her, not taking his eyes off her but always with the utmost discretion. Or so he thought. Then, when summer came, Rose left town for the holidays and the cello behind for good. A vacant Max in abandoned Toulouse went to have a drink at the same outdoor café, also empty, where only a few patrons were to be found—mainly tourists, but also, what do you know, the fierce bearded fellow, with whom Max struck up a conversation.

It didn't take long for the talk to turn to Rose. Mouth agape, Max soon learned that it was about him that they had talked. It was Max himself they discussed, she going on about him nonstop, to the point where the bearded chap sometimes had to suggest she sing a different tune for a change. It turned out that Rose hadn't dared approach Max any more than Max Rose, the latter having only once ventured to ask him for a light. And worse still, according to this fellow, the only reason Rose frequented this café every day was that she hoped to see Max, believing that he was a regular there. At this news, Max remained frozen, in arrest, in apnoea, remembering only after a minute that man needs to breathe, to inhale some air, especially when he's overcome by an enormous desire to weep. But where is she now, he pleaded, how can I find her, is there an address where she can be reached? Well, no, the other answered, she's gone now, her studies are over and she moved to God knows where.

Since then, Max had spent a good part of his life expecting, hoping, waiting to run into her by chance. Not a day went by without his thinking about it for a few seconds, a few minutes, or more. Now this isn't entirely rational. After thirty years, Rose could have been living on the other side of the world, already having, according to his informant, some predisposition in that direction. Or perhaps she was even dead, having had, on that score, no less predisposition than the rest of us.

FIVE

UP AT TEN-THIRTY, Max discovered his half-full glass next to the bed, went to empty it in the sink, and then, standing naked in the kitchen, made some coffee.

He would wash up only at the end of the day, before going out to perform or see friends. For now he donned soft, practical, fairly ample garments, such as a sweatsuit or an old wrinkled beige linen shirt and canvas trousers that were no longer very white. Moreover, it seemed that, these days, all his buttons were dropping off one by one; his shirts had lived full lives and showed it. Two or three times a week lately, at the slightest excuse, whether through overly zealous washing or ironing by the cleaning woman or washing machine, muscle stretch, awkward movement, or spontaneous decay, a worn thread would give way, the button would leave its mooring and fall like a dead leaf, ripe fruit, or dry acorn, bouncing and rolling protractedly on the ground.

Then it's the same daily routine: after coffee, piano. The time

21

is long past since Max did exercises before getting down to business, scales and arpeggios serving only to loosen up his fingers before a concert, like limbering-up exercises to gently warm the muscles. He works directly on the pieces that he will soon have to perform, polishing up a few phrases of his own invention, ruses and technical manoeuvres adapted to such-and-such an obstacle, for three or four hours at a stretch. He sits at his keyboard in a feverish mix of excitement, discouragement, and anxiety, although after a while anxiety gains the upper hand. At first lodged in the pit of his plexus, it then invades the surrounding areas, mainly Max's stomach in an increasingly oppressive, convulsive, and pitiless way, until, mutating at around one-thirty from the psychic to the somatic, this anxiety metamorphoses into hunger.

In the kitchen, Max now searched through the refrigerator for viable solutions but, as Alice had done no shopping, nothing stood out with sufficient conviction to sate this hunger on its own. Which was so much the better, since eating at home alone isn't exactly a thrilling prospect; anxiety can then overtake hunger to the point of eliminating it, preventing you from eating, while the hunger, for its part, grows larger and larger—it's terrible. As usual, then, Max went out to eat in the neighbourhood, where the ethnic brew had fermented into a proliferation of African, Tunisian, Laotian, Lebanese, Indian, Portuguese, Balkan, and Chinese restaurants. There was also a decent Japanese that had just opened two blocks away. Japanese it is; Max slipped on a jacket and went out. He left his building, headed up the street, and there, reaching the corner, he ran into her. No, not Rose. Somebody else.

This somebody else, let's not mince words, was also a supernaturally beautiful woman. Not the same type as Rose, although, yes, perhaps there was something. Max had noticed her some time before, but he didn't know her, had never spoken to her, had never even exchanged a single glance or smile with her—although she apparently lived in Max's neighbourhood, maybe even on his street, perhaps only a few yards away. He had seen her off and on for years, who knows how many—maybe eight, ten, twelve years, or even more; he didn't remember when the first time was.

Always alone, she might be spotted twice in the same week, but months might also go by without Max seeing her once. She was a tall woman, touching and dark and gentle and tragic and profound and, once past these adjectives, which mainly applied to her smile and her eyes, Max would have had a devil of a time trying to describe her. But that smile, those eyes—tightly linked to each other, as if interdependent, and, to Max's great regret, never directed at him, being reserved for other privileged and unknown persons—were not the only attributes of hers that he found intriguing. There was also, in the midst of this lower-class, noisy, multi-coloured, and overall rather bleak and shabby neighbourhood, an extreme elegance in this woman's bearing—in her walk, her posture, her choice of clothing—that one could hardly imagine existing outside of the pretty, calm, rich neighbourhoods, and maybe not even then. Anachronistic wasn't the word; anatopic would be the word, but it doesn't exist yet, at least not to Max's knowledge. For him, this unattainable creature was a kind of variation on the Rose theme, a repetition of the same motif. Meeting her in person, Max also tried to meet her gaze, managed to do so for only a fraction of a second without glimpsing any particular sign of interest on her part and two hundred yards farther on was the Japanese. Sushi or sashimi?

Sashimi, for a change. Then he returned home and sat down again at the piano, having no further reason to be out. Two or three times he had to answer the phone, which seldom rang to begin with, and which, as Max almost never called anybody, now rang even less. At around six he heard Alice come in, but that was no reason to interrupt his practising: he would spend the rest of the afternoon refining a few nuances of two movements, "Presentiment" followed by "Death", of *Piano Sonata 1.X.1905* by Janáček, after which he'd go up to find Alice busy in the kitchen. "Hmm," he'd say, "fish." "Yes," Alice would reply, "why?" "No reason," Max would say, setting the table, "I like fish. Where do you keep the fish forks?" Then they'd eat together, more or less telling each other about their day, and then they'd spend a moment in front of the television which that evening was showing *Artists and Models*—a film already familiar to Max, who interrupted its progress shortly after Dean Martin had lathered sun lotion on Dorothy Malone's shoulders while singing "Innamorata" to her. Then, each in their own room, they went to bed.

SIX

WITH A WEEK gone by since the concert at Salle Pleyel, Max still had some fifteen days to live, and one early morning he was speeding back to Paris in a TGV from Nantes where, the evening before, he had appeared on-stage at the Opéra Graslin with an all-Fauré programme. As usual, the terror of this recital had barely had time to fade from Max's body and mind when, at the prospect of performing again tonight at Salle Gaveau, a new panic had already taken hold of him. In an attempt to dilute it, to give himself something to do, Max left his seat and headed for the bar, unbalanced by the train's motion, grabbing headrests from behind.

He did not have to go very far to reach the bar, which at this hour was nearly empty. From here you could watch the country-side in peace, even though thick horizontal shafts across the middles of the windows, incomprehensibly placed just at eye-level, forced you to bend down or crane up on tiptoe to enjoy said countryside, which wasn't very interesting to begin with. Having ordered a beer, Max reached into his pocket and pulled out a phone, on which he called a number.

"Hello," Parisy answered almost immediately, "how can I help you? Oh, it's you. So how did it go in Nantes?"

"Oh, not bad," Max replied, "but the hotel was a disgrace."

"Oh, right," said Parisy, his mind elsewhere, "I see."

"Listen, what were you thinking," Max asked, "getting me a room for the handicapped?"

Indeed: special bed and raised toilets, support bars attached to every wall, open-work seat in the bath, window with northern exposure overlooking a section of car park that (as symbols on the ground indicated) was also reserved for the disabled. The clinical-looking accommodation had nothing about it to brighten the mood of a man alone, especially of an artist alone, and more particularly of a terrified artist alone.

"I know," said Parisy, "I know, but there really wasn't anything else available. There must have been some kind of convention or something going on in Nantes, all the hotels were full."

"I understand," said Max, "but still."

"You know," Parisy went on, "that kind of room isn't all bad. It's much larger than the other kind, for instance. And did you notice, the doors are wider."

"Why wider?" asked Max.

"Because," Parisy explained, "they need to be big enough to fit two wheelchairs."

"Why two?" Max asked, surprised.

"Even the handicapped are entitled to love," pronounced Parisy.

"I understand," Max repeated, "but, well, really, there wasn't even a minibar."

"The handicapped are sober," Parisy remarked coldly.

"All right, fine," said Max, "whatever. Talk to you later."

And then, having downed his beer, he bought three little bottles of alcohol that he stuffed into his right pocket before returning to his seat.

In First Class, Smoking Section, Max had a group of four facing seats all to himself. One good thing about the TGV, at the time, was that in Car 13, First Class Smoking was next to the bar, which tended to make matters simpler. Coming from the Non-Smoking section, a man walked up to ask if one of the seats was free, adding that he wouldn't stay long, just long enough for one or two cigarettes. "Please," said Max with a gesture of hospitality, as if he were at home. While thanking him and producing cigarettes and a lighter, the man gave Max a slightly prolonged glance, making the latter wonder if the former had recognised him. After all, since his face sometimes appeared in newspapers and specialised magazines, on posters and record covers, it happened occasionally that people came up to talk to him—oddly enough, more often on public transport than anywhere else. It was never unpleasant, of course, even if sometimes embarrassing, but on this particular morning, in this particular train, Max, who was finding the time hanging heavy on his hands, wouldn't have minded a little conversation. But no: having incinerated his Marlboro, the other man suddenly went to sleep right there in front of him, mouth hanging open, and Max could clearly discern a dark filling in the upper right of his jaw. Oh well, so it goes, isn't that always the way. When you know you're a little famous, you're always a little more or a little less famous than you think, depending on the situation. So what shall I do with myself? Shrugging figurative shoulders, Max dug into his pocket for the first of the miniature liquor bottles.

Upon the train's arrival, well before it had come to a stop, the passengers stood up from their seats, retrieved their bags, and crowded around the doors. All except Max, who climbed down slowly from the carriage after everyone else. Bernie, who was waiting for him on Platform 8 at Montparnasse station, could see right away that all was not well. He rushed up and took Max's arm, labouring to stick to the straightest possible course towards the station exit while talking incessantly, informing the pianist that the reviews of the last Pleyel concert had been uniformly laudatory (anyway, that's what I heard, I never read the papers), that Gaveau would surely be packed tonight, that the States had called asking about a month-long tour, that the honorarium offered by the Fougères festival was scandalously unacceptable according to Parisy, and that, the complete Chausson being very much in demand, Japan was pressing them to know what date they should reserve for the Cerumen studios (couldn't they find something more inviting, as names go?), as well as a host of other things.

On the escalators, all this only provoked in Max knowing little snickers, which, in conjunction with the smell of his breath, made Bernie supremely nervous.

"By the way," said Max, "how did it go the other night with Parisy? You know, your rise."

"Well, actually, not badly," answered Bernie, "but it'll depend a bit on you."

"Never fear," said Max, tripping over a step, "it'll be fine. And if it's not fine, we'll get rid of him. You can always change managers. We make a good team, you and I, and Parisy is an idiot."

"Now really," Bernie objected.

"Shut up," Max ordered. "He doesn't know the first thing about music. He has the artistic sense of a yogurt. On top of which," he persisted, missing another step, "he's completely tone-deaf."

"Now really," Bernie repeated, gripping Max's elbow more firmly.

"He is, he is," Max developed. "He's so deaf that his ears are only good for holding up his glasses. And besides, he doesn't understand a thing about my project. But then again," he generalised, "no-one understands my project. Not even me."

As it was now twelve-something, after dropping Max off in front of his building in a taxi, Bernie walked down Boulevard

Barbès in search of a restaurant. He found one, ordered the daily special, and went downstairs where the telephone and toilets languished as usual. He used the latter, then picked up the former and dialled Parisy's number.

"So?" worried Parisy. "How is he?"

"Not too good," said Bernie. "I get the feeling he isn't too good."

"What!" exclaimed Parisy, "is he pissed again? This early already?"

"He's tired," Bernie allowed. "He looks really tired to me."

"Listen, Bernard," Parisy said sharply, "that's your problem, understood? It's your responsibility. You remember what we agreed the other day? I don't have to tell you that if the concert suffers for it, the deal's off. Go and do your duty now."

After Max had lunched at home at Château-Rouge, where Alice had left some cold chicken in the fridge, he dozed off a moment on the studio divan, was startled awake by the return of the fear that he tried to exorcise with a drink, managing only to potentiate it. When Bernie reappeared at his door late that afternoon to escort him to the concert as usual, Max looked even less sure of himself than he had at the station; Bernie had to guide him towards his shower before helping him get dressed. Then, at the corner of Rue Custine, he hailed a cab and they jumped in.

"Parc Monceau," Bernie announced.

"Parc Monceau again?" Max complained. "Why do you always take me there?"

"Parc Monceau is good," answered Bernie. "It's handy, it's pretty, it's easy to get to. It's near where I live. And anyway, it's all I could think of."

A dark grey sky hung over the boulevards filing past. The air was heavy with chilly gusts, little intermittent slaps that entered through the lowered windows of the taxi; Max was constantly opening and closing his raincoat. "Hey," he observed when the taxi pulled up in front of the gilded fence, "it's raining."

"Wait a minute before getting out," Bernie anticipated. "I'll cover you. And I'd like a receipt for that, please," he said to the driver before rushing around to the other side of the car, producing a telescopic umbrella. This he deployed above Max, who stumbled as he got out of the cab under the fine rain.

They again entered the park. Bernie had to contort himself somewhat to support Max by one arm while continuing to maintain, at the end of his other arm, the umbrella perfectly centred over Max's skull, as the latter protested, "Cover yourself, too, you're going to get soaked!"

"I've got my hat," Bernie reminded him.

"Listen," said Max, "suppose we go to your place instead and have a little drink, just one little beer, where it's nice and warm?"

"No, Monsieur Max," said Bernie in a firm voice.

"Listen," Max insisted, "you know the rain isn't good for my hands. It plays havoc with my fingers. I'm freezing, I feel my arthritis taking hold, I can feel it coming on. At this rate, I won't be able to play at all."

"Monsieur Max," Bernie moaned desperately.

Sensing his opponent falter, Max thrust a hand into a pocket of his raincoat, pulled out one of the miniatures bought on the TGV, and brandished it threateningly like a grenade. "Look at this," he said. "If this is what you're afraid of, I have some on me in any case. It can only warm me up. So here's the deal, it's very simple: either a beer at your place or I drink this right here. Would you prefer that?"

"This is not good," Bernie capitulated, "this is not good."

"*What's* not good?" Max persisted. "Where's the harm? And anyway, where'd you say your place was, exactly?"

"Rue Murillo," Bernie answered in a doleful voice, "just over that way."

"I know it well," said Max. "So hey," he snickered unpleasantly, "you live in a pretty fancy neighbourhood."

"It's tiny," Bernie protested limply. "It's on the top floor, just enough space for my stepson and me. It was in the family."

"Let's go," said Max.

A resigned Bernie followed more than led Max towards the park's south gate, still taking care, out of principle, to avoid the monument dedicated to Chopin—where the composer, sculpted in mid-action at his piano, continues hammering out some mazurka or other while the inevitable young woman seated beneath the instrument, her hair covered with a veil and her feet curiously huge, apparently quite enthralled, covers her eyes with one hand while in the grip of ecstacy—God, that's beautiful!—or exasperation—God, get me away from this creep!

Number 4 Rue Murillo is in fact quite a handsome building, but Bernie's lodgings consisted of three maids' quarters merged into one, overlooking the courtyard. Bernie ushered Max into the main area, which combined the functions of living room, kitchen, and dining room, and which also contained his bed. Through an open door, Max noticed some very state-of-the-art computer equipment in the room of the very intelligent stepson, who seemed to be absent. Bernie, as agreed, served Max a beer, into which, to his great consternation, the other emptied half the alcohol exhibited in the park. Then the little man attempted as usual to distract the pianist, to make him forget the approaching moment of the concert, seeking out arguments and ideas with all the more difficulty in that Max's intoxication worsened with each passing minute—although, to look on the bright side, it seemed to have dampened his stage fright.

At around seven-thirty, holding each other up as best they could, they slowly made their way down Avenue de Messine towards Salle Gaveau. And at eight o'clock sharp, after a fair number of efforts to keep Max on his feet, Bernie propelled him towards the piano using his habitual technique. What was not predictable was that the other man walked with a firm step towards the instrument, even though, in his vision clouded by imbibition, the keyboard was no longer its usual single maxillary but an authentic pair of jaws that this time was preparing, as sure as anything, to draw him in, chew him up, and spit him out. Now, as the entire room stood up to applaud him the moment he appeared on-stage, in an interminable Niagara of acclaim that was even livelier than last week, and as the ovation grew only more enthusiastic with no signs of abating, Max, who was no longer in full possession of his faculties, deduced that the concert was over. He therefore bowed deeply to the public several times and headed with a no less resolute step back towards the wings, under the horrified eyes of Parisy—but, without a second's hesitation, Bernie gripped Max by the shoulders, spun him around, and, with a hearty shove, vigorously sent him back on-stage and so off you go: sonata.

"Well done, Bernard," said Parisy. "That was good. That was really good."

"It's not always easy, you know," Bernie pointed out. "It can be quite a physical job, at times."

SEVEN

TWO HOURS LATER, sobered up by the trial of the concert, nerves
at rest but mind at zero, Max Delmarc was dozing on the back
seat of a taxi. When it then came to a halt, Max, opening his eyes,
recognised his building before noticing, in front of the door, a
very large and immobile dog staring fixedly in his direction. Once
the driver was paid, the dog continued to stare at Max as he got
out of the cab: it was a truly voluminous beast, of Newfound-
land or mastiff proportions, apparently peaceful and friendly,
which then left, pulled by a long leash whose taut line Max's eyes
followed in a tracking shot to arrive at a person of the female sex,
viewed from behind. Now even from behind, even from afar, even
under street lamps fifty percent of which were burnt out, Max
had no trouble recognising the extraordinarily beautiful woman
whom he occasionally ran into in the neighbourhood. Here she
was now, walking away, followed by her animal, towards Square
de la Villette, and at this time of night.

Max is really not the sort to accost strange women in the street, especially at this time of night. It's a matter of principle, of course, but not entirely: even if he wanted to, he would be incapable. Still, maybe as a delayed effect of all the alcohol consumed that day—no doubt, but perhaps not only—he was now starting to follow this woman with the firm intention of speaking to her. He had no idea what he would say, didn't really care, and wasn't even surprised that he didn't care—he'd find something at the last minute. Alas, coming up behind her, he was suddenly surprised to hear her talking to herself, until he noticed that she was conversing with a mobile phone. No chance of accosting her under these conditions, so he passed her with a quick step as if he had other intentions, without turning around or even knowing where he was going, forced to look like he was heading somewhere, improvising a target that would in fact be Square de la Villette three blocks away. Not many people at this hour in the small streets of the neighbourhood: the noise of his footsteps echoed too loudly, seemed to ricochet against the dark façades and, as it made his gait awkward, Max uneasily imagined himself seen from behind. Then, arriving at the square, he formulated a very simple plan: he would double back to cross paths with the woman and this time he'd speak to her. He still had no idea what he might say, but this, oddly enough, struck him as negligible.

Having reached the square, then, he retraced his steps and spotted her from a distance coming towards him, the dog walking in front of its mistress in hazy silhouette. As this silhouette became more precise, making it clear to Max that she was still talking into her little phone, he could only abstain once more from accosting her. Head lowered, staring at the tips of his shoes, he passed by her as quickly as possible and dashed off to take refuge at home—she must have noticed my little act, at worst I must look like a nutter, at best like an idiot, and in any case it's a disaster. He pushed open the main door of his building, registering that the lights were still on in Alice's rooms but not slowing his pace. Then, entering his studio, he tossed his raincoat carelessly on the divan, not lingering awhile as he usually did but heading directly into his bedroom, where he threw off his clothes in a rage and went to bed in a rage. But after a moment of immobility, he was hurriedly throwing them back on again, perhaps inside-out, recrossing the studio, and walking hastily out. She must be home by now, but you never know, still no idea what I might say but basically what do I have to lose? But wait, what do I see: there she is. She's there, the dog is there, they're there.

Max approached, determined. The dog again began staring at Max benignly, without emitting any growls or showing the slightest glimpse of fang, seeming as gentle as he was huge—can somebody please tell me what dogs like that are good for? She too watched Max approach, showing no surprise at all, and without the slightest trace of a frown or self-protective spray made from natural pepper extracts.

"Don't be afraid," Max stammered a little too fast, "I'll just take a second. The thing is, I've been seeing you around for a long time."

"That's true," she smiled. That's good, Max said to himself, she's noticed me, that's already something.

"And so," said Max, "the thing is, I just wanted to know who you are." Cheeky fellow.

"Well," she smiled, "I live at number 55, and as you see I'm walking my dog" (I'm at number 59, myself, Max calculated). "Normally it's my children" (ouch! Max said to himself) "who walk him, but tonight they're out." Silence and another smile. It was high time to wrap this up if he didn't want to look like a . . . Max, who emphatically did not want to look like a . . . , bowed slightly, smiling in turn as broadly as he could. "Well, then," he said, "I bid you an excellent night."

Crossing through the courtyard once more, Max again saw the light in Alice's window but he refrained from going in to say goodnight. And yet he often went to see her after a concert, to tell her how it had gone, how was your day, that kind of thing, but tonight, no, not possible. He wouldn't have been able to prevent himself telling her what had just happened. He had already made enough of an ass of himself as it was, and besides he was too agitated. So he paced for a while around his studio, naturally poured himself one last drink, lifted the fall board on his piano only to close it again, leafed through a newspaper without reading it, and ended up putting himself to bed: long thought for the woman with the dog, barely a tiny thought for Rose, my sleeping pill, and goodnight.

EIGHT

OVER THE FOLLOWING DAYS, Max met the woman with the dog at an unusual rhythm, much more sustained than over all the past years. After their brief encounter a few nights before, they now had to greet each other, and even smile at each other since their rapid exchange had transpired in perfect civility. These smiles, however, proved to be of variable amplitudes and models. One evening when he saw her looking more elegant than usual (to be that elegant, she must have been going to some social event, and who knows with whom—you might even wonder if Max was starting to get a bit jealous, things can move so fast in this kind of situation), she gave him an amused smile, almost collusive, or merely indulgent, that seemed to prolong itself even after she had turned her back on him—which had the effect of making Max feel ridiculous, then flattered, then ridiculous at feeling flattered.

Another time, late in the morning, he observed her coming from the other end of the street, dressed in a jogging suit—a jogging suit from Hermès, of course, but a jogging suit all the same—and dragging a shopping trolley behind her—shopping trolley from Conran, granted, but a shopping trolley nonetheless. That morning she was less made-up than usual, her hair less managed, less victorious and arched; she must simply have been coming back from doing the shopping and not have appreciated overmuch being spotted like this, because her smile, this time minuscule, struck Max as noticeably cooler. On yet another day, he saw her in front of number 55 trying to park her car in the rain—a small black Audi, Max noted—in a space that was somewhat tight for the vehicle's dimensions. Twisted all the way around in her seat toward the Audi's rear window, apparently absorbed by her task, she flashed Max a smile that this time had a more complicit nuance, given the difficulty of the undertaking— one of those smiles that make you gently raise your eyes heavenward, that take you aside as witness to life's little challenges, especially since on top of it all it's raining and since this movement of the lips is further softened by the mist and mobile reflections of the streaming windows. Max, who didn't own a car, who hadn't known until then that this woman had one, immediately committed her number plate to memory. In each of these instances the dog was nowhere to be seen and, on each of these occasions, Max made a point of showing himself as discreet as possible, responding to those smiles with a courteous reserve, or a half-tone just below, in short behaving like a perfect gentleman. Still not wanting to risk looking like a . . .

The day of that complicit smile, Max was expecting a visit from Parisy. It was the first time the impresario came to his home, anxious to verify the performer's good spirits before the taping of a televised concert. Prestigious orchestra, exceptional soloists, live broadcast conditions in a studio at Radio-France, and audience by invitation only, but the show would be pre-recorded, then screened late in the evening on the cultural channel. Although Parisy, dressed that day in a dark suit meant to absorb and conceal sweat, came on the pretext of having a last look at the scores, of fine-tuning a few technical details, he mainly wanted to reassure himself that Max, nervous as always during the past few days at the prospect, was not going to misbehave beyond reason while awaiting the concert hour. Normally the impresario delegated this surveillance work, but this time the stakes were too high to be supervised by Bernie alone. Max nonetheless seemed rather distracted, mixing up the figures embossed on the Audi's number plate and the bars on his score.

"Aren't you thirsty?" said Max. "Don't you want something to drink?"

"Listen," Parisy began, "let me just say straight away that I'd rather you—"

"Never fear," Max interrupted, "no alcohol today, don't worry. I'm not even sure what's the matter with me, to tell you the truth. I don't even feel like any. Coffee?"

"Gladly," said the other.

Via the intercom, Max asked Alice to make some coffee,

inviting her to join them. Then, closing the score, he dropped on to the divan with a yawn.

"Everything O.K.?" worried Parisy. "Not too nervous?"

"Oddly enough, no," said Max. "TV doesn't affect me the way concert halls do."

"And anyway, it's not live," Parisy reminded him. "You have nothing to worry about. If need be, they can always retake a passage if something goes wrong."

"Yeah, yeah," said Max, standing up to go and cast a few sullen glances out of the studio window. Under the combined effects of the rain and wind, there was nothing and nobody to see in the street, except that they were still offering the usual twenty-five percent off the linoleum rolls lined up on the pavement, the green neon of the pharmacy cross was blinking as always, and at the second-hand clothes shop next door everything was still ten francs an item. Whereupon Alice appeared, carrying a tray.

Nearly as tall, even thinner, and two years younger than Max, hair as white as his, slightly awkward, barely made-up, adorned only with a thin gold chain around her neck, Alice was wearing a very lightweight, light-coloured grey ensemble, very loose-fitting and very neutralising. Having set the tray on a chair near the divan, she walked smiling up to Parisy, who rose sharply from his seat to bow stiffly before straightening up again. Looking at her gravely, he seemed impressed to the point of starting to stutter and sweating outrageously the moment she addressed him. Max looked on in surprise at his manager, not used to seeing Alice produce such an effect on a man, but amused to see this one so off-balance. Parisy, so as to regain his bearing, forced himself to make a little joke, and Alice immediately burst out laughing. As with some not-very-pretty women, it didn't take much to provoke her hilarity, and so she laughed a bit too often even though her laughter sounded raucous, like a cry of rage or suffering, as if laughing were painful, as if she were trying to expectorate something with great difficulty.

Parisy, however, did not seem to be shocked by this laugh as much as was Max, who normally had such a hard time coping with it that he carefully refrained from saying anything even remotely funny in her presence—except that something that wasn't funny at all could still make her burst out laughing, provoking a chain effect of further laughter, in ricochet, increasingly inextinguishable and frenetic the more one tried, more and more sternly, to check the process. Max, in any case, decided to clarify the situation.

"Well then," he said, "let me introduce my sister. I don't believe you two know each other."

NINE

YOU, ON THE OTHER HAND, I know perfectly well; I know exactly what you're thinking. You were imagining that Max was yet another ladies' man, one of those classic schemers, charming and all that, but a touch tiresome. First Alice, then Rose, and now the woman with the dog: these episodes led you to assume the profile of a man drowning in amorous intrigues. You found this profile rather conventional, and you wouldn't be wrong. But that's not it at all. The proof is that, of the three women who up until now have figured in the life of this artist, one is his sister, the other a memory, the third an apparition, and that's it. There aren't any others, you were wrong to worry; so let's get back to it.

They'd had their coffee, during which time Parisy hadn't taken his eyes off Alice until she'd left the room. Then he'd pointed out that it was getting late and it was time to get a move on and that his car was parked on Rue de Clignancourt, so Max went off to don his pianist's uniform. And there again, even though he proceeded without nervousness, and even with unusual calm, two more buttons chose to desert his garment, one rolling off to hide under a chest of drawers, the other going underground in a crack in the floor. It must have been a season in the life cycle of Max's outfits, some autumn of his wardrobe. But for the moment, they were too rushed to indulge in long searches. Alice, summoned back, indicated she wouldn't have time to intervene, and Max had to swap his dress shirt for a more ordinary model. It was annoying but he'd make do, and they left in haste in Parisy's Volvo towards the sixteenth *arrondissement*, which if you leave from Château-Rouge is almost at the opposite end of Paris, the intramural equivalent of New Zealand.

"Rotten weather," muttered Parisy. "We'll try to avoid the centre of town."

The rain, in fact, having continued to fall, certainly would not fail to produce its usual coagulation of obstructions. To avoid losing time by crossing through a congested Paris, they agreed to take the outer roads. They first followed rectilinear Rue de Clignancourt, then took a right on to Rue Championnet to get to Rue des Poissonniers, before reaching the outer boulevards named after marshals, whose pavements were sporadically populated with very young women of Nigerian, Lithuanian, Ghanaian, Moldavian, Senegalese, Slovakian, Albanian, or Ivorian nationality. Skimpily clad beneath their umbrellas, they were more or less constantly observed by four categories of men: first the Bulgarian or Turkish procurers scattered about the vicinity, snug and warm in their high-octane sedans, having made the standard recom-mendations (At least thirty tricks a day; fewer than twenty-five and we break your leg); secondly the customers for whose benefit, day and night, they declaimed in every tone the same perfect alexandrine, classically balanced with caesura at the hemistich (It's fifteen for a blow and thirty for the works); thirdly the forces of law and order that, for their part, emerged especially at night, though not too aggressively (Hello hello, it's the police, do you have ID papers? Nothing? You sure? Not even a photocopy?); not to mention, fourthly, the television crews making sure that, when the nth report on the subject was broadcast after prime time, in accordance with the law on the protection of privacy, the faces of these working girls appeared duly pixelated on the screen. These young women, these young girls, who often were not even eighteen, began to thin out after Boulevard Suchet, then were completely gone by Rue de Boulainvilliers, along which Parisy's car glided up to the Maison de la Radio.

Recording was supposed to start at six, but they'd need a little time to get used to the studio, negotiate with the lighting techni-cians and sound engineers, and go over two or three details with the orchestra one last time, even though everything had been set-tled after several weeks of rehearsals. Then they'd move on to make-up, filing before the mirrors in groups of three, in the hands of specialists who were often quite pretty and who han-dled matters with attentive indifference. In any case, they were only putting make-up on the soloists and the conductor; the bulk of the troupe would remain in its natural state, with just a little touch of powder for the melancholics and the sanguines. Although only a minimal space was needed to contain the orchestra, the studio was still much more cramped than it would appear on-screen, but it's always the same story with television: space, screen, ideas, projects, everything is smaller there than in the normal world.

After disembodied voices had given the countdown, the concert could begin. The conductor was fairly exasperating, full of mannered grimaces, unctuous and enveloping motions, coded little signs addressed to different categories of performers, fingers on his lips and inopportune thrusts of his hips. Following his lead, the instrumentalists themselves began to act like smart alecks: taking advantage of a frill in the score that allowed him to shine a little, to stand out from the masses for the space of a few bars, an oboist demonstrated extreme concentration, even overplaying it to win the right to a close-up. Thanks to several highlighted phrases allocated to them, two English horns also did their little number a moment later. And Max, who had very quickly lost the scrap of stage fright that had come over him that day and was even starting to feel bored, himself began to make pianist faces in turn, looking preoccupied, pulling his head deep into his shoulders or excessively arching his back, depending on the tempo; smiling at the instrument, the work, the very essence of music, himself—you have to keep interested somehow.

Then, once it was all wrapped up, it was time to go home.

47

Taking advantage of the fact that for once he might look good, Max opted not to have his make-up removed. When Parisy apologised for not being able to drive him back, he set off on foot. The rain had abated and he crossed the Seine over the Pont de Grenelle up to the Allée des Cygnes, a fragment of the river's spine lined with benches and trees that he followed up to the Pont de Bir-Hakeim, via which he reached the Passy *métro*. His plan was to take Line 6 of the urban network, change at Place de l'Étoile, and, from there, head back to Barbès. The elevated Passy stop is very pretty, very airy and chic, overhung by tall buildings as distinguished as flagships, so handsome that they look un-occupied and strictly decorative. Max waited calmly for the train to appear.

Once it arrived, as it was emptying itself and being filled by several passengers, another train pulled in from the opposite direction, heading towards Place de la Nation; it stopped, emptied out and filled up like the others. And once Max was aboard, standing against a windowed door, who did he see, or at least think he saw in the facing train at just the same level as his, which was about to leave? Rose, of course.

Rose, dressed in a dark grey suit beneath a pale-beige, much-pleated raincoat, apparently lightweight, cut from what must be called soft poplin and belted at the waist. The garment wasn't familiar to Max, naturally, but that aside, she didn't seem to have changed much in thirty years.

TEN

EMERGENCY. Although the warning signal had just sounded, Max rushed perilously out of the carriage: he jumped off in profile, Egyptian-style, to avoid the doors that briefly slammed into his shoulders and had closed before he landed on the platform. From there, he tried again to make out Rose through the superimposed windows of the two trains, one of which, his, was now rolling towards Étoile. It left the other one more visible for an instant, before the latter started off towards Nation two seconds later, and without Max being able to verify that it did in fact contain Rose. He wasn't completely certain it was her but, for the space of an instant, the resemblance had struck him as indisputable; a resemblance wearing a raincoat in which Max, while he had never seen it before, recognised what he believed he'd surmised of Rose's sartorial tastes, thirty years earlier.

Nothing is certain, but you never know. Max started to run down the platform towards the long transfer corridors, bounding up the stairways four steps at a time to reach the opposite plat-form, where he waited for the arrival of the next train. Which took a ridiculous amount of time. The whole enterprise was absurd. You don't follow a tube train. But then again, why not? While waiting, to make time go faster, he feverishly reread the *métro* regulations—making sure that the five categories of passengers who ride for free still included, albeit in last place, unaccompa-nied persons who have lost both hands. The train arrived, Max got on. Although this train abounded in unoccupied seats, Max remained standing, posting himself next to a door through the window of which he could inspect the platforms of the stations to come. Once they had left Passy via the Bir-Hakeim bridge, he had another opportunity to examine the Seine, after which, between the ensuing stations, he could once more ponder the city.

It's just that the Étoile–Nation line, which provides the link between the affluent and working-class neighbourhoods—although these adjectives, melding together to the point of leapfrogging over each other, of taking themselves for each other, are no longer what they used to be—runs above ground for the most part, enjoying as no other line the light of day, from which nearly one station in two benefits. It constantly emerges from the earth only to plunge back down again in a sinusoid, sea serpent or roller coaster, ghost train or coitus.

But already, the platform of Bir-Hakeim station, first stop after fording the river, bore no trace of the raincoat. Nor was there any glimpse of beige at Dupleix, a clear and well-lit station beneath a sky of double-sloping glass; and as they began to pick up speed beside the buildings, eye-level with kitchens and bathrooms, living rooms and bedrooms and hotel rooms, and as dusk began to fall and electric lights threatened to go on, Max began to see his enterprise as highly dubious. Although the building windows were most often masked by curtains, nets, or blinds, he caught fugitive glimpses of the scenes in the flats. Three men sitting around a table. A child illuminated by a desk lamp. A woman passing from one room to another. A cat, or maybe a dog, lying on a cushion. After not finding the slightest trace of Rose at La Motte-Picquet-Grenelle, Max's doubts about the viability of his project deepened further. He was almost at the point of giving up, but no, he persevered. Better that than doing nothing.

After a while, he accorded no more than a summary glance to the station platforms parading by. Instead, he inventoried what came between them, the individuals and objects decorating the balconies and terraces that he saw from the rushing train at a downward angle—laundry stretched on a line or a clothes horse, mopeds leaning against a lowered shutter, shopping trolleys, push-chairs, and broken down washing machines, soaked cardboard boxes, garden chairs, rugs, ladders, footstools, plants and flower boxes in which geraniums claimed the lion's share, old broken toys, plastic basins, washbowls, and pails with mop handles thrusting out at an angle. Not to mention, months after New Year's Day, the old Christmas trees of which only a rusty spine remained, nor the parabolic antennae all facing in the same

51

direction like vertical fields of sunflowers, nor the idle women in various states of dress, leaning on their elbows against railings and watching the elevated *métro* pass by, full of single men like Max, who stared back at them.

After Pasteur station, Max, who had lost all hope of finding Rose and ended up taking a folding seat, cast only an absent eye towards the platforms. As long as the *métro* remained elevated, he observed the landscape and, when it plunged underground, he pondered the two men on the seats opposite his, but in that regard there was nothing very attractive to see: one, with a suitcase at his feet, offered a view of the cut on his scalp; the other, with an expressionless face, was consulting a brochure entitled *How to Recover Your Alimony Payments.* Max opted to study his *métro* ticket.

As nothing special is happening in this scene, we might as well take the time to look more closely at this ticket. There's actually a lot that can be said about these tickets, about their secondary uses—toothpick, fingernail scraper, or paper cutter, guitar pick or plectrum, bookmark, crumb sweeper, conduit or straw for controlled substances, awning for a doll's house, micro-notebook, souvenir, or support for a phone number that you scribble for a girl in case of emergency—and their various fates—folded lengthwise in halves or quarters and liable to be slid under an engagement ring, signet ring, or wristwatch; folded in six or even eight in accordion fashion, ripped into confetti, peeled in a spiral like an apple, then tossed into the wastepaper-baskets of the *métro* system, on the floor of the system, between the tracks of the system, or even cast out of the system, in the gutter, the street, at home to play heads or tails: heads magnetic stripe, tails printed side—but perhaps this isn't the moment to go into all of that.

When the *métro* re-emerged from under the ground, Max might also have absorbed himself in the viaducts they were rumbling over, good old handsome viaducts, good solid iron architecture, intelligent and dignified, but no: as his plan of pursuit came un-done before his eyes, soon wilted like a poppy, here he was getting off the train at Nationale station. Then, as he had nothing left to do, he began to walk, without imagination, still following Line 6, but in the open air, crossing the savage, cursory, and poorly laid-out space that runs beneath those viaducts like a path. This space sometimes contains various pedlar's carts, flea markets, stalls, or impromptu basketball courts, but it's mainly a place for the rela-tively anarchic parking of cars: a cold narrow corridor, a no-man's-land beneath the prickly metal noise of the convoys, where no-one ever ventures without a vague sense of disquiet. And so Max walked, following this route up to the Seine, which he crossed in the opposite direction from before, then continuing up to Bel-Air where, exhausted, he waited for the next train.

ELEVEN

BEL-AIR is an elevated station isolated between two tunnels, an island that hangs over the depopulated Rue du Sahel like an oasis. Supported by two rows of five columns, awnings of painted wood shelter the platforms, extended by glass canopies. These platforms appear shorter than in other stations, and overall Bel-Air gives off an aura of humility. It calls to mind a small village station, poor cousin or disowned sister of George V.

We would have no reason to linger on this station, except that it was here, against all likelihood, that Max believed he again recognised Rose. This is how it happened: Max arrived on the empty platform, Nation-bound side, when a train pulled in from the opposite direction, towards Étoile—this train business never ends. Passengers got off, almost none got on, then the train set off. Max distractedly glanced at the travellers as they made their way towards the platform exit before disappearing into the stairway. Now among them, from the rear, in three-quarter view, it indeed appeared to be her again, apart from the fact that this time she was wearing navy-blue slacks and an apple-green zipped-up jacket, or something like that, he didn't really have time to look, all of this transpired in a mere couple of seconds. Still, Max did not take the time to reason it out, to deem it odd that Rose should be getting off a train in that direction whereas he, less than an hour earlier, had begun tailing her in the opposite direction—not to mention that she wasn't even dressed the same. Neither space nor time nor clothing matched, but never mind, let's go. Run for it.

He began running under the twenty-four pairs of uncovered neon lights that reached to just above his skull. He ran skirting the classic attributes of a *métro* platform, monitor screens, fire extinguishers, plastic chairs, mirrors, pictograms warning against the dangers of electrocution, and rubbish bins—four rubbish bins on the side going to Étoile while only two on the Nation side, why is that? Does one have less to throw away when coming from the rich neighbourhoods? Max did not have time to deal with this question right now, but even so, as he rushed back out of the station, the idea flashed through his mind that he'd just used up a ticket for nothing.

When he found himself back on Rue du Sahel, once again there was nothing to be seen, neither to the left nor to the right. He decided to take a footbridge at the edge of the station, straddling the tracks and protected by a fence against which rested empty and more or less battered cartons (Orangina, Coke,

Yoplait), six pebbles, a litre bottle with star-shaped cracks, an un-usable pair of Air Force-blue espadrilles, a little green plastic sand shovel without its pail, all surrounded by a palpable silence, the famous silence of the twelfth *arrondissement*.

And in the midst of this silence, nothing and no-one as far as the eye could see. Right. Let's analyse the situation. It's one of four things. Either it was Rose at Passy in a beige raincoat. Or it was Rose at Bel-Air in a green jacket. Or it was Rose in both in-stances, having changed clothes in less than an hour to take the *métro* twice in opposite directions, which wasn't very likely. Or it was she in neither instance, which was all too likely. Go back home. Take the *métro* again, plunge back underground. That's right, buy another ticket. And stop making that face.

And for the entire duration of this long return, fourteen stops and two transfers, the *métro* seemed to him dirtier and more de-pressing than ever, despite the zeal of the cleaning services. We all know that in the beginning (historical factoid) the immaculate tiling of the subway system, modelled on that of clinics, was in-tended to lessen or even eliminate worrisome ideas injected by the subterranean depths—darkness, dampness, miasmas, humid-ity, illness, epidemic, collapse, rats—by disguising this burrow as an impeccable cloakroom. Except that they ended up with exactly the opposite result. For there exists a malediction of cloakrooms. Even a slightly dirty cloakroom always looks dirtier than a much dirtier non-cloakroom. It's just that on any white expanse, be it ice floe or bed sheet, it takes almost nothing, the tiniest suspect detail, for everything to turn, just as it only takes one fly for the entire sugar bowl to go into mourning. Nothing is sadder than a stain between two white tiles, like dirt under a fingernail or tartar on a tooth. Once back home, Max didn't even feel like taking a shower.

But the next morning, as he emerged from his building, he again ran into the woman with the dog. This time she was displaying her customary elegance—neighbourhood elegance, half-way between that of her supposed evenings out and the outfit in which she did her shopping—and no sooner had he spied her than she walked straight up to him.

"Good morning," she immediately said. "I saw you last night on television, by chance, as I was channel-surfing." She paused for a moment to smile, as if in apology for this verb. "Ah," she resumed, "I didn't realise we had a famous musician in the neighbourhood. I'm going to tell my husband" (ouch! Max said to himself again) "to buy your recordings." She smiled at him again, differently this time from all the other times, before walking off on her very narrow high heels, and Max, turning back protractedly to watch her move away, thought that you can say what you will, but music has its advantages.

TWELVE

SEVERAL DAYS LATER, Max had to attend a benefit for he wasn't sure what, but something that Parisy deemed couldn't hurt in terms of public image. A succession of musicians were to follow one another on stage for brief performances; Max knew most of them, almost all friends, relaxed atmosphere, zero stage fright. The atmosphere in the hall was also much more relaxed than usual for a concert: families paying very little attention, huge number of children, not exactly the typical audience profile for classical music. When the time came for Max, who was in fact due to play Schumann's *Scenes from Childhood*, he sat at the piano amid an astounding hubbub: from the seats came a cacophony of calls, chatting, laughter, and crinkled wrappings that he had never experienced while playing—for, despite what they say, the public for classical music is fairly well behaved; even when it disapproves, it generally keeps quiet.

Without letting the noise deter him, Max thus attacked

"From Foreign Lands and Peoples" in an environment so festive that he could barely hear the opening bars. Still, as he continued to play, he felt the noise begin to dissolve like a cloud, open on to a silent blue sky; he noticed that he was circumventing the audience, drawing it to him like a bull, focusing it, holding it, pulling it taut. Soon the silence in the room was as loud, magnetic and nervous as the music itself; these two fluxes bounced back and forth and vibrated in harmony—without Max mastering in the slightest what his ten fingers were doing on the keyboard, without him knowing where this was coming from, from his work or his experience or from some other place, like lightning, like a great unexpected ray of light. The phenomenon is rare, but it can happen, and twenty minutes later, no sooner had he finished "The Poet Speaks" than, after a pause, an instant of suspended amazement, an ovation burst out that Max wouldn't have swapped for a triumph at the Théâtre des Champs-Elysées.

Champagne. It was the least he could do, he had to recover a bit. Champagne, of course, but soon the programme organisers came up, asking Max to sign a few CDs by popular demand. Of course, said Max, just one more little glass and I'm all yours. He went back into the room where they had set up a small table for him, behind which was a chair, and in front of which a rather considerable queue had indeed begun forming. Very quickly, the *Scenes from Childhood* that Max had recorded two years earlier would be out of stock, then almost as quickly Schumann in general, then any other Romantic music they had available. These went to a long queue of intimidated men with smug smiles, excited women with ready smiles, and even very well-groomed children with serious smiles, and Max signed, signed, signed, ah, all the times in one's life that one has to write one's name.

After a while, the turn came for a man of rather handsome appearance, with an open face and well-cut suit, who deposited three CDs in front of Max while leaning towards him. "You don't know me," he said, without a smile, "but you know my wife and my dog."

Max, immediately understanding what was what, thought his hour had come. We ourselves, knowing that his death is nigh, might have reason to believe that his passing was imminent, but no, nothing of the sort—we could even say things went quite well. The man's spouse must have told him about their rapid nocturnal encounter, apparently without this triggering any reaction of jealousy or homicidal vengeance. The man himself, he explained, practised a profession that was not unrelated to the artistic sphere.

"What name should I make them out to?" Max asked hopefully.

"They're for me," the man said. "My name is Georges and I came alone, without my wife and children." It would not be that day that Max learned the name of the woman with the dog.

Everything went quite well, then, but Max was still a little nervous when leaving the site of the benefit concert. While he hadn't, for lack of stage fright, felt the need to drink before playing, he had on the other hand downed a good amount of champagne afterwards with his colleagues, in decreasing numbers until none remained and he had to leave in turn. Then he passed alone through several bars that he also successively closed down, after which, my word, it was indeed time to go home to bed.

It is late, it is cold, it is drizzling or dribbling, it's still with a fairly steady gait that Max advances in his empty street at this hour of the night. Then, as he approaches number 55 en route to his building, he casts a semi-circular glance ahead to verify that the husband of the woman with the dog isn't lurking in a recess, having reconsidered and lain in wait for Max's return with evil on his mind. No, no-one. But would that Max had cast that glance behind instead, for suddenly he feels himself grabbed by the collar of his coat, thrown down on to the pavement, and now he's lying stretched out on his back with two fellows on top of him, masked by scarves—but, scarves or no, Max has thrown his forearm over his face in protection—who undertake a systematic rifling of his person. To do this, they tear open his raincoat violently, with so little care that two or three new buttons jump off and roll together towards the gutter—no doubt about it, it's plain to see, this really is the season of buttons.

The men methodically extract everything they find in Max's pockets and, after a moment, as the latter reckons that this is all beginning to drag on, it occurs to him to cry out, oh, not cry out for real, cry out just a little bit, you know, for form's sake, in case it could summon someone. But first, he manages to emit only a feeble and timid whine, like a slightly peevish whimper, and second, he feels a hand clamp on to his mouth to shut him up. He could, of course, push that hand aside to keep shouting; it's only a small hand of adolescent size. But he's afraid that another hand, not necessarily larger but holding a weapon, might administer a more radical treatment, and more to the point, he notices the briny, grimy taste of that hand on his lips, which he prefers to shut tight out of hygienic reflex.

And besides, truth to tell, he decides it's better just to lie back, to simply let himself go, let things take their course. He is suddenly enveloped by an almost comfortable, almost shamefully voluptuous resignation, in the renunciation of all and the vanity of everything. It works the same as when you decide, screwed if you do and screwed if you don't, to give yourself over to the anaesthetist, who fixes a mask over your face in the perfect scialytic light and ideal calm of the operating theatre, under the eyes of skull-capped surgeons. And correlatively, even though this entire process unfolds at top speed, time seems to Max to distend and multiply, as if all this were happening in slow motion despite the nervous fever of the two fellows installed on top of him.

He knows he shouldn't do it, but sometimes one has troublesome reflexes: Max stops protecting his eyes to see who these guys are—they're obviously very young, but what do they look like?

But their faces are hidden by scarves, and Max, seized by a jolt of exasperation and before he realises what he's doing, rips one of them off. He uncovers a rather indistinct, and indeed very young, face, on which he barely has time to glimpse an expression that quickly veers from bewildered to furious, indignant to vengeful, then the time to notice a foreshortened arm raised above him, prolonged by a stiletto that the unmasked young man, surely no less horrified than Max, drives deep into his throat, just above the Adam's apple. The stiletto first pierces Max's skin, before its momentum carries it through his tracheal artery and oesophagus, damaging large vessels of the carotid and jugular type, after which, gliding between two vertebrae—seventh cervical and first dorsal—it severs Max's spinal cord, and there is no-one left on the scene.

Everything is dark in the surrounding buildings; all the windows are black; no-one is looking at anything except the dog of the woman with the dog, still awake at this hour on the fourth floor of number 55. He's a sweet and meditative dog, as Max had immediately noticed, a good pensive dog who, suffering from bouts of insomnia, sometimes stares out the window at night to pass the time, and who has just witnessed this regrettable incident. If the beast's dreamy nature predisposes him towards visions, perhaps it will now see, as a little encore, Max's soul rising gently into the welcoming ether.

II

THIRTEEN

NO.

No, no ascension, no ether, no big to-do. And yet it seemed that even after he was dead, Max continued to experience things. He found himself naked in a single bed that occupied about a quarter of a small, dark room whose walls, painted ochre with patina effects, absorbed the light of a weak bedside lamp standing on a bedside table, the dimness increased by a fringed maroon cloth spread over the beige lampshade. Once he had opened his eyes, and after several minutes spent looking around without seeing much of anything, Max pulled away the cloth without this revealing a great deal more of his new environment. A few more minutes passed, during which he mustered feeble efforts to understand what could possibly have happened, but in vain. Giving up, he finally got out of bed, fighting off a brief dizzy spell before gathering up his trousers, which he found carefully folded over the back of a chair. He pulled them on, then set off towards the door that he assumed, for no particular reason, would be locked.

It wasn't. But although this door opened without difficulty, it led only to a long, empty corridor, punctuated by other closed doors between which, at regular intervals, wall-lamps gave off the faint halos of night-lights. The corridor was so long that you couldn't see either end of it; so empty that it was nothing, revealed nothing, provided no more information than if the door had in fact been bolted. Max, bare-chested, was about to close his door again when he noticed, far down the corridor to the left, an indistinct figure wearing a yellow dressing gown who detached himself tentatively from the wall, evidently venturing out like Max. Max was hesitating about which course to take, whether to wave or hide, uncertain as to the nature of this figure, when he saw it jump back at the arrival of another silhouette.

White in colour and emerging from who knows where, this second figure seemed gently but firmly to admonish Yellow Dressing Gown, who immediately vanished. Apparently White Silhouette then noticed Max, who watched it walk towards him, become transformed in its approach into a young woman who was the spitting image of Peggy Lee—tall, nurse's blouse, very light hair pulled back and held with a hair-slide. With the same implacable softness, she enjoined Max to go back into his room.

"You have to stay in here," she said—moreover, in Peggy Lee's voice. "Someone will be along to see you soon."

"But," started Max, getting no further, as the young woman

immediately negated this incipient objection with a gentle rustling of her fingers, deployed like a flight of birds in the air between them. When you got down to it, she did look phenomenally like Peggy Lee, the same kind of big, milk-fed blonde, with a fleshy, dimpled face, full figure and broad forehead, invasive cheeks, wide mouth, and excessive lower lip forming the permanent smile of a zealous cub mistress. More reassuring than arousing, she exuded complete wholesomeness and strict morals.

Back in his room, Max examined things more closely. There wasn't enough space for much furniture other than his bed and the bedside table, both made of mahogany; a minuscule cupboard, perhaps made of oak and containing a few spare clothes in Max's size; an elegant little table roughly the size of a sideboard; the chair on which his trousers had been folded, and that was it. No decoration on the walls, no knick-knacks, no magazines, not a book in sight, no Gideon Bible in the bedside drawer or tourist brochure that might indicate where he was, what he could do there, what there was to see in the area, with all the usual timetables and price lists. In sum, a sober, comfortable room, the kind probably found in certain abbeys that have been refitted as spiritual retreats, intended for souls who dispose of equally comfortable incomes. An air-conditioned space, perfectly quiet owing to the fact that, alas, there were no windows, and still more so because it contained neither radio nor television. A door made of some translucent material led to a decently designed bathroom, even though there was no mirror above the sink. As Max tried to see his reflection in this translucent material, he vaguely made out a dark patch at the base of his neck. But something made him hesitate before bringing his hand to it, and in any case, at that same moment, the door to his room unexpectedly opened to reveal a visitor.

The visitor was perhaps a bit taller than Max, clearly a bit thinner, well built and of elegant bearing—things that Max would ordinarily find rather irksome. The man displayed a casualness bordering on insolence, reminiscent of a fair number of clowns that Max had known in his professional life: art directors or publicity heads of record companies, critics or producers of specialised festivals in some narrowly defined sub-category of Baroque. His light, loose-fitting clothes also fitted him a bit too well, beige linen suit over an anthracite T-shirt and docksiders. He seemed excessively aware of his appearance; his hair denoted just the right amount of negligence, thick and brushed back with one discreetly rebellious strand falling forward. With his manicured nails, weekly ultraviolet treatments, and exfoliated skin, he radiated gym clubs, hair salons and beauty salons, fitting rooms and tea rooms. "Hello, Max," he uttered without warmth, "pleased to meet you. My name is Christian Béliard, but you may call me Christian. I'll be looking after you."

All of this—and those who know anything about Max can see it coming—does not augur well. Max does not particularly like it when a stranger calls him by his first name straight away, like an American; he does not appreciate very much that this stranger is addressing him in a nonchalant tone and hardly looking at him; and he especially does not care for the relaxed, professionally indifferent attitude displayed by this stranger who, while talking to him, is casting distracted glances around the room as if conducting an inspection. On top of which, Max really doesn't see why this chump, for whom he feels an immediate dislike, claims to be looking after him, or who the hell he thinks he is. He would prefer that someone first explain to him, politely, what he's done to deserve all this distant solicitude, and what they, in fact, are actually doing here, and particularly what he, Max, is doing here at all. But, dislike or not, the man must be fairly intuitive, or at least sufficiently trained to understand what is rumbling spontaneously through Max's nervous system. "Not to worry," says the aforementioned Béliard, who breaks into a half-smile while sitting at the foot of the bed, "everything will be just fine. I'll explain briefly."

It turned out from his explanation that Max was, right here and now, in transit. Right here, in other words, in a kind of specialised Orientation Centre, or so he gathered. Something like a triage area where his fate was to be decided. The time needed to rule on his case, which would be handled by a duly appointed committee, should not exceed one week, during which Max could rest and enjoy the Centre's facilities at his leisure—you'll find, incidentally, that the cuisine is excellent. As for the decisions that this committee would be handing down, their nature couldn't be simpler: there were only two possibilities, following the either/or principle. Depending on the outcome of their deliberations, Max would be sent to either one or the other of two predetermined destinations. "But don't worry," said Béliard, "each one has its good points. In any case, you'll have a better idea of what I'm talking about in five minutes. Kindly get dressed."

They left the room and headed down the corridor, along both sides of which were aligned doors identical to the one to Max's room, separated by those wall-lamps that were like little torchères of gilded wood. These unnumbered doors were closed, except for a single one, half open, that afforded a glimpse of a cell also identical to his own. It seemed that someone was cleaning it, for from behind, through the opening, Max fleetingly noticed two chambermaids in action, dressed in immaculate bodices and remarkably short black skirts, with a metal cart behind them holding an array of cleaning products and piles of clean sheets, pillowcases, flannels, and towels, as well as bundles of rumpled sheets, pillowcases, flannels, and towels, all of it under the muted whine of a vacuum cleaner and in a light perfume of deluxe disinfectant.

Then, to their left, another door opened and out came the nurse whom Max had met half an hour earlier, and who stopped at their passage. Max greeted her with a respectful nod, then turned towards Béliard, whose face tightened.

"Number 26 is rather agitated," the nurse said in a concerned voice. "I don't know what to do with him."

"Listen," Béliard said coldly, "you know perfectly well that 26 is a bit of a special case. Do you know the treatment or not?"

"Of course I know it," said the nurse, "but I've tried everything. Nothing seems to work with him."

"That's not my department," said Béliard. "That's *your* area of expertise, isn't it? Assuming you have one," he added in a cutting tone. "And besides, can't you see I'm busy? Go and see Mr Lopez if you can't handle it, maybe they'll give you a transfer. I think they might be short-handed in the kitchen. Later."

They parted without warmth. "That girl," Max ventured to remark, "she's really not bad. It's amazing how much she looks like Peggy Lee."

"She *is* Peggy Lee," Béliard said indifferently.

"Come again?" went Max.

"Yes," said Béliard. "I mean, she was Peggy Lee. Why, do you know her?"

"Well, gosh," said Max, no longer astonished by much of anything, "she was pretty famous, after all. I've seen some of her movies. And I even think I had one or two records."

"Oh, right," Béliard said indifferently, "that's true, you were in music, weren't you?"

"Not exactly the same type of music," said Max, "but even so, I was interested in other things, too. I mean other types."

He fell silent for a moment, looking at his hands, planting a diminished seventh chord in the air. "Besides, I have to admit I'm eager to get back to it," he continued. "I start to miss it pretty quickly when I'm away from my instrument."

"Ah, as for that," Béliard interrupted, "I'm afraid that's going to be a bit difficult. You'll have to reconsider the matter."

"I beg your pardon?" went Max.

"What I mean is," Béliard specified, "you're going to have to change professions. That's how it is when you come here. It's not my decision, you understand, the same rules apply to everyone."

"But what do you expect me to do?" worried Max. "I don't know how to do anything else."

"We'll find you something," said Béliard. "We find solutions for everyone. Take Peggy, for instance. She had to change jobs, too. She needed to find another trade. So fine, she chose health care, and she's not doing too badly. Besides, she has the right physique—though no matter what we do, she can't quite rid herself of her little movie-star habits. She gets like that now and again, and sometimes we have to take her down a peg."

"I see," said Max. "I thought I noticed some tension between you two."

"It's not just that," said Béliard. "It's also that I don't really like that kind of girl."

"What kind?"

"Oh," Béliard said with a wave of his hand, "big blondes and such. I know them all too well."

At the far end of the corridor they could make out a bend, past which they reached a kind of vast foyer where the light of day finally entered, pouring in through two large picture windows that faced in opposite directions. One of these windows looked out on a city that could have been a sister to Paris, as it displayed the same classic landmarks—various towers bespeaking different periods and uses, from Eiffel to Maine-Montparnasse and Jussieu, basilica, assorted monuments—but seen from very far away and on high. It wasn't possible to determine which angle they were seeing this city from, or precisely where they were, as such a view of Paris was not possible from any standpoint Max could envisage. Whatever the case, this Paris, or its twin, seemed to be smothered under a black, synthetic rain expelled by clouds of pollution, brownish and swollen like udders. The light arriving from that side was opaque, depressing, almost extinguished; whereas it flowed in gently, affectionately and brightly from the other side. This other side overlooked an immense park, a vegetal mass with soft contours forming a vast array in every shade of green, from the darkest to the most tender. Undulating at various points beneath a more clement sky, the expanse seemed to spread into infinity, as far as the eye could see, with no perceptible boundaries.

"Basically, this is what's awaiting you," said Béliard, indicating the two opposing axes. "These are the two possible orientations, you see, the park or the urban zone. You'll be assigned to one or the other. But again, don't worry, there's no bad or good solution. Both sides have their good and bad points. Anyway, as I mentioned, residence at the Centre is limited to about a week. Which means that since today's Thursday, you should be all set by next Wednesday."

"Aha," Max said unenthusiastically. "And couldn't I just stay here? It's not so bad here, I think I could get used to it. I could even help out a bit."

"That's completely out of the question," Béliard shot back. "This is just a transit station."

"Yes, but what about Peggy, for instance?" Max insisted.

"Peggy is a special case," said Béliard with an evil smile. "She's an exception. She has protection, you understand? She managed to get herself placed. The system has loopholes. Favours are done here just like anywhere else." Max didn't dare ask from whom or thanks to what Peggy Lee could enjoy such preferential treatment.

As Max, thoughtfully rubbing his chin against the grain of an already noticeable beard—which hadn't been shaved in how long, exactly? How much time separated the scene on the pavement from his awakening? Could one get information on this point?— was about to run his hand mechanically under the collar of his shirt, Béliard promptly checked his movement.

"Don't touch your wound," he said. "We're going to take care of it. On top of which," he added, knitting his brow, leaning closer to Max and examining him with a professional eye, "we'd better take care of it sooner rather than later. We can't leave you like this. In the meantime, you'd best keep to your room. You know the way."

"Yes," said Max, "but now that I think of it, I'm a bit hungry. Couldn't I have something to eat?"

"With the shape your throat is in," said Béliard, "I wouldn't advise it for the moment."

"What's wrong with my throat?" asked Max. "I don't feel anything. I feel perfectly fine."

"That's normal," said Béliard. "You're being given a special treatment until we perform the operation. You can eat afterwards. In the meantime, you're forbidden to swallow anything whatsoever; in any case, it wouldn't go through. But I'll take care of all this; someone will come and see you in a little while."

FOURTEEN

MAX WENT BACK to his room, which they had taken the trouble to clean up a little in his absence, bringing it to a relatively high-starred level of comfort. The little table now held a tray of exotic but forbidden fruit under cellophane—kiwis, mangoes, bananas, with a preponderance of papayas—plus a matching bouquet of flowers. Easy background music also played at low volume, a loop of placid, traditional, non-threatening works, no doubt selected by a middlebrow sensibility, its volume adjustable via a knob integrated into the bedside table.

As a dozen books were also piled up on the bedside table, Max examined them. They were all identically bound in reddish leatherette as if they came from the same book club, and apparently had been chosen following the same principles as the music. It was a selection of classical works: Dante and Dostoevsky, Thomas Mann and Chrétien de Troyes, things like that, despite the jarring presence of a copy of *Materialism and Empirio-Criticism* that had wandered in, and that Max leafed through for a few minutes. After he had again tried in vain to see his wound in the frosted glass of the bathroom cabinet, he decided to lie on the bed, resisting the temptation to peel a banana, abandoning Lenin to open at random *Jerusalem Delivered* in the old Auguste Desplaces translation (1840).

He didn't have time to pursue his reading very far, as someone soon knocked at his door. Béliard again, no doubt, but no, it wasn't he. It was a valet classically dressed in black and white who entered his room smiling, Good day, sir, except that in place of the habitual meal tray balancing on his open left hand, he carried a metal stem attached to a bag filled with translucent liquid, from which emerged a flexible tube ending in a needle—in other words, what is commonly called a drip.

This valet was another tall young man, with wavy, gelled black hair and a Latin smile, ironic and charming à la Dean Martin. Up close, in fact, he looked exactly like Dean Martin, down to his dancer's bearing and brown eyes sparkling with blue reflections. He bore such a resemblance to Dean Martin that Max, at the point they were at and given the precedent with Peggy Lee, began wondering if he wasn't the genuine article. Knowing that this was delicate territory, he nonetheless decided to broach it.

"I beg your pardon," he said, "but you wouldn't by any chance be Dean Martin, would you?"

"Sorry, sir, afraid not," the valet answered, his smile more Martinesque than ever. "Sad to say. I wish I were."

"It's amazing how much you look like him," Max remarked in an apologetic tone.

"So I hear," the valet smiled modestly. "People have actually told me that on more than one occasion. Now, if you would kindly roll up your sleeve. No, the right one, if you don't mind."

For the following hour, Max remained lying on his bed while a hydrating solution of glucose, vitamins, and mineral salts spread through his system. Then there was another knock on his door— God in Heaven, don't they ever stop—and this time it was again the smile of Peggy Lee, exuding more than ever an aura of vegetarianism and Christian Science. Still fresh and perky, she was followed by a young man dressed like a stretcher-bearer, who, for his part, didn't look like anyone famous. They asked Max to get undressed and to put on a kind of smock, clap a bonnet on his head, and slip on shoes made of blue synthetic fabric that crumpled like paper, then to lie down on a very tall stretcher, upon which he again set off, pushed by the young man, down the long row of corridors. This time they took the opposite direction to a service lift as huge as in a hospital, as fast as in a skyscraper: they must have been descending at top speed from a very high altitude, since from the heights of his stretcher Max had to force himself to swallow several times to open his eardrums, blocked by the race down to Basement Level 3.

Then new corridors flooded with white light and pierced by wide swinging doors, one of which opened on to an operating room that was no different from any other operating room; nor did the surgeon call to mind any celebrity. "Just a little repair job," the doctor explained, planting another needle in Max's forearm—the left one this time. "We're going to fix you up with a small cosmetic procedure, since of course vital functions are no longer an issue." It would just be a matter of cleaning the wound, sewing up the pieces of his lacerated throat, then reconstructing the damaged elements, especially around the spinal cord—a delicate area—before plugging up and masking the hole created by his attacker's weapon. Max plunged into chemical sleep before the other had finished his explanations.

He awoke with a start, took a moment to recognise his room, but immediately identified Peggy Lee at his bedside, sitting on a chair and flipping through the pages of a magazine. As he was opening his mouth to ask a question, she gently placed her right hand on his lips, posing on her own a finger of the left. "Don't try to talk," she said softly, "it's too soon, it could hurt. But don't worry; it will go very quickly from now on. In your condition, it heals pretty fast. You'll see, you'll feel better by tomorrow." Although he didn't understand a word of what she was saying, Max nodded with a knowing air, glanced briefly at the IV that was lodged once more in his right arm, then dropped off to sleep again like a stone.

The next time he opened his eyes, there was no-one in his room, which he now recognised instantly. No sound came from anywhere: they must have disconnected the background music to ensure that he get some rest. No way to know what time it was, evening or morning, day or night. For lack of anything else to do, Max reviewed all the information he had gathered since arriving at the Centre, making a synthesis, then reflecting on what was now liable to happen to him—what zone they were going to assign him to. By all appearances, aesthetically speaking, the park seemed to be a good solution, even if it would be smart to check it out more closely. Since Béliard had indicated the decision would be made by studying his file, Max visualised the future with optimism, having a fair amount of confidence in the balance sheet of his life.

For it seemed to him that he had always behaved rather well. Taking a survey of his existence, he came to the conclusion that he hadn't seriously lapsed in any domain whatsoever. Naturally, he had suffered from doubt, alcoholism, and acedia; naturally, he had occasionally succumbed to laziness, allowed himself a few minor tantrums, or indulged in bouts of pride, but what else could he have done? Overall, it all seemed decidedly venial. If one was granted access to the park based on one's merits, Max couldn't really see what might stand in the way of his acceptance, but it was no doubt premature to speculate on his fate before getting more information—and at that moment, the door opened to reveal Béliard.

FIFTEEN

"WELL," PROFFERED BÉLIARD in the martial tones of a senior consultant, "how are we feeling this morning?" So it was morning. The next day, unless it was the day after that. But before Max had a chance to answer, someone knocked at the door: this time it was the valet carrying an actual meal tray.

"You've noticed everything moves very quickly here," noted Béliard, handing Max a pocket mirror. "Don't even need a bandage, the healing is almost done." And in fact, in the mirror, Max saw at the base of his throat only a slight pale line bordered by a barely perceptible row of dots. "You're going to be able to start eating again," Béliard added, pointing to the valet, who promptly cleared the table before setting down the tray, then busied himself with removing the IV. After extracting the needle from Max's forearm, he briefly swabbed the area with alcohol, the swipe of a dust cloth over a waxed canvas, and zip zip zip, a little square of sticking plaster on top, and end of story. "There," said Béliard, "that's taken care of. Now you can get dressed."

"It's just a light meal, sir," the valet apologised under his breath as Max slipped on his shirt. "Because of your operation. A little convalescent diet, not very exciting, I grant, and I sincerely hope you won't hold it against us. You'll soon be able to enjoy more varied menus." In fact, this one consisted of white rice and steamed vegetables, a slice of boiled ham, yogurt, and fruit compote, washed down with mineral water. "Will this be to your liking?" worried the valet, while meticulously arranging the silverware in parentheses around the dish.

"Cut it short, Dino, cut it short," exclaimed Béliard, who seemed to derive great pleasure from bossing the junior staff around. He tried to dismiss the domestic abruptly, the moment the latter had finished his task, but Dino, since Dino he was, took his sweet time with a distant, smiling, indifferent, calm indolence.

"Now that you're recovered," said Béliard, "I'll show you around the place a bit." They took the same lift that had carried Max to the operating room and, as they went down, Max tried to worm some information out of Béliard about Dino.

"Why?" the other asked coldly.

"I don't know," said Max, "I like that young man. I find him very pleasant, even rather special."

"I can't answer that," said Béliard. "He doesn't like people talking about him. He prefers not to have anything known about him personally, which I respect. People have this right in our institution. But I won't hide the fact that he annoys me sometimes. Truth be told, I find him a bit too casual."

This time, the lift stopped three floors above the surgical level, at the ground floor of the Centre. They followed a new network of corridors, wider, better decorated—fresh bouquets of flowers on console-tables, neoclassical statuettes on pedestals, fantastical landscapes—and more populated—chambermaids and factotums, secretaries wearing glasses and buns who, hugging their folders under their arms, gave Béliard timid and respectful greetings when crossing his path, which he vaguely answered with a brief movement of his chin. Corridors and more corridors that finally ended at a gigantic foyer lit *a giorno* by gleaming crystal-and-bronze chandeliers framed by oblong pastel windows, and from which rose a monumental staircase with two revolutions. "Here we are," said Béliard. "This is the entrance of the Centre." Past a revolving door one could in fact make out, punctuated by water fountains and clumps of vegetation, the kind of vast stretch of gravel that one often sees in front of grand mansions—usually strewn with long motor cars, stained by oil from their sumps, and furrowed with traces of their tyres, but here, as far as Max could tell from where he stood, there was no stain, no trace of any tyre, no car beneath the clear sky.

Nor did there appear to be a security guard on duty inside the foyer or in the surrounding area. No sentinel, no watchman, not a single video camera, ah, wait, there's something: hidden behind the architecture of the staircase, Max spotted a small, discreet booth, in frosted glass to waist level and containing a desk, behind which a sexagenarian dressed in traditional grand hotel concierge garb—black frock coat over white waistcoat, his lapel sporting two crossed keys—seemed to be in a dream, oblivious to the world.

"It doesn't look like you have a very large staff," Max observed. "People can come and go as they please, can they?"

"It's not quite that simple," Béliard moderated, "but it's a little like that. We work on the honour system, if you like. Surveillance is very low-level, everyone is responsible for himself. I'll show you around the park tomorrow, if that sounds all right. In the meantime, let me introduce you to the director. Would you like to meet him?"

"Oh, yes," said Max, "good idea. I'd like to meet the director."

"Let me make sure he's in," said Béliard, setting off towards the concierge's booth. "Good morning, Joseph, is Mr Lopez in his office at the moment?"

At Joseph's affirmative reply, they took the staircase, on the landings of which several bellboys stood or circulated—very young subjects, barely pubescent, dressed in woollen dolman jackets and striped trousers, white collars, gloves, and caps, and engaged in apparently farcical activities that Max and Béliard's passage momentarily disrupted. On the second floor was a large double door guarded by an usher who, with a grave salute to Béliard, let them pass. They crossed through a string of vast rooms that were sometimes empty, sometimes sectioned off into cubicles separated by glass partitions behind which, here and there, one could make out a silhouette bent over its job. After they had crossed another antechamber, Béliard knocked on the next door, which immediately opened on to a huge directorial office. We'll choose not to describe this office in much detail; let us simply note that its furnishings and decorations matched—perhaps in a slightly duller and sadder way, and a little less well maintained—the style of the rooms Max had thus far walked through.

Directorial or not, the office was occupied only by one thin, stooped, standing man, bent over thick bundles of yellowish documents spread out over a desk. This person was of average height, tightly dressed in inexpensive grey. His long, waxy face denoted a poorly balanced diet; his rheumy eyes were tearful. He sported the anxious air of an underpaid clerk, depressive, apologetic more than displeased about being so anxious, but resigned to it. He must have been a secretary or accountant, or one of the undersecretaries or under-accountants working for the director, whom he was, no doubt, going out to notify.

Or maybe not. "Mr Lopez," Béliard uttered gently and with deference, "this is Mr Delmarc, who has recently joined us. He was admitted this week and he wanted to meet you."

"Ah," the other said confusedly, raising an intimidated eye towards Max, "well, welcome." He did not even ask Max a few questions for form's sake. At first glance, he seemed a bit frightened; his questioning look made him appear overwhelmed by events—although one might wonder if this wasn't some kind of ruse, a trick he used so as to be left in peace; if in fact he knew, better than anyone, all about Max. "What did you say his name was?" he asked Béliard, who repeated Max's last name for him, spelling it out. "Yes," said Lopez, "I see. Just a moment." Bending once more over the desk and rifling through the scattered documents, he eventually pulled one out and handed it to Béliard. The latter first skimmed it rapidly, then, in the general silence, began rereading it more closely.

Standing at a cautious distance, Max nonetheless glanced over at the object. It was a rectangular, lined index card, 5 x 8 format, its edges yellowed and slightly frayed, almost entirely covered in a fine, close handwriting traced in brown ink: apparently it was not of recent vintage, like most of the documents piled up on Lopez's desk. It was reminiscent of those other index cards that people used to consult in public libraries, before their catalogues went digital.

"Hey," Max allowed himself to observe, "you aren't computerised here?"

"Did I ask you anything?" Béliard answered without raising his eyes.

Meanwhile, Lopez had sat down, brushing imaginary dust with the back of his hand from the surface of his desk, which he stared at vacantly. Then Béliard, having finished reading, glanced quickly at Max before handing the card back to Lopez. "Right," he said, "I think I basically get the picture."

"What's the matter with them?" Max asked himself. "What's there to see, in particular?"

Two fried eggs were waiting for him in his room, accompanied by a beer and a slice of melon, the first discreet sign of an improvement. As of the next day, in fact, his lunch would offer more depth, then dinner would be frankly worthy of a five-star restaurant. Max had to spend that entire second post-operative day in his room, leafing through the books he had, but without enthusiasm and not really able to read, at first distracted by anxiety over the index card he'd seen in Lopez's office, then, as of early afternoon, more profoundly distracted by boredom. Dino still handled the service with his smiling and detached discretion, although it was still impossible to make him be anything but evenspoken; then Béliard came by for coffee. When evening fell, Max fretted to him about his schedule in the days to come.

"It's just that I'm starting to go a bit crazy here," he had to admit. "Couldn't I just go out for a little walk now and then?"

"But you're absolutely free," Béliard assured him. "Your door is open. At this point, nothing is stopping you from coming and going as you please in the establishment. As for distractions *per se*, we'll see about that later. Cigar?"

SIXTEEN

THE START of the next day would prove to be pretty depressing. It's just that it was Sunday and, even in a place as cut off from the world as the Centre, Sunday produced, as always and everywhere, its effect of indolence and emptiness, of pale expanse and hollow, sorrowful resonance. First there would be an interminable morning, during which Max would keep to his room, pondering the matter of Lopez's index card, until somebody served him one of those cold meals that you get when there's no-one in the kitchen. Besides, it wasn't even properly served to him: when he started feeling hungry and opened his door to watch for Dino's arrival, he found the tray set down in the corridor at his feet like a doormat. And Béliard, like Dino, was no doubt taking advantage of his weekly day off, unless he already had lunch plans, since he didn't show up for his daily coffee with Max. Max now felt fully recovered from his operation and, once fed, he decided to take a spin around the Centre. With a little idea in the back of his mind.

It wouldn't exactly be easy. He had to reconstruct, by himself, the path he and Béliard had taken the day before. Emptier even than usual, the corridor on his floor gave off the glacial echo of a deserted boarding-school during holidays, when all the others have gone to be with their families and you remain behind, alone with the staff, whether out of punishment or orphanhood. Except that Max didn't come across any staff. He could have sworn he made out the rumbling of a vacuum cleaner in the distance, the dim clanks of a mop in an empty pail but, as there was no-one to be seen, these could just as easily have been slight auditory hallucinations produced by the silence itself. He had no trouble finding the lift and, once its doors had closed behind him, as the mechanism made no sound, Max was shut into a higher silence, a silence within the silence, a cubed silence that didn't bespeak anything good. It was with a troubled index finger that he took aim and pressed the button for the ground floor; then the descent was long enough for his entire life to pass before him, until the concluding *dring* of the lift brought him back with a slight start.

As on the day before, the lift doors opened on to the same network of hallways that were better decorated than upstairs. The rooms from yesterday were now deserted, and Max could linger at the doorways, looking at what must have been offices, exhibit halls, and conference rooms furnished with coffee machines. He ventured into what looked like a reception hall, a huge space whose decoration suggested a vaguely Soviet aesthetic: stucco and mouldings, thick damask curtains, carpets with indistinct designs, and large ungainly furniture, heavy with good will and coiffed with table mats. At the far end of the room, there was even a piano. A concert grand. Well, well.

Seeing it, Max realised that for the past several days he had almost forgotten about music. And yet music was his life, or at least it had been. But he had hardly even mentioned it to Béliard, just long enough for the latter to intimate that he would now have to give it up. Max remembered, moreover, that he hadn't been particularly devastated by this news at the time, but the piano, well after all. A piano. Max approached it very slowly, as one might draw near a wild animal, as if the instrument were threatening to fly off with a squawk at the slightest sudden movement. Taking advantage of Béliard's dominical absence, he felt the desire to see what this model had under its hood, the urge to make it talk. But first, prudently halting a few feet away, he tried to make out its label. Neither Gaveau nor Steinway nor Bechstein nor Bösendorfer nor anything: no signature on the gold plate under the music desk. A big, anonymous machine, black, sleek, shining, solitary, and closed. Inching closer on tiptoe, Max silently turned his hands supine but, when he gently risked the tips of his fingers towards the instrument to open the fall board, he noticed that it was locked, making the keys inaccessible. Max insisted, trying to force the cover, but no, nothing doing, it was bolted. Bernie, among his many talents, would have been perfectly capable of prying open the lock in two beats of three movements, but there was no more Bernie. Bernie, too, had been his life.

Max had to be content with circling for a moment, not more than two or three times, around the closed piano. Without much conviction, he also tried to lift the instrument's lid, if only to examine its sounding board and wrest plank, caress the strings and run his fingernails over them like a harp, but in vain: locked shut like the rest. During these two or three turns around the piano, the little idea grew in the back of Max's mind.

This idea led him to retrace fairly quickly and easily the path towards the main entrance. He moved forward in the same thick silence that, not merely amplifying the sound of his steps, also brought forth other various and indistinct sounds, distant moans and grunts, whines, creaks, and buzzings that stopped dead the moment Max became aware of their untraceable origin, their possible genesis inside him, his cranium acting as their echo chamber. When he found himself back in the foyer, it was equally devoid of any guard: even the concierge was absent from his glass booth. Max nonetheless made a show of examining the place as nonchalantly as you please, distracted but exhibiting a complete curiosity, like a tourist set loose in a chateau without his guide, coming and going with no discernible method on open-house day. Nevertheless, a goal directed his wanderings: to amble closer, by concentric circles and oh so casually, to the foyer's revolving door; and then, having reached it, to give it a slight prod to make sure it wasn't blocked; then, this being verified, to push it more firmly, slip into its space, and stroll out as naturally as could be. He experienced a brief sensation of claustrophobia when he found himself, for the space of three seconds, enclosed in the door's rotating airlock, while the once little idea now left the back of his mind to swell and invade his head completely—I'm getting out of here, God help me, I'm getting the hell out of here.

To go where? No idea. Once outside, the main thing was to get as far away as possible; after that, we'd see. The exterior consisted of a minimal landscape: past the gravelled esplanade that stretched before the Centre, a summarily tarmacked pathway opened up, its pavement gradually splitting into plates of asphalt that were increasingly unconnected, among which grew tufts of weeds. This pathway soon became a stony dirt road, barely suitable for traffic and lined by dry shrubs with outlines like stick insects, with nothing in sight but sterile undulations on either side, stretching to infinity.

Nothing in this landscape suggested either of the ones Max had seen from the windows: it was an intermediate stage, grey, neutral, and chilly in nature. Max decided to follow this dirt road, shivering a little, and in any case having no choice, nor the slightest idea of where he was going. After roughly five hundred yards, he thought to turn around and get a look at the Centre. It was, as the lift had defined it from within, a very tall building, almost a skyscraper, about forty storeys high, grey in colour and flanked with long, low wings and annexes. The whole thing must have been able to house a huge number of people.

He walked another mile or two along this deserted road in the middle of the countryside before he made out the faint whine of a rather shrill engine, no doubt a two-stroke, slowly growing louder behind him. Max took pains to act as if there were nothing untoward until he heard the engine slow down right near him, behind his back, humming gently in neutral. At that point he had to turn around and look: it was a service vehicle of a model unfamiliar to Max—moreover, as with the piano, no manufacturer's mark was visible. Halfway between a Mini Moke and a golf trolley, it was a small, topless, all-purpose conveyance, rather stylish in its very simplicity. Max had no trouble recognising Dino sitting behind the wheel, even though he'd swapped his valet's livery for a well-cut electric-blue business suit. He was also wearing a hat that he pushed back slightly while opening the passenger door with the other hand, not saying a word but grinning irresistibly with the full range of his enamel.

It was clear that there was no discussion to be had; Max could only get in quietly and sit down. Dino manoeuvred the vehicle and they set off with no comment towards the Centre, at first in silence. Then, as if sensing that this silence might begin to weigh on them, Dino began delicately humming a melody that Max immediately identified: "The Night Is Young and You're So Beautiful"; then he started to sing it for real, with lyrics, at half-

95

volume, while improvising a rhythm section by tapping his fingers on the steering wheel. Not only did Max recognise the song, but he recognised more and more precisely the timbre of Dino's voice—that crooner's voice, a bit ironic, nonchalant, and gifted, but aware and making fun of its own nonchalance: obviously Dean Martin, of course Dean Martin. It was no less indisputable than it was intimidating—because, after all, Dean Martin.

But it was also a chance to know the artist a little better, even while not letting on that he'd been recognised, the other having made it very clear that he wished to remain incognito. If Dino didn't want to be identified, that was his business, and Max wasn't going to pester him about it. Still, they could talk a bit, broach a host of other subjects, like, well, I don't know.

"Dino," he said once the other had finished singing, "would you like to have a drink one of these days? I'd enjoy getting to know you better."

The other, who up until now had been nothing but relaxed and friendly, suspended his smile for an instant, albeit without hostility, and, turning politely towards Max, he answered calmly, "No-one can know me, sir," before redeploying his dazzling whites. Max took care not to insist: Dino was a tranquil and secretive man, and as Béliard had said, one had to respect that.

As they drove towards the Centre beneath a sky that was almost as white as that smile, Max began to ponder the awful trouble that was surely awaiting him on his return. He could hardly imagine the disciplinary measures that might follow his attempt to run away or escape—the very nature of his crime was still to be defined—but there must be a punishment for such conduct. What? Penitence, imprisonment, reprimands, forced labour, appearance before a disciplinary committee followed by expulsion pure and simple—although where could they expel him to? And yet, for the moment, none of this seemed worth worrying about to judge by Dino, who continued to tap his fingers casually on the steering wheel—although it wasn't really sympathy that emanated from his behaviour, more like he didn't seem to give a damn, and more generally didn't seem to give a damn about anything, and not only seemed, at that.

Still, arriving back at the Centre, Max was not greeted by a row of impassive armed guards or nurses brandishing syringes, nor dragged to a jail cell or before an assembly of men in black. Dino merely accompanied him back to his room, where Béliard, sitting on the single bed, was waiting calmly while looking at his watch. Max feared remonstrations or even threats, for on top of everything else, he had probably ruined Béliard's Sunday, his one day off all week—but no, the other proved to be as benevolent and detached as Dino. And even fairly thoughtful. As Max was about to launch into jumbled explanations, Béliard pre-empted him with a wave of his hand.

"Don't worry about it," he said. "Everyone has tried at some point. Well, not exactly everybody," he qualified. "But you know, we don't really have anything against this kind of initiative. On the contrary, it's very healthy, it's a good reaction. It's especially a sign that you're completely healed. And now, if you'd be good enough to get your belongings ready," he added with a circular gesture.

"I don't have any belongings," Max reminded him, worried.

"Forgive me," said Béliard, "it was just an expression. It's only that you're going to change lodgings."

Max was still expecting the worst—dark dungeon, padded cell, cooler—but instead, no, not at all, it seemed that they had even decided to upgrade him. Located on the same floor, larger and especially better lit than the first, his new room included double French doors leading to a balcony, from which one could enjoy an unimpeded view of the park. That evening, Max would again have dinner in his room, and Béliard, having invited him to lunch at the restaurant the next day, lent him a pair of binoculars thanks to which Max, while the daylight lasted, could get an overall idea of how the park was laid out.

Bringing Max's tray, Dino, who was attired in his livery once more, marvelled at the new room, sparing no praise for the furnishings, the functional arrangement, and the colour of the walls. "It's much better than my place," he observed. "And just look at that view. Wow!"

Uttering this interjection, he looked so much like what he obviously was that Max, no longer able to stand it, cried out, "Come on, Dino, please, I'm begging you, just admit who you are."

"Who I am?" The valet darkened.

"You know perfectly well what I mean," Max said, exasperated. "I'm sure it's you. I know you, I've often seen you in the movies, I even saw you in a Tashlin film on TV not more than a month ago. I owned some of your records. Come on, admit it, it'll be our secret."

"Sir," Dino declared firmly, "I like you, but I would appreciate it if you did not bring this subject up again. O.K.?"

SEVENTEEN

THE NEXT DAY at around half-past twelve, Béliard came to find Max, saying it was time to socialise him a bit. "It's not good for you to stay all alone in your little corner; you can't keep yourself cut off from the world. A little conversation never hurts." This would therefore be Max's first meal outside his room, at the door of which they met Peggy in the corridor. There she was, apparently just hanging around with nothing special to do, as if she were just waiting to run into Max. And although he, as we have said before, had never exactly been what you'd call a seducer, never been sensitive to the more or less subliminal signals that might have been addressed to him, since he was never sure enough of himself to consider them such, it seemed to him that Peggy looked at him more closely, smiled at him more acutely. Even her make-up and her gait, suppler and more light-footed than usual, weren't the same as the other times, as if something—well, who knows. Anyway, what are you rambling about? Who do you think you're fooling?

"It's not the only restaurant in the Centre, of course, but this one isn't bad," Béliard announced, leading Max through yet another network of corridors that this time did not pass by the lift doors. "Otherwise we could never manage," he continued. "In fact, there's one on every floor. We're divided into sectors, you see, with people grouped by geographical area. The ones you're about to see didn't live very far from your neighbourhood. You might even run across some fellows you knew. In any case, they're only here for a week, like you."

"Fine," said Max, "but why only fellows?"

"Ah," went Béliard, "I neglected to mention that the Centre isn't co-ed. The women's section is somewhere else. I know that sounds a bit old-fashioned. The point has been hotly debated with the management team, but for the moment that's how things stand. We'll see. We have time. We have all the time in the world. Besides, here we are. After you; I insist."

They entered a space able to contain some two or three hundred persons, sitting around about forty tables that were each set for six. There were mainly elderly men, of course, who ate slowly and little without looking around, but there were also some younger ones, sometimes of Max's age, who gaily asked for more wine. Among the latter, one could count a higher proportion of accident victims, murder victims, and suicides who for the most part exhibited souvenirs of serious injuries—puncture wounds, impacts from projectiles, traces of strangulation, and skull fractures. Of course, the surgeons must have treated these lesions as they had operated on Max's, making their scars barely visible, but nonetheless some of these stigmata remained distinguishable and, depending on how each man looked, one could have made up a game of guessing what had happened. Whatever the case, past events did not seem to ruin the appetite of any of them. "Well," said Béliard, "I'll leave you now. You'll be taken care of, and I'll see you later."

A headwaiter in fact came up to them, leading Max to a table where a free seat was available. As Max didn't recognise any of his tablemates at first glance, and as none of them took the initiative to speak to him, he used the opportunity to study the place, and after it the staff. It was, then, a room of huge proportions, monumental angles, and vast perspectives, but in no way reminiscent of a refectory, mess hall, or company cafeteria. On the contrary, everything suggested the decor of a very expensive restaurant: pleated curtains, loaded chandeliers, cataracts of hanging green plants, immaculate embroidered napkins and tablecloths, heavy engraved silverware, prismatic knife-rests, fine porcelain monogrammed with indecipherable interlacing, gleaming crystal, and guilloched carafes, with small copper lamps and assorted bouquets on each table.

The service was supervised by a headwaiter wearing a black dinner jacket, starched shirt with wing collar, black bow tie and white waistcoat, black socks, and matt black shoes with rubber heels. He was assisted by front of house waiters in black evening coats, waistcoats, and trousers, starched shirts with wing collars, black bow ties, black socks, and matt black shoes with rubber heels. These latter oversaw a brigade of assistant waiters in white chequered spencer jackets, buttoned-up black waistcoats, black trousers, starched white shirts with wing collars, white bow ties, black socks, and matt black shoes with rubber heels. As for the sommeliers who constantly verified the levels in each glass, they wore black tailcoats, waistcoats, and trousers, starched white shirts with wing collars, black bow ties, and aprons of heavy black cloth with patch pockets and leather strings; an insignia depicting a gilded bunch of grapes was pinned to the left lapel of the tailcoat.

Lower down in the hierarchy, servers assisted by attendants provided the link between the tables in the service of their assistant waiter and the kitchens, unseen areas in which, under the authority of a head chef, as in any worthy establishment, there must have been an army of sauce cooks, pastry chefs, coffee makers, silver polishers, dishwashers, glass washers, cellarmen, wine stewards, and fruit arrangers—and at the top of the pyramid, gliding along the margins of the tables and keeping a wary eye out for trouble, the restaurant manager was wearing a jacket and waistcoat of grey fabric with black flecks, a starched white shirt and collar, a grey tie, striped trousers, black socks, black shoes, and impeccably silver hair.

No doubt having arrived at the Centre before Max, thus necessarily better informed, the fellows around the tables seemed much more knowledgeable than he about their two possible destinations, park or urban zone, each one wondering about his own fate without neglecting to comment, sometimes rather cattily, on that of the others. They were speculating high stakes, bets were placed under the table, and Max listened. Before learning of the gender segregation, he had briefly nurtured the ever-possible idea of finding Rose at that restaurant, but let's not go into that. Let it pass.

Since the stays lasted a week, some, already there for the past five or six days, had had time to start conversations and had got to know the others. Max felt like the new boy who needed to be broken in. They passed him the salt without a glance and barely said a word to him. It seemed that the only glimmer of sympathy he received was from the meat carver in immaculate kitchen togs who, circulating among the tables with his little chrome cart, sliced the roasts to each diner's specifications after having presented to each the various cuts: it seemed that the choices that day were spring chicken à la Polonaise or saddle of venison with Cumberland sauce. Once he had opted for the spring chicken, Max consumed what was on his menu, including coffee, simply waiting for Béliard to come to fetch him.

Later, in the lift: "So," asked Béliard, "did you run into anyone you know?"

"No," answered Max, who, having spotted no familiar faces in the restaurant, but whom the presence of Peggy and Dino at the Centre—even if the latter clung to his anonymity—had impressed, hinted at his disappointment in not meeting other celebrities.

"On that score, you needn't waste your time," said Béliard, who explained that, while one of the Centre's principles was to recycle old personalities as part of the staff, there were nonetheless quotas to be respected. The whole thing was carefully regulated: no more than two per floor. "For instance, on the next level down," he specified, "they've got Renato Salvatori and Soraya." Some of these past luminaries found themselves exempted from the choice between urban zone and park and were appointed permanently. Their status was without risk, of course, but also without much of a future.

Max was about to have him develop this point about the future when the lift's discreet bell notified them that they had arrived. We won't elaborate on the new corridors that led, this time, to an entrance vastly different from the one through which Max had tried to escape. Here, there was no revolving door reminiscent of an old colonial hotel, no booth, no vista on to a gravelled courtyard: here, two high, wide glass doors led straight out to nature.

"Come on," said Béliard. "Follow me. A little after-dinner stroll, what do you say?"

"With pleasure," said Max.

To begin with, they climbed up a hill from which Max could view the overall structure of the park. It was a huge verdant expanse, roughly circular in shape, but of such vastness that a tour of its horizon seemed to exceed the usual three hundred and sixty degrees. It was composed of remarkably varied landscapes, felicitously combined, a montage of every imaginable geomorphological entity—valleys, hills, steep slopes, canyons, plateaux, peaks, and so on—among which snaked a very complex hydrographic network: here and there, transient or fixed, areas of brilliance revealed or suggested rivers, streams, lakes, ponds, basins, spouts, waterfalls, and reflecting pools, at the horizon of which one could make out a seashore.

Once they had arrived back at the foot of the hill, Max saw a green profusion begin to stretch towards that horizon, a concert of trees and plants in which cohabited every species growing in the most varied climates—pine juxtaposing elm and yew rubbing against terebinth—as one sees in certain Portuguese gardens, but much more exhaustive, to the point where not one of the thirty thousand varieties of trees inventoried in the world seemed to be missing.

"Let's keep going," said Béliard. "We'll take a closer look."

They embarked on a path of a style quite different from the one Max had taken the day before, abundantly floral, bordered by fruit, ornamental and forest trees, and prickly, intertwined vines. In the heart of this vast flora, of course, the fauna was not to be outdone. Rabbits bolted in the bushes like furtive little machines; flights of iridescent hummingbirds striated the sky between the branches; and at mid-level buzzed de luxe insects, hand-picked— varnished dragonflies, lacquered ladybirds, metallic beetles. Further on, certain ill-mannered monkeys hung from the vines screeching like morons while other monkeys, calmer and better disciplined, gathered fruit in the pear trees, the handles of lovely wicker baskets nestled in the crooks of their elbows.

After a while, and seemingly at a great distance, small houses set far apart could be distinguished among the trees that were equally varied in appearance. These constructions bespoke various cultural origins, from traditional hut to yurt and from isba to tea pavilion, but one could also make out more modernist edifices, gas-inflatable structures, concrete dwellings with glass appendages, one-piece abodes of diverse materials, monoshell capsules made of plastic, and even a prefab bungalow. Every one of them had two peculiarities. First, each one was of reduced size, designed to house one or two people at most; and second, each one seemed as if it could be quickly dismantled and rebuilt at short notice, when they weren't simply mounted on wheels. Seeing Max's surprise, Béliard explained that geographical mobility was a way of life among park occupants, a nomadism encouraged by its ample dimensions. Scattered throughout the landscape, these mobile structures generally stood at a decent remove from one another, although certain more sedentary residences, installed in the tree branches, might form a network linked by suspended catwalks, running from plane tree to sequoia. But Max could only see these houses, in which one occasionally glimpsed an occupant or two, from too far away to really make them out in any detail.

"Couldn't we get a little closer?" he asked.

"No," answered Béliard, "we can't. We mustn't disturb them, they don't like that. They value their privacy. And besides, you have visitor status, you see. I can't let you mix with the residents. I can tell you in any case that they're comfortable, all of them at home in their own little spaces, which they designed themselves. It's a very popular solution. Since the park is so vast, they can live here in peace, without being on top of each other. But sometimes they get together. They have the use of sporting equipment. There are golf courses, tennis courts, yacht clubs, the works. I have to say, the amenities aren't bad. They also organise small concerts from time to time, little shows, though of course no-one is required to attend. Everyone does as they please. Actually, I *can* take you to visit one of the units from closer up. We can go and have a look; it's unoccupied at the moment."

He guided Max towards a minuscule English-style cottage flanked by a modest garden teeming with roses and anemones, phlox and love-in-a-mist, cleomes and poppies, under fleeting rainbows unfurled by the automatic sprinkler system, in the shadow of mastic and sweet gum trees. "Just look how lovely that is," marvelled Béliard, "they can even tend their gardens. And besides, there are as many fruit trees as you could want in the park, you see, you can eat anything you like. Well, when I say 'anything', in reality it's mainly papaya. There are practically no seasons here, the climate is ideal. So it grows constantly, papaya, it never stops. Just between you and me, it helps if you like papayas—personally, I have trouble digesting them. But here, let's have a look at some more exotic houses. We'll take advantage of the fact that no-one's in them right now. No surprise, really, since they aren't nearly as comfortable. They mainly serve as stop-overs."

And so Max was able to admire, by turns: a lodge built on oak pillars, with chestnut beams and willow poles, the whole thing thatched with layers of pine needles arranged on a wicker trellis; a circular cabin whose frame, walls, and roof were formed of interlaced reeds, bamboo, and rushes; a low-lying shed covered with palm fronds woven together with goat's wool, and in which the heavy canvas of the walls and roof were stretched and held in place by thick, braided cords; a conical hut with A-shaped rafters built on layers of brick that were coated with a mortar composed of mud, mashed grass, and horse manure, and bonded together with a cement made of peat and cowpats.

"I grant it all smacks a bit of a natural history museum," admitted Béliard. "It's fairly ethnographic. That's enough of these. But you also have less exotic things, look over there." Max in fact noticed, as they walked, miniature Mediterranean villas, fishermen's cottages, workers' units, and even, still more roughly assembled, refurbished caravans, estate cars, or mini-vans, customised bunkers and blockhouses, and inverted boat hulls. "You see," said Béliard, "there's a little of everything. Whatever the client wants."

"Yes," said Max. "And how are they heated?"

"The climate is carefully regulated," Béliard smiled. "You don't need heating here, ever, any more than you need fans. Anyway, there it is," he concluded. "This was just to give you some idea of the park; in any case you'll be assigned tomorrow. But you can see how comfortable you'd be, no?"

"Oh yes," recognised Max. "The only thing is, I'd be a little afraid of boredom."

"Ah," said Béliard, "there's the rub, of course. Right. Well, it's getting late, time to be heading back."

As he was returning to his new room, Max again ran into Peggy in the corridor. She stopped alongside him, all smiles, will you be needing anything? "Everything's fine," Max assured her, "everything's just fine."

"So, you were able to visit the park, you saw how pretty it is?"

"Magnificent," certified Max, "truly gorgeous."

"Well, I'll let you go, I've finished my shift," Peggy indicated, "so I'll say goodnight."

"Goodnight," said Max, "goodnight."

They parted company with prolonged smiles, intent looks. Max hadn't been in his room three minutes when there was a knock at his door. It was Peggy again, who entered on a flimsy

pretext, claiming that the chambermaids had left something behind, looking for that something in vain, then turning impetu-
ously towards Max and, against all odds, rushing into his arms.
And that was how Max Delmarc, one fine evening, possessed
Peggy Lee.

EIGHTEEN

NIGHT OF LOVE with Peggy Lee

NINETEEN

THE NEXT MORNING, Max woke up very late and alone in his bed. As he turned over, eyes still shut, the first spontaneous movement of his brain was to recall the previous night. At first, the episode with Peggy seemed so highly improbable that he suspected it was just a dream. But once he opened his eyes, then sat up with a start and gave his sheets a quick once-over, the state they were in confirmed the reality of the facts. He fell back again, pulling the covers over himself and letting out a contented sigh. Then, after revisiting the high points of the evening, came the second movement of his brain: it was today, he remembered. It was today, according to Béliard, that he would be informed of his fate.

In anticipation of the verdict, Max attempted once again to take stock of his life, as he had done after his operation but in a more strictly canonical fashion: exhaustive examination of conscience following the accepted protocol. Let us recapitulate, then: I've never killed anyone, practically never stolen anything, no memory of bearing false witness, and I rarely swore. I always made sure to rest on the Sabbath, and as for my parents, I think I did the best I could. While I never had a chance to explore the question of adultery very fully, there was certainly the more general matter of coveting my neighbour's goods, wives included, on which I perhaps haven't always been entirely above-board. But fine, nothing excessive. Then, of course, there's the problem of divinity, which I believe I handled reasonably well. Sceptical but honest. Hesitant but respectful. Apart from that, I really can't think of anything. I admit I sometimes had occasion to drink excessively, but first of all, given my profession, I think there were extenuating circumstances, and besides, it seems to me that nothing in the Ten Commandments directly addresses the question of alcohol. What else? Overall I believe I can say that I behaved, yes, rather well. It should be fine. It should go smoothly. Although the park, well, I don't know that it appeals all that much, but we'll see.

Basically satisfied with this panorama, Max then re-projected the film of his night with Peggy. She really was pretty amazing sexually, very imaginative as far as he could judge—he who, for lack of experience, since he had never known much in his life other than two or three unhappy love affairs and a few call girls, could only suppose that she had in fact been full of ideas. Even though in this domain one can rarely surpass the ten or twelve possible deployments with their many variations; after that, it's always pretty much the same thing. For example, during a good part of the night, she had performed long and remarkably so-phisticated blow jobs that Max, back when he would listen to her singing, would never have imagined she could conceive of, despite her artistic talent. He would never have thought of her that way.

It was a little before noon and he, still in bed, was at this point in his reflections when Béliard entered his room with an unaccus-tomed albeit very discreet look on his face, halfway between reprobation and amusement. "Is everything O.K.?" asked Béliard. "Did you sleep well?"

"Not bad," answered Max, wondering if by some chance the other could know about the details of his night.

"Good," Béliard said abruptly. "I have your results. I've come to give you the report; they ruled this morning."

"Go ahead," said Max.

"I'm terribly sorry," said Béliard, "but you're being sent to the urban zone."

"Well, all right," said Max, wondering again if by chance his night with Peggy might have weighed in the verdict, constituting an infraction of the non-co-ed principle that might, just as easily, extend to a more generalised intolerance of sexuality. Just as eas-ily. Still, despite the slight reticence he had exhibited about the park—which was in fact only a bit of coyness, based on his cer-tainty that he'd been assigned there automatically—anxiety seized him. When you got down to it, they hadn't really told him anything about the urban zone, and besides, what was so special about that idiotic name that they'd taken from an old *métro* map?

"To be honest, I don't really understand," he said. "It seems unfair. With the life I lived, my devotion to art, I thought I could expect a little more indulgence."

"You know," Béliard softened, "I won't deny that there's always some measure of subjectivity in these deliberations. It's not automatic. It often happens like this, it's almost standard practice. And besides, we have to maintain the quotas," he added without further details.

"And there isn't any way," Max coughed, "there isn't any way to appeal?"

"No," said Béliard. "That, on the other hand, is not at all standard practice. But don't worry about it, don't take it badly. And besides, frankly, just between you and me, the park isn't always a picnic. You can definitely get bored at times. Of course, you've got the sun all the time, but I'm sure you'll agree that the best part of sunlight is the shade. There are even some who have a very hard time dealing with it at first, and then eventually they get used to it. Fact is, they don't really have a choice."

"Fine," said Max, "I'm willing to go along with the programme, but what exactly is this urban zone about?"

"Very simple," said Béliard. "People form all sorts of ideas about it, but you'll see it isn't so bad, either. In a nutshell, we're sending you back home, there you have it. Well, actually, when I say back home, I mean to Paris, you understand."

"Until when?" worried Max. "When does that part end?"

"That's all there is," said Béliard. "It will never end. It's rather how the system works, if you like. But if it makes you feel any better, remember that it never ends for those in the park, either." And as Max was about to console himself that returning home would at least allow him to find his loved ones again, see people again, resume normal activities, Béliard immediately intercepted his thought.

"There are only three basic rules in the urban zone," he specified. "First, it's forbidden to contact people you knew in life, forbidden to make yourself recognised, forbidden to renew contacts. But that," said Béliard with a knowing air, "shouldn't be a problem."

"And why is that?" Max wanted to know.

"We're going to modify some small aspects of your appearance," Béliard announced, "just some little things. But don't get upset, it's very subtle."

"But I don't want that!" Max protested vehemently. "I refuse."

"I told you not to get upset," said Béliard. "When we put you back together the other day, we already took care of a few details."

"What details?" panicked Max, running his hands over his face.

"You see?" said Béliard. "You didn't even notice. You're going to have a little more plastic surgery, nothing very complicated, just a few finishing touches, some minor touch-ups here and there, and after that no-one will be able to recognise you. As far as your appearance is concerned, we'll handle the entire thing. As I said, nothing too drastic. And let me reassure you straight away, it won't change very much for you. People can't imagine how peaceful it is to be incognito.

"The second point is that you also have to change identity, naturally. That will be your responsibility to take care of. You'll have to see about obtaining identity papers and such."

"Hold on a minute," Max objected plaintively, "give me a chance. I don't know anything about all that. I wouldn't have a clue how to go about it."

"That's not my problem," Béliard said harshly, with his former abruptness. But, seeing how lost Max looked, he ended up digging into his pocket and pulling out an address book, which he leafed through. "I could give you an address," he said, "but it's in South America, and I'm not even sure it's still valid. Still, I'll try to arrange a little excursion for you."

"But I don't know that part of the world," Max repeated. "I don't even know how to get there."

"We'll give you a hand at first," said Béliard, "but after that it'll be up to you to find your way. Right. The third rule, as I've already mentioned, is that it's forbidden to resume your old activity. In the broad sense, I mean. That includes any professional practice related to the one you used to have. You won't be able to play the artist as before, you understand, you'll have to hold down a real job like everyone else. You'll need to find something. But there again, you'll have a little help at first."

"And what about money?" asked Max.

"We've thought of that," answered Béliard. "We'll also give

you a little something to start off with. Well, I think I've covered everything. Your operation is scheduled in twenty minutes, and you'll be leaving immediately afterwards. I'll come back to fetch you in a while."

No sooner had he shut the door behind him than it opened again on Dino, whose smile was a notch below its habitual register. "So you'll be leaving us, sir," Dino said gravely.

"Yes," Max said in an anxious tone. "They're sending me back home. I don't really know what's going to happen."

"So I heard, sir. I'm sorry."

"Dino," Max suddenly thought, "could I get a little something to drink? I think I could use one right now."

"I'm afraid that would be difficult, sir," said the valet. "Your stay here is over. To tell the truth, I just came to prepare the room for the next occupant, you understand, they never stay empty for long. That's the problem with this job, the turnover is very fast and you never have much time to get to know people."

"I understand," said Max. "I understand."

Béliard reappeared just then, accompanied by the stretcher-bearer, and Max said a quick farewell to the valet. "Right, well, good-bye, Dino, thanks for everything and sorry to have bothered you."

"Bothered me, sir?" said Dino. "Come now, not in the slightest, never."

"Yes, I did," said Max. "You know, that question I asked you."

"Really, sir," went Dino, again displaying his classic smile, this time seasoned with an unaccustomed wink—a direct quote from a scene with Raquel Welch in the film *Bandolero!*, which explicitly answered the question.

"Come on, come on, let's go," said Béliard impatiently.

Back in the operating room, Max was offered no commentary by the surgeon, who in any case wasn't the one from the other day. Nor, to put him under, did they use an injection, as he expected: this time it was an anaesthetising mask, promptly clamped over his face, that once more plunged him into artificial slumber, without leaving him time to wonder where, when, how, or even if he would one day wake up again.

III

TWENTY

HE WAS AWAKENED by the chaotic bucking of a hydrofoil, a small yellow craft in the white of dawn slapping over a wide river the colour of glue. Opening his eyes, Max noticed, in the distance to his right, a city of respectable proportions and shabby appearance built near the water. "Iquitos," the pilot soberly announced—a young fellow with a pencil moustache, a face of ochre marble, and dark fake Ray-Bans treated with iridium.

Now immobile, the hydrofoil rocked gently on the surface of the waves, in the extreme heat already rising at that hour of the day. After a few minutes, the young fellow clicked a latch on the door, pointing with his chin to a motorised canoe that approached at top speed and then came to a halt next to the vehicle's floats. Max thanked the pilot with a wave of his hand before jumping on to the canoe, which immediately started up again towards the port terminal located upstream from the city. The canoe driver was as uncommunicative as the hydrofoil pilot, and

Max was carrying only a small bag of unknown origin, containing a few basic toiletries that he didn't recall having purchased. Nothing else, no change of clothes, just an envelope holding a small bundle in a local currency unfamiliar to him, along with a slip of paper bearing the address of a hotel and a telephone number preceded by the name "Jaime". This bundle might be enough to live on for a short while in a country with a weak exchange rate, which at first glance, from afar, the rather miserable aspect of the place suggested that it might be. Max didn't dare ask the canoe driver where exactly in South America they were; it might have sounded strange, and in any case Max spoke neither Spanish nor Portuguese. Whatever the case, he'd have to figure out how to buy something to wear, for at the moment he had on only a shirt, a pair of canvas trousers without a belt, and yellow shoes that pinched his feet.

Located to the north-west of the South American continent, at equal distance from three borders, squeezed between the tropical forest and the Amazon river, Iquitos is a city of 300,000 inhabitants built on the right bank of this considerable estuary. It was officially designated an Amazonian port by the sole clause of Law no. 14702 on January 5, 1964. Its average temperature is 36°. Surrounded by the river and several of its branches, Iquitos might also appear to be a kind of island, since no road leads there; the only way to reach it is by air or water. Along the bank is a series of small docks like the one they were approaching, at the far end of which sat a Ford occupied by two men named Oscar and Esau, who eventually extricated themselves from this vehicle to come and welcome Max.

Much younger than Esau, more talkative and plump, short-sleeved shirt and a gold chain around his neck, Oscar spoke excellent French. Without explicitly naming Béliard, he intimated that he was aware of his influence and the formalities Max needed to handle, before inviting him to get in the car. They turned on to the dilapidated road that must have led to the centre of town. Dark suit, tie, slicked-back hair, thick glasses with large frames, Esau contented himself with driving, silently and slowly, the dented old air-force-blue Ford. The seats and steering wheel of the car were covered in a yellowish plush, and a horizontal band along the bottom of the windscreen was covered by a protective runner of quilted red velour with gold fringes. As this unstable runner kept sliding from its support, falling at the slightest pothole, Esau spent most of his time patiently setting it back in place with one hand, his primary concern apparently being the maintenance of this object that Oscar sometimes helped readjust. Constantly distracted by his task, Esau drove at an average speed of twenty miles an hour, with a fair number of dips to about twelve. When for no apparent reason one of the two windscreen wipers spontaneously began working, scraping the heavily pocked windscreen with a raucous screech, Esau vainly tried every knob on the dashboard to switch it off before letting the matter drop. It was getting hotter and hotter in this car with no air conditioning, and as for the protective runner that continued to slip off, Esau let that drop, too.

In Iquitos, at the corner of Fitzcarrald and Putumayo, the room that they had reserved for Max on the second floor of the Hotel Copoazú was as elementary as could be, its window looking directly out on to a solid wall. Iron single bed; little hospital-style TV attached to the flimsy wall; plastic chair; a bedside table holding a lamp, a telephone, and the television remote control: nothing more. The bathroom was meagre, and Max put off as long as he could checking in the mirror to see what he looked like now. Lying on the bed, the back of his neck twisted by the flimsy pillow propped against the metal headboard, he skipped through some forty public and private channels of local, neighbouring, and North American origin. The three national stations broadcast election results, which Max, although he grasped very little of the language, seemed to understand were being contested. Still, he couldn't stop thinking about his face, with a mixture of fear and impatience, dreading what he desperately wanted to see.

He finally decided to have a shave, comb his hair, and brush his teeth as an excuse to get himself into the windowless bathroom. As the neon light above the mirror naturally didn't work, he could only view himself in silhouette, but from that perspective, at least, nothing appeared significantly different. He waited another long while in front of the television before calling the front desk to ask in his rudimentary English if someone could come and replace the bulb—*Please could you change the light in the bathroom, it doesn't work*—*Sí, señor*—which also took a fair amount of time.

Then, once the repair was made and Max was alone again, he took a deep breath before daring to go and look at himself.

Nice work. They hadn't made a mess of it. While Max was patently unrecognisable, you couldn't attribute his transformation to anything in particular. Not his nose, forehead, eyes, cheeks, mouth, or chin—nothing had changed. Everything was there. Rather, it was the arrangement of these features, the relationship between them, that had been imperceptibly altered, although Max himself couldn't have said exactly how, in what order or which direction. But the fact was, he wasn't the same any more—or rather, he was the same but incontestably someone else: his face might appear vaguely familiar to someone who had known him, but it would surely go no further than that. He tried opening his mouth wide to make sure they had left him his teeth: they had. He recognised his old fillings and his little crown, but there again an indefinable new maxillary order seemed to reign.

Perplexed, at once relieved and horrified, Max turned on the tap to give himself a glass of water. But on the one hand, he was trembling so hard that it took several attempts to fill the vile cup, and on the other the water from the tap, which under European climates has to pass sixty-two quality parameters to be deemed potable, must in Iquitos have had roughly a few dozen, at the most. So Max called down to the front desk again to ask for an *agua mineral* to be sent up. And while they were at it, considering that this kind of thing doesn't happen to you every day, judging moreover that after his week of relative abstinence at the Centre he certainly deserved one, why didn't they also bring him a bottle of pisco, with ice and some lemon. Sí, señor. While waiting, he went back to look at himself again in the mirror. He'd get used to it. He didn't have any choice, of course, but fine, he'd get used to it, maybe even quicker than he thought. He switched off the neon light, left the bathroom, and, just as he was turning up the sound on the television, someone knocked at his door.

It was the manager with his tray, holding everything Max had asked for. Once the manager had left, Max uncapped the bottle of pisco and eagerly poured himself a drink, but the taste of the alcohol was repulsive, vile, unbearably emetic, and Max had to run to spit it out in the sink. What's going on here? Very strange. And yet pisco is actually quite good. Whatever the case, after having washed and carefully wiped his glass, Max rinsed out his mouth with *agua mineral*, opened his bag, removed the envelope, opened the envelope, took out the piece of paper with the telephone number jotted on it, sat down on the bed, pulled the telephone towards him, and dialled the number.

TWENTY-ONE

AFTER HANGING UP the phone, Max left the hotel with his empty little bag, which he spent the afternoon filling by doing some shopping in the streets of Iquitos: clothing suited to the climate—light jacket and shirts, cotton trousers, pack of underwear; basic necessities, such as a belt, razor-blades, soap, and shampoo; as well as a larger bag to hold it all plus the folded smaller bag. Back at the hotel, he ate alone, the clink of his silverware producing sinister echoes in the empty restaurant dining room. Then he went upstairs and soon got into bed. He slept fitfully and, having risen early, decided to leave this establishment without further ado.

That morning, Max quickly found two rooms to let in the dilapidated mansion of a former rubber tycoon. The façade of this residence was covered with glazed ceramic tiles, beautifully decorated though now mostly cracked; *azulejos* that, in the days of his splendour and Iquitos's prosperity, the tycoon had had shipped from Portugal via fluvial and maritime routes, on the same ship that carried his dirty laundry each week to the Lisboan laundries. The barred windows looked directly out on the Amazon past Avenida Coronel Portillo and, from his room, Max could thus enjoy a view of the wooden houses built at river level, some floating, others on stilts. Large sea-going vessels passed by in the distance, motorbikes spluttered on the tarmacked avenue, birds circled above the traffic of the canoes, and small children played in the rubbish. Max absently surveyed this spectacle, daydreaming, developing his thoughts in two directions. First, he would have to get used to living with his new appearance, while waiting for the documents bearing his new identity that they would deliver in a few days at the airport cafeteria, as agreed the day before on the phone. Second, while his rent for the two rooms wasn't exorbitant, Max had nonetheless felt a twinge of worry when calculating the fraction it deducted from his little bundle. The identity forgers surely weren't in it for the good of the cause, and what he had left wouldn't take him very far. We'll wait and see.

Resigned to spending his money, he soon came across a place where he could take his meals: the Regal restaurant, located in an iron building on Plaza de Armas, above the British consulate. The iron had the drawback of amplifying the heat like a cymbal, but you could eat fish from the river while watching the girls who strolled across the square in tight, inaccessible groups and the men who gathered around the sewer drains, amusing themselves by fishing for rats with some line and a bit of omelette tied to the end. And here, as in every tropical restaurant in the world, you could see huge fans reflected in the concavity of the saucers, spoons, and ladles like gigantic insects or tiny helicopters. Max stared at all of this with an interested but detached eye, the eye of a man resuscitated, restored to the world and looking at this world as if through a pane of glass.

As he didn't speak to anyone and no-one spoke to him, his main activity consisted in systematically and thoroughly perusing the local and national press, which soon gave him an elementary grasp of Spanish. On the heels of an obviously fixed recount, the controversy over the electoral results still occupied the front pages in bold headlines, but Max was more interested in the back sections. Entirely photographic, these related in detail the social lives of the local and neighbouring ruling classes. Thus one could see, in the context of various inaugurations, receptions, premières, marriages, and cocktail parties, groups of personalities flashing wide smiles at the paparazzi with glasses in hand. Evening gowns, dinner jackets, champagne, and pisco sours, general gaiety, dizzying multiplicity of faces, none of which, of course, was familiar to him. Max, whose stay at the Centre had made him neither forget his cares nor lose his habits, continued to verify automatically if Rose might perchance figure in one of these photos. Naturally, such a hypothesis was highly improbable, but when you got down to it, having disappeared so completely, she could just as easily turn up married to an Argentine banker or a Guatemalan indus-trialist, or maybe a Paraguayan senator.

One can get used to Iquitos fairly quickly—more so than to those yellow shoes that Max still hadn't managed to replace. It's fairly easy to get around, and one finds oneself not too badly off. Apart from his money worries, which he kept putting off think-ing about seriously, Max felt as if he was on holiday by the end of his third day. But that was the day of his meeting with the iden-tity broker, at Francisco Secada Vigneta Airport, located two and a half miles from the centre of town. To get there, Max had to take one of those motocars whose drivers were constantly offering him their services. The motocar, a covered scooter with a seat in the back, is the Amazonian equivalent of the rickshaw, though lacking the side panels and with a slightly different body from its Indian counterpart. Unlike the latter, it is not spangled with po-litical or pious transfers—just a tiger or two, at times, painted on the seat—and isn't equipped with a meter. But as we all know, a rickshaw meter isn't worth much. We all know just how unreliable it can be, and so the fare for a ride is debated from the start no less bitterly with a *motocarista* than with a Tabul rickshaw-wallah, a Beninese *zemidjian*, or a Laotian *túk-túk* driver. As for the comfort provided by each of these vehicles, it is more or less comparable in every case.

Arriving at the airport, Max had no difficulty finding the cafe-teria nor, virtually alone in the middle of it, the aforementioned

Jaime to whom he'd spoken three days earlier on the telephone, sitting before a steaming double espresso. Jaime must have been about Max's age; the small, ironic spectacles of a presbyopic filtered his knowing gaze. Left arm in a cast buried under a sweater buried under a jacket buried under a coat buried under a scarf buried under a hat—but, despite the steamroom atmosphere, these superimpositions did not seem to bother him overmuch. No sooner had they started talking than an old shoe-shine boy, haggard and dressed in rags, came to squat at Max's feet and, without asking his permission, immediately began to polish his shoes, which Max let him do without overseeing the operation.

"Right," said Jaime, "everything is almost ready. All we need now is an ID photo. If we could have it by the day after tomorrow, the papers could be ready at the end of the week."

"Fine. And tell me," worried Max, "do you know exactly how much this is going to cost?"

"Hard to say just yet," Jaime eluded. "We haven't drawn up the final invoice."

Then, concerning the shoe-shine boy who had finished his task and was now standing, trembling lightly in silence and staring fixedly at him, Max asked the same question.

"And what about him? How much should I give him?"

"A one-sol coin will do," decreed Jaime.

Max paid the shoe-shine boy without looking at him and arranged a second rendezvous with the forger, who then walked away. Left alone, Max cast a glance at his shoes. For lack of yellow shoe polish, no doubt, Max's footwear had been made violet, a beautiful and spectacular violet. Maybe they really weren't any worse like that, but still. Max stood up and left the airport, staring at the new colour of his feet. Well, if one was going to change identity, might as well start from the ground up.

TWENTY-TWO

THE DAYS THAT FOLLOWED didn't go nearly so well. Time passed ever more slowly and Max grew ever more concerned about money. For whatever one might think, despite his stay at the Centre and the tragic event that had preceded it, his personal situation did not prevent him from experiencing the classic feelings and needs of the organism. Hunger, heat, thirst (even without pisco), the desire for elementary creature comforts—all this raises problems that only money can solve. The humblest lifestyle is still subject to a budget. But Max could see his resources dwindling visibly, inexorably.

Added to this was an increasing sense of isolation. While discovering Iquitos had initially been enough to occupy him without his needing to speak to anyone, by now Max had had enough of tourism; by now he couldn't stand the solitude of this godforsaken hole any more. No way to share a few words with anyone on Plaza de Armas, neither the pretty girls nor the rat fishermen.

And if he sometimes managed, in his budding Spanish, to chat a bit with natives, mainly the ageing waiters of the Regal, it was only to hear pessimistic and resigned news of the city: exploding suicide rate, omnipresence of religious cults, massive drug traffic, practice of black magic, and I'll spare you the rest. All this was pretty discouraging and didn't exactly inspire Max to try to settle here. He had bouts of depression, days of boredom, the kind of listless boredom engendered by the union of solitude and modest means. He sometimes lost all desire to walk around Iquitos, what's the point, and once he even spent the entire day shut up in his two rooms, pacing restlessly between them, a caged beast who only stopped now and then to contemplate, through the bars of his window, the river with its unchanging colours.

That day, to take his mind off things, Max decided to write to his sister, thereby breaking the strict regulations that Béliard had recited to him. He spent a good hour composing his letter, in which he explained everything, recounted everything, complained about everything, and even had the nerve in conclusion to ask Alice for money. But once he had signed, read, and folded his letter, slipped it into an envelope and licked the adhesive strip, the troubles began. First, Max cut his upper lip on the flap of the envelope—a wound that, although very fine and benign, proved to be disproportionately painful; second, the rancid fish taste of the glue spreading through his mouth was abominable; third, Max stopped to think about the problems he was courting if Béliard were to press an investigation, now that he'd left behind some compromising saliva—the Centre's doctors surely hadn't gone so far as to alter his DNA. And finally, reflecting on, fourth, the extreme distress Alice might feel on receiving it, Max opened the envelope, read his letter over one last time, then ripped it up and burned the pieces.

At the Tropical Paradise Lodge on Putumayo Boulevard, where he had gone to nick a few leaflets for reading matter, he was offered the opportunity to take his mind off things by enjoying a canoe ride down the river. It would be another expense, of course, but what the hell, the half-day was still within his means. From several angles, the dark blocks of the Amazonian forest some-times called to mind certain areas of the park he'd visited with Béliard. Infested with mosquitoes, the waterways were lined with trees that grew following a bizarre logic, as if prey to a hereditary insanity, which went no small way towards fostering a sense of unease. They came across other canoes, rowed by silent locals transporting crates, bags, rubbish bins, or chickens in cages. They saw dogs, and once a fat iguana on a protruding branch, or more precisely a fat, female, pregnant, flabby iguana, which the canoe driver tried to capture to steal her egg—nothing tastier, the man assured him, than soft-boiled iguana egg.

On the appointed day, Max took another motocar back to the airport. Jaime was there, again swaddled in the convection-oven temperature, this time sitting in front of a hot chocolate. He handed Max a small bag made of embroidered cotton—local craftsmanship, handmade, he pointed out, a gift—containing the perfect copy of a French passport in the name of Salvador, Paul André Marie, French nationality, born on the same day as Max with Max's photo beneath, accompanied by no children on page four and authentic French fiscal stamps on page five. On page seven, in the first empty space reserved for visas, there was even a stamp attesting to his arrival in the country's capital, several weeks earlier, at Jorge Chávez International airport. It all looked impeccable.

While Max leafed through this object, Jaime withdrew from his pocket and handed him a folded sheet of paper on which a long number was inscribed. This number, the amount of the invoice for the passport, corresponded precisely, down to the last centavo, to what Max was carrying that very moment in the pockets of his new trousers: apparently they had kept close tabs on him, watched over his slightest expenditures, meticulously calculated what he had left, and now Max was utterly broke. As this must have shown on his face: "What's the matter?" said Jaime. "Is something wrong?" Max didn't have time to answer before the other, smiling as if he had been waiting only for this, was already making him a proposition so classic and devoid of imagination that it's embarrassing to report it. It would involve, as is only too common in this sort of caper, transporting a certain something abroad—to France, as it happened—for a certain remuneration. The situation is so common that there isn't even any need to specify the nature of this something, enclosed in a lizard-skin valise with locked, gilded-metal clasps, that Jaime, bending down, pulled out from under the table and placed on top.

"Here, this is all you'll have to carry," he explained. "It's nothing. Discreet, easy work, and paid. Not in local currency, trust me on that. You'll get dollars, the freshest bills around."

"Sure," said Max, "I don't mind, but when would I be going?"

"Right away," answered Jaime. "Your plane leaves in forty-five minutes."

"And what about my things?" worried Max.

"No problem," said Jaime, bending down once more, "I've got them right here. They stopped by your place to pick them up after you left." He handed over the belongings, carefully folded in their bag, and here are your tickets and here's your money. Max took a moment to count this money: dollars indeed, but very few of them, barely enough to last two or three days in Iquitos, in other words two or three hours in France. But for now, what else could he do?

"Right," said Max. "Fine."

TWENTY-THREE

MAX, HIS SUITCASE, and his bag did not have long to wait: immediate boarding. In the lounge at Iquitos airport, locals departing for Lima crossed paths with clusters of holiday-makers come to tread the limbo of the Amazonian forest, study the natives, consult their shamans, and have their minds exploded by the ingestion of *ayahuasca*. The luggage of both groups was carefully and suspiciously sniffed by two dogs kept on a leash and muzzled, whose absence of reaction at the passage of the lizard-skin suitcase at least allowed for the hope that it didn't contain any narcotics. Then, as soon as Max was seated in the small plane it began moving at top speed, attaining its altitude and cruising velocity in the blink of an eyelid, attesting to the professionalism of the pilots. This country, in fact, maintains a long tradition of virtuoso aviators, taking off at the appointed time and landing at the exact moment without getting bogged down in considerations or niceties—never hesitating to dive towards their goal, for instance, almost on a vertical trajectory and ignoring the stages of decompression entirely, heedless of the passengers who clap their hands in unison over their eardrums and howl in pain.

On the other hand, Max had a longer wait in Lima, where he passed the time reading through the newspapers, pleased to note his dazzling progress in Spanish, but anxious about what awaited him in Paris. Then, once on board, he dispensed with the mimo-drama of safety precautions performed by the stewardesses, who then distributed among the passengers orange juice and sweets, blankets, and headphones featuring various musical programmes. A knob embedded in the armrests allowed one to choose among these programmes: selections of easy listening, jazz, ethnic, and classical music. As the aeroplane began to taxi, Max put on his headphones to have something to do, automatically stopping at the classical selection where he immediately identified an *Impromptu* by Schubert in midstream, the Allegro in E-flat from Op. 90. But no sooner had he recognised the work than he also recognised his own performance, recorded five years earlier at Cerumen. He pretended not to notice, the way one feigns not to see a bothersome acquaintance in the street, except that this time the acquaintance was himself. He immediately changed programmes, then finally gave up; in any case the headphones were hurting his ears like an ill-fitted prosthesis. Max preferred listening to the sound of the Boeing engines, which was deep and penetrating, fundamental like an endless breath, not like those little Airbus motors that give off the sound of an old cultivator. Then he eventually fell asleep.

It was raining hard in Paris when the aeroplane touched down at Roissy-Charles-de-Gaulle, the kind of heavy rain that seems to fall from very high up and that Max had noticed, several days earlier, from the windows of the Centre. After customs, where, nothing to declare, no-one bothered to inspect the contents of his bag and suitcase, he passed through the doorway to the main hall unimpeded. There, facing the flow of arrivals, several individuals seemed to be waiting: two wives equipped with children ready to throw their arms around the first available neck, three unknown persons holding cardboard signs with names on them. Max did not immediately react when he spotted, on one of them, his new identity written in capitals; then, remembering, he walked straight up to it.

The unknown person holding it was absurdly wearing a beard, hat, dark glasses, and a raincoat buttoned to his Adam's apple. Still brandishing a card with Max's name even as he watched him approach, he dangled at the end of his other arm a suitcase of moderate size that he immediately held out to Max, without, for lack of available prehensile organ, shaking his hand.

"I'm Schmidt," he said, "and here are your belongings. I trust you have the suitcase."

"Here," said Max, handing it over.

"Good," said Schmidt, taking it. "Let's go and get a taxi."

A fairly short queue at the taxi rank, after which the so-called Schmidt gave the driver an address, an odd number on Boulevard Magenta. Max discreetly studied this improbable Schmidt, with his exaggerated surplus of anonymity attributes—although in truth, he wasn't certain they were really artifices; all of it could have been entirely normal for him. Then, deciding to cut short his contemplation—Schmidt probably didn't much appreciate people looking at him—Max turned in the other direction to ponder the landscape. It felt as if he was coming home after a very long absence, even though his combined stays at the Centre and in Iquitos had probably lasted no more than two weeks, but under the circumstances it was understandable to think that way. Through the taxi window, he saw the flat low-rise buildings and tall towers of the eastern suburbs that are visible around Bagnolet, when you return from the airport on the A3 motorway. Max had always found it hard to believe that these buildings contained real flats housing real people, with real kitchens and real bathrooms, real bedrooms where they authentically coupled, actually repro-duced—it was scarcely imaginable.

But as it happened, the lodgings selected for him by the ser-vices of the Centre would be hardly more desirable. Schmidt, after remaining silent on the motorway, specified the route to fol-low once they hit the peripheral boulevard and, on Boulevard Magenta, halfway between Place de la République and Gare de l'Est, the taxi pulled up at an hotel. While not exactly luxurious, this establishment, named the Montmorency, wasn't quite a flea-pit, either. It possessed a foyer, two conference rooms, and a bar. They didn't take the lift: without stopping at the front desk, where a shapeless receptionist was marking time, Schmidt immediately beckoned to Max to follow him up a steep staircase that did not appear to have been built for the use of the clientele. On the uppermost floor, two rows of brown doors, opposite each other and very closely spaced, filed down a dark yellow corridor. Schmidt pulled a key from his pocket and the fourth door on the right opened on to a narrow room, wall-papered with faded flowers and fitted with flimsy furniture apart from an overly large bed, with a washbasin as its sole sanitary facility.

"Here you are," said Schmidt, "this is your home. There's a shower and a toilet on the landing."

Max walked up to the French window, pulled back the curtains, whose metal rings squeaked on the metal rod, and opened it on to the tumult of the boulevard that immediately began roaring and bounding into the cramped space.

"One problem," Max reminded him, immediately closing the window. "I have practically no money."

"The first month's rent is taken care of," Schmidt indicated. "After that, it'll be up to you to pay out of your salary."

"Salary," Max repeated uncomprehendingly.

"Of course salary," the other confirmed. "You've been assigned to the bar. I'll show you."

They therefore went down to the cellar of the establishment. As the bar was empty at that hour of the morning, Schmidt introduced him to his future work area, the multicoloured collection of bottles, the glasses of all sizes, the utensils, saucers, cocktail shakers, strainers, juice extractors, and spice racks. On a hanger in the cupboard hung a worn red jacket; a gilded metal rectangle was already pinned to its lapel with the name Paul S. engraved on it.

"Here you are," said Schmidt, "your work uniform. You have two days to get over jet lag, and on Monday you start. The management knows the story, if there are any problems you take it up with them. We will surely not have occasion to meet again . . . good luck."

Back in his room, Max pulled from his bag the items he had bought in Iquitos: garments that were too exotic and lightweight for the climate here, still impregnated with tropical aromas that he breathed in nostalgically before putting them away in the narrow white melamine armoire. Then he opened the suitcase that Schmidt had given him. It contained a dark grey suit, a pair of black trousers, two white shirts, a black tie, and three pairs of Y-fronts, as well as a pair of black shoes wrapped in a newspaper from the day before. All these clothes, of synthetic fabric, approximate size, and mediocre quality, seemed to have been worn by countless others before being put through numerous industrial washes. Welcome to the urban zone.

TWENTY-FOUR

MAX SPENT HIS TWO DAYS OFF walking around Paris. First he tried a few experiments in his old neighbourhood of Château-Rouge, as a way of verifying the effect produced by the plastic surgeons' work. He went incognito to see the shopkeepers he had habitually frequented, whom he used to call by name, and who for their part had ended up, despite his not exactly sociable nature, considering him a nominal regular. He observed their reactions when he entered their shops, making a few small purchases—a pack of Kleenex here, the evening paper there—looking them in the eye more and more intently, but without the others ever showing the slightest sign of recognition.

It even happened on the first day that, as he was leaving his ex-pharmacy, he ran smack into the woman with the dog, flanked by the latter to her left and her husband to her right. It was the first time Max had seen the three of them together; they looked rather content to be that way but showed no reaction when they crossed his path: they even met his gaze for a few seconds, then walked off as if he didn't exist. Only the dog, after a brief latency period, turned back towards Max with a perplexed expression, braking for an instant and knitting his brow—that odour reminds me of something, confound it, I've already sniffed that somewhere, but where? To give himself time to study the question in depth, the animal even stopped to piss lengthily against the right rear tyre of a Fiat Panda while examining Max, who for his part, wanting to verify once more the transformation of his appearance, leaned discreetly and symmetrically towards the vehicle's left rearview mirror. Then, yanked by his leash, the dog seemed to drop the matter, letting his attention drift toward a band of soaked, hirsute, rumpled pigeons who—the proof that they're aware of their filth—had come to take a lustral bath in a gutter of flowing water before flying heavily off again.

Since he was in the neighbourhood, Max decided to brave it still further by going to see his sister. He would just try to get a look at her, without making contact, merely to reassure himself that she was all right. He would proceed carefully, without exposing himself to Alice's view, for, despite the know-how of the Centre specialists and given what had just happened with the dog, it wasn't far-fetched to think that his own sister—blood thicker than water, etc.—would recognise who he was. Accordingly, he took up a position not far from the entrance to his building, inanely hidden behind a newspaper; and in fact, after an hour or two of waiting, he saw Alice come out, stop in front of the doorway, and look at her watch. And then, surprise surprise, here was Parisy emerging from the building in turn to come and join her and take her arm. Parisy's bearing, a slight nonchalance in his suit along with something lighter, more familiar, in his behaviour, suggested that the impresario had finally made it with Max's sister, perhaps had moved in with her, and perhaps had, troubling perspective, even taken over Max's studio. It nonetheless seemed to Max, from a distance, that Alice was speaking a bit harshly to Parisy, who answered while waving his other arm in agitation—in short, it seemed as if they were already fighting. Max watched them walk away, not following them, then set off again. He continued to look at all the people he came across in the street, wondering about each one's status: maybe there were others like him, who had passed through the Centre before coming back here; maybe there were many of them; maybe, when you got down to it, they were even in the majority.

Once his two days of recuperation were over, Max, as scheduled, began his new vesperal service as a bartender. It turned out that the bar was not only empty in the morning; it was that way almost all the time. Not empty enough, however, for Max to take it entirely easy: there was always, at some advanced hour of the evening, one customer or other, sometimes alone but much more often accompanied by a woman. And Max, noticing that it was usually the same woman but not the same customer, and that their brief stays at the bar (whispered confabulations in which numbers played a part) most often concluded with the ordering

of two drinks or a bottle to be brought to a room, soon understood what was what. So there weren't a lot of people there to
pass the time with, which didn't keep him from being asked now
and again for atypical cocktails that were a real bore to make.
Alcohol itself was no longer something to pass the time with: it
seemed that, since his attempted pisco in Iquitos, Max's appetite
for it had curiously evaporated.

And every night at around 1.30 a.m., he returned to his room
after having done the till and wiped down the bar. He took off
his red jacket and the rest and immediately went to bed, reviewing
his cocktail recipes in a special book and taking pains to memo-
rise them. Then he had trouble falling asleep in his large bed, for
large beds, let's not forget, are made for two people to find each
other in beneath the sheets, and these sheets themselves are designed to be folded by a couple. Just see how a man trying to fold
his large sheet alone soon ends up in an awkward position, entan-
gled in himself as much as in the sheet; see how his short arms
struggle to attain the required breadth. Whereas a couple, folding
the sheet together while talking about other things, have it much
easier—not to mention the additional interest, the intimate strat-
egy, of anticipating, on either side of the dividing sheet, which
direction the other will turn it in so as to harmonise with his or
her movement.

But then see, too, how things work out. After several painful
weeks of solitude in the depths of his red jacket, Max ended up
meeting someone. As often happens in life, this would occur at

his place of work, at the hotel itself. The receptionist. Not at all as shapeless as he had originally thought. She was, on the contrary, a tall reddish-blonde, not fantastically wonderful-looking, but not too bad, always dressed fairly sexily, with high heels up to there. He might have noticed her earlier, but the truth is, during his first days at the Hotel Montmorency, Max hadn't noticed anything at all, not even that it was raining all the time.

Now one day, when the sky was promising enough to clear up, Max ran into the receptionist not far from the hotel, right in the street, lit by a shaft of gentle sunlight. She was with a small boy in the four-five range who was complaining in an anxious voice that something black kept following him, that something was there and it didn't want to go away. "It's just your shadow, darling," the young woman explained. "It's nothing. Well, it's not nothing, but it's just your shadow." That sentence persuaded Max, who felt pretty shadowy himself, to take an interest in this young lady. He would proceed gradually. He had time.

He had time, but things nonetheless went faster than expected. One Wednesday Max suggested they go for coffee—O.K. Bought her some flowers—very O.K. Then invited her to dinner, next Sunday when he wasn't on duty at the bar—all the more O.K. in that the receptionist's son would be spending the night at his grandma's. Risked complimenting her overtly—absolutely O.K., and Max, as it happened, neither restrained nor recognised himself: you're so feminine, he told her, tracing rounded figures in the air, you're the very definition of feminine. To which she responded with a very pretty laugh. She was a single mother named Félicienne. What a beautiful name, Max enthused. And how well it suits you. So well, in fact, that their evening ended in a hotel, neither very far nor very different from the Montmorency.

TWENTY-FIVE

THEN, after his shift the next evening, Max went to see Félicienne at her place, and on the nights that followed he would no longer sleep much in his room at the hotel. The receptionist lived in a three-room apartment, hardly bigger than Bernie's on Rue Murillo: a living room and two bedrooms, the larger one being occupied by the kid, whose IQ they hadn't gauged yet and who answered, or didn't, depending on his mood, to the name of William—though in general, they just called him the kid.

At first, Max spent only his nights at Félicienne's, joining her after having closed his register and changed jackets, but always escaping from her place the moment he woke up. After breakfast in a nearby café, he would go back to the hotel to take a shower, then set off again to walk around Paris, sometimes stopping in a cinema—better to see a film than to watch the time pass on the ceiling of his inhospitable room, stretched out on his bed as if dead. But little by little Félicienne persuaded him to have breakfast with her, use the bathroom after her, accompany her to the babysitter's to drop off the kid, then escort her to the Montmorency. Not quite to the entrance: no sense in the whole staff knowing about them. They usually separated one street beforehand.

That was in the first stage, for it happened that things moved quickly—very, then too quickly. Max soon found himself being given a copy of the door key, along with a shelf in the cupboard for his change of clothes, which would rapidly land in the laundry basket next to the washing machine, after which, since according to Félicienne Max had nothing to do all day long, he saw himself being handed the iron. Responsibility for this iron was soon followed by the bestowing of shopping lists, on which figured a fleet of cleaning products whose directions Félicienne taught him to read and then apply, having already introduced him to the mop and broom cupboard, which would keep him busy until it was time to go and collect the kid from the babysitter's. From that point on, Max went to the cinema less often, now spending the free time he had left after shopping and cleaning in front of Félicienne's video, taking advantage of her subscription to a video club.

This evolution is hardly enviable, but then again, since things were going well with Félicienne sexually, this shared life was basically as good as any other. For lack of other alternatives, at least there was this. And so the time passed. Having finished his shift, Max joined Félicienne who was asleep, who on awakening gave him a little love before setting off to the hotel to receive the customers and answer the phone, leaving Max, sorry, leaving Paul to take care of the housework, and returning home just as he was setting off in turn to put on his red jacket and concoct spritzers, bronxes, manhattans, and flips for a clientele that, truth be told, was rapidly deteriorating. Plainly put, the vague provincial businessmen who took advantage of their brief stay in Paris to buy themselves a girl for the night were being replaced by a growing population of locals who fancied that kind of girl, and who often weren't even guests of the hotel; in short, there were more and more whores, often the same ones and often quite nice. Max wasn't offended—on the contrary—by this shift in population, which paid less attention to the dosage and quality of the cocktails that he still had some trouble mixing by the book.

Given their work conditions, Félicienne and Max hardly saw each other any more, except on Sundays when they took the kid out for some air—which kid, initially shy with Max, ended up letting himself be won over to the point of becoming very familiar, then more and more familiar, and soon much too familiar for Max's taste. They went to the Champ-de-Mars on Sundays, they went to Les Halles, to the park, they went for a walk down the Champs-Élysées. It always gave Max a funny feeling when Félicienne suggested Parc Monceau. He no longer dreaded the statue of Gounod next to the drinking fountain, nor even the one of Chopin not far from the children's playground, where the kid constantly stamped his feet to have yet another turn on whatever it was.

Nonetheless, Max began to feel bored. While he'd grown accustomed fairly quickly to his new physical appearance, strangely enough he had much more trouble with being called Paul, but perhaps someday he'd get used to that as well. And so time passed as if in a waiting-room, with a sense of leafing through magazines as worn-out, faded, and mind-numbing as Félicienne herself. On top of which, what did he really know about Félicienne, other than that she dwelled on insane claims about the past, bitterly insisting that in her youth she'd had measurements to kill for, a gift for languages, and perfect pitch? But, raised in modest surroundings, she'd had to enter working life early, thereby sacrificing a triple career as a world-famous top model, international interpreter, and renowned concert performer, having been forced to abandon the piano. Max, slicing the Sunday roast, masked with his indifference the intense relief produced by this third piece of information.

Indifference, yes, they would reach that point. Soon the arrangement with Félicienne would no longer be working so well. It's just that love—well, when I say love, I'm not sure it's the right word—is not only evanescent, but soluble. Soluble in time, money, alcohol, daily life, and a host of other things besides. Sexually, for example, it was not going well at all, Félicienne refusing his advances more and more often. In fact it was going so badly that Max, often, dreamily played a record he'd found one day at a discount shop near the Porte Saint-Denis, *The Best of Peggy Lee*, about which Félicienne, demonstrating a real hostility as if she suspected something, would sourly ask him how he could waste his time listening to that shit.

"No, no," said Max, "no reason. I just like it."

Nor did it help matters that he found it harder and harder to stand the kid, who, technologically very precocious, demanded the video-recorder for his own exclusive use, depriving Max of being able to watch one of the two videos with Dean Martin— his all-time greatest roles, in *Some Came Running* and *Rio Bravo*— purchased that same day at the same discount shop.

Several increasingly lack-lustre weeks flowed by like this until one night when, in the bar, while turning over and over the different ways of putting an end to this business with Félicienne, Max was artlessly preparing an alexandra—the composition of which is not all that complicated: three equal parts cognac, whipped cream, and crème de cacao. As he was struggling with the whipped cream, which was too firm after a prolonged stay in the fridge, he saw a man come in at the far end of the room, fairly short in stature and flanked by an immense redhead dressed in almost nothing.

Max knew the redhead a little, one of the new regulars he liked well enough, a sweet girl who ran on whisky-fizz, which is a refreshing drink served directly in a tumbler, very simple to prepare. Too absorbed in his task, he paid no attention to her new admirer, who sat down with her at a little table in the back, then, standing up again after a few seconds, started walking towards

Max, no doubt to impart what he wanted to drink. Now, Max had better things to do at that moment than to take an order, having just spilled all the whipped cream into the shaker, and, head down, he was just about to rebuff the outsider, when: "Monsieur Max?" uttered the outsider.

TWENTY-SIX

MAX JUMPED, sending the whipped cream spewing even further and raising his eyes to the outsider. Bernie.

"Monsieur Max," Bernie repeated with delight. "What are you doing here?"

"It's a long story," said Max, wiping a spurt of cream from his sleeve. "But how did you recognise me?"

Bernie didn't seem to understand the question. "Well, it's you," he said. "Why?" (One's true friends, Max melted inside.) "I'm really happy to see you," declared Bernie. "I've often wondered what became of you."

As he didn't seem to know about any of it, Max avoided going into the matter. "And how about you?" he asked. "What have you been up to?"

"I had some problems with Parisy," answered Bernie, "didn't he tell you? I got fed up, you see, he wasn't true to his word, and I left right after your concert at Gaveau, do you remember? I haven't seen him since."

"Of course," eluded Max, understanding that Bernie, who still maintained he never read the papers, must not have heard about what had happened to him, neither his disappearance nor, of course, the rest.

"But I immediately found something much better," Bernie continued. "I'm in show business now. I've completely broken with the classical crowd. I organise shows. Well, not exactly—I'm a concert promoter, if you like, and it's going pretty well. Ah, I never would have expected to find you here."

"Yes," said Max, "I needed to get away from what I was doing before, you understand, the milieu and all that. I needed a break myself."

"Right, right," Bernie said dubiously. "So you're happy here?"

"Not really," said Max, "but it's just for now. It's temporary."

"Even so, a man of your stature," lamented Bernie, "ending up here. I've never been to this place, but it doesn't strike me as all that great. I was just coming in for a drink with my friend."

"Of course," said Max, with a wide smile for the friend, which caused Bernie to glance down at his shoes.

"Listen," he said timidly, "if you ever wanted to make a change, I might be able to help."

"You think?" Max pretended to wonder with a detached air.

"Oh, definitely," said Bernie. "I'm sure I could find you something. Are you still playing the piano?"

"Well, actually, that's a bit complicated," said Max. "But anyway, what can I get you in the meantime?"

"It's mostly cocktails here, right?" said Bernie.

"Alas," admitted Max.

"Well, in that case, I'll have a rainbow," Bernie stated. "Hold on a minute, I'll ask my friend what she's drinking."

"Don't bother," said Max. "I think I know."

When Bernie returned the next day, alone, Max was wiping his tumblers while casting distracted glances at the two or three girls settled in that evening with their clients. While he was relieved that someone had finally recognised him, he was also a bit concerned about flouting Béliard's instructions. But after all, he himself hadn't done anything; it was Bernie who had recognised him, Bernie who had acted on his own, Bernie who was coming back to see him. It was also Bernie who had looked into things: an acquaintance of his named Gilbert had just opened an establishment off Rue d'Alésia.

"Very up-market," stressed Bernie, with a gesture towards the girls. "Not at all like here. Kind of a nightclub, very distinguished, very quiet, and they're looking for a pianist. What do you say?"

"In principle, I really shouldn't," said Max, "but what the hell." Yes, what the hell, what would the staff of the Centre know? Of course, it would again mean working in a bar—which, given

Max's past, bordered on just retribution, or repetition compulsion—but it was perhaps, and particularly, a welcome chance to rid himself of Félicienne. Although he didn't quite know how to go about it, as he explained in detail to his former bodyguard. "I tell you, Bernie, I can't take any more of that woman. And I don't have the first clue how to get away from her."

"Nothing could be simpler, Monsieur Max. Here's what we'll do."

TWENTY-SEVEN

AND THE FOLLOWING SUNDAY, after they had walked the kid, Max announced to Félicienne that he was taking her out to dinner that very evening, which would give him an opportunity to introduce her to an old friend of his.

They met in front of a large seafood restaurant on Place de l'Odéon. Bernie was already waiting, very elegant, standing very straight in a chic black unstructured suit, nothing like the outfits Max was used to seeing him in. Max only had the sordid grey suit left by Schmidt to wear; a striped tie bought by Félicienne failed to raise its sartorial level. From the moment they went in, the staff treated them with an attentiveness that rivalled the restaurant in the Centre. Félicienne, impressed by the setting and Bernie's elegance, tried not to show it. As she went to powder her nose before they were shown to their table, Max briefly took Bernie aside.

"There's just one thing I forgot to mention," he said.

"Yes, Monsieur Max?" said Bernie.

"Listen carefully, tonight you don't call me that, O.K.? Just call me Paul. I'll explain later."

"That's fine with me," said Bernie. "It's my stepson's name. It'll be easy to remember."

It must be obvious by now that Max is not exactly the world's jolliest fellow, the most relaxed or talkative person around, but as soon as they sat down at their table, he became someone else. Maintaining a smile that was by turns affectionate, complicit, seductive, kind, relaxed, and generous, he took the floor from the start and did not let it go, segueing gracefully between myriad anecdotes and light pleasantries, attentions and compliments, bons mots and witticisms, subtle observations and rare quotations, imaginary memories and historical comparisons, without ever getting bogged down or seeming as if he was hogging the spotlight. Bernie was convulsed with laughter at the slightest remark from Max, while Félicienne, dazzled, looked at him with a new tenderness and wide, emotion-filled eyes.

From aperitif to dessert, Max thus staged a spectacular performance. Hanging on his every syllable, Félicienne and Bernie smiled and laughed non-stop, she turning several times to Bernie to take this charming friend of Paul's as witness to her happiness, Paul's charming friend sometimes laying a discreet hand on Félicienne's shoulder to punctuate his hilarity. At times both of them looked at each other, delighted like enthusiastic spectators sitting in adjacent seats thanks to the luck of the draw of their tickets, who spontaneously, without knowing each other, connect in their enchantment. Charming ambiance, delectable evening. From the diners sitting around them to the waiters themselves, the whole room cast seduced, almost envious glances at this trio led by a Max in excellent form.

When suddenly, at the turn of a phrase, he immobilised both the fork above his plate and his smile, freeze-frame on the image, his gaze fixed on Félicienne and Bernie in a glacial stare. Disconcerted silence around the table.

"No, really, both of you," he said in a changed voice, "you think I haven't noticed your little game? You seriously believe I don't see what you're up to? You somehow imagine I'm going to put up with this right under my nose?"

And, standing up, Max pulled from his inside pocket a wad of notes that he dropped on the table before taking his leave for ever, without another word, wearing a bitter expression of wounded pride.

And the next morning, he met Bernie in a café near Châtelet.

"So," said Max, "how was I?"

"Excellent, Monsieur Max," said Bernie. "You were perfect."

"I owe it all to you, you know," said Max. "It was your idea. How did she take it?"

"The poor woman," said Bernie. "She didn't know what hit her. She needed consoling, so I took it upon myself. I saw her home and then, you know how it is."

"Very good," said Max, "you did well."

"So there you have it," said Bernie. "I'm seeing her again on Thursday."

"Just be careful," Max warned. "She's not exactly an easy customer."

"Oh," said Bernie, "I'm used to that. But now where are you going to live?"

"I don't want to go back to the hotel," Max indicated.

"No problem," said Bernie, "you can just come and stay at my place."

"I've been to your place," Max recalled. "It's too small."

"I've moved since," said Bernie. "Now I live on Boulevard du Temple. It's not as fashionable as Monceau, but I have a lot more room. I have the income for it now—you saw my suit last night, didn't you?"

"Speaking of which," said Max, "I owe you for dinner."

"Oh, don't worry about it, Monsieur Max," said Bernie. "We'll deal with that later. In the meantime, let's go and see Gilbert."

The establishment that Gilbert had recently opened was large, dark, and silent at this hour, as was Gilbert himself at all hours. The decor was elegant, sober, and distinguished, as Gilbert turned out to be as well.

"So you're a pianist," he said.

"Gosh," Max qualified, "let's say I used to be."

"Monsieur Max is a great artist," Bernie testified, his eyes bulging.

"You see," said Gilbert, "the fact is, I need someone reliable. I know all about the problems you can have with musicians. Would you mind submitting to a small audition?"

"Really, Gilbert," Bernie said indignantly, "you can't just insult him like that. You forget you're dealing with an artist of international stature."

"No problem," said Max, "as you wish. What would you like to hear? Classical or piano bar—whatever you prefer."

As Gilbert left the choice up to him, he performed "Laura", "Liza", "Celia", one after another, followed by one or two polonaises.

"That should do perfectly," judged Gilbert, but just at that moment the door to the establishment flew open and, visibly furious, Béliard made his appearance.

TWENTY-EIGHT

WITHOUT A WORD OF GREETING, without a glance at Gilbert or
Bernie, Béliard walked straight up to Max with a determined step.

"What did I tell you?" he began, screaming. "If you think we're
not watching, you've got another think coming. What you're
doing here is a double violation, it's not right, it's a double infraction of the rules. Not only did you let yourself be recognised——"

"You can't blame me for that," Max interrupted him, pointing
to Bernie. "*He* recognised *me*. It's your doctors' fault for not doing
their job properly."

"Maybe so," shouted Béliard, "but then on top of it you're
practising your former profession."

"Not in the slightest," pleaded Max, pointing to the piano. "I
was just showing these gentlemen what I can do."

"Fine," said Béliard, calming down a bit too quickly, "I'll let
you off this time."

He had changed since the Centre. He no longer displayed the

haughty, distant, and condescending composure that had antago-
nised Max from their first meeting. He now seemed hyper-tense,
taut with emotion, flying off the handle just as quickly as he'd
then let the matter drop. Gilbert and Bernie chose to move away
from the piano, sidling over towards a back room.

"Let's get out of here," Béliard decided, nodding his head in
their direction. "We'll be able to talk more freely outside."

They went out. The street. The cars passing by. The various
kinds of music escaping through the lowered windows of the
cars. Sometimes it was just rhythmic blips, sometimes heavy bass
lines that sent a shiver up the spine. At first they walked without
saying anything; then Béliard resumed speaking.

"I've come to put things back in order," he stated calmly. "So
now you're going to do me the favour of going back to your job at
the bar, all right? At the hotel where you've been assigned."

"Absolutely not," Max declared in a firm voice. "I don't ever
want to go back to that bar. I don't think I've done anything to
deserve that."

"You're beginning to get on my nerves, Delmarc," Béliard
started shouting again. "You're making my life very difficult.
You're not a very easy fellow to deal with, do you know that?"

"First of all, what are you doing here?" asked Max. "I thought
you always stayed at the Centre."

"They reassigned me," said Béliard. "I've been rather tired
lately. And anyway, as I said, I needed to deal with you. I'm going
to stay here a few days, long enough to put you back on the

straight and narrow. And besides, I have another, more important problem to take care of. I've got someone who escaped from the park—you remember the park?—who I have to bring back. It's work, it's really a lot of work."

"First you should get some rest," Max pointed out. "What hotel are you staying at?"

"I don't know," said Béliard, ready to collapse, "I just got here, I haven't had time to deal with it. Do you know of one?"

Advising him against the Montmorency, Max recommended the Holiday Inn on Place de la République. "It's not bad," he emphasised, "it's comfortable and centrally located. And on top of which, I've got a friend who's offered to put me up on Boulevard du Temple, which is just a stone's throw from République. We won't be far from each other, we can get together whenever you like."

"Maybe," said Béliard, letting his shoulders sag, "I don't know. I'm exhausted. Yeah, maybe that's what I'll do. Is République far from here?"

"A bit," said Max. "You'll be better off taking a taxi."

"Fine," said Béliard. "All right." Then, pulling himself together and wagging his finger: "But don't get any ideas about acting like a bloody fool behind my back, all right?"

"No acting like a bloody fool," said Max. "Go and get yourself settled. You get settled in, get some rest, and I'll call you in the morning, all right?"

"All right," said Béliard. "That's what we'll do."

Max hailed a taxi into which the other man jumped without

another word and which Max watched drive away. The fact is, Béliard seemed utterly depressed.

"It was nothing," said Max once back at Gilbert's, "just a friend who's going through a bad patch. Anyway, where were we? Shall I play you something else?"

"That won't be necessary," said Gilbert. "I thought you were very good."

"Right," said Max, "so when do I start?"

"How about Monday?" suggested Gilbert.

"Ah, I'm so happy," Bernie exclaimed ten minutes later, in another taxi that was carrying them towards Boulevard du Temple. "Monsieur Max, I'm proud of you."

"I should be thanking *you*," said Max. "Furthermore, you can call me just plain Max from now on. Or Paul. Whichever you like."

Bernie's new flat, at number 42, was indeed roomier than the one on Rue Murillo but also much noisier, as it looked directly on to the boulevard. Since the stepson's room was still unoccupied—"He's in Switzerland now," explained Bernie. "A big private school in Switzerland. He just keeps getting smarter and smarter"—Max moved into it without bothering to fetch his things from the hotel. An advance from Gilbert would allow him to buy all new clothes as of tomorrow, after he had met Béliard as arranged.

Béliard was decidedly less agitated than the day before. "I slept well," he informed Max. "I got some rest. I needed it." Without

Max having to plead his case, he made no more fuss about the new employment at Gilbert's. "I admit that business with the Montmorency was a bit harsh," he judged. "Basically, you can do as you wish, I'll smooth things over with Schmidt. I'm going to take advantage of being here to do a little sightseeing. Do you have plans for this afternoon?"

"Just some shopping," said Max, "for some new clothes. But we can have dinner tonight if you like. Why don't you drop by at Bernie's, he'd be happy to meet you."

So Béliard dropped by at Bernie's, got along with Bernie, came back the next evening then the evening after that, to the point of dropping by for dinner almost every evening until they eventually got used to his being around.

While Max persisted in his new-found sobriety, it seemed that Béliard, on occasion, gladly yielded to the call of the spirits. One excessive evening, he opened up a little, evoking in a jumble his daily life at the Centre—"It doesn't seem like much, but it's hard working there. You might not think so to look at him, but Lopez can be a holy terror"—and a few episodes of his professional career. As he emptied glass after glass under the worried eyes of Max and Bernie, he pastily alluded to a so-called mission during which he'd had to look after a young woman in dire straits. He was just starting out at the Centre at the time, he laboured to explain, he was in training and it was especially horrible to be a trainee, he assured them, pouring himself another one, they force you to be small, ugly and mean, I who love only what is beautiful and good, but anyway, he'd had to go through that stage. He was clearly delirious.

As the days went by, Béliard, who had started drinking a lot, at times from early in the morning, called in at Boulevard du Temple on a daily basis, to the point where they soon had to take care of him full-time. Bernie arranged for another room for him and they took him for walks, brought him to the Louvre or the Musée d'Orsay, dragged him out to the Mer de Sable amusement park and the Palace of Versailles, made him breathe the clean air of Buttes-Chaumont park. Having no further objection to Max's job at Gilbert's, Béliard accompanied him there every other evening, sitting at a table very close to the piano with an infinitely refillable glass and insisting on loudly giving his opinion of the music afterwards.

But this saturation soon twisted him up, as is sometimes the case, in knots of depression. When Béliard started complaining continuously about his loneliness, despite the fact that he was always on their backs, they searched for new solutions. Bernie even offered to introduce him to girls. Not difficult girls, he hastened to add, but nice, simple girls, the kind you might for example find in abundance at the bar of the Montmorency; but Béliard flatly refused. "My condition," he slurred with a drunkard's gravity, "forbids me." Without making any comment, Max deemed his refusal to associate with mortals rather snobbish.

They went through a difficult period, then, in which Béliard started moaning so much, and so constantly, that they ran themselves ragged trying to help him. They recommended he see someone—but in spiritual medicine he had no confidence. Max, who remembered going through similarly difficult periods, offered to obtain anti-depressants of all kinds, things with lithium that at the time had brought him a little relief, but Béliard refused these as well. He refused everything they suggested. They didn't know what to do with him.

TWENTY-NINE

AND THEN, who knows how or why, the situation gradually improved. After several weeks, Béliard started feeling better. Without going so far as to swing into a manic state, the classic alternative to depression, Béliard's mood took a more serene turn: they saw him begin to smile again, start conversations, even take some initiative. Soon Max and Bernie no longer needed to rack their brains finding distractions for him: he went out all by himself in the afternoons, the entertainment listings in his pocket, and they didn't see hide nor hair of him until it was time for the aperitif—towards which, moreover, he seemed to be practising a certain moderation.

He who, since his arrival at Bernie's, had never lifted a finger to help out with day-to-day life, might now come home carrying—on his own initiative—some shopping for dinner. Truly Béliard was making progress, tidying his bed as soon as he got up, helping with the dishes and the housework, cleaning the bath before leaving the bathroom. Willingly he accompanied Max to the supermarket, nor did he hesitate to change a light bulb or cart the empty bottles to the green receptacle on the corner of Rue Amelot, even without anyone having dared to ask him. The ideal guest: pleasant, cooperative, and so discreet that sometimes Max, coming home late from his job at Gilbert's and consequently rising late as well, didn't see him for the entire day.

On one of those days when Béliard had disappeared—to the Sainte-Chapelle, the Grand Rex, or the Drouot auction house—Max took advantage of his free afternoon to go to the Printemps department store, with the prosaic goal of underwear renewal. Having quickly dispensed with this, he wandered around the store's various floors, with no desire to buy nor any aim other than to pause here and there in front of things for which he had no need whatsoever, a multi-functional shower head, a wide-screen plasma TV, or a panoply of knives—for vegetables, tomatoes, bread, ham, and salmon; for de-boning, slicing, or hacking. All the while, he listened vaguely to the various loudspeaker announcements, which might encourage shoppers to check out this week's bargain on curtains, discounts on household appliances, twenty-percent-off awnings, or Madame Rose Mercœur to please report to the customer service desk on the ground floor.

Of course, it wasn't that rare a first name, but then again, why not? Nor had it been, at the time, Rose's family name, but anyone can get married. In short, it was even more improbable than at Passy or Bel-Air, but he had time to kill, so why not go and have a look? However, the situation was clearly making him nervous, and he advanced discreetly towards the lift without seeming to be in a hurry, with the same detached air and pounding heart as if, having just committed a robbery, he was afraid of being watched—careful not to give himself away by suspicious behaviour under the eye of the surveillance cameras. In the lift, Max continued to display this nonchalant slowness; then, having reached the ground floor, he searched a bit more feverishly for the customer service desk and, once he had found it, believe it or not, this time it was her, it was absolutely her.

It was immediately apparent that Rose, who hadn't changed much in thirty years, in other words, no more than would be expected, had had her nose remodelled, about which Max experienced a wisp of annoyance. We recall that this nose, at the time, might not have been her loveliest feature, but even so, even so. Slightly too hooked, it was so well framed by a perfect face that it ended up being, at the time, all the more endearing. Fine, well, now it had become as pretty as the rest; it was rather a shame, but why quibble? It was, in any case, a handsome job of plastic surgery, wholly worthy of the surgeons at the Centre. As for Rose's outfit, she was wearing at the customer service desk none of the clothes he had spotted the day of his pursuit in the *métro*. It was fairly classic, a camel-coloured cashmere twin set and speckled tweed skirt—Max noted with a pang of emotion that the label of the twin set, having escaped the cardigan, was curled up on the nape of her neck.

She was alone. She appeared to be waiting. Max wanted to go up to her, but she surely wouldn't recognise him—understandable, given the time gone by, not to mention the treatments he'd undergone at the Centre. So she obviously wouldn't identify him, but then again, trying to seduce her with his new name and appearance might even be rather exciting after all these years. Max was dying to approach her, but something held him back; he was embarrassed by his pathetic clutch of shrink-wrapped underpants no less than by the risk, as always, of looking like a . . . although that risk, this time, seemed less likely than it had with the woman with the dog. He nonetheless waited a while, giving his heart time to stop pounding so hard and himself a moment to imagine how he might dare go up and speak to her.

It was then that, from across the store, Max saw Béliard cross the entire length of the perfume department and walk up to Rose, accosting her head-on and without preamble, as if he'd known her for ever. Between Chanel and Shiseido, they immediately launched into an animated discussion, easy and smiling, at the start of which Max, horrified, witnessed Béliard fold the label of Rose's jersey back inside with a familiar movement. After which he seemed to be stressing a point, making his case with eloquence and with the use of gestures, always the same gestures and therefore, no doubt, always the same point. As the conversation went on, Rose for her part showed more and more signs of acquiescence, provoking in return wider and wider smiles from Béliard.

Max could not help starting to walk towards them, like a ghost, but let's not forget that he is only a ghost, then stopped several yards away. As Béliard noticed him at that moment, he beckoned to him to come closer, maintaining his wide smile, come over here so I can introduce you. "This is Paul," he uttered, "a friend of mine. And this is Rose, an old friend I hadn't seen for quite some time." Béliard smiled more and more broadly. "I had almost given up ever finding her again." Max bowed clumsily to Rose, who, as anticipated, gave him merely a slight nod without showing the least sign of recognition. "Well, we'll be leaving now," Béliard announced. "We have a small errand to run."

"Wait just a minute," said Max. "Excuse me, but this person— I think *I'm* the one who was supposed to find her."

"Yes," Béliard said with a cold smile, "I know. I'm perfectly aware of all that, but I'm still the one leaving with her. You see, this is what it's like in the urban zone. This is what it consists of. In a sense, it's what most of you call Hell. So, are we agreed?" he segued, turning back to Rose. "I'm taking you back to the park? My dear Paul, I bid you farewell for the time being."

Standing frozen by the customer service desk, a crushed Max watches as Rose and Béliard proceed towards the glass doors, push them open, and leave his field of vision; then, as if in a trance, he sets into motion as well. Once outside the store, he again spots them walking up Boulevard Haussmann in a westerly direction, but he stops there, follows them only with his eyes, without trying to catch up. At the corner of Rue du Havre, Béliard looks back to give him a little wave, and Max, deader than ever, sees them resume their walk, growing smaller on the receding boulevard before turning right and disappearing into Rue de Rome.

The
GREEN GRAVES
of BALGOWRIE

by

JANE HELEN FINDLATER

NORWICH:

The Walpole Press, 36 Elm Hill

1930

9th Edition

Dedication

From this grey town beside the Forth,
Go, little book, up to the North,
With greeting that your author sends,
To Margaret, dearest, best of friends ;
And as she reads you, bid her smile,
Bid her remember all the while,
(Reading of broken faith—of tears)
Our happy, undivided years.

THE GREEN GRAVES OF
BALGOWRIE

I

"*THEIR graves have been green for ninety years and more,*"
*said my grandmother, as she finished telling me the tale of
Henrietta and Lucie Marjorybanks; "so you may make
what use you like of their story."*

"*Don't tell me it's true,*" *I said—for my eyes were wet.*

"*Well, that is the story as my mother told it to me; and she had
seen Lucie face to face—she was the Maggie Pelham of the tale.*"

"*Ah, Life, there are stranger things in you than were ever
written!*" *I said.*

And I have held to that opinion ever since.

*   *   *   *   *   *   *   *

The old house of Balgowrie stands on a rising ground,
and looks seaward over a wide bay where the tide rushes
in with a long tumbling surf. To the back of the house the
country is wooded, and is intersected by deep and very muddy
roads. Once upon a time the Balgowrie garden, which lay
to the south and was protected by high walls from the sea-
winds, blossomed and brought forth; but now the walls are
broken down, and the salt winds whistle over the flowers.
Veils of fog-like grey moss cover the apple trees, and the
fruit is green and sour that grows on their neglected branches;
the rose bushes are all gone to leaf, and each rose has a little
mossy green heart; the jasmine has grown into a great tree

that hangs all to one side over the south wall, and path and turf have long ago been merged into one.

The house itself is little more than a ruin now. Its old gables are stained to half a dozen hues with the damp of years, and yellow sea-lichen has crept over the slates, colouring them like autumn sunlight. House-leek covers the rounded steps that lead up to the door, and wall-flower is growing bravely in every chink. The only memorial that " envious time " has left of Henrietta and Lucie Marjorybanks in the place that once knew them, is a heart cut upon the west turret window, with the name " Lucie " scrawled above it, and underneath, the words " United hearts death only parts," with over all the date 1775.

Some wild pigeons—far-away descendants of the fan-tails that once fed from Lucie's hand—still flutter round the doo-cote : they are the only living things about the place.

But even in its better days Balgowrie was a lonely—an eerie spot : rat-hunted, and with a reputation for being ghost-haunted too, which had kept it empty for years before it came into the hands of Mrs. Henry Marjorybanks in the year of grace 1766.

The widow, with her two little daughters, aged respectively nine and twelve, had not been long settled at Balgowrie before the neighbouring gentry came jolting over the miry roads in their yellow coaches to pay her their respects. But these overtures of friendship were received with great coldness, and the only return made was a week later, when John Silence, the widow's man-servant, went round the neighbourhood, leaving his lady's card upon those families who had honoured her with a visit. This, in an age much more punctilious than our own in matters of etiquette, was considered an outrageous breach of good manners, and Mrs. Henry Marjorybanks was not disturbed by more visitors.

This was exactly what the widow had desired. Her object in taking a lonely house in a lonely neighbourhood had been to cut herself off, so far as is possible in this life, from the world of living men. Her success was admirable. After the first few weeks no stranger ever passed through the gates of Balgowrie, and the two little girls, Henrietta and Lucie, grew up in as complete isolation as any castaways on a desert shore.

The only communication which Mrs. Marjorybanks kept up with the outer world was by letter. She corresponded with but one person, a certain Mrs. Pelham, then residing in London, and her reasons for choosing this lady as her friend were of a piece with Mrs. Marjorybanks' other eccentricities, as the following story will show: The late Henry Marjory-banks, in the days of his youth, had fallen deeply in love with a beautiful girl, who rejected his addresses, and married another suitor, Charles Pelham by name. Marjorybanks was inconsolable. He fell, indeed, into very poor health, and adopted peculiar and rather pessimistic views. While in this state he made the acquaintance of the woman who was afterwards to become his wife. She was considerably his senior, but their ideas seemed wonderfully harmonious ; according to herself, she had tasted " the pleasures of this world and proved their hollowness." Presumably, however, she had now a desire to prove the hollowness of matrimony, for she exerted herself not a little to gain the affections of Henry Marjorybanks. This she never did ; but she gained his hand, which was the next best thing to do, and retired with him to a lonely village in the south of Scotland, where the curious couple lived for many years. Here Henrietta and Lucie were born and spent the first years of life, and here their father died when the children had reached the ages of twelve and of nine. Whether Mrs. Marjorybanks had, after her own strange fashion, been attached to her husband, or whether she only imagined that she had been, she certainly assumed all the most profound trappings of woe when he died. The place became hateful to her, and she cast about for some equally lonely house where to bury herself and her unfortunate daughters. At the same time she opened a correspondence with Mrs. Pelham by returning to her several letters which she had found among her late husband's papers. Mrs. Pelham had also become a widow. Of several children, only one remained to her, a daughter of nearly the same age as Henrietta.

The similarity of their circumstances struck Mrs. Marjory-banks. " You are bereaved like myself ; you have a daughter whose age corresponds with that of my Henrietta ; above all I see that you were my husband's first love," she wrote to Mrs. Pelham, at the same time praying her to continue the correspondence.

" The woman must be mad ! " Mrs. Pelham had exclaimed on receipt of this letter, and the impression did not wear off as the time went on, and her unknown correspondent continued to ply her with the most voluminous letters ever penned.

In these letters Mrs. Marjorybanks poured out her ideas on every subject under heaven. She expressed herself cleverly, and there was a strong flavour of originality in all her views. These were not the conventional views held by every decorous woman of the day. Mrs. Marjorybanks had evidently been born several generations too soon. Her religious beliefs—or want of belief, for she boldly named herself " atheist "—would only be considered a bore now, when every sensible person is weary of " doubts ; " in these days they were mentioned under the breath. In politics she was a radical ; before the days of socialism she was a socialist ; wherever opportunity offered, she placed herself in opposition to established use and wont. " I count it one of my greatest mercies," she wrote in one of these exuberant epistles, " that I have children to educate. My daughters are intelligent ; they shall not be trained like every other woman in Britain ; their personalities will be allowed free scope ; my daughters shall not be turned out like ninepins."

Mrs. Pelham, a gracious, womanly " fine lady " of the old school, seeing that her opinion was of some weight with her extraordinary unknown friend, tried a little remonstrance here.

" It would be better to concede a little to the generally received views upon education," she wrote ; " and your daughters, I feel sure, would benefit by mixing with other gentlewomen."

But the widow was immovable.   She had formed her own ideas of what her daughters were to be, and she held to these with determination.

The children who had fallen into such strange hands for guidance were very unlike each other both in appearance and in character.

Henrietta, the elder of the two, was a tall girl for her age, with dark, lank hair and grey eyes, while Lucie was like a child in a picture, with fair curls and brilliantly blue eyes. Henrietta had her mother's peculiarity of character—though in the daughter it had not that harshness which made Mrs. Marjorybanks unpleasant;   yet, Henrietta never did everything exactly like other people, never expressed herself in a commonplace way, and, indeed, had far too pronounced ideas of her own on every point.   Lucie was nothing more or less at this time than a child—as sweet and fresh as only children can be.

What would have struck any outsider rather painfully in coming into this household at Balgowrie, was the dread which the children had of their mother.   She never ill-treated them in any way, and did not even believe in severe punishment, yet every year the children seemed to draw farther away from her—farther and farther into a close little world of their own. their dread had been quite instinctive and unacknowledged till one day,—it was a damp November afternoon, and the physical oppression outside may have affected the child,—as Henrietta stood by the hall window watching her mother, who was coming up the steps from the garden, wrapped in her long black coat, suddenly little Lucie pulled her sister by the sleeve, and in a choking whisper, as if afraid of her own voice, cried out—

" Oh, Harrie, I'm frightened ! "

" Frightened, Lucie ?   It's not dark."

" Of . . . of *her*," cried the child.   Harrie would not, from her superior pedestal of three extra years, have admitted to Lucie the sudden panic that overcame her also at these words. Fear is so much worse when we acknowledge it.   For a moment she thought blindly of " running " somewhere—

anywhere—away from this terror. Then she said only,
" Nonsense, Lucie ! " and established her supremacy for
ever over Lucie's weaker character.   They never spoke of it
again.

II

THE first object of Mrs. Marjorybanks' Educational
System was the development of character rather than
the acquisition of knowledge.   " No character,"
she maintained (in one of those prolix letters which she
devoted to educational subjects), " can take its individual bent
if it is subjected to the authority of an elder mind too soon ; "
and, following this idea, Henrietta and Lucie ran wild and
lessonless for the first dozen years of their lives. By the phrase
" the authority of an older mind " Mrs. Marjorybanks seemed
to imply its influence rather than the usual meaning of the
word " authority," for she exacted implicit obedience from
her children in all physical matters, and only left them without
a guide in the more perplexing ways of the mind. If, as all
intelligent children will, they asked her questions, she had
none of those ready-made answers which are safer satisfactions
to the growing mental appetite than anything else ; instead
of these, Mrs. Marjorybanks bade the children " think for
themselves," or " come to a decision for themselves," and
their decisions on many subjects were very quaint in conse-
quence.   They grew up utterly ignorant of the outside world,
and having only a verbal knowledge of any of the facts of life.
Reading, which, with the addition of writing, was their only
accomplishment, will not, after all, teach a child much if
nothing it reads is explained to it. " They will grasp the
forces that sway the world better, if they come to understand
them without preconceived ideas," wrote Mrs. Marjorybanks.
  So the children had lived on year after year untaught, and
probably would have remained ignorant even longer, if an
accident had not sent them a teacher who happened to please
their mother.

One damp November afternoon, a few months after the arrival of Mrs. Marjorybanks and her daughters at Balgowrie, as they returned from their usual walk, a riderless horse feeding by the roadside attracted their attention. Mrs. Marjorybanks looked up and down the lane for the owner of the horse, then she stepped up to the beast, and, taking it by the bridle, turned its head towards Balgowrie.

"Someone has met with an accident," she said. "We will send Silence to the village to make inquiries."

The little girls were quite pleased by this amusing episode. It was so delightful to try to keep up with a horse—it got over the ground at such an amazing pace with no effort at all! They took little runs beside it and laughed. But as they came round the turn of the lane, the rider lay across the path, a sight that checked their mirth.

"Hold the horse, Henrietta," said the widow shortly, bending over the figure on the road.

"Oh, madam, is he hurt—is he dead?" cried the children. They knew that something called Death existed, and used the word glibly enough.

Mrs. Marjorybanks knelt down and examined the man.

"No; only drunk," she said, "and stunned."

"Drunk? what does that mean?" the children asked each other by signs, for the word had no meaning for them.

But as they spoke, the man sat up and began to look about him in rather a bewildered fashion. He was a handsome elderly man, with thick grey hair, and a fine smooth skin.

"Come, sir," cried Mrs. Marjorybanks, "get up, and thank your good luck you can. Had I not come this way, you might have lain here long enough, to be ridden over by the first waggon that passed. Here, get up—I will help you."

"It seems I've had something of a tumble, madam," he said, feeling the back of his head meditatively with his ringed hand. "That horse is the very deuce to shy when the light is bad."

"A good rider should be surer of his seat than that," returned the widow.

She prided herself on administering home truths, and always judged of people by the way in which they received such remarks. This man seemed quite to understand her. He only laughed, and asked Mrs. Marjorybanks to be kind enough to help him to rise.

" For, faith, madam, as you insinuate, I'm perhaps not so steady as might be," he said, laughing again.

His straightforwardness quite won the widow's heart. She helped the stranger to his feet and inquired after his injuries.

" You're all right, now, whatever you were when you fell, sir," she said, intending to be amiable. "But since your head has suffered, you had best take my arm to Balgowrie, and rest there for an hour or two."

The stranger, however, professed himself quite able to walk unaided, and at a slow pace they made their way through the lane, the older people first, Henrietta and Lucie behind, leading the horse.

When they reached the house, Mrs. Marjorybanks bade the children run away to Hester, and herself ushered the unknown gentleman upstairs.

Hester was the old servant who united the functions of nurse, maid, and housemaid at Balgowrie. Hers had indeed been the only care that Henrietta and Lucie had ever known. She it was who cut out and made for them the curious garments they wore ; she had even taught the children to read and write, for Hester had been a farmer's daughter from the south country, and prided herself on her genteel speech, very different from the rough Doric speech of Silence and the kitchen " lass," who, together with the gardener, formed the rest of the domestic staff at Balgowrie. Hester did not quite approve of Mrs. Marjorybanks' views on education, but knew her place too well to interfere with them. The little girls, meeting her on the stairs, stopped her to ask with wide eyes, " Hester, what is *drunk* ? " And Hester with great prudence replied, " A weakness gentlemen suffer from, misses," but would not say more.

" It must be very uncomfortable," said Lucie sympathetically. " I hope he will soon feel better."

Later in the evening, when the children came down to the drawing-room, the unknown guest sat by the fire, looking quite well.   He and Mrs. Marjorybanks seemed to be talking very earnestly together.

Henrietta came forward into the fireside, curtseying low to the stranger, as she had been taught to do.

" I hope that you find yourself better, sir ? " she said, with with her funny grown-up manner.   " You seemed to be so sadly drunk in the afternoon."

It would have been impossible to suspect intention in such an earnest-faced, sympathetic little speaker.   The stranger held out a plump white hand to her and answered her question as gravely as it was put.

" Yes, my little lady, I find myself much better."

Then he flung back his head against the high-backed chair and laughed till the gaunt Balgowrie drawing-room echoed with his mirth.   The children were startled, and shrank back, hand in hand, into the shadow.   Then the stranger rose from his seat, wiping his eyes, which streamed from the force of his laughter, and turned to Mrs. Marjorybanks.

" Ah, madam, you must pardon me ! Children are so delightful, they go to the point as we never can."

He called to them to come nearer, and asked their names and their ages, not in the perfunctory way common to " grown people," but as an evident preface to friendship.   When he sat down again, Lucie came and stood beside his chair, placing her tiny fat hand on his knee, and Harrie, understanding the unspoken compact between them, began to turn his ring round and round on his finger.

" What are you called, sir ? " she asked.

" I am called Dr. Hallijohn, Henrietta, and I am minister of Eastermuir, if you know what that means," he said gravely.

III

D R. CORNELIUS HALLIJOHN, at the time I speak of, was perhaps as manifestly unsuited for his calling as a man could well be.   But his father, a hard-living, impecunious country gentleman, had been the patron of

Eastermuir, and having a son to provide for, and little prospect
of having much to leave him, had sent Cornelius into the
Church.   Ten to one Eastermuir would be vacant by the
time Cornelius was ready for it, he had calculated, looking
upon the grey hairs and tottering gait of the then incumbent.

And Cornelius, having been born with a silver spoon in
his mouth, had stepped comfortably into this fat living at
the age of three-and-twenty, and at the close of a genial
pursuit of divinity at St. Andrews.   His father, a few years
later, died almost bankrupt, but the lucky Cornelius very
shortly after this fell heir to an uncle's money, and settled
down, lonely, it is true, but possessed of most ample means,
and a nature admirably fitted to enjoy them.

These were not the evangelical days when even a country
minister, by industriously bearing upon his heart the souls
of his parishioners, can be busy in spite of a sparsely populated
district.   The handsome, idle young man found small amusement here, and sought it eagerly elsewhere.   Now for twenty
inactive years the minister of Eastermuir had done nothing
beyond the compulsory duties of marrying, burying, baptiz-
ing, and preaching.   Twice each Sunday he had preached—
vain repetitions that fell from careless lips upon deaf ears.
The sick died with scant prayers to ease their going ; the
funerals were hurried oftentimes ; the baptisms delayed.   But
souls from the parish of Eastermuir appeared before God none
the less and gave in their account of the things done in the
body, without reference to the aids of the Church.   As for
the children, they got baptized some time, provided their
parents exercised sufficient patience, and Dr. Hallijohn generally patched up a tardy christening by a very welcome crown
piece.

In twenty years of life in a small place a man must do
one of two things : he must wed himself to the place and its
interests, or he must divorce it from him, and clasp some other
bride.   Dr. Cornelius Hallijohn had chosen the latter course.
Eastermuir and its people were to him a bugbear and a bondage
to be forgotten and escaped from as best might be, and he
joined himself to pleasure gaily.   He was not, strictly speaking,

a sober man, but it would have been equally unjustt to call
him a drunkard; his lapses from sobriety were infrequent, and
were owing far more to a social disposition and love of good-
fellowship than to love of liquor.   Just now and then, as on
the present occasion, he went a little too far.   But ministers in
these happy days were not expected, as they are now, to be
absolutely perfect, and allowances were made for " Dr. Cornelius," as he was familiarly called in the parish.   Among the
upper classes there were too many in glass houses to admit
of much stone throwing; and the working people, who
dearly love a gentleman, overlooked a good deal in Dr.
Cornelius because of his high-handed, fine-gentleman manners,
and laughed indulgently at the ways of the gentry.

So the parish of Eastermuir had been shepherded for nigh
on twenty years.   Dr. Cornelius was growing grey in its
service, and no one breathed of reform in church matters.

Dr. Cornelius rode home late on the night of his rather
ignominious introduction at Balgowrie.   He did not hurry
his horse as they passed along the silent, miry roads, but went
at a foot pace, the reins hanging loosely from his hands.   The
night was very dark, and so silent it was in these deserted
lanes, that the creaking of the saddle leather, and the soft
hoof-falls on the fallen leaves that carpeted the road, seemed
to intrude upon some sanctity of nature.

The Manse stood in a walled garden; an iron-studded door
admitted the outside world.   It was a large and very comfortable house, but the study was perhaps the most delightful
room in it.   Bookshelves lined the walls from floor to ceiling,
and the room smelt spicily of the calf bindings.   To-night, as
Dr. Cornelius came in from the dark November fogs to its
warmth and lights, it seemed a very picture of comfort.   He
walked up to the blazing wood fire and stood looking down
into it for a moment.   Then he turned and looked round the
large firelit room, taking in, as if he had been a stranger, all
the comfort and plenty of its atmosphere.   But these cannot
have been what struck him, after all, for suddenly he spoke out
what must have been the end of some train of thought—

". . . But—O God, pity my empty house—my empty heart ! "

He crossed to the side of the fireplace and sat down. Like many lonely men, Dr. Cornelius sometimes spoke to himself. Just now, as he sat looking into the fire, he uttered his thoughts aloud.

". . . That woman ! I wonder, is she mad ?| Near to it, I fancy ; . . . but ah, the children—the children ! "

He sat silent for a little, and his thoughts must have strayed away from Balgowrie, for when he spoke again, he seemed to be addressing some one :—

". . . I think I have forgiven you, Penelope, for that —for everything except for the children that might have been mine—children like these I saw to-night. The paternal instinct seems to die harder than the other. I'm incapable of love nowadays, but I'd sell my soul for children like these."

He rose and began to pace up and down the room, then laughed gently, heartily, as a man laughs only at his own foibles.

" Yes, sell my soul, but never marry some good, intolerable woman, and take all the horrible, beautiful worries of a family on my shoulders ; that I will never do now."

As he spoke, the door opened, and James, the manservant, looked in.

" Will ye be for anything the nicht, sir ? " he asked.

" No, nothing to-night. I am going to bed, James. You may put out the lights," said Dr. Cornelius.

He went upstairs slowly, and, closing his door behind him, stumbled across the room in the dark to where the window was indicated by a faint square of light. He drew up the blind and stared out into the night. There were neither moon nor stars, and the fog had turned to rain, that fell with a dispiriting drip upon the slates.

" No, no, Cornelius," he said. " You are joined to your idols, and God has left you alone."

IV

AFTER this manner, then, Dr. Cornelius Hallijohn gained admittance to Balgowrie, and by reason of those very grave inconsistencies which would have shocked other people, he seemed to find favour in the eyes of Mrs. Marjorybanks.

It tickled her rather malignant sense of humour to see the chosen minister of Christ subject to all the commonest frailties of humanity.

With more even than the genial hospitality of the times, she pressed the Doctor to taste her vintage on the occasion of his next call at Balgowrie ; while he, with the connoisseur's horror of " women's wine," courteously declined the proffered refreshment.

But the widow was insistent ; she drank excellent wine, and was aware of it.   Dr. Cornelius was not allowed to refuse, and found his opinion of the Balgowrie cellar change with his first sip.

" Your glass is empty, sir," said Mrs. Marjorybanks then, poising the decanter in her long white fingers ; and the Doctor had held it out to be refilled, when, glancing up, he caught a gleam of amusement in the widow's eye.   For a moment he hesitated, then—

" Thank you, madam," he said.   " I find your port excellent."

She poured the red liquor slowly into his glass with a sort of icy satisfaction in the act ; and said Dr. Cornelius to himself as he watched her, " Circe—you won't find it so easy to bewitch me as you think.   Two glasses of port are not the way—I can carry more than that."

Which was true enough.   But after this the widow never could persuade Dr. Cornelius to go beyond one glass.   He had taken her measure once for all.   There sprang up between them an intimacy of the kind which sometimes exists between " two of a trade "—neither trusted the other, both were on the defensive, yet were willing to accept each other with their limitations.

The widow had frankly expressed her feelings regarding him to Dr. Cornelius.

"I like you, sir," she said. "For you are no hypocrite; you really do not profess godliness—only a palpable form of it; and no one can doubt for a moment that your only reason for remaining in the Church is the fat living you get out of it."

Dr. Cornelius bowed. "Perhaps you are right, madam; but do you not consider that my sermons smack of hypocrisy?"

"I have never heard them," said the widow, "and never intend to. But, after all, it is the life that preaches, not precept; so, if you preach like Paul and live like Bacchus, there is no doubt about which will be the sermon."

"None whatever," assented the Doctor.

He, on his part, was equally candid, seeing that candour was the "open sesame" to the widow's heart.

"You must know, madam," he said, sipping the fragrant port, "that I consider your views extreme and your ideas impracticable. In this low-toned world the true wisdom is to tune oneself down to its tone, otherwise one is always out of harmony with it. The average of wit is extremely low. The greater part of mankind cannot take in a new idea —let them jog on with the old ones."

"If the rest of the world is witless and without ideas of progress, I see all the more need for mine," said the widow.

"Except that the witless world will call you a fool," said Dr. Cornelius.

"'Twas ever the fate of reformers," she said.

So through endless arguments this odd friendship ran upon its way. Arguments on religion, on politics, on education— on all things in heaven and earth. And ever at the close of the interminable conversations Dr. Cornelius would say as he rose to go—

"And the children, madam? May I see my young friends to-day?"

The widow would bid him look in the garden on his way out. "They are generally in the garden," she added.

And so they were, even on the chilliest November days.
The steps that led up to the sundial were a very favourite
playground with them, and there they were to be found
playing the delicious imaginative games of lonely children,
and would rise demurely when Dr. Cornelius appeared, to
curtsey to him and let him know what their game was.   Even
in that stately-mannered age there was an inimitable quaint-
ness in their ways, and Henrietta, from diligent perusal of
long-worded, half-understood books, had picked up the
strangest collection of words and phrases imaginable.

"You find us engaged in our favourite pastime, sir," she
would say, indicating by this fine sentence a very simple
amusement they never seemed to tire of.

They pulled bunches of house-leek from the walls, and,
sitting on the sundial steps, crushed the succulent leaves with
stones, and filled bottles with the juice.

"We are apothecaries, you see, sir," explained Henrietta.
"I am Court apothecary to His Majesty King George, and
Lucie is my assistant.   We are extremely busy to-day, for
there has been an outbreak of the small-pox, and all the
resources of our skill are called into use."

"Oh, I see!" said Dr. Cornelius, entering into the game
with that imperturbable gravity which wins a child's heart
immediately.

He sat down beside them and pulled up his coat sleeve.

"As you see, Dr. Marjorybanks, I have sustained a serious
injury ; perhaps your skill can prescribe for it," he said,
indicating a bruise which discoloured the womanish whiteness
of the flesh.   "I received this blow two or three weeks ago—
one afternoon when I had the ill fortune to fall from my horse,"
he explained solemnly.

"Oh, it's blue !" screamed Lucie, quite wild with delight
at such unexpected excitement being added to the game.   But
Henrietta reproved her junior assistant with great sternness.

"I fear you are suffering severely, sir," she said, poking
the blue mark gingerly.   "May I prescribe some of our celebrated mixture?   Dr. Lucie bring a bottle of our best mixture
immediately. I shall apply it myself, sir, with your permission."

"I am fortunate to have such advisers," said the Doctor, surrendering his arm to the tender mercies of the Court physicians with his finest bow.

The bruise lasted a wonderfully long time, in spite of the celebrated mixture; and when this, which was after all a summer game, though it was played far on into autumn, was peremptorily stopped by a snowstorm, Dr. Cornelius even found his way to the attics, where the children played in winter, and invented quite new games there. Henrietta would meet him at the head of the attic stair, with her demure curtsey and—" Dear sir, we have been thinking all the week of the various amusements you suggested to us last Saturday, and if it meets with your approval, we think we will play at a levee, if you will be King George."

Then how grandly Dr. Cornelius extended the royal hand, while Henrietta and Lucie, in all the glories of an old brocade dressing-gown and a tablecloth respectively, trailed past their gracious monarch and saluted his white fingers.

The garrets at Balgowrie were hideously cold, but imagination lights a fire that mere external chilliness is powerless to put out, and Henrietta and Lucie would not have given up the freezing levees of the attics for the warmest playroom you could have offered them.

As time went on, the villagers seeing Dr. Cornelius so often at Balgowrie, declared that he and the widow were to "make a match of it," and concluded that their ages were very suitable. They would have marvelled much if they could have read the thoughts of the supposed suitor each day, as the door of Balgowrie closed behind him.

"That woman and her ideas! her talk! she is enough to drive a man out of his reason. I wonder how long I can go on listening to her. Have I gained any influence over her in all these months, I wonder? She is wonderfully set in her ways for a woman—most of them divagate off their theories constantly, but she is always on the same trail—one-ideaed. That is where her touch of madness comes in, and yet she is sane enough!"

No, certainly Dr. Cornelius was not in love—not in love with a woman, and that woman the widow—but in love with childhood—uncared for, worse than motherless childhood—childhood at the mercy of whims and theories ; a helpless living sacrifice ready to be offered up.

V

WINTER in 1766 was a stern reality. Frost was frost, and when the snows fell they lay for weeks. People were more real too, I fancy, and were made of such much sterner stuff, that even in these bitter seasons it never occurred to the ladies of 1766 to wear anything more comfortable than those low-necked gowns which look so picturesque as shown in the miniatures of the day, and must have been so chilly—as judged by our modern ideas. Even children were brought up in this Spartan manner, and poor Henrietta and Lucie used to scamper through the draughty Balgowrie passages, or play in the freezing attics, in little scanty muslin frocks with short sleeves and low necks. Mrs. Marjorybanks would have laughed at the idea of protecting them from the cold. It was not the fashion of the day.

One icy afternoon, the second winter after the widow's arrival at Balgowrie, when the roads were deep in snow and the big gaunt drawing-room filled with the staring white light reflected off the snow-covered ground, Dr. Hallijohn was announced to pay his repects to Mrs. Marjorybanks. The widow was sitting beside the fire—it was a small one—in a straight-backed chair, reading her favourite author, Voltaire, the arch-heretic of the day. She laid aside her book at the Doctor's entrance, and greeted him with her finest cutrsey.

" To tell you truth, sir," she said, " I was wishing to see you. It is some time since you have honoured us with a visit, and I have been considering various things in the meantime."

"The roads must be my excuse, madam," said the Doctor.
"They are heavy for man and beast in this weather."

"Better say your ministerial duties at once," said the
widow, who never lost an opportunity of sneering at the
cloth.

The Doctor leaned back against the mantelshelf, a handsome, unclerical figure enough in his long riding boots. He
laughed gently.

"As you suggest, madam—my clerical duties ; but I ask
you, what right have men to die or to be born in such weather
as this ? "

"So you have been cheering some passing soul, as I
divined ?—or is it the holy rite of baptism that you have
administered ? "

"Both—both, I can assure you, madam. A man must
die at Eastriggs Farm, seven weary miles from here, and
over his grave I must offer petitions this day, to the tune of
the north wind, and with six inches of snow on the ground.
As for the baptism, that was at Selton, seven miles the other
direction, an it please you, and ' would Dr. Hallijohn hasten,
for the child was near death '—seven miles, in haste, with the
horse's feet balling every mile of the way."

"You are the slave of the public, Dr. Hallijohn, and
to-night will sleep the sleep of the just, after such a day of
usefulness."

Nothing can be more monotonous than sarcasm. The
Doctor was weary of the widow's sneers. He sat down
and brought the conversation round to her own affairs.

"You mentioned that your own time had been occupied,
with the best of all occupations—thought. May I ask for
the result, madam ? "

"It is the education of my daughters which has occupied
my thoughts so much," said Mrs. Marjorybanks ; and with
this result, Doctor, that I wish you to undertake their education."

"Oh ! " said Dr. Cornelius, drawing out the little mono-
syllable expressively.

" You see, sir," she continued, " I think I can trust you not to teach them any of the follies of religion.   You evidently do not believe in ' religion ' so called,—your life evidences that,—and from what I know of your character, you are too honest to teach my daughters what you disbelieve."

" But," interrupted the Doctor, " I am not too honest to preach religion."

" Tush ! we have argued that before.   'Tis a palpable farce your preaching, sir, whereas your teaching of my daughters would be serious earnest.   I have explained my educational views to you often enough, and you must understand that I wish my daughters to reach years of maturity without all the network of preconceived ideas that clogs the mental machinery of half the world.   Women especially are degradingly superstitious, just the fools of priests and the dupes of worn-out beliefs.   Of course my daughters, as you know, have no beliefs, luckily do not understand the meaning of the wretched word—I wish them to have no foibles either."

Dr. Cornelius was not in the least surprised by this request. For the last twelve months he had been working for nothing else, and had expected his efforts to be successful sooner or later.   It had been a long fight unspoken, unconscious on Mrs. Marjorybanks' side, between their two very acute minds. " She has far too many ideas of her own for a woman," Dr. Cornelius had said to himself ; " but if she is given her head, without contradiction of any kind, she will come in time to believe that my ideas are her own, and will trust the children to me to educate—then I can see what can be done." So when the request was made, he sat silent for a few exultant minutes, as if considering the matter very gravely.

" Well, madam," he said at length, " you ask a great deal of me.   But, to tell you the truth, I am fond of the children, and I will undertake it on one condition."

" And that is—? " queried the widow.

" That I take my own way with their education."

" Your own way, of course, Doctor, but on my lines."

" My own way, on my own lines.   If you have sufficient confidence in me, from what you know of my character after twelve months' study of it, to trust me with the children at all, you may trust me with them altogether."

" And what will you teach them ? what will you begin with?" asked the widow, with a shade of distrust in her voice.

" Well, I shall teach them many things they are ignorant of at present, madam ; but, as I said before, if you think that I am the sort of man to train your daughters as you wish, then trust them to me ; if not, let somebody else conduct their education."

Mrs. Marjorybanks was unaccustomed to firmness in those about her. Her servants and the children were like wax in her hands ; she had expected to bind down Dr. Cornelius with promises and conditions as many as she would. His distinct refusal to be answerable in any way for his teaching startled her. Their eyes met in the last struggle of this unspoken battle of will ; the widow's questioning, uneasy glance asking as plainly as words, " Can I do as I like with this man ? "—the Doctor's hard, unconcerned stare answering, " No, you cannot." She accepted its reply.

" Sir, I will trust you with my daughters," she said.

" Without conditions ?—I teach them what I think they ought to know, as I think it should be taught, and when I think they should learn it ? "

" Yes."

" Then the matter is settled. I shall have great pleasure, madam, in teaching your daughters, and I hope your confidence will not be misplaced."

Mrs. Marjorybanks rang for the usual refreshment it was her habit to offer, and they drank their accustomed glass of port together over educational schemes.

" I must see my young pupils," said the Doctor, as he made his adieus in the fast falling dusk.

" They are probably upstairs," said the widow. " Silence will find them for you."

But Dr. Cornelius did not ask the assistance of Silence. He stumbled up the dark attic stairs towards the chink of light that showed under the playroom door. At the sound of his voice it flew open and the children ran forward to meet

him. He sat down on the top step of the stair, taking Lucie
on to his knee.

"Ah, Loo, my own, what cold little hands!" he said—for
he petted Lucie extravagantly.

Henrietta stood beside them: she was growing now into
a tall, plain-looking girl. When they played together, the
sisters seemed wonderfully of an age, except for Henrietta's
curious, pedantic speech. But every now and then, when
the games were over, she would turn into quite another
creature, and the three years dividing her from Lucie might
have been ten.

As she stood just then looking down at Lucie and Dr.
Cornelius, she had taken one of these grown-up turns. Her
great dark eyes glowed with tender admiration for all Lucie's
babyish charms as she lay nestled against the Doctor's arm,
with her yellow curls and dimpled cheeks.

"You really make a mistake sir," she said. "We are
not cold—it is only superficial. We have been playing that
delightful game of the robber and the balls that you invented
for us with the bowls.

"Come and sit here, Harrie," said Dr. Cornelius, making
room for her on the step beside him. "I have something
to tell you."

"Yes, sir, we are all attention," said Henrietta, settling
her stiff little skirts as she sat down.

Lucie, too comfortable to raise her head, let herself be
included in this speech.

"I have been speaking to your mother" said Dr. Cornelius,
"and she and I have agreed that I am to teach you lessons
now; you are to come to my house every day for them."
Lucie buried her face in the Doctor's cambric frills,
rather sleepily saying—

"I do not like lessons, sir; I had rather just come to see
you, please."

"And you, Harrie?" he asked.

Henrietta turned and looked straight into his face. Then,
resting her hand suddenly on his knee, she spoke with an
arresting earnestness.

" Shall I *know*, sir ? " she said.

There was a penetrating wistfulness in her voice, a deep and hungry question in her eyes.

" Know what, Harrie, my dear ? '"

" Everything—I wish to learn something—oh I do not know what it is !—something I cannot understand."

" Ah, Harrie, you have started on a long quest ! " he said.

VI

LIFE took on quite a new complexion for Henrietta and Lucie after this. Their days, instead of being spent in aimless, undisciplined play, were planned out for them into hours for learning and saying their lessons. Every afternoon they walked down to the Manse under the care of Silence, and were duly escorted home by him two or three hours later.

But all this sounds grim enough, and does not express in the least the rush of happiness that had come into their lives. For at the Manse they found a whole new world of interest for their inquiring little minds. There was an atmosphere of comfort and cheerfulness here that was wanting in the bleak Balgowrie rooms—the fires were so large, and the sun seemed to be always shining in at the south-looking windows, so the little girls were soon quite as much at home in it as in the house that bore that often misapplied name for them. Henrietta specially liked the spicy leather-smelling study, and would stand before the bookshelves running her fingers softly along the bindings, like a genuine book-lover. For Lucie there was no place so dear as the housekeeper's room. It lay at the end of a long yellow-stained passage, and the children always chased each other along the passage when lessons were done, to be welcomed by Mrs. Allan, the housekeeper, with ample cordiality and jelly scones. She had two little stools waiting for them before the fire, and on these the children sat, munching their scones and chattering gaily, till Silence, all too soon, appeared with his inevitable punctuality, and the same invariable form, "We maun be movin', young leddies."

It required some ingenuity on the part of Dr. Cornelius to educate Henrietta and Lucie together ; for not their ages only, but their characters and capacities, were so widely different. Dear Lucie was never a scholar; it took infinite trouble and petting to coax knowledge into her pretty little head, and Dr. Cornelius invented easy tasks, and explained them to her every day with unfailing patience. But Henrietta leapt into the knowledge so long withheld from her. She could not now study hard enough, and her mind began to expand as suddenly as the crumpled bud of a field-poppy furls out when once the restraining green outer sheath has cracked open. It was well she had fallen into wise hands that restrained her stretching ambitions, and held her down to unimaginative everyday studies, for Henrietta would have been a temptation to most teachers, and would have worked her little brain stupid if she had been allowed to. As it was, she galloped through the elements of learning at an amazing pace. It was not only her knowledge that increased, however; she was sezing on every new impression and idea with that eager young intelligence. Every day she had fresh questions to ask and fresh puzzles to propound. It had dawned upon her, with a delicious thrill of pleasure, that in Dr. Cornelius she had found someone who would never refuse to explain anything to her, and she took full advantage of the discovery.

"You say you *never* find it trouble you to answer my questions sir ? " she said. And, "Never, Harrie my dear, never," said Dr. Cornelius from the bottom of his heart. But he soon found that Henrietta was apt to be embarrassing in her investigations after truth.

One afternoon, as was her way when she wished to ask for an explanation, Henrietta came and laid her hand on her teacher's knee.

"Eh—yes, Harrie ; what is it ? " Dr. Cornelius asked.

He was reading a letter at the moment. The room was very quiet. Lucie, dear child, had fallen asleep in the arm-chair over the preparation of one of her tiny tasks.

"What is it to be ' damned,' sir, if you please ? "

"Why, Harrie, where did you find these words? I do not think it is in your lesson-book, is it ? "

"No, sir, I heard you say it. Yesterday, when James came to the door and said that Robert Yule wished to speak to you, you said, ' Robert Yule be damned.' What is it to be ' damned,' sir ? "

"In its original meaning, it meant, I believe, to go to hell. Are you nearly done with that verb, my child ? "

"Yes, sir, very nearly. And where is hell ? and why was Robert Yule to go there ? "

"Oh, woman, woman ! Theology has a fatal fascination for you at all ages ! " ejaculated Dr. Cornelius. " I suppose I must teach you that next."

"Shall I get the atlas ? " queried Henrietta innocently, but was bidden instead to sit down beside her teacher, and there received her first outline of the doctrine of a future state. It is a staggering one when communicated to a young mind for the first time. But Henrietta did not take it in much just then.

"That will be something quite new to think about," she said in a very satisfied tone. " But what a very bad man Robert Yule must be, sir ! "

"Very far from it, Harrie."

"Then why ? "—Henrietta stopped bewildered, and Dr. Cornelius, seeing himself hopelessly incriminated, could only put a brave face to the matter.

"Ah, Harrie," he said, " I should not say things like that ; 'tis what is known as swearing—a most unministerial habit, in truth ! "

"Then why do you do it, sir ? "

"Why ?—why do I do many things and say more, Harrie ? " he said, with a shrug of his shoulders.

And Henrietta made this little note in that curiously acquisitive mind of hers, that *Dr. Hallijohn sometimes swore ; that is to say, he said he wished people to go to hell, which is another world, situated somewhere, but not marked on the atlas ; and he said it was wrong to swear, therefore Dr. Hallijohn must sometimes do what was wrong. It was all extremely puzzling, was it not?*   A conclusion, this, which was to be verified in another way before very long.

Lessons were not conducted after a very conventional fashion at the Manse. On cold days they were often said round the fire, and when they were over, Lucie always sat on the Doctor's knee for half an hour, while Henrietta was given, as a special honour, " the parishioner's chair " all to herself on the opposite side of the hearth. How they chattered and laughed in these delicious half-hours—laughed as they never did at home, and chattered with a freedom that was unknown to them in their mother's presence. They were only half-conscious themselves of the chilling personality that awed their home life ; but revelled to the full in the freedom and genial atmosphere of the Manse.

Mrs. Marjorybanks, if she had known what a cheerful, wholesome life the children led there, would probably have found some excuse for changing their instructor. For the good lady did not approve of open-air methods ; she considered their results too commonplace ; she was anxious to educate her daughters in as peculiar a manner as possible. But, quite without any idea of deceit, the children were silent on the subject of their lessons. They told their mother what " studies " were given them, and Dr. Cornelius gave her business-like reports upon their progress every month, but none of the pleasures of the case were entered upon, so the widow was quite contented.   " Pleasure is dissipating " was one of the senseless formulas which she habitually practised upon her daughters, sometimes even going the length of preparing slight disappointments for them—" Disappointment braces the mind," she used to say. It was no wonder that the children hid their pleasures from her almost instinctively.

On the long summer afternoons lessons became very nominal at the Manse. There were bunches of little blood-red roses that clustered round the study window, nodding in the most inviting way, as if saying, " What a wasting of time to be indoors ! " and in the kitchen-garden there were

red gooseberries of enormous size to be eaten at all hours ;
and then there were the bees to watch. Lucie was afraid
of the bees, having once been stung, and required a reassuring hand to lead her up to the hives ; but Henrietta loved the
wise, diligent little workers, and insisted upon visiting them
every day.   Best of all, there was Barnabas, the Doctor's
horse, who fed in a paddock, and came to eat carrots from
their delighted hands. Barnabas was very gentle, and the
children were mounted on his unresisting back every day,
and rode round the field, screaming with pleasure at the
jolting of his long backbone at every step.

"And do you know, sir," said Henrietta one day as she
was lifted off, " the first time I saw Barnabas, that day when
you were so drunk, on the road, I was quite frightened of
him ; I was alarmed, I think, by his height. Mother directed
me to take hold of the bridle. Do you remember ? "

"Yes," said the Doctor rather curtly, giving Barnabas a
slap that sent him capering over the field.

Henrietta continued her musings. "How fortunate it
was for us, sir, that you should be taken ill like that, for had it
not been for that, I fear we would never have made your
acquaintance. I hope that you will not suffer in the same
way again, however," she added, with quick sympathy.
Dr. Cornelius did not reply, and Henrietta concluded that
the subject was a distasteful one.

Summer merged into autumn, and winter fell over
Eastermuir again, with its cruel frosts and long, long snow. A
year now—such a short, happy year—had passed since Henrietta and Lucie had begun their education. In it the great
need of childhood as well as age had been supplied—they
had found someone to love and trust. Older pupils might
have very easily discovered faults in Dr. Cornelius, but
Henrietta and Lucie did not consider him capable of wrong-
doing ; there were no spots on their sun. They poured out
a fulness of love and confidence upon him.

One bitter afternoon, when they came in, Dr. Cornelius
was walking up and down the study rather impatiently.
" Late ! " he said, and Henrietta, curiously business-like

for her age, glanced at the clock—by her way of reading the clock they were early, but she said nothing, and they sat down to their lessons. Before they were well begun, Dr. Cornelius interrupted them.

" Give me a drink, Harrie my dear," he said, indicating a bottle which stood on a small table beside the fire. It was a well-known object to the children, looked upon and handled with the greatest respect. Three bottles were contained in the one, welded together, but having separate mouths, and each mouth was stoppered with a dainty silver cork. It was the Doctor's custom to have a drink every afternoon when lessons were done, and the children had the privilege of handling the sacred Dutch bottle day about. But to-day it was far from the canonical hour. Henrietta obeyed with surprised alacrity.

" 'Tis very early to-day, sir," she said, as she crossed the room, balancing the glass in both hands.

" I'm put out and cross, Harrie. Here, give me another," he said, disposing very expeditiously of the liquor.

Henrietta obeyed, and they resumed lessons. Lucie stumbled a little in the conjugating of her verb, and Dr. Cornelius rose impatiently and began to pace up and down the room. Then Henrietta began her verbs. She seldom faltered over her tasks, but to-day something seemed to have gone wrong. She made two mistakes in succession, an unknown fault with her.

Dr. Cornelius strode across the room angrily.

" So this is what you call preparing your lessons, is it? What do you mean by it?" he said, and shook Henrietta roughly. She found it impossible to believe that Dr. Cornelius was really angry.

" How well you pretend!" she cried, with a delightful little scream of laughter at this bit of the histrionic art introduced into lesson hours.

But a second glance at the face above her made Henrietta silent with terror—its expression was unmistakable.

" By——, I'll teach you to laugh at me!" said Dr. Cornelius He sent the Latin grammar spinning from his hand, but

his aim was unsteady, and the book flew past Henrietta and
fell upon the floor.   There was a moment of tense silence,
then Henrietta gripped Lucie's hand, and whispered the
one word, " *Run.*"   Dr. Cornelius had turned in his walk
up and down, and in another moment the children had reached
the door and made their escape.   Along the yellow-stained
passage they fled, scarcely feeling the ground under them in
their terror, and fell against the door of Mrs. Allan's room,
too frightened to feel for the handle.   It seemed a century
to them before the door opened, and they saw in the pleasant
brightness beyond the familiar figure of Mrs. Allan.

" My conscience, Miss Harrie, what's wrong ? " she
cried ; for Henrietta, still holding Lucie's hand, stumbled
across the floor and buried her face against the old woman's
skirts in an agony of sobs.

" Ah, Mrs. Allan, I do not know !   It is dreadful—it is
Dr. Hallijohn !   Oh, do not let him come here ! he is angry
with us.   Oh, I hear him coming !   Oh ! oh ! "

She clung to Mrs. Allan and sobbed, almost screamed
with terror.

" Tut, tut, Miss Harrie ! there's no one has a mind to hurt
you ; here's Silence himself beside ye," said the good woman,
exchanging a hurried glance with him as she spoke.   Then,
moving to the door, she barred the threshold with her ample
person.

" The young ladies are away home, sir," Henrietta heard
her say.   She stopped her sobs to listen to what Dr. Cornelius
was saying.   She could not quite make out, for his kind
voice sounded changed somehow.

" Tut, tut, Doctor ! " said Mrs. Allan then—her invariable reproof.   She closed the door, and stood with her back
against it.

" Ye'll take the young ladies home the back way, Mr.
Silence," she said.   " His reverence is none so well to-day,
I'm thinkin'.   Miss Lucie my dear, there's a fine bit ginger-
bread for each of ye on the table."

Silence pressed the bonnie brown cake into Lucie's plump

little hand, who found the substantial comfort very pleasing but Henrietta would not touch it.

"No, I thank you, Mrs. Allan; I do not feel inclined to eat anything. I only wish to get home," she said, extending her hand to Silence for protection.

The homeward way was very quiet—Henrietta would not speak; the silence was broken only by the munching of Lucie's gingerbread. On the steps Henrietta paused, assuming her most grown-up air.

"Silence," she said, "please do not mention this to Hester or to Mrs. Marjorybanks."

"Very good, Miss Henrietta," he responded, being a staunch upholder of the Church.

That was a very long night to Henrietta. Lucie's deep, dreamless slumbers fell over her like a mantle when her head touched the pillow, but Henrietta tossed about till the breaking of the day. A child's first disillusionment is terribly bitter. For Henrietta it was not so much disillusionment, indeed, as despair. She did not in the least understand the cause of Dr. Cornelius' behaviour; she only knew that, whereas she had trusted him with all her heart, she could now do so no longer. She would always be expecting this horror to fall on her again. She would never feel the same beautiful confidence. The idol had feet of clay. And there was no one to tell it to. Lucie seemed suddenly separated from her by gulfs of age—a child to be protected and reassured, not frightened by mentioning this horror they had witnessed. With a sudden hot rush of despairing tears she thought, "Only yesterday, I would have told Dr. Hallijohn, but *I can't tell him about himself.*" Was the kind, dear friend gone for altogether now? Was everyone false and disappointing? Was there anyone in the world to trust and love wholly? With these sorry questions beating through her head, Henrietta fell asleep as the morning came in, and woke an hour or two later, feeling, oh, so old!

VII

THE children did not discuss this sad matter together. Lucie only said tentatively the next morning, " I suppose we will go for our lessons to-day ? " and Henrietta replied, " Yes, certainly. We must prepare them very well, Lucie."

But when they reached the Manse gate, the children drew very close to Silence. Mrs. Allan herself opened the door.

" Ah, misses, here you are ! and I was just to send up Thomas with a message. The Doctor's not so well to-day ; I think maybe he'll not be for seeing you to-day."

Henrietta took up a resolute stand on the doorstep.

" I am very sorry, but I should like to see Dr. Hallijohn. Perhaps Lucie might sit with you, Mrs. Allan, and I might see him alone." Her face was white, and her eyes very red.

Mrs. Allan hesitated. " I'll just see, Miss Harrie," she said, preceding her to the study door. " This is Miss Henrietta, sir," she said, with an introductory cough, speaking into darkness, for all the study blinds were drawn down.

" Come in, Harrie," said the voice that Henrietta loved.

She gave a quick tug to Mrs. Allan's gown and whispered, " I am not afraid—not very. I will just go in, if you will leave me."

The door closed behind Mrs. Allan, and Henrietta groped her way across the dear familiar room that was so horribly dark. She stood still in the middle of her journey, saying in a very faint little voice, " 'Tis very dark, sir." Her heart stood still with terror ; would that horrible, unknown Person arise in the darkness to meet her ?

Dr. Cornelius was stretched on two chairs beside the fire. He stirred it at the moment of Henrietta's entrance, and the room was suddenly lit up by the leaping flames, showing her as she stood shrinkingly in the middle of the floor.

" Harrie—Harrie, dearest child !—it cannot be that you are afraid of me ? " he said, rising and coming forward to meet her.

" No," began Henrietta, and then, quickly drawing back towards the door—" Yes, oh yes, sir—dreadfully ! " she cried.

With her whole heart, she longed to turn and fly towards Mrs. Allan and safety, yet her wounded love drew her irresistibly, against herself, towards its object.

Dr. Cornelius returned to the fireside, sitting down so that the bright light played across his face.

" Look at me, Harrie ; I am just as usual," he said.   " Can you not come and sit by me ? "

Henrietta drew nearer and nearer, till she stood in the circle of firelight, looking with those terribly searching eyes of hers straight into the Doctor's face.

" What was it ? " she asked slowly, when she had finished the examination.

Dr. Cornelius did not reply for a full minute, then he held out his hand to Henrietta and drew her close to him.

" Would you rather love me with your eyes shut or with your eyes open, Harrie ? "

" Which is best, sir ? you know," she said, in spite of her shattered trust.

" Open, Harrie ; but the process is painful."

" Will I feel the same ?—that is all I wish, sir ; for oh I do not feel as if I ever could ! " she cried, gulping down her tears.

" Why, Harrie, you are grown into an old woman in a night.   Now, by all that is dear to me, child, I have nearly broken my heart thinking how I frightened you yesterday."

" Will you do it again sir ? Oh, please do not ! Oh, will you explain to me, sir ? "

" Yes ; I suppose it must be done.   I drank too much yesterday, Harrie—that's the whole matter."

" Is that ' drunkenness ' ? " asked Harrie in an awestruck voice.

" Well, a degree of it ; I was not actually drunk yesterday, Harrie, only excited with it."

" I would not wish to see you ' actually drunk,' sir.   You are not nice when you drink too much.   Why do you do it ? "

" I do not do it very often, Harrie ; and why I ever do it
at all I know not ! But it's a habit I confess I've given little
thought to till to-day."

Henrietta withdrew her hand from the Doctor's, and stood
silently looking into the fire for a little. Then she said very
slowly—

" I must always love you, dear sir, for your great kindness ;
but I think it will not be possible for me to trust you again
as I have done. Are my eyes open now ? "

These were the great drinking days, when priest and
layman alike drank and spared not, and Dr. Cornelius had
spoken truly when he said his own lapses from sobriety had
never troubled him much ; but Henrietta's words went like
a knife to his heart.

" Ah, Harrie, Harrie, don't say that ! Forget, and you
will never see me like that again. I give you my word for it.

" It would make no difference, sir, whether I saw it or
not, if you continued to do it," she said, with a cold sorrow
in her voice. " I would not forget that you might be—like
yesterday—when I was not there."

The firelight sparkled suddenly on the familiar bottle,
standing in its accustomed place beside Dr. Cornelius' chair.
Henrietta watched the dancing gleam for a moment, and then,
snatching up the bottle, she flung it down on to the stone
hearth with a passionate gesture. The delicate necks of the
curious old flask cracked across as it touched the stone, and
the liquor hissed among the wood ash. She watched it for
a moment and then ran to Dr. Cornelius and flung her arms
round his neck.

" Dear sir, I cannot do anything but love you, whatever
you do ! " she cried.

Dr. Cornelius stroked her hair softly. " You are true to
your sex, Harrie ; but we have been destroyed by that very
tenderness from the beginning of all things," he said.

" I fear I do not quite understand you, sir."

" No, I should suppose you did not. We will close this
subject for evermore between us. So you have broken my
Dutch bottle ? that is a simple cure, if it prove one."

"I am very sorry; it was not mine to break, sir," said Henrietta, looking down ruefully at the shining fragments now that the heat of her anger was past.

Dr. Cornelius stooped down and felt among them.

"Here, Harrie," he said, "here is a memorial of a very unhappy half-hour." He held the three silver-topped corks in the palm of his hand.

"No, I thank you, sir; I think I will not require a memorial," said Henrietta.

"What! do you refuse these fine corks for the 'celebrated mixture' bottles?" he said lightly. He had been treating the whole matter too seriously, he thought; it would be better now to pass if off with a joke.

But Henrietta did not see it in the same light.

"I find myself doubting whether we will ever play at 'Court Physicians' again," she said sadly.

With the wisdom of fourteen years, and a broken idol. she seemed to herself to have put away childish things.

VIII

FOLLOWING the precedent of a certain class of story-book, it would now be pleasant to relate that Dr. Cornelius after this renounced the devil and his works for ever. But although this is the way of the story-book, it is not the way of the world. Dr. Cornelius still drank his port as usual, and occasionally came home drunk from the meetings of Presbytery. He was only careful that the children should know nothing of this. The Dutch bottle was not replaced, and the subject received decent burial at both their hands—which, perhaps, was the best thing that could be done. Dr. Cornelius having once repented of the fright he had given his little pupils, gave the matter no further attention. Sentiment had no part in his nature; there was no reason, by his way of thinking, why he should deny him-

self his wine because he once made a mistake, and had he
been told that there was, he would have called it sentimental
nonsense.

But I doubt if Henrietta ever was quite a child again after
this incident. She had learned life's bitterest lesson early,
and where disillusionment comes in, childhood goes out.
Not that her love for Dr. Cornelius suffered any diminution—
that was an impossibility to her nature; but the former
divinity was now only a fellow-creature—and there is a
difference between the two. Dr. Cornelius was a little annoyed by her quietness for a time. She was unnaturally
eager over lessons, and indifferent to play; but he began to
think the child was really growing up, and forgot to connect
her gravity with his own conduct. Lessons became a more
serious matter, and Lucie began to be left very far behind
on the path of knowledge.

The teacher acknowledged with a sigh that children had
an unfortunate way of growing up, and addressed himself
in earnest to the task of keeping pace with the rapacious
demands of Henrietta's mental appetite. But sometimes,
as he sat sipping his port, Dr. Cornelius would find himself
wondering how his experiment would end. The girls
were unquestionably growing up, he would admit with a
frown, and growing up very unlike the rest of the world;
they required direction from a woman's hand now, it was
evident. And this they were not likely to get. Whenever
he left home nowadays, Dr. Cornelius took careful note of
the girls he met, and these observations all tended to confirm
his impression of the oddity of poor Henrietta and Lucie.
Even his masculine eyes discerned the absence of any pretence
at following the fashion in their dress; Hester's dressmaking
was elemental in its simplicity, and was not calculated to
display their best points. Dr. Cornelius would sit and mourn
over his pupils to his old cousin, Matilda Hallijohn, each
visit he paid her in Edinburgh. She, good lady, would suggest all manner of schemes for the relief of the little prisoners—
they were to be sent to stay with their relations, their father's
people, or they were to come and visit her, or they were to

go to London to visit the Pelhams. But to each and all of
these propositions Dr. Cornelius found a negative. Mrs.
Marjorybanks held no communication that he knew of with
either her own or her husband's relations. She would never
permit her daughters to visit a stranger ; and as little would
she permit them to visit in London.

"Easier far to get a prisoner out of the Tolbooth, Matilda
than to get these poor children from Balgowrie," he would
conclude.

"'Tis clear then, Cornelius, you must do just your best
for them yourself," said Miss Hallijohn. "You're not the
man I would have chosen to educate young women, but
strange instruments are chosen under Providence," she would
add, smiling, for the cousins were very good friends.

This was, indeed, the only conclusion that anyone could
have come to. Mrs. Marjorybanks had her own ideas on
education, and would hold them against the advice of all
the world. The girls must take their chance, and turn out
as best they might. Dr. Cornelius, it appeared, was to be
their only teacher—he must do all in his power for them,
and leave the rest to Fate. At least he could educate them
well—that was always something ; then perhaps—perhaps—
strange are the freaks of fortune—relations might interfere
—Mrs. Marjorybanks might die—it was surely impossible
that things could go on for ever like this. So, comforting
himself with this thought, Dr. Cornelius continued his
instructions, looking as hopefully as might be towards the
future for help. And Henrietta and Lucie, quite unconscious
of all the anxiety they occasioned, lived on their quiet lives
from month to month and from year to year, leaving childhood behind them so gradually that they scarcely knew it
was gone, entering into life insensibly, through long, eventless,
and, on the whole, happy weeks.

IX

A S time went on, Mrs. Marjorybanks, herself an indefati-
gable correspondent, determined to establish communication between Maggie Pelham, the daughter
of her own unknown friend, and Henrietta.

The girls had a good deal in common, she had discovered,
in a kindred love of study, so they began to correspond upon
the simple, girlish subject of mathematics.   It is possible
that Maggie Pelham was not so single-eyed in her devotion
to study as her letters would at first have indicated ; the
truth was that kind-hearted Mrs. Pelham, whose heart ached
for the unknown children she heard so much about from their
mother, thought that this was the best way of establishing
an intimacy between them and her own daughter.   She
was acute enough to see that Mrs. Marjorybanks would never
permit her daughter to correspond with an entirely unintel-
lectual correspondent, so Maggie's studious tastes were put
well to the fore, there was no great mention made of relaxation
or pleasuring, and every now and then a kind message was,
sent—" Would the girls not come up to London and see
their unknown friends there ? "   As yet these hints had been
quite disregarded, but the correspondence continued.   It
gradually assumed a less formal tone, and Henrietta and Lucie
came to love the bright tales of London ways and manners,
and to look forward to the monthly budget.

In reply Henrietta sent long outpourings on books and
ideas, mixed with quaint enough pictures of the home life
at Balgowrie.   These letters, of which Maggie Pelham had
a whole bundle, were such letters as are never written in the
degenerate days of the penny post.   They were several pages
in length, and written in a handwriting most exquisitely minute
and delicate.   Selecting one at random from the bundle,
it runs thus :—

" MY DEAREST MARGARET,—It is with great pleasure that I
take up my pen for the ever pleasant task of writing to you. But,
immersed as you are in the gaieties of the capital, I can hardly

expect to gain your interest in our homely provincial affairs. You ask what we have been about in these long winter days, so I must gratify your curiosity by giving you some account of them.

"For myself—who am a tiresome bookworm, and only care for grubbing away among my favourite authors—the time has not seemed long. Do you not find, dear Margaret, as you go on with life, an increasing interest and curiosity regarding its ultimate issues? Each day, as I follow some train of reasoning as found in one of the books I love, I say to myself, ' Shall I find it here? ' Yet each day, a I close the volume, I find myself confessing that the problem is still a problem to me—will it always be so, I wonder? Among the books I have found most deeply engrossing is one which my dear teacher, Dr. Hallijohn, has directed my attention to. He considers it the pivot of ancient as well as of modern thought; it is named *The Bible*. He does not believe all its teachings, but thinks every well-informed person should have some knowledge of them. They appear to me wonderfully short-sighted in some respects, wonderfully long-sighted in others—as, how will you reconcile these apparently dissimilar axioms : ' Love not the world, neither the things of the world ' ; and ' Make to yourselves friends of the mammon of unrighteousness, that when these shall fail, it may receive you into everlasting habitations ' ? Dr. Hallijohn has taught me all the generally received ideas about the Bible, but my mother, it appears, does not agree with him in admiring its teaching, so till lately the book itself was not put into my hands. Now, I am happy to say, I am allowed full liberty in my reading. I have thought much upon what is contained in this book about *another life*—it seems a curious idea. Why should we require another life? this one, it appears to me, is tremendous enough without another. Dr. Hallijohn tells me the idea is ' specially held by those who have broken hearts.' Is there no mending of them here? It seems a clumsy arrangement. . . .

"But I weary you with these matters, as I am sorry to say I sometimes weary my dearest Lucie. Her interests are far

other than mine. Did you hear her play and sing you would
I feel sure, be enchanted, for, young as she is, her voice is
sweetness itself. She is never weary of this, and will sit
for hours at a time at the spinnet. Then she loves all the
outdoor creatures. Every morning she will be out across
the courtyard, even in these heavy snows, to feed the hens !
The peacock is her special favourite, and even the cow she
must visit daily. You mention in your last letter the elegant
new work you occupy your leisure with ; I feel sure that were
Lucie with you, she would be anxious to try to emulate you—
for a needle is seldom out of her fingers ! it is her implement,
just as the pen is mine. She is making for herself, and for
me, who am so clumsy with my needle, a set of tucked night-
dresses of extraordinary fineness.

" It would amuse you to see our old Hester's look of
contempt as she sweeps past me sitting over my books, to
give Lucie her advice on the setting of the innumerable
tucks. Hester does not consider that study is womanly,
and cannot praise Lucie's handiwork too highly. If she
were not my dearest joy, I might indeed be nettled and teased
by the constant interruptions she occasions, for Hester is
always coming up to nudge my elbow, saying, 'Miss Henrietta,
will you cast your eye on this seam for a moment ? Did
ever you see such stitching ? Miss Lucie has a real taste
for her needle.' Then I will look up, rather crossly sometimes
saying, ' Don't bother me, Hester, I am busy,' and she gathers
up the work and carries it off. Lucie sits always in the west
turret, which looks seawards, and receives all the afternoon
and evening light. She has a lark in a cage there, and sits
whistling to it over her sewing half the day. We do not
now go daily to the Manse for our lessons, but twice a week
we have that pleasure. I am now beginning to study Greek,
but Lucie has rebelled at that, and Dr. Hallijohn sides with
her. He is of opinion that Greek is not essential to a girl's
education.

" For me I cannot learn enough ; I must learn everything
it is possible for me to acquire. While I am at my Greek
lesson, Lucie goes into Mrs. Allan the housekeeper's room

and bakes gingerbread or plum-cake. Lucie is strangely
fond of cookery. Then, when I am done, we—Dr. Hallijohn and I—come in and watch the baking—Lucie has her
sleeves rolled up and wears a large apron ; sometimes she will
insist upon our tasting the cakes, which are always very good,
before they are packed up and given to Silence to carry home
for us—for Dr. Hallijohn will never eat sweets ; he says they
' coarsen the palate.'   In the evenings we play whist, or my
mother reads aloud to us. We are reading the works of
Voltaire at present, which I find deeply interesting. I have
indeed given you a long description of our employments,
dear Margaret, and must crave your patience in their tedious-
ness.

"I shall hope very soon for another of your most charming letters which seem to link us on with the great outer
world of which we see so little. Meantime with kindest
remembrances from all our circle to you and to Mrs. Pelham
—I remain, ever most affectionately yours,

"HENRIETTA MARJORYBANKS."

But the story of Henrietta and Lucie as told in these letters
would be a very long one. The bundle of yellowing manu-
script lies in a drawer now, together with a port-folio tied
up with ribbon strings, containing the minute pencil sketches
which formed one of the occupations of Lucie's existence.
There is a drawing of Balgowrie, where every turret and
crow-step gable is etched in with extraordinary veracity of
detail, and Henrietta's hand-writing supplies the verses that
are placed below this picture of the house that was called
home by the two solitary girls.

X

MRS. MARJORYBANKS had ideas of her own upon
manners as well as upon education. When Henrietta
and Lucie had reached the ages of sixteen and thirteen
respectively, she had announced to them that it was now time

for their "polite education to begin." And this branch
of education had been continued ever since.

"So that you may hold your own in the world, it is necessary
that you learn its tone," she had said.

"But, madam," Henrietta ventured to ask, "are we not
going to live always at Balgowrie?"

"It may happen not," the widow had replied.

The walls of Balgowrie had truly been a close enough prison
those many years now, for the two young creatures penned
in between them. Although travelling was not very common
in those days, still even then there was something unusual
in girls of their age who had never been out of one lonely
parish for so many years.

"I suppose we shall get out of it some day," Henrietta
used to say.

But, like the captive accustomed to his chain, they did
not yet rebel at all against their captivity. Henrietta was
wrapped up in study of every kind, and Lucie was still too
much of a child to feel anything singular in the solidude of
their lot. As seen from the outside, the girls were strange
enough. It must be remembered that they had never spoken
to a young person of their own age and had passed their
time exclusively in the society of a very eccentric woman
and an elderly man of somewhat easy morals. Henrietta's
manners bore traces of this—they were a mixture of precise-
ness and of mannish brusqueness. Lucie was too entirely
feminine by nature to acquire any masculine traits, but she
was a quaint little lady enough, even at thirteen. Dressed
by their mother quite without regard to the fashions of the
day, they needed all the peculiar charm that was their greatest
gift, to carry off the impression of strangeness they produced
at first sight.

"We shall have a reception every Thursday evening, and
I shall instruct you in the art of conversation, in dancing,
and in deportment," said Mrs. Marjorybanks.

On Thursday evening the girls were bidden to put on their
best frocks—curious sprigged muslins they were—and to
come down to the drawing-room.

They found Mrs. Marjorybanks in full evening dress (of twenty years old fashion) standing at one end of the drawing-room. She advanced to meet them with a sweeping curtsey, while instructing them *sotto voce* to do the same. Then ensued introductions, which were given at great length, and where chairs took the place of human beings, Mrs. Marjorybanks would sweep up to an arm-chair, saying, " Allow me, Sir Horace, to present to you my daughter, Miss Henrietta Marjorybanks ; " and then, with such a wave of her gloved hand, and another billowy curtsey—" Sir Horace Walpole. Henrietta, our . . ."

Poor Henrietta, overcome with the honours of this presentation, remained dumb after she had made her curtsey, till the widow indicated that she, as Sir Horace, was ready to enter into conversation upon all the topics of the day. Surely the angels must have laughed, if they did not weep, to watch these ghostly receptions of bodiless guests, and listen to the talk that was carried on in the echoing old room. When conversation flagged the dancing began. Lucie supplied the music ; perched upon the high stool before the spinnet, she tinkled away sometimes for an hour at a time, shivering and nodding by turns over the notes. Then Henrietta would take her place, and Lucie would dance. Mrs. Marjorybanks was incapable of fatigue, and would have paced the minuet all night if the fancy had taken her. As it was, the receptions went on from seven till eleven,—four weary, weary hours,—and then the girls stole off to bed, cold and tired. Thursday evening became a black spot to look forward to through the week, and as time went on, the receptions became more and more irksome. Monotony, more than any grief, wears upon young creatures—it has a deadening quality all its own. The girls complained bitterly of the infliction to Dr. Cornelius, who was wise enough to laugh at it, and professed himself anxious to join in the game.

" Why, you used to like the levees in the attics," he said. " This must be the same thing on a more majestic scale ; pray invite me next week."

But Henrietta shook her head.

" It was quite different then, sir.   I began to see that where the element of coercion comes in, there pleasure ceases."

" I wonder if you are a budding philosopher, Harrie—something must surely come out of these magnificent sentences of yours," said the Doctor.

He was beginning to realise more and more seriously every year, the oddness of his poor young pupils.   He would pace up and down the study o' nights, revolving plans for their release—plans that ended in nothing, for the widow was inflexible in her views upon the beneficial effects of solitude upon the young mind.   All that a man could do Dr. Cornelius had done.   But experience of life, of men and of manners, of that great teacher we call the world, cannot be imparted second-hand.   " They must awaken up some day to find themselves in the thick of a great struggle, where every man's hand, and specially every woman's, is against them, and they unarmed against their foes—they will only realise that they have foes by the wounds they will receive. Ah, poor lambs !—it's cruel—I could almost pray they might never leave the curious fold they are in.   Only, what a waste of Harrie's powers and Lucie's looks !—why, the child will be lovely a few years hence."

So moaned Dr. Cornelius month by month and year by year.   He even tried some remonstrance with Mrs. Marjorybanks.

" Would you not allow your daughters to make some friends of their own age, madam ? " he asked.   " Would you not go into Edinburgh for the winter months, and give them the advantages of society ? "

But Mrs. Marjorybanks only smiled.

" I have established a correspondence between Henrietta and the daughter of my friend Mrs. Pelham.   I consider that correspondence is fully more stimulating to the character than friendship.   Henrietta writes an excellent letter, and enters, indeed, into all the topics of the day with Miss Margaret Pelham."

As you have seen, " all the topics of the day," as they existed for Henrietta, were mainly dissertations upon religion, mathematics, and philosophy—her only interests in life, and Maggie Pelham, a gay young maiden just entering on the pleasures of a London season, would sometimes laugh a good deal over the funnily-worded letters.   But there was a touch of rareness in all that Henrietta did which made her lengthiest epistles worth the reading.   She struck out new phrases and ideas constantly, and when she came down from the clouds to describe their daily life at Balgowrie to her unknown friend, she made it all so real and unconsciously touching that Maggie Pelham would cry out with moist eyes to her mother—

" Madam, do you not think we might invite Henrietta and Lucie to visit us ? "

And Mrs. Pelham would shake her head regretfully, saying, " We might ask them very often, Maggie my dear, and have always the same reply.   I fear Mrs. Marjorybanks is demented, poor lady or something very like it—'tis a sad pity for the poor girls."

So time wore on, and this long lane of life that hedged in Henrietta and Lucie seemed no nearer a turning than when they had first come to Balgowrie nine long years before.

Henrietta was one-and-twenty and Lucie eighteen when an event occurred which changed the current of their lives at last.

XI

SO," said Dr. Cornelius, sitting looking into the fire, and speaking to himself, " So the time has come. I see trouble ahead."

Strange things had been happening at Balgowrie.   For the last ten days a visitor had been there—and that visitor a man, young, and extraordinarily good-looking, and of pleasant address.   " Lessons," properly so called, were at an end now that Henrietta and Lucie were grown to years of discretion, but Dr. Cornelius still " directed their studies," as Henrietta phrased it, and directed their lives too, so far as

it was in his very limited power to do.   So the advent of this
disturbing stranger had given him much food for thought.
" Very good for the girls," he had said at first, but a nearer
acquaintance with Captain Dan Charteris, in his more un-
guarded moments over a bottle of claret, and in the absence
of the ladies, had caused Dr. Cornelius some little anxiety.

" 'Pon my soul !   I never knew I was so squeamish before,"
he said, with a smile.   " It's Lucie, I see ; " and then added
slowly, as an after-thought, " happily."   He sat silent after
this for a little, and then rose and stood gazing into a little
oval mirror that hung over the mantelshelf, examining himself closely, as if with some quite new interest.

" Why, Cornelius, how old are you now ? " he said.
" Let me see—fifty-two, is it—or fifty-three ?—and your
hair grey—grey as silver.   Heavens ! what a fool you are ! "

The glass reflected a very personable man, however, for
all his grey hairs and fifty years, and Dr. Cornelius was not
slow to recognise the fact.   The gentleman of last century
had admirable constitutions in spite of their potations ; and
those which Dr. Cornelius had indulged in had left no trace
upon him beyond the slightly deeper tint than nature's which
suffused his fine, smooth skin, giving him, when taken in
conjunction with his grey hair, something the effect of
wearing rouge and powder.   He leaned his arms on the
mantelshelf and continued to gaze at this comely reflection.
He was quite sufficiently conscious of his own attractions ;
and, following the precedent of ninety-nine men out of a
hundred, finished his survey by the remark, " Most women
would have me ; " but toned down the vain-glorious thought
by the heartfelt addition—" except Harrie, she is unlike all
other women.   I believe it would shock and wound her to
think I ever thought of her after this fashion ; and, besides,
she cares for none of these things.   Why, I doubt if the child
would know what I was driving at if I made love to her.
Yet one cannot wait for ever.   If Lucie and this Charteris
were to make it out, there might then be a chance for me,
but those girls are twined together like the strands of a
rope. . . ."

So he mused on, as men and women, too, will do to the end of time when it is a question of love. The fire died down into a little heap of white ash, and the eight-day clock in the hall struck twelve in its ponderous, sure-footed style, before the musings came to an end.

* * * * * * *

And meanwhile, at Balgowrie, Henrietta and Lucie were entering, all unknown to themselves, into women's kingdom. The stranger had arrived on one of the Thursday reception evenings. It was a lovely May night, and the long, sweet-scented dusk tantalised the girls with thoughts of what the garden would be like were they only at liberty to stray through it, instead of going over the long played-out farce of the receptions. Lucie was specially petulant this evening. As she and Henrietta were donning their evening gowns together, she broke out in bitter complaint. "It is too hard, Harrie! How long do you suppose this is to go on ?" and then, lowering her voice and drawing nearer to her sister, she added, ; *I believe mother is crazy, Harrie"*

Henrietta tightened her lips for a moment. Then she said gently, " You must get ready, Lucie. It does no good, but rather harm, to complain. Come and let me fasten your ribbons, dear."

Lucie plumped down on her knees before Henrietta, bringing her white shoulders on a level with her hand ; but just as the ribbons were being gathered up into a neat little favour, a tremendous knock echoed through the quiet house. The girls held their breath to listen, and, in the silence that followed, they heard the startled rats scamper off through the walls.

Lucie was on her feet in a moment. " What can it be, Harrie ? Dr. Hallijohn never knocks, and there is no one else to come " (she was unconscious of the pathos that lay in the statement). " Let me look out," she added, pulling aside the toilet table, and squeezing into the window niche. " Why Harrie," she cried, " it's a horse—a horse I have never seen before."

"The horse could not knock, child; who is on it?" laughed Henrietta.

"I cannot see; I shall go and look down the passage."

Lucie ran to the door and stood with her head turned in the direction of the front staircase, listening intently. Presently she returned to say incredulously, "It is a man, Harrie, and he has come upstairs."

"It *must* be Dr. Hallijohn; you have mistaken about the horse," said Henrietta, with composure, slipping on the hair bracelets which formed her curiously ungirlish ornament, and clasping a tiny gold chain, to which a miniature was suspended, round her throat. "I wish Dr. Hallijohn had not come," she said "I dislike that even he should see this and I fear that mother will not forego the reception on any account. Let us come downstairs, Lucie."

On the stair they met Hester, with an almost awed expression on her face. "I am to tell you, young ladies, that Captain Charteris is in the drawing room."

"*Who?*" said the girls in a breath.

"A gentleman, calling himself Captain Charteris, misses, and that is all I know of him," said Hester.

Henrietta and Lucie exchanged glances of entire amazement, and, Henrietta leading the way, they entered the drawing-room.

Mrs. Marjorybanks stood in her usual reception dress at the far end of the room; no chair, but a living, breathing man stood beside her. To understand the feelings of Henrietta and Lucie at this sight, it must be remembered that this was literally the first young man to whom they had ever addressed a word—almost, indeed, the first young man they had ever seen.

He was a very pleasant specimen of the new species to look upon—tall, and carrying himself bravely, with a crop of dark red curls, and eyes of wonderful blue; altogether an uncommon man in appearance and in address. He came forward to meet the girls, who stood still for a moment in slight embarrassment.

"This gentleman, Captain Charteris, has been sent here

by our friend Mrs. Pelham," said Mrs. Marjorybanks ; " and unused as we are to the exercise of hospitality, I am honoured to entertain any friend of Mrs. Pelham's."

Henrietta held out her hand awkwardly and in silence, but Lucie said very sweetly, " The Pelham's seem dear friends of ours, although we have never seen them.   Have you ridden all the way from London, sir, or did you come by coach ? "

" By sea from London, and rode from Edinburgh.   I had a mount from a friend there.   Forty miles, is it not ? and a long forty at that, Miss Marjorybanks," he said, running his gallant eyes over Lucie for a moment.

But further conversation was interrupted by Mrs. Marjory-banks, who said firmly, " It is our custom, Captain Charteris, to go through the outward forms of society every week in our secluded home, and if you will excuse us, we will just proceed with our reception as usual.   If you are fatigued by your ride, Silence will show you to your room ; but if not, perhaps you will join in our entertainment."

The young soldier was rather perplexed by this announce-ment.   What did the " outward forms of society " mean ? However, as it seemed the best way to spend his evening, he signified to the widow his pleasure at being included in their party.

Poor Henrietta and Lucie !   Was it possible they had to go through this farce before a stranger—to converse in his presence with a chair apiece, and be introduced with stern formality to the sofa ?   They hardly dared to look up as Mrs. Marjorybanks began her introductions ; their tongues seemed to cleave to the roof of their mouths with shyness and the smarting sense of the stranger's inevitable ridicule.   He leaned back against the mantel-shelf for a few minutes, listening and taking it all in, then suddenly sprang forward and bowed low before Lucie, while Mrs. Marjorybanks brought out a long-winded introduction.

" Gad ! " he said ; " it's a better game than some I have played !   Permit me, madam, to take the place of this gentle-man ; " and with that he shoved aside the inanimate partner that had just had the honour of introduction to Lucie, and placed himself in its stead.

"Now," thought Lucie, "there is no more need to feel shy—I am not speaking to a chair;" and, her tongue being unloosed, she chattered to the Captain as though she had known him all her life. Lucie was, in fact, rather like those tropic birds we read of in traveller's tales, who, having never seen the cruel monster man, are quite without fear of him, and will alight on the very barrel of his gun without dreaming of danger. Her ignorance of men and manners was so profound that she was not even self-conscious.

"It is quite amusing to us to see a stranger, I can assure you, sir," she said; "for, as you see, our receptions are not very crowded."

"Beauty has always her court," he said, with his finest bow. But Lucie was not sophisticated enough to appreciate the compliment, so he went on—"Have you agreeable neighbours here, Miss Marjorybanks?"

"Neighbours?" queried Lucie. "We have Dr. Hallijohn. He is the only person we ever see."

"The only person?"

"Yes. He used to give us lessons, but since we have grown up, we have stopped that partially—at least I have. My sister Henrietta is very fond of books."

"And what do you do with yourself all day, if I may make bold to ask?" said the Captain.

"I sew, sir, and I play upon the spinnet, and I feed the hens, and we walk out each afternoon; and in the evenings we read aloud the works of Mr. Hume—at least we are reading them at present; they are very instructive, but I would prefer a romance."

"Miss Pelham warned me I was coming among learned ladies," said Captain Charteris, laughing. "She has a great opinion of Miss Henrietta's learning."

"Oh, will you tell me about Miss Pelham, sir? Will you describe her to me?" cried Lucie delightedly. "We have corresponded for a very long time, but we have never met, and I should like beyond all things to hear about her."

" What shall I tell you then ?   Miss Pelham is a very
lovely young lady, the toast of half London by now, and as
sweet as she is lovely, report has it."

" Then you do not know her yourself, sir ? " said Lucie.
The Captain shrugged his shoulders lightly.

" We were good friends enough once, Miss Marjorybanks,
and are still, for that matter ; but I've been out of London for
two years now, while Miss Peggy has been entering society
with a flourish of trumpets, so we are scarce as intimate as we
once were."

" Society ? how singular it must be to ' enter society' ! "
exclaimed Lucie in her artless way, and Charteris laughed.

" I suppose you will do it some day yourself," he said.
But Lucie shook her head.

" I do not fancy that I ever shall.   Tell me, sir, is it very
delightful to ' enter society' ?—and there is another phrase
which I have heard Dr. Hallijohn employ—' seeing something
of the world.'   Have you ' seen something of the world' ? "

" Well, yes,—I fancy I have," he said, laughing a very
pleasant laugh, that impelled Lucie to laugh also.

" Ah, tell me about ' the world ' then, that will be delightful"
she said, turning her blue eyes up to the Captain's face in that
charming way she had.

And he, nothing loath, set himself to the task.

" 'Tis a wide word ' the world,' " he said, and I've seen
but a small part of it after all.   What shall I tell you about ? "

" Wars.   Have you ever been in a battle ?   I should like
to hear about that," said Lucie, settling herself down to listen,
like another Desdemona, to the tales of bloodshed.

" I had the good luck to see active service when I was a
boy ; but these are old stories now—we've fallen on peaceful
times, the more's the pity, unless we get some fighting with
the colonies."

" Ah yes, in America ; but you have not told me about your
battles," pouted Lucie.

" Let me see—what can I tell you ?—'tis so long ago,
Miss Marjorybanks, I've forgot the most of it."   But, in
spite of this protestation, Charteris found one or two stories

to tell.   He broke off in the middle of one of them at sight
of Lucie's blanching cheeks.

"Ah, go on," she cried; "I am so silly, I go white when
things stir me, sir.   I do not wish you to stop—pray continue
your story.   May I ask my sister Henrietta to join us ? 'twould
interest her vastly—and she does not whiten as I do at nothing."

But Charteris would not finish the story.   He said they
had had enough of it ; nor would he go over any of the former
stirring tales for Henrietta's benefit.   He did not seem to
find her such a sympathetic listener.   So, instead of conversation, he paced the minuet with Lucie ; and with this and
supper, the hours, generally so leaden in their passing, slipped
away unheeded.

The girls had plenty to talk of that night.

XII

CAPTAIN CHARTERIS had not intended to pay a long
visit to Balgowrie.   He had only thought of claiming
the widow's hospitality for a few nights in passing on
his way through Scotland, but the few nights extended to seven
or eight, and still there was no mention made of his journey
being resumed.

The unusual presence in the house necessarily brought
about a change there in some respects.   Mrs. Marjorybanks
remarked to her daughters that it was their duty to entertain
the visitor, but she made no suggestions as to how it was to
be done, only said, "You are worth but little if you cannot
amuse an idle man for a day or so ; " and with this undeniable
truth she left the girls and shut herself up to pen one of her
interminable letters.   It was more like the idle man entertaining them, as it proved ; and for this kind of thing Charteris
showed himself admirably fitted.

"Do you not ride ? " he asked Lucie, on the second
morning of his stay at Balgowrie.

He was standing beside her in the west turret, looking along
the great curve of beach that lay below the house towards the
west.

" Those are sands for a gallop indeed," he added.

" No, sir ; my mother has never kept a horse," said Lucie.
" But why do you not ride out by yourself on this fine
morning ? "

" I find myself poor company, you see," he said, looking
down into Lucie's blue eyes.

" I feel sure that Dr. Hallijohn would ride with you.   He
rides every day.   Shall I send Silence down with a note to
him ? " asked Lucie innocently.

Even two days of determined pretty speeches had not
taught her how to take a compliment.

" No, no ; but—let me see—would Dr. whatever-his-name-
is not lend you his horse ?   I shall be proud to be your teacher
in horsemanship."

Lucie flushed with delight.   "I should like it beyond
everything.   I am sure he would—only I fear mother would
not allow me to—she does not like us to enjoy ourselves,"
she added naively.

" But this is not enjoyment—at least, we shall not call it
so.   We shall say that it is a lesson.   Every lady should know
how to ride ; it is quite necessary, I can assure you, Miss Lucie."

" We might ask her, at least," said Lucie.

" Oh, I'll do that—let me ask Mrs. Marjorybanks," he said,
and strode out of the room in search of his hostess without
wasting more time.

Lucie was in a fever of excitement and delight.   How often
she had longed to ride ! and there was a delicious excitement in
the teacher too.   Life had acquired a sudden saltness after its
long vapidity, and she walked about the room clasping and
unclasping her fingers, dreading to hear that the proposed
pleasure had been forbidden.

The Captain returned very soon.   " Mrs. Marjorybanks
is quite pleased.   Will you send Silence for the horse ?   And
your mother even tells me she has a habit for you."

"Oh yes, I have often dressed up in it!" cried Lucie, breathless with pleasure. "And are we really going? Ah, but why can Henrietta not come too?" she said, her happy face clouding over.

Charteris drew in his breath in a half-whistle of intense inward amusement. "If she was not as innocent as a dove, wouldn't that have been a coquette's question?" he said to himself; but aloud—

"I fear we cannot furnish ourselves with three horses, Miss Lucie; it is a sad pity, but perhaps Miss Marjorybanks, who is so studious, would despise it for wasted time."

"Oh no. But why should Harrie not go instead of me?" said Lucie, struck with a fresh thought.

"Ah, but you were the first I proposed to instruct," said Charteris quickly. "And before the morning loses its freshness, can we get the horse?"

Lucie ran off to write a note to Dr. Cornelius, praying for the use of Saul (who had succeeded Barnabas when that long-suffering steed went the way of all horseflesh), and ended her note with an ecstatic girlish postscript, "I am so much excited," that made Dr. Cornelius smile. But in the meantime a new difficulty had risen—a side-saddle.

"What the deuce am I thinking about?" said the Captain. "The parson doesn't ride side fashion, I fear."

Lucie's face fell—the cup was to be dashed from her lips after all. But the Captain was determined. There was an inn, was there not? he asked—was there ever an inn without a side-saddle? So Silence, when he at last appeared grimly leading Saul up to the steps, was bidden return to the village and search up a saddle. "Fine ongoings," he muttered under his breath as he departed reluctantly, relinquishing Saul into the hands of Captain Charteris.

Henrietta and Lucie had both come out on to the steps to meet the well-known steed, and Lucie had to get carrots and sugar immediately for her favourite.

"Dr. Hallijohn had another horse we liked even better," she said. "He was a dear beast, black, and with a white star on his nose. We were deeply attached to Barnabas, but he had to be sold two years ago ; he became too old. Now we are very fond of Saul although we hardly think his colour so impressive."

" Not so like a parson, perhaps," said Charteris, slapping Saul's sleek bay coat approvingly.

It seemed as if Silence would never return. Saul was fed until the Captain remonstrated, and yet the laggard did not appear. At last he hove in sight, with—yes—the saddle riding triumphantly on his head. Lucie did not wait for further sight of the prize, but flew upstairs to don her habit.

Ah, what a picture she made some minutes later as she came out a little shyly on to the steps ! The habit cut in the fashion of thirty years before, was of bright blue cloth, and trimmed profusely with tarnished gilt buttons. She wore along with it a small feathered hat with the plume falling over one side of her bright face. The habit, made for her mother, was much too long, and she had some ado to gather up the voluminous folds in her little white fingers. Her cheeks were like blush roses with excitement and pleasure.

" Ah ! " said Charteris appreciatively, drawing in his breath ; but to himself—" Fancy that habit in town ! "—the picturesque and the fashionable go not always hand in hand.

" Now, are you frightened, Miss Lucie ? " he asked ; " or do you think I can take care of you ? "

" Oh, I could not be frightened of Saul, I know him so intimately," said she. " But you know, sir, he is of great height ; I fear you must lift me up."

The Captain did not demur. It was far pleasanter to put a hand on each side of that dainty little waist and toss her upon to her saddle like a feather, than it would have been to go through a lesson in the art of mounting—that could come another day. He gathered up the reins and gave them into the little white fingers, with great emphasis upon how to hold them ; then sprang into his saddle and turned the horses' heads towards the shore. Did any man ever ride like Dan Charteris ? Horse and man seemed one in an indescribable harmony of motion. To see him ride past was to feel you should applaud such a gallant sight ! For such an expert horseman he had wonderful patience with a beginner in the art.   Lucie was not nervous, in spite of being perched up so high and being pitched about in her saddle at every stride of her steed : she laughed and joked over it all—her curls flew out from under her hat and blew about her face in the fresh salt wind—she was a bewitching pupil.   They paced up and down the sands slowly at first, and then a little less cautiously as Lucie got a better seat.

" Ah, this is the most delightful day of my life," she said, as they pulled up the horses to let her regain her breath a little.

And Charteris was nearly of the same opinion as he watched her glowing cheeks and clear blue eyes.   It was a little damping to have her say, " If only Harrie were here ! "— but she would learn greater wisdom before long.

" I must stay another day or two if Mrs. Marjorybanks will extend her hospitality so far, and by that time I will have made a first-rate horsewoman of you," he said.

" But then I will have no one to ride with," said Lucie, with a fascinating little pout, turning her eyes up to his.

She was getting on a little already, he thought, as he looked down into them.

Henrietta had been rather anxious meantime.   She went up to the west turret window and watched the riders as they cantered along the sands.   Something almost intangible stirred at her heart—was it jealousy or an uneasy feeling that, after all, Captain Charteris was only a stranger to them ? She could not say.

" Oh, is he not nice ? " said Lucie that night, as the girls were alone together.

" He—he is pleasing," said Henrietta, with a more distinct tug at her heartstrings this time.   After only two days !

XIII

THE Captain's visit lengthened out.   He had found favour in the eyes of Mrs. Marjorybanks by assuring her that he considered all forms of faith equally vain, and by appreciating the contents of her cellar.   " He is a

gentleman of the old school," the widow said.   So she gave
him of her best, and did not play the chaperon at all.   She
scorned such conventionalities.   Certainly the visitor was a
wonderful addition to the strange little circle at Balgowrie.
The house put on an air of habitation that it had never known
before.   Its long passages echoed to the Captain's laughter
and whistling, and the snatches of gay little tunes that were
ever on his lips.   In the evenings he and Lucie sang together,
or in the long dusks of May they would wander about the
garden, amusing themselves with nothing, as all young
creatures can if they are left alone.   Henrietta, of course,
was always there, for Lucie would not go alone ; but it must
be said that her position became not altogether a pleasant one.
She could not help acknowledging that Charteris, for one,
would have preferred to be alone with Lucie.   " I suppose
this is what in romances is termed *Love*," she said, with
infinite scorn.   She knew very little about love and cared
less ; for her it was a figment of the popular fancy, a curious
superstition that had somehow become universal—a name.
The realities of life, for Henrietta, were only study—the
pursuit of knowledge under any form—and her love for
two people—Lucie and Dr. Cornelius.   Between these two
sisters, so unlike in character, there had grown up that
exquisite intimacy which is so close as to be unconscious of
its own preciousness.   There was, as it were, one heart
between them ; the gropings of speech were superfluous.
As you may sometimes see two branches of a tree almost
grown together by continued pressure one upon the other, so
these characters, that started on their journey so far apart,
had been welded into one by their dependence on each other.
Now a thin edge of the outer world's dividing wedge began
to push itself between them, and Henrietta winced sharply
and sorely as the intruding presence asserted itself beyond a
doubt.   The first pin-prick had been the thought that Charteris
was in love with Lucie—but like a knife at her heart came
the conviction that Lucie was in love with him.   Where
confidence is absolute there is seldom much speech—most
things are understood.   Lucie said no word to Henrietta of

the sudden summer in her heart—it would have seemed quite unnecessary to her to do so. But she laughed and sang out of the fullness of her happiness, and Henrietta did not need to be told about it. And from her calm standpoint Henrietta at first smiled too ; for Lucie did not take love very seriously. It was only a delicious frolic then, new and intensely exciting, the first sip of life.

But when Charteris had been now three weeks at Balgowrie (a long enough visit, in all conscience, for a self-invited guest), the frolic came to a sudden end. Lucie woke up to find that she had staked her happiness at this fascinating game, and Henrietta, watching, trembled and held her breath to see such high play.

It was one of those May evenings when the light seems unwilling to say good-night to the budding world, and lingers very long in a splendid after-glow. The apple trees were a sheet of blossom, and little puffs of wind came up from the sea, smelling salt and fresh, to mix their saltness with the heavy scent of the blossom. It was a delight to draw breath in such sweetness. Lucie and Charteris had gone out to the garden, and were leaning over the low wall at the end of the orchard, looking towards the sunset. An interruption was the last thing they looked for, and the appearance of Silence, bearing a salver, on which lay a large crested envelope, was not welcome. Letters were no everyday event in 1775, and Silence presented the missive with a bow of solemn reverence.

" A letter ? " said Charteris carelessly. " It grows too dark to read it now—eh, Lucie ? "

He ventured upon her name for the first time under cover of the reassuring dusk. The retreating figure of Silence, as he disappeared among the apple trees, seemed to leave them doubly alone.

" Oh, I think you could still see to read it, sir," she said, catching up the big envelope, and slowly spelling out its address.

" Well—here goes," he said, taking it from her with a lingering touch of her little white hand. " Come, and we shall read it together ; I shall let you into all my secrets."

He spread out the sheet towards the glow that indicated where sunset had been, and they bent their heads over it in the effort to decipher its contents. The letter was inscribed under His Majesty's seal, and summoned Captain Dan Charteris to London with all speed.

"To-morrow, that means," he said blankly. "Gad! but the time has wings in Scotland, I think."

Lucie said nothing; for her heart had stood still in a moment of utter dismay, and now she was gulping down her tears, and could not trust herself to speak. Charteris probably understood the situation. He put his arm very gently round Lucie's neck and kissed her.

"Never fear, Lucie. We'll meet again this side the grave," he said lightly.

"I—I hope so," she stammered. "I should not care very much for the other side;" and, yielding to the soft pressure of his arm, Lucie buried her face on his breast and sobbed out of very joy.

Charteris did not take very long to kiss away her tears. He did not say much; but kisses are wonderfully reassuring.

"We must go in, Dan," she said at last, remembering how long they must have been absent from the house; but before they turned to go, she looked up into her lover's face, to stamp it on her memory for ever. As he stood there in the dull red glow, Charteris seemed like some sculptured bronze knight. His colouring was indistinguishable in the dusk; his hair looked black as night, and his blue eyes, except where a reflection from the sky gave them a flash of scarlet, might have been coals for blackness.

And Charteris, taking a farewell look also, saw Lucie like a little white ghost against the dark tree stems behind her.

"Why, you might be on t'other side already, child," he cried, laughing, and passing his arm through hers.

"The other side of what?" queried Lucie.

"Of the grave, you little white ghost!" he said.

XIV

THE drawing-room was quite dark when Lucie and Charteris came in. Mrs. Marjorybanks had a curious habit of pacing up and down the room like a caged beast at times, and to-night she had one of her restless fits upon her. She passed from end to end of the long room without a moment's pause for breath, moving with almost a man's stride. At the window Henrietta sat, holding a book close to her eyes to catch the last rays of light. Mrs. Marjorybanks did not stop for a moment as they entered, but said shortly—

" You are late," and passed them on her rapid walk.

Charteris fell into step with her, however, and forced conversation by the announcement of his summons to London. The widow did not seem to be disturbed at all.

" Everything comes to an end, you see, Charteris," she said. " We have enjoyed your company, and now we must enjoy your absence."

He had learned to laugh at her queer speeches,—a condition of life at Balgowrie. So he laughed at this, and they paced up and down together for a few more turns, before Charteris remembered that his effects must be packed that night, to catch the Edinburgh coach on its way through the village in the early dawn. He excused himself, and went off to his packing, whistling along the passage very light-heartedly.

Lucie had gone over to the window where Henrietta sat. They did not speak, but Lucie slipped her hand into Henrietta's, and gave it a little excited squeeze, then she went into the west turret and leaned against the window frame, looking out across the darkness to the long red bar that still lingered in the western sky. Standing there, she heard Charteris come into the drawing-room again and ask where she was.

" I am here, sir," she said softly; and he crossed the room, and stooped his head to pass through the low entrance to the turret.

" I am come to ask a favour of you, Lucie," he said. " And must you call me ' sir,' by the way ? Well, this is it. Why, it is too dark to see here. I wished you to mend my laced coat for me."

"Oh, I can do that with pleasure! I shall get a light if you wait one moment," said Lucie.

She rang for Silence, who came in with a lamp, and grumbled under his breath when sent for another for the turret.

"My sewing things are here," Lucie explained, as if explanations were necessary for her wish to be alone with her lover.

Charteris spread out all the gaudy bravery of his laced coat across her knee. Some of the gold braid had been torn, and the lace was come loose from its ruffling.

"Small use I have had for it ; I thought to wear it at Holyrood," he said, with a grimace at the finery.

"Oh, I should like to see you in it, above all things ! " cried Lucie, with all a woman's enthusiasm for uniform. It was the first she had ever set eyes upon, and she could not but admire it infinitely.

"Ah ! who knows ? Perhaps some day you may," said the Captain, indicating where the repair was needed in a very utilitarian way.

Lucie's fingers played long with the laced coat. You may be sure she put her best sewing into it, but at last she had to confess the pleasant task was done.

"You will remember me when next you wear it," she said shyly, as she folded it up with beautiful exactness into the proper folds.

"And what will you remember me by ? " said Charteris.

"I am in no danger of forgetting, sir—Dan, I mean," said Lucie softly.

Charteris was standing beside the little turret window, and as Lucie spoke, he drew the diamond ring from his finger, and began to draw something on the pane.

"Oh, what is it ? " she said, starting up to look at what he did, and letting her hand rest on his shoulder for a moment as she leaned forward.

"A heart, little lady—yours or mine," he said. "And here goes your name above it, and 1775, and D. R. C. for my name ; and what shall we have underneath ? "

" Whatever you like," said Lucie.

Charteris went on scrawling some words on the pane.

" See—does that please you ? " he asked at length.

"'United hearts death only parts,'" read Lucie slowly. " Ah, Dan, that is beautiful ! "

But further sentimentalities were stopped by the announcement of supper, a meal which Charteris partook of with his wonted perfection of appetite, while Lucie could not even make a pretence of eating.

She did not make much pretence of sleeping either ; for oh, the hours passed quickly enough that were bringing her nearer and nearer to " Good-bye "—they would have flown with intolerable swiftness in dreams.

Charteris rode away in the splendid morning sunshine, and Lucie and Henrietta stood on the steps to watch his going. His farewells had been quite unemotional ; he only pressed Lucie's hand a moment longer than Henrietta's.

The sisters stood together watching till the last glimpse of horse and rider had disappeared. Neither spoke, but Henrietta passed her arm round Lucie's neck. Faithless Lucie ! the caress only brought to her mind the remembrance of another, the same, but so different, and her tears fell fast. She pushed away Henrietta's arm and sprang down the steps and along the orchard walk till she reached the old wall where she had stood the night before with Charteris.

" He is away—he is away ! and not even Harrie can make up for him ! " she cried. And, leaning her head on the old wall, she tasted the bitterness of first parting. Dan was gone— had ridden away into the great busy world in which he played his graceful, daring part ; while she stayed here, penned up alone in this garden, as much out of his world as if she were in the moon and he on earth. Every step of his horse was at that moment carrying him farther and farther away from her, into the unknown and far away, where she might not follow— whence he would not come for—oh, centuries ! And the whole world was black and dull, except just that happy spot where he chanced to be. Lucie wept on till she was too tired to weep any more, then she dried her eyes and smiled a faint watery smile, remembering that, after all, it was happiness, not grief, that she had found.   Then she thought of Henrietta with a pang of self-reproach, and the thought sent her racing down the orchard towards the house.

Henrietta, who did not love the sunlight as Lucie did, had gone indoors.   She was sitting in the library as usual, a book open before her, her face supported on her hand ; but as Lucie came nearer, she saw that the book was all blotted with tears. Henrietta, it is true, was reading at that moment a hard lesson in the book of life.   As was their habit, the sisters did not waste words.   Lucie knelt down beside Henrietta, and they cried together silently.   It was quite as sad a thought to Lucie as to Henrietta that someone from the outside had stepped in between them.   At last Henrietta said pensively—

" You are not my little sister any longer—you are as old as I am all of a sudden."

At this Lucie rose with great dignity, saying, " Older, Harrie ; I am in love—what we have heard so much about."

And then they both laughed, and Henrietta said in her heart· " Lucie is a child still."

XV

SO Lucie was child enough to be delighted for a time with her new sensation.

But as you will sometimes see a child that is smitten by some sad and wasting illness play about merrily enough at first, then become daily quieter, as the burden weighs heavier and heavier in its flesh, till at last all the games are forgotten and the toys are put away—so Lucie became very sober after a time, and her usual occupations seemed to have lost all zest for her.   She did not sing as of yore over her work, and would sometimes let her diligent needle fall unregarded on to her lap for a minute or two, and sit gazing out vacantly into the garden. Then all the little incidents of Dan's visit that it had been her delight to go over in conversation with Henrietta became prohibited subjects, and gradually even his name died out of their talk; for, alas! Dan seemed to have forgotten all about Balgowrie.

Henrietta was distracted.   She tried by every art in her power to interest and amuse Lucie, but, after all, what had she to offer as a balancing interest to this great absorbing one that filled her sister's heart?   Abstract subjects demand before everything that an undivided mind be brought to their consideration, and philosophy and mathematics roused no enthusiasm in Lucie when another and a very concrete subject filled the foreground of her mind.   The only interest she found in anything was in Maggie Pelham's letters.   They were a slight link of connection with Charteris, and welcome on that score.

At last Henrietta could bear it no longer.   She must speak to someone—get some help.   It was a simple matter in one way, for she had no difficulty as to who should be her adviser—there was only Dr. Cornelius.

So she walked down to the Manse one afternoon " with a book."   But the book was a transparent excuse, as Dr. Cornelius was quick to see when she turned her troubled eyes to his.

" There is something wrong, Harrie," he said.

Henrietta, who never could say a thing like other people, did not tell her errand at once.   She entered upon the subject in one of her long-winded sentences, that were like the preparatory remarks of her favourite novelists.

" Sir," she said, " I have been coming to conclusions regarding love.   I believe now, what I have disputed with you, that it is one of the vital forces of the world."

" Ah, you have come to that conclusion, Harrie?   Well, you never come to conclusions without having good grounds for them—may I inquire further? "

But here Henrietta broke down.   She clasped her hands in a queer tragic attitude she had, just like a stage posture rather overdone, and turned to Dr. Cornelius with streaming eyes.

" Oh, sir, it is Lucie—my dearest, my own Lucie!   She cares for that man, and for no other thing on earth.   You must have noticed that she grows thinner and paler each day. I am breaking my heart over her."

"Tut, tut, Harrie! you take matters too seriously; 'tis a childish complaint we all pass through," said Dr. Cornelius lightly, and he patted Henrietta's shoulder encouragingly.

"But she lies awake half the night, and weeps when she thinks I do not hear her; and she does not care about the pigeons, or the hens, or her lark any longer."

"We have all lain awake—no—I believe you have not— I have, many a time, though, and see me now," said Dr. Cornelius. He certainly had not suffered materially from his vigils: Henrietta allowed herself to feel comforted by a glance at his smooth face, where even fifty and odd years had written no wrinkles as yet.

Seeing her a little reassured, Dr. Cornelius began to look at the other side of the picture.

"It is not a very wholesome process all the same, Henrietta," he said; "I agree with you there—Lucie looks ill and thin—she requires change before anything. Would nothing induce your mother to send her away from home?"

"You know my mother, sir," said Henrietta hopelessly.

"I only know one thing of her, that you cannot really calculate exactly upon her actions in any way: there is just a fractional chance that if you proposed this at the right moment, Mrs. Marjorybanks might suddenly consent to it."

"And where would Lucie go? We have no friends that I know of."

"To London—where her heart is—to your friend Mrs. Pelham. Henrietta, I shall write to Mrs. Pelham myself about this, with your consent."

"I fear, I fear, sir, it is useless!" and then with a sudden lowering of her voice and a passionate, despairing movement of her hands, "Only God can help us, sir—our mother is mad!"

"My dear, my dear!" said Dr. Cornelius soothingly, but to himself he ejaculated, "Has she only found that out now?" Aloud he said, "Now we play the parson—you should not speak of that Aid as the last resort."

" I have only two—you and God—I came to you first,"
said Henrietta simply.   She had hewn out some rudimentary
religious beliefs for herself, but she was so destitute of conventional religiosity that her expressions might sometimes, as
in the present instance, seem to savour of irreverence.   But
irreverence was very far from Henrietta's nature.   After she
had said this, she sat looking at Dr. Cornelius silently.

" Cornelius," she said suddenly (it was the first time she
had ever spoken his name, and he started to hear it from her
lips),—" Cornelius, I never like you so little as when you say
things of that sort."

" Of which sort, Harrie ? "

" ' Playing the parson.'   I know enough to know that if
there is a God you should not make a joke of serving Him ;
and if there is not, or if you think there is not, you should
scorn to live on the teaching of lies."

Henrietta spoke with eyes that flashed and a ringing voice,
and Dr. Cornelius, watching her, felt a throb of triumph at his
heart.   He listened to her quietly, then stepped forward and
took her hand in his.

" One cares something for the man one finds such heavy
fault with, Harrie," he said.   " And since when did you
become old enough to rebuke me by my Christian name ? "

" I do not know—since we seemed to become the same age,"
said Henrietta. looking into his face with her steady eyes.

Dr. Cornelius hesitated for a moment—had the right time
come at last ?   Then he took Henrietta's face between his
hands and turned it up towards his own, and kissed her lips.

" We are not teacher and pupil any longer, Harrie, but man
and woman—I found that out some time ago.   I was waiting
to see when you would make the discovery."

" 'Tis very pleasant, sir."

" And will you find it very pleasant to marry me Harrie ? "
There was a long pause then.

" Yes, I think I shall—but Lucie ? "

The lover is proverbially impatient, so perhaps it was not
surprising that Dr. Cornelius should be provoked at this.

" Lucie, Lucie, Lucie ! " he cried.   " Can you never forget her for a moment? This is not the time to think of her, Harrie—surely your own affairs and mine might occupy you for a little?" He could not be angry with Henrietta, but he came very near it just then.

"My affairs and Lucie's are the same, I think," said Henrietta; but Dr. Cornelius questioned this statement firmly.

"No, no, Harrie; you must make up your mind to take your separate ways at last. She has got her lover, and you have got yours. Your affairs are very different, instead of being identical."

He had risen, and stood now leaning against the mantelshelf. Henrietta rose also. She was playing a part that was quite new to her, and in which she did not feel easy as yet. She was not one of the women to whom love-making comes by nature; she found no sweet words waiting on her tongue, and the very fullness of her feeling hindered its expression. To help out her halting words she came up to Dr. Cornelius placing her hands on his shoulders with a quick, gentle movement, and looking into his face.

"You must not mind, sir," she stammered out. "You—you are my—my lover . . . but oh, Lucie is my very life!"

He laughed at her shyness, stroking her hair, and looking deep into her eyes to read their baffling honesty, that had never had a thought to hide. "There's not one woman in a thousand could stand that test, Harrie," he said, for she turned up her face to his like a child.

"You have not said anything about Lucie," said Henrietta, and at this Dr. Cornelius laughed more loudly than before.

"Ah, Harrie, Harrie, you will never act like other women—never! I can swear that you have just heard the first words of love-making you have ever listened to, and instead of being fluttered by them, you return to your starting-point as if nothing had happened! So it appears we must settle Lucie's affairs first?"

"If we did, I could then think more undisturbedly about my own," said Henrietta.

Dr. Cornelius made a grimace and shrugged his shoulders.

"Madam is business-like," he said. "Pray be seated, then,

and let us finish the first subject before we begin on the second.
I have only one advice to give.   Send Lucie to London.   I
shall arrange it.   Give me three weeks or so, Henrietta, and I
will see if it can be done.   Keep your mind easy about Lucie—
' men have died, and worms have eaten them, but not for love,'
as your favourite Shakespeare has it."

"Yes ; men," said Henrietta curtly.

"And women less so—women are not so constant as they
are represented to be.   We all console ourselves, and so do
they.   Now, are you at leisure to discuss our personal
affairs ? "

"Yes, I am ; but you must speak, if you please, sir, for I am
so unaccustomed to conversation like this that I cannot say
what is in my heart—you must understand it."

"Oh, love is easily learned.   Come and say, ' I love you,
Cornelius ;' surely that is easy enough, and it is all I wish."

"I have never done anything but love you for all these
years ; I do not need to tell you."

"Then will you leave Lucie and come to me ? "

"Yes, some time.   You could not ask me to leave her now."

"Remember my grey hairs, Harrie.   I shall have a shorter
lease of happiness than most men."

"Then it must be all the deeper," said Henrietta.   "If we
had met each other when you were young,—the same age with
me—I could never have felt as I do to you now.   Why, you
have been my father and brother and lover all in one, and I love
you with the love of all the three ! "

"I used to think you were not meant for marriage, Harrie,
—you are not the domestic angel woman,—but I am losing
that impression now."

"I—I have one or two womanly feelings, sir," said Henrietta reflectively.   "I cannot love sewing and baking, but
really my heart is not hard ; I care for a few things besides
study."

"And you are the one woman in the world for me.   I love
your inky fingers and your learned sentences beyond all the
womanly virtues of the veriest Dorcas.   Ah, and some day I

shall be proud of you !—some day the world will hear of you, Harrie, and the learned sentences will come to something."

" I doubt if I shall ever do much ; I think that God has shut in my life between walls."

" But you are going to break through the walls. You will come out into the world with me, dear, and forget the prison-house, and see men and things new and strange, and it will be like entering a new life.

Henrietta's great eyes glowed, and her queer, expressive face was lighted up with pleasure. She sat gazing into the fire, and repeated his words slowly in the silence that followed—

" *I shall see men and things new and strange. . . and it will be like entering a new life.*"

XVI

AFTER Henrietta had gone, Dr. Cornelius sat thinking for a long time over what had passed. He was not entirely satisfied. The affection Henrietta had for him was beautiful, ideal in some ways,—the steady, natural out-growth from their earlier relation of teacher and scholar,—but did it not want just the one thing needful ? " She is too sure of me," he reflected ; " women adore an element of uncertainty. I am ever with her, and all that I have is hers, and she knows it. I shall go away, like Lucie's cavalier, and see if the like salutary effects follow. I would give something to see Harrie grow thin and pale for me ! If I thought she would give up study, and sit looking at the moon and sighing, I would stay away from her dear presence for a year of Sundays ! But she does not love me after that fashion yet. Well, I shall go to London, and take Lucie with me, and perhaps Made-moiselle may find time heavier on her hands without us."

Dr. Cornelius accordingly laid his plans for going to London, and some three weeks later came to announce them at Bal-gowrie. He had written to Mrs. Pelham, as arranged, and knew that by this time her invitation to Lucie must have arrived.

The news of his intended journey (a great one it was considered in those days) was received with astonishment.

" You are going to London ? " cried Henrietta incredulously, and not without a momentary feeling of pique ; she had hitherto heard long beforehand of the smallest change in Dr. Cornelius' plans. " Why, sir, I do not remember that you have quitted the parish, except to go to Edinburgh since we we came here," she added.

" Then you see there is all the more need of my going, Harrie ; the moss grows over a man in a place like this. Once upon a time I went to London whenever the fancy took me ; but nowadays my ministerial duties are so pressing that London does not see much of me."

He glanced at Henrietta as he said this, to see if she was sufficiently provoked by his levity ; but Henrietta affected not to understand his intention, so he added—

" But these are not matters to joke upon ; the ministerial calling is a solemn one—eh, Harrie ? "

Henrietta refused to reply, however, so Dr. Cornelius had to change the subject. He went directly to his point, addressing Mrs. Marjorybanks now.

" I have been wondering, madam, if you would not think of allowing Lucie to come up to London with me ? I do not think she is looking well, and I see she makes no progress with her studies ; she requires some stimulous ; perhaps you might arrange for her pursuing some course of study under fresh auspices in town if you thought of letting her go there for a time."

" I do not approve of change for young people," said the widow, with great finality of tone,

" I was not urging the advantages of change, madam, but of stimulus—of emulation, incentive, ambition. Lucie is apt to be lazy in her studies ; but if she were placed among other girls, and fired with the desire to keep pace with them, she might become more industrious. Henrietta needs no incentive to study ; but after considering Lucie's temperament carefully, I have come to the conclusion that emulation alone will make her work. Of course it is for you to decide. I only proposed that she should accompany me to London as it seemed a good opportunity for her going, and as I remembered your good friend Mrs. Pelham had so often invited your daughters to visit her."

" I had an invitation from Mrs. Pelham to-day for Lucie," said Mrs. Marjorybanks.

" And will you not consider it as a possibility, madam, now that you know Lucie would have a responsible escort ? "

" It is a possibility," said the widow ; and Lucie, sitting at her work beside her, held her breath, and broke her needle across, in the effort to direct it with such trembling fingers.

" It would be a pleasure to me," said Dr. Cornelius.   " And before leaving town I would see that all arrangements about Lucie's studies being properly carried on were completed. I would myself interview her proposed masters, and let them understand that the object of their pupil's coming to London was entirely that she might benefit mentally, and not that she might enter upon all the frivolities of town life."

Dr. Cornelius spoke with extraordinary gravity.   He even rose and walked over to where Lucie sat tremblingly at work, and laid a hand on her shoulder, saying in his sternest tones—

" It will be no laughing matter this, Lucie.   Some people have an idea that London is a place to amuse oneself in ; but you will find that you will be compelled to work there, however dilatory you may be over your studies here."

He stood as he said this with his back to the widow, and even as the severe words fell from his lips, Lucie saw his eyes laugh reassuringly into hers.   She said—

" Yes, sir," very meekly, and waited to hear the upshot of the discussion.

Dr. Cornelius returned to his seat beside Mrs. Marjorybanks.

" I fear I shall hurry Lucie's preparations," he said, taking it for granted now that she was to be allowed to go with him, " for I intend to leave for London at the end of the week. But I am sure, madam, that you do not think it necessary to make any great preparations for a stay in the capital ; and should any little changes of toilet be desirable, Mrs. Pelham will arrange about them, no doubt. The boat sails for London from Leith Harbour on Saturday morning. Can Lucie be ready to go to Edinburgh with me on Friday?"

It seemed a century to all the impatient listeners before Mrs. Marjorybanks spoke. "Yes," she said at last, and Dr. Cornelius had triumphed. He did not show any signs of surprise or of pleasure.

"I thought you would agree with me, madam," he said. "We are so generally agreed upon most subjects that I felt sure it was only necessary to point out this matter to you to gain your consent to my plan."

Then he rose and bade them all adieu, and Henrietta's heart felt heavy in the prospect of her coming loneliness, and Lucie's very soul sang for joy.

XVII

IT was a chilly October dawn that saw Lucie start on her travels—an excited, sobbing little person, clad in weird garments made after no known canons of fashion past or present. The Edinburgh coach passed through Eastermuir at six in the morning, and Henrietta had come down to the village to see the travellers off in it. Her heart, too, was in her mouth as they stood together in the chill morning dusk, waiting for the arrival of the coach. The sisters had never been parted before, even for a day, and now that the moment of separation was come, both of them would have been willing that the London visit should be renounced, that they might stay together.

Lucie's courage was entirely gone, and she sobbed openly under her odd green silk bonnet, and clung to Henrietta,— indeed, it is doubtful whether she would ever have gone if Dr. Cornelius had not been her escort. But there was an infectious cheerfulness in his solid, handsome presence as he appeared, rolled up in a long driving coat, and carrying for his own and Lucie's benefit an armful of wraps.

"A stage-coach is the last place for sentiment, Lucie," he said ; " its discomforts are too practical to admit of it ; so you must dry these sweet tears, and set your mind to facing the trials of the way with heroism. By the time you have jolted for two or three hours in the coach, I doubt your tears will be falling for yourself, not for Harrie."

"You seem very cheerful, sir, in the face of all that is before you," said Henrietta demurely, and Dr. Cornelius laughed, assuring her that he rather liked discomfort as a change.

"I shall take you to London next, Harrie,—to see men and things," he said.

Lucie did not understand the allusion, or why Henrietta blushed suddenly and hotly at his words. For Henrietta had told her nothing of what had passed between herself and Dr. Cornelius. "If she had been happy, I must have told her," she thought ; " but it would kill her just now to think that I even dreamed of leaving her." So the blush rather mystified Lucie.

The coach came rumbling up then—mud-spattered, with steaming horses. The driver, a red-faced man encased in a multitude of coats, greeted Dr. Cornelius heartily—

"You're for the road, Doctor ? " he cried, and pulled up his cattle alongside of the little group.

The moment of parting had come, and Lucie flung herself upon Henrietta's neck, clinging to her as if she would never let her go, till Dr. Cornelius remarked gently that the coach could not wait any longer.

He lifted Lucie into the inside of the vehicle, and turned to say good-bye to Henrietta. She was crying unrestrainedly now, and with a movement of impatience he recognised that she wept for Lucie's going, not for his. He waited for her to speak, but she had no words, so, pressing her hand silently he jumped up beside the driver and wrapped his coat about him in the keen air.

With a strain of the horses at the collar, a jolt of the coach, and a great splash of mud from the heavy roads, off they went ; and Henrietta, standing forlorn among the puddles, watched the two people who formed her world disappear like shadows into the mists of the morning.

It was perhaps as well that Lucie was the only inside passenger for the first stage of the journey ; for she crept away to one end of the coach and nearly cried her eyes out. The road lay along the shore at first,—by the edge of the sands where she had ridden with Charteris, and the remembrance made her sob all the more as they rumbled along round the great curve of the bay. The breakers were tumbling in with the same roar that had sounded in her ears from childhood. She was leaving all that was familiar and dear, and going out into the unknown and terrible world, and at the thought poor Lucie sobbed more and more bitterly.

But as they left the well-known shore behind, and the road turned inland, Lucie dried her eyes, and began to look about her. She had never been more than ten miles from Balgowrie since they came to it, and her recollections of life before that date were too indistinct to count for much. Now they were passing through villages and past houses unknown to her even by name, and it was wonderfully interesting. A greater interest than the scenery, however, appeared very soon, in the person of another passenger, a stout country-woman, carrying a baby. Now, strange as it may seem, Lucie had never, in the whole course of her nearly eighteen years' pilgrimage, seen a baby so close at hand. Mrs. Marjorybanks did not approve of the girls visiting their poor neighbours, and they had never even spoken to the people as they passed on the roads. So when Lucie was brought face to face with this, one of the wonders of the world, she held her breath for delight. After a little she moved across the coach and sat down beside the woman, as if irresistibly drawn towards the little bundle she held in her arms.

" May I—may I see the baby ? " she faltered out at last ; and the woman opened up her shawl immediately, to display the little waxen sleeping face to Lucie's wondering eyes.

" Oh, it is beautiful, most beautiful ! I suppose it is asleep just now ? Will it waken if I touch it ? Might I touch its

head ?—it looks so soft," she cried, and the woman said something which she took to be an assent from her amused smile.
She leaned forward and touched the soft little head gingerly.

" How *delightful* it is ! " she exclaimed.   " I should like
beyond anything to hold it for a little."

" They're an unco fash," said the unemotional mother.

Lucie did not understand what " fash " meant in the least,
but the woman placed the child in her arms, and she sat watching its gentle breaths come and go, breathless herself with
excitement.

When it opened its eyes and cried it was a new wonder
(" Just like a doll come to life," said Lucie) ; and when,
restored to the parental arms to receive substantial material
comfort, the little creature spread out its tiny dimpled hand
against the mother's breast, Lucie cried out for pleasure.

" I had no idea they were so delightful," she said, speaking
as if of an unknown species.

The mother fairly laughed.

" In a' the warl', woman, whaur are ye come frae ?   A
body'd say ye'd ne'er set eyes on a wean afore."

Lucie thought it necessary to reply.   " I come from a
village called Eastermuir."

" An' hae they nae bairns in Eastermuir ?   My word, it
maun be a fine place thon ! "

" Oh yes, there are children in the village, but I have never
spoken to one before—not that I have spoken to this one
either.   Can it speak yet ? "

" Sakes she's fair daft, I'm thinkin' ! " exclaimed the amused
mother.   " He'll no' hae his tongue for twa year yet."

" Two years ! that seems a long time," said Lucie reflectively, gazing at the child.

Now that the comversation had begun, the woman seemed
anxious to continue it.

" Yon's ' Doctor Cornelius,' as they ca' him, on the top,"
she said, indicating the roof of the coach with an upward
nod.   " Ye'll ken the Doctor, maybe ? "

" I *know* Dr. Hallijohn very well," said Lucie doubtfully.
" He is taking care of me on the journey."

" He's a fine man the Doctor," said the woman quickly, restraining an inclination to gossip over his delinquencies as she saw Lucie was a friend.

Just then the coach drew up before an inn, and the " fine man " came to help Lucie out, for they were to breakfast here. She noticed how the people about the place seemed to know Dr. Cornelius, and he would pass a word with each of them, as if they were old friends. They all looked curiously at Lucie too, and even the bucolic mind seemed to find something a little curious in her appearance, for as she and Dr. Cornelius passed into the parlour where they were to breakfast stood smiling and whispering to watch her.

Lucie had a pretty good appetite in spite of her morning of weeping, and sat down to discuss cold ham and oatcakes with great pleasure. She had to describe to Dr. Cornelius her wonderful encounter with a real live baby of only two months old, and she did so with an enthusiasm that made him smile.

" You are intended to be a mother, Lucie, without doubt," he said.

" Ah, you are laughing at me, sir ; but do you not find them very delightful little creatures ? "

" They do tug at one's heart-strings," said Dr. Cornelius sentimentally, as he carved another slice of ham. " Here, my dear, you must have some more ; remember what a long day is before you."

" Why have you never married, sir, when you are so fond of children ? " asked Lucie after a minute's silence.

" Why ?—oh, every man has his story, I suppose," said Dr. Cornelius evasively. " To which fact I owe any popularity I possess. I am a wretched parson, Lucie ; I cannot for the life of me reprove a man, and for that very reason I hear all their stories."

" Do good ' parsons ' always reprove people, sir ?—they must be very disagreeable, I think, if they do."

" Not at all—it is sometimes exquisitely pleasant to be reproved—it altogether depends upon who does it."

Dr. Cornelius gazed out through the window in the direction

of Eastermuir with a reminiscent smile about his lips, forgetting his breakfast in a, for him, most unusual way.

"I do not think you are eating as much breakfast as I am,
sir, said Lucie.

Which was perfectly true. The fresh horses were being
yoked below the window, and Lucie rose and stood looking
out at them.

Dr. Cornelius paced up and down the narrow panelled
parlour, stopping to look at the prints on the walls, He
seemed occupied with something else, however, Lucie
thought; then she heard him say, with great decision—
"'Henry'—yes, of course."

"Who is Henry?" she asked, turning round in surprise.

"Did I speak! A stupid habit of mine, Lucie—someone
I was thinking about," said Dr. Cornelius.

"Henry was my father's name: Henrietta was called after
him," said Lucie.

"Called after her father? Exactly as it should be;
children should always be named after their parents. My
dear Lucie, we must come downstairs; the coach is ready to
start."

And down they went, and Lucie was bundled into the
stuffy vehicle again to resume her journey.

The way seemed interminable. Lucie felt as if she must
have reached the end of the earth when at last the coach
drew up in the High Street of Edinburgh. And the confusion! and the noise! In absolute terror of the unknown
faces, the jarring sounds of the streets,—the first she had ever
trod,—and the tall frowning houses overlooking her, Lucie
clung to Dr. Cornelius. It was well they had only a few
steps to go through the street before reaching the close where
old Miss Hallijohn was to bid them welcome. Lucie was
bewildered, almost weeping with fear when they stood at last
under the shelter of the doorway.

"Oh," she gasped, "is this what a town is like? Sir, I
am so much alarmed, I fear I shall be in your way."

Dr. Cornelius laughed. "It is an attempt at a town, Lucie:
what will you say to London town itself if this scares you?

Well, we must come upstairs, and I shall present you to my good cousin."

Miss Maltida Hallijohn sat at work in her panelled room looking out over the street. She was a fine old lady, with silver hair dressed high on cushions after the fashion of the day, and a dress of stiff brocaded black satin. Lucie had never seen hair dressed after this prevalent mode, and gazed at it in mute astonishment. Balgowrie made no concessions to the foibles of fashion. The old lady received them with great cordiality, and remarked to Lucie that " Cousin Cornelius had often spoken of her and of her sister."

But at the mention of her sister poor Lucie broke down. She had a sudden vision of what it would be if Harrie could come into this unfamiliar room—how it would seem like home in a moment, and fear and strangeness would vanish away.

" Tut, tut ! the bairn's tired out, Cornelius," said Miss Hallijohn. " Come away and lie down, my dear ; " and she led Lucie up to a little fusty-smelling bedroom at the very top of the house—so high up that it must be among the clouds, Lucie thought. It had one tiny window set into an extra-ordinarily deep window niche, and the room seemed to contain nothing but a bed, so massive in size was the yellow-curtained, four-posted resting-place that stood at one end of it. Miss Hallijohn drew back the curtains and patted the pillows enticingly ; but the strange, town-smelling room was terrible to poor home-sick Lucie. How could she rest in that unknown bed, behind these sober yellow hangings, without one familiar object in sight ? But suddenly, with a little cry of joy, she ran forward to the window ; for through the smoke over the roofs and chimney-cans, beyond the distant fields, and indeed, almost indistinguishable in the creeping October mists, her country eyes had discerned a dim blue line dotted with white and brown sails.

" Oh, it is the sea—the sea ! " she cried. " Oh why is it so far away ? "

" To be sure it is the Forth, my dear—the same sea you look out on at home," said Miss Hallijohn reassuringly.

She could scarcely get Lucie to leave the window and lie

down, for, tired as she was, the poor child could not tear herself away from this newly-found link with home—the same sea that was washing up over the sands at Eastermuir—the sands where Henrietta was probaby walking at that very moment. And at this fresh thought of Henrietta Lucie began to cry again more sadly than before. Miss Hallijohn led her away from the window at last almost by force.

"Things will appear quite differently after you have rested for a few hours, Lucie," she said.

She could not find it in her heart to address this forlorn little person as Miss Marjorybanks.

"I shall send Joan my maid to waken you at six o'clock. We drink tea at that hour. Come, my dear, you must compose yourself and lie down quietly."

So Lucie composed herself as best she could behind the yellow curtains. She was glad to be alone at last, and employed her first half-hour of solitude in shedding many soothing, unobserved tears. Then she lay and listened to the unaccustomed noises that floated up from the street. Strange strange, they seemed to her country ears! the rolling of wheels and the monotonous footfalls on the paving-stones. As evening drew on, there were the cries of hucksters in the street—then an oyster-woman came down the close and stood below the window and gave her melancholy call, suggestive to the uninitiated of all that is weird and desolate rather than of the pleasures of the table. Lucie sat up, quite alarmed by it, but as nothing seemed to happen, she lay down again. Very gradually the noises became indistinct; the roll of passing wheels turned into the surf that broke along the sands at home on the wild winter nights; these footsteps could only be her mother's, pacing as usual up and down the drawing-room at Balgowrie; and the oyster-seller's cry resolved itself into the old brown owl that lived in the holly tree.

"I wonder if it has caught a mouse?" Lucie asked herself sleepily, and remembered nothing more.

Downstairs, Miss Hallijohn sat engaged in conversation with Dr. Cornelius.

"You are surely never going to take that poor child to

London like that Cornelius," she said.   "She is far more peculiar than I had anticipated even from your descriptions—and a pretty girl as ever was, too, had she the ordinary advantages of dress and of manner."

"But, Matilda, her manners are those of the lady that she is," said Dr. Cornelius.

"A lady certainly; but there is a peculiarity.   She is unlike the young people I see about me she is so strangely nervous and discomposed."

"Oh, I assure you her manners are charming as a rule—the child is over-excited and wearied out to-day.   In general she is not nervous at all."

"But with strangers, Cornelius?   How will she comport herself in London society if she is so overcome here?"

"That will pass off.   Remember she has never left home before in the seventeen and a half years that make up her sum of life."

Miss Hallijohn shook her head profoundly.

"And her dress is most peculiar, Cornelius—every young woman of any social standing wears her hair dressed high at present, and a hoop.   Now poor Miss Marjorybanks is wearing her hair much as nature arranged it, and her gowns are as flat as my hand.   She is most peculiar to look at, in spite of that lovely complexion and those eyes.   Your first duty on reaching London must be to procure new clothes for her at any cost—it should have been done before she went. 'Tis cruelty sending a child among strangers dressed after such a fashion."

"I was thankful enough to get permission to take her as she is.   If you knew the difficulties I had to contend with, Matilda, you would congratulate me on my cleverness, instead of finding fault with me."

"I fear the mother is quite demented," said Miss Hallijohn. "And what of the other sister?"

"Henrietta?   Henrietta is very different from Lucie," said Dr. Cornelius slowly.   "I daresay you would consider her fully more peculiar—she is in some respects; but she has—

oh, she has a thousand qualities that Lucie has not got—
originality, strength of purpose, courage, perseverance "—

He stopped suddenly, afraid that he had said too much,
and added in an off-hand manner—

" One finds out these differences in character after teaching
children so long."

" Is Henrietta a child ? " asked Miss Hallijohn, picking up
a stitch in her knitting with extreme elaboration.

" That is the worst of cousins—they think it permissible
to search out one's affairs as much as they like," said Dr.
Cornelius ; and at this Miss Hallijohn laughed gently.

" I did not know that Henrietta Marjorybanks' age formed
any part of your affairs, my good cousin, but since you assure
me that it is so, I am compelled to believe you."

" Well, I trust you are pleased by the intelligence ? "

" Let me see," said Miss Hallijohn, laying down her knitting
with deliberation, and assuming an air of calculation. " How
long ago was it ? Yes—twenty-five years ago, Cornelius,
you came into this very room, and told me you would hang
yourself for love of Penelope North. It was immediately
after she jilted you. I told you then you would live to marry
a better woman, and advised you to defer the hanging for a
time. I confess I had almost despaired of seeing my prophecy
come true ; even yet the young lady is unknown to me, so I
can scarcely judge between her and what I remember of
Penelope North after more than a score of years."

" You would find them strangely different, of that I am
certain. Henrietta is no faint reflection of my first love."

" Not by all accounts. Do you remember Penelope at the
Commissioner's ball in '51 ? "

" Yes," said Dr. Cornelius slowly. " I have a very good
memory. But if she could stand beside Henrietta in all the
beauty she wore that night, I would not even remember to
look at her once."

" Cornelius, Cornelius, you will be a boy to the day of your
death ! And tell me, why are you leaving your charmer in
this way ? for you tell me you will make a considerable stay
in London."

" I am leaving her because she hardly loves me enough yet—does that seem a good reason to your wisdom ? "

" Ah, come ! now I think better of Mistress Henrietta," cried the old lady. "The best women need a second asking —they do not give their hearts away too soon ; but I admit that at your time of life cousin, it is trying to have a wavering bride—you are none too young."

" Oh, my age be—— Pardon me, Matilda ; 'tis your own fault entirely, for reminding me of what I am striving to forget."

" Well, well, cousin, your wife will have several faults to correct in you," said Miss Hallijohn. " And when she has succeeded in that, you will make her a good husband. Kindly ring the bell for me now ; I must send Joan to waken our young friend."

Lucie looked very sleepy when she appeared, but after they had drunk tea together, she awakened up and became more like herself. Dr. Cornelius went out later, and Lucie was left alone with Miss Hallijohn. When he returned, it was to find Lucie sitting close by the old lady hand-in-hand with her, her cheeks pink with pleasure, and no trace of tears to be seen.

" Oh, sir," she cried, jumping up to meet Dr. Cornelius, " Miss Hallijohn is most kind ! I have told her all about Harrie, and all about Balgowrie, and—and everything. And when I return from London, Harrie and I are to come and visit Miss Hallijohn together. She thinks she will like Harrie quite as much as we do—and indeed she could not be disappointed in that, could she, sir ? "

" Not by our way of thinking, Lucie. But, Matilda, I am surprised that *at your time of life* you have not more sense than to keep this child up so late. Are you remembering that the boat sails at nine to-morrow morning from Leith, and Lucie requires a good night's rest before she starts ? "

" Tut, tut, Cornelius ! none of your airs of a family man for me. Your toddy is waiting you by the fire. Come away, Lucie my dear ; we will leave my gentleman to himself, since he wishes to be rid of us."

Lucie laughed gaily, and ran up the corkscrew stair so quickly that her hostess was left far behind, and she had to turn back to meet her again.   The little bedroom did not seem at all melancholy to her now and she fell asleep dreaming of the time when she and Henrietta would occupy it together—when they would laugh at the strange town noises and waken to see the dawn coming in over the hundred roofs below.

<h2 style="text-align:center">XVIII</h2>

DR. CORNELIUS began to realise that he would have his own difficulties with Lucie on the journey to London.   For after they had bidden adieu to Miss Hallijohn, and were jolting down to Leith in the coach, Lucie became very apprehensive.   The coach was crowded and the strange faces seemed to fill her with uneasiness.   She drew close to Dr. Cornelius, and shrank behind him to escape observation—which, indeed, was not to be wondered at, for the poor child's dress was sufficiently odd to attract attention to her anywhere, and, added to her pretty face, made the rough-mannered passengers stare at her unmercifully.   But when the coach drew up at Leith pier, things became much worse.   Dr. Cornelius left Lucie for a moment to look after the shipping of their luggage, and was just coming leisurely back up the quay to find her, when he saw the little crowd of people beside the coach parting as if to let someone pass, and Lucie ran towards him, holding out her hands with a pitiful gesture of terror.   Some of the crowd laughed loudly, and from the better-class passengers there was a ripple of amused comment upon the odd little figure flying down the quay.

" My dear Lucie," exclaimed Dr. Cornelius, " what is the matter ? "   He took the cold little hands she held out to him and smiled into her white face.

" I—I do not know, sir.   I felt bewildered after you left me.   The people seemed to press on me.   I must look peculiar, surely, for they were all laughing.   Oh, you must never leave me again."

" Come away with me," said Dr. Cornelius, but with rather a sinking heart he thought, " Matilda was right ; her dress is cruelly peculiar. I should have thought of it before." He led her on board, and sought out a sheltered corner of the deck. There he sat beside her, and treated Lucie to a little good advice. " You must not give way to these nervous feelings, Lucie. No one is wishing too hurt you ; you are perfectly safe, and I am never very far from you. If your dress is not very fashionable, we shall get you new garments in London—never mind it just now ; and, indeed, if you are like most amateur sailors, it is not much use you will have for your clothes for the next day or so."

They watched the other passengers come aboard, and Lucie, feeling once more sheltered and protected, was vastly entertained by the sight. A great many fine people, it appeared, were travelling by this boat, and Dr. Cornelius could tell her who they were individually. He even seemed to know some of them, and, after they had set sail, several people came up to speak with him. Lucie shrank into the corner behind Dr. Cornelius, and watched and listened. Wonderfully fine the ladies looked to her eyes in their hoops and tall headdresses, the like of which she had never dreamed of before.

Everyone seemed charmed to recognise Dr. Cornelius ; in especial one young lady who was travelling along with her father, a rather severe-looking elderly man, whom Dr. Cornelius addressed as " My lord."

" We are sure of an amusing voyage when you are on board, Doctor," she remarked, smiling very sweetly.

And Dr. Cornelius bowed and made her some pretty speech in return. He introduced Lucie very carefully to the girl (Lady Mary Crichton by name), explaining to Lady Mary that his young charge was not accustomed to travelling, and requesting her kind oversight of Lucie in the ladies' cabin."

At which Lucie cried out in dismay, " Oh, sir, shall I not have a room to myself ? "

And Lady Mary laughed till she cried, saying, " I must be very repulsive, Miss Marjorybanks ; had I been a toad, you could not have looked more frightened."

She was a good-humoured, handsome young woman,
dressed in the extreme of the fashion, and wearing a great
deal of rouge—a thing which Lucie had never even heard of,
and which impressed her vastly. She volunteered to take
Lucie down to the cabin, and could not understand her
reluctance to go with her, till Dr. Cornelius laughingly told
her that Lucie was afraid of all strangers, he feared.

"Afraid? *of me*!" said Lady Mary incredulously, but she
soon saw that it was too true. Lucie refused to move from
Dr. Cornelius' side.

"If you please, sir," was all she said, but in such an appealing
voice that it was irresistible.

"Well, if I do not ask too much, Lady Mary," said Dr.
Cornelius, "will you not sit down by us? and when Miss
Marjorybanks knows you better, she will change her opinion
of you."

Lady Mary was nothing loath, and sat down to enter on a
brisk one-sided flirtation with Dr. Cornelius. She chaffed
him gaily upon his country life, his infrequent appearances in
Edinburgh society, his grey hair—every imaginable subject.

Lucie sat by and received her first lesson in flirtation, but
she began to feel less fear of Lady Mary, and once or twice
joined in the conversation with a timid little remark. At last
she crossed from Dr. Cornelius' side amd seated herself beside
Lady Mary, with one of the graceful, sudden little movements
she had.

"I feel I am not in the least afraid of you now, madam,"
she said, "and I shall be much less alarmed among the other
ladies if you are with me."

"Oh, you must not ' madam ' me, madam," laughed Lady
Mary.   "I am not so much older than yourself—'tis only the
dress I wear," she added, sweeping a rather amused eye over
Lucie's sorry garments.

The breeze freshened, and they went rocking down the
Forth, past the low green shores of East Lothian, and out, out,
out, into the wide fresh sea. Dr. Cornelius bade Lucie stand
up, and pointed over to the land—miles away, and veiled in a
blue haze.

" There is home, Lucie," he said,—" home, and Henrietta.
Are you sending your heart over to her ? "

It was too much for poor Lucie, and she broke down once
more into pitiful sobs. She began to look very white and
miserable, too, with the ship's motion, so Lady Mary took her
briskly by the arm.

" Come, Miss Marjoribanks, let me have the pleasure of
showing you our luxurious quarters," she said, and led Lucie
down the companion ladder.

The days that followed were not pleasant ; for Lucie proved
a very bad sailor indeed, and had to remain in her berth all the
time. She would have fared very badly without good-
natured Lady Mary, who came and sat beside her whenever she
was able, and entertained her with all that was going on above.
Lucie was amused to see how much she thought of Dr. Cornelius ; it was quite a new idea to her that anyone should consider
him young.

" Why, Lady Mary, I think of Dr. Hallijohn as my father,
with the deepest respect," she said one day, and Lady Mary
laughed.

" Yes, I am sure you do ; to tell you the truth, if I were in
your place, I should be in love with him ; his grey hair and
fine complexion are irresistible. Confess now, my dear Miss
Marjoribanks, they are singularly attractive."

" *In love* with Dr. Hallijohn ? " said Lucie so wonderingly
that the other girl laughed.

" 'Pon my word, Miss Marjoribanks, I think that he has
taught you very insufficiently. I do not think you know
what the phrase ' in love ' means. I shall tell Dr. Hallijohn
that to-night."

" I—I think I understand what it means," said Lucie,
and her white cheeks were suddenly bathed all over with the
loveliest rose-colour.

" Oh, oh ! " cried Lady Mary ; " I thought we were too
much out of the world at Eastermuir to have ever seen a
young man to fall in love with, but I see we are just like other
young women, are we not ? " And she bent down and
kissed Lucie's pink, pink cheek. Lucie was weak and tired

and at these words turned away from the light, and felt an inclination to cry, that was become painfully common with her nowadays. Lady Mary averted the coming tears by a change of subject.

" You should keep your preceptor in better order, Miss Marjorybanks," she said. " The dear man drinks quite a shocking quantity of wine for one of his calling. Indeed, my father tells me 'tis the reason why Dr. Hallijohn has never been Moderator of Assembly—and he such a popular man too,"

" Does Dr. Hallijohn drink much wine ? " said Lucie—a far-away incident of her childhood had almost passed from her memory now, and nothing had happened since to revive the remembrance. The note of disapproval in Lady Mary's remarks gave her a feeling of uneasiness.

" Indeed he does ; why, last night I doubt if he quite knew what he was saying."

" Oh ! " said Lucie, mystified and shocked.

" Did you not know ?—how curious, when you are such friends ! Well, a great many do the same, and no one thinks twice of it. 'Tis just because everyone likes Dr. Hallijohn so much that they remark on it."

Lucie thought a great deal over this conversation, and decided to write all about it to Henrietta, which, perhaps, was not the happiest conclusion she could have arrived at.

In spite of her terror for strangers, Lucie made friends wonderfully fast, and before they had reached London, seemed to have known Lady Mary half a lifetime. She poured into her good-natured ear all her tremors and fears, her despairing sensations of terror when left alone with strangers, and her dread that her clothes were peculiar. This undoubted fact Lady Mary was too honest to deny. She even pressed Lucie to allow her maid to dress her up in one of her own dresses, so that she might arrive at the Pelham's in more everyday attire. But Lucie would not consent to this, having a good deal of pride, so they agreed that her first expedition in London must be to the shops. Lady Mary tried to fortify Lucie's courage and assure her that her nervous fears would soon disappear, but when at the end of the week they came into dock, Lucie was, if possible, more terrified than ever. The terror of the crowd "pressing on her" was like a nightmare, and she became quite faint with agitation. Dr. Cornelius had some ado to get her safely into the Pelhams' coach when it was at last discovered among the crowd of other vehicles, and she could only articulate a feeble little word of good-bye to Lady Mary, who came to the door of the coach to see the last of her curious fellow-passenger.

"I shall come and see you, Miss Marjorybanks," she said, nodding gaily to her. "Good-bye, and keep up your courage, my dear." And with a parting word of chaff with Dr. Cornelius, she disappeared in the crowd.

A minute later Lucie saw her drive off with her father in a large yellow coach, with powdered men standing on the rumble. She turned to smile into Lucie's coach as she passed and to wave a reassuring hand.

Lucie was thankful to be on land again, and once out of the crowd, quite enjoyed her drive up from the docks. When the traffic became very dense she felt a little scared, and drew nearer to Dr. Cornelius, hoping that the horses would not put their noses through the windows; still, she was not on foot among the crowd, so did not really mind it much.

They drew up at last before the Pelhams' door. Dr. Cornelius helped Lucie out. The ground seemed to rock under her as they walked upstairs, and then in alarmingly loud tones the butler announced her name. She shrank back, but Dr. Cornelius said, with quite extraordinary sternness—

"Go into the room first, Lucie, and speak to Mrs. Pelham."

So, dizzy with fright Lucie obeyed, stumbling blindly forward to where Mrs. Pelham stood holding out both hands in welcome, her kind face lighted up with smiles.

XIX

SO this is Henry Marjorybanks' child!" said Mrs. Pelham. She stooped down (for she was a very tall woman), parted Lucie's curls from her forehead as if to see her better, and kissed her on the cheek.

A girl rather older than Lucie came from the far end of the room and greeted her after the same fashion. She was tall like her mother, fair, and walked with a fine easy motion, like a ship under canvass. As she bore down upon her across the room, Lucie felt an inclination to turn and fly, but as she bent to kiss her, Maggie Pelham smiled—her smile revealed the most good-natured of dimples, and she spoke in a voice that was like a caress.

"I am so delighted that you are come at last, Lucie," she said. "I am sure we shall be happy together."

Lucie was reassured, but still far too frightened to speak. The strange, rich house and these unknown women struck her silent—she was oppressed by the feeling that she should speak and yet had nothing to say. Her eyes filled slowly with tears, and she could only press Maggie Pelham's hand in response.

Dr. Cornelius was speaking now with Mrs. Pelham, but Lucie's heart stood still when he came up to her, smiling and holding out his hand.

"I must leave you with your friends now, Lucie," he said, "having brought you here. I shall come to see you very soon, but I daresay you will have forgotten me altogether in the pleasures of town."

Lucie caught hold of his arm desperately.

"Oh, sir, do not go! Oh, dear sir—dearest Dr. Hallijohn, do not leave me all alone!" she cried, turning her face up to his in piteous entreaty, the tears running down her cheeks.

"My dear Lucie," said Dr. Cornelius, quite sternly for him, "you are forgetting yourself. You are with the kindest of friends, you are not alone. Come, say good-bye to me, my child, and dry your eyes."

But Lucie clung to him all the more.

"You must not go, sir! I am so much alarmed! I have no one that is known to me. Oh, Harrie, why did I ever leave you!"

Mrs. Pelham exchanged glances with Dr. Cornelius who shook his head sternly.

"I must go, Lucie. You have never disobeyed me before, and surely you will not do so now?—you must stop crying, and not distress Mrs. Pelham any more. I shall come to see you to-morrow."

He disengaged himself from her clinging little hands, and made his adieus to Mrs. Pelham, who. much perplexed by her strange guest, would have had him stay with all her heart. But a significant frown from Dr. Cornelius warned her not to press him to remain. As the door closed behind him, Lucie sprang forward.

"Oh, let me go with Dr. Hallijohn!" she cried. "I cannot stay here without him."

She caught the handle of the door, and in her terrified haste could not even turn it. Like some wild creature that has strayed into the haunts of men, and, blind with fear, cannot see how it entered she ran across the room and then back to the door again, hardly knowing what she did. Mrs. Pelham laid her hand on her shoulder, and spoke words whose prosaic kindness was soothing.

"My dear Lucie, you are very tired. What will you have to eat ? Do you drink wine ? or will you have a dish of tea ? or some milk ? "

Lucie sank down on one of the sofas, sobbing violently, ashamed of her own conduct now, but as yet too much upset to control herself. Maggie Pelham came and sat beside her, and stroked the limp little hand that Lucie yielded into hers.

"I think she would like some tea, mother," she said. "Do you not think it would revive her after her long drive from the docks ? See how cold her hands are."

"Oh," began Lucie through her sobs, "you must think me sadly unmannerly. I—I—cannot tell you what it is. I—I—know you are good and kind. It is something that rises in me when I see strangers that I cannot fight against. I felt the same when I arrived in Edinburgh, but there Dr. Hallijohn did not leave me, now — " She sobbed again and again.

"I quite understand all you are feeling," said Maggie in her caressing voice—she who had never known what the feeling of shyness meant. "But you will very soon forget that, dear, and remember that we really know you quite well—

it is only our *faces* that are strange to each other. Why, remember how many letters we have written to each other ! "

This seemed to cheer Lucie a little ; it joined the dreadful, unusual present on to the peaceful and familiar past—to Henrietta sitting in the window niche writing—writing to the girl who sat holding her by the hand at this moment. Lucie dried her eyes and smiled faintly.

" I suppose it is our solitary life hitherto that has given me this feeling of alarm when I come among strangers. I feel sure you will pardon me, madam," she said, addressing Mrs. Pelham, who had taken up her work again and sat beside them.

" My dear Lucie, you need never think of it again," she replied. " And tell me, how is your mother ? and your sister Henrietta, whom we seem to know so well from her delightful letters ? "

Lucie was wiled into conversation quite easily now. An hour later no one would have recognised her for the same girl as the half-wild creature who ran round the room crying for escape. She laughed and talked gaily, telling all the little incidents of her voyage from Leith, which seemed quite as great a feat to her as a voyage to the Antipodes is to other people. Mrs. Pelham amd Maggie were charmed, and concluded a little rashly that, the initial difficulties being over, all would go smoothly and well. Lucie made a very pleasing and piquant visitor—her outlook on life was, naturally, extremely fresh, her comments on everything entirely unconventional. Now she would have Maggie rise and let her examine her dress, and must handle with gentle, inquiring fingers the huge erection of cushions which graced Maggie's beautiful head. She laughed merrily over it, and over Maggie's vast hoop and high-heeled brocade shoes.

" And Lady Mary tells me that I must procure the same for myself immediately, madam," she said, addressing Mrs. Pelham.

" Well, I think, unlike your mother, that some concession to fashion is necessary, Lucie. Perhaps it will be as well to buy you some new gowns—we shall see."

While expressing herself so moderately, Mrs. Pelham decided conclusively that Lucie could not possibly go out in her present garments, and that no time must be lost in procuring other clothes for her use. To prevent exposing Lucie to remark in the shops, however, Mrs. Pelham decided to send for the milliners and dressmakers to take her orders at home, and, in the meantime, she must be kept indoors if possible.

So, among a feminine gossiping over ribbons and modes—what would be most becoming in colour and texture and make—ended Lucie's first day in London.

XX

IT was rather a delicate matter to suggest to Lucie next morning that she must stay in the house, owing to her very peculiar appearance : for she declared herself quite rested, and anxious to go out and see some of the wonders of London. Mrs. Pelham was specially anxious that no painful consciousness of her own oddity should strike Lucie—she was quite shy enough without this added torture. So, when she expressed her wish to go out, Mrs. Pelham could only reply evasively, " My dear, I feel sure you would be better to remain indoors to-day."

" Ah, madam," cried Lucie, " pray allow me to go out ! I am accustomed to a country life " (as if she needed to tell them this, poor child !), " and cannot bear to be a day in the house ; —the walls choke me. Indeed, indeed, madam, my health will not suffer from the fresh air."

" You must be weak still, Lucie, after such a prolonged sea-sickness. You are exceedingly pale to-day," objected Mrs. Pelham.

" Ah, but, madam, I shall remain pale if I stay indoors—it is but the air I need. Can you not allow me to go out ? "

Mrs. Pelham moved to the window—ostensibly to look at the sky, really to take a hurried survey of the Square. It looked very quiet certainly at this early hour in the forenoon, and the garden which the Square surrounds was quite deserted.

No doubt the air would do Lucie good, and there was no danger of her exciting remark at this hour and in the quiet Square. Mrs. Pelham, after making these calculations, gave her consent.

"You may go out, then, Lucie, but not beyond the gardens, or round the Square. Your strength cannot be equal to prolonged exercise," she said. "Maggie will go with you, as I am busy."

Now Maggie Pelham, albeit good-natured, was also a very fashionable young woman, and she did not relish the idea of walking out with such an oddly habited companion, even in the chaste solitudes of the Square; but she was as curiously obedient as were all young women in the good old days, so she had just to conquer her feelings and profess herself delighted to accompany Lucie.

They sallied out together—as queerly matched a couple as ever trod London streets. Maggie, tall, and seeming taller by reason of her cushioned head, her ample skirts, and her high-heeled shoes; Lucie, her slim girlish figure disguised by the hideously ill-fitting black silk sacque she wore over a long and perfectly limp skirt, her sweet face and golden hair engulfed in a mighty green silk bonnet, under which, by her mother's direction, it had always been her habit to assume a white nightcap whose frilled edge fitted all round her face like a frame.

With the first breath of the outer air Lucie's colour began to freshen. She looked round her on every side most eagerly.

"So this is London—London, that I have dreamed of so often. Do you know, Maggie, that last summer I dreamed every night that I was in London? I did not know then what a city was like, except from prints, but I knew in my dream that the place was London."

"How strange! what could make you do that?" said Maggie in rather a pre-occupied tone, and quickening her steps to reach the gate leading into the gardens. For she had become aware that three rude little message boys were following close behind them, pointing at Lucie's great silk bonnet, and making audible fun of her. Maggie was a fine lady, and they were most insignificant errand boys, but their ridicule was acutely painful to her all the same, so she directed Lucie's steps into the gardens, where the hooting urchins might not follow. Their Cockney speech was happily quite unintelligible to Lucie who walked on unheedingly.

But, rather to Maggie's surprise, Lucie did not seem to care about the gardens much. " The pavement felt so delightfully *new* under my feet, Maggie," she said, after they had paced about under the sere-leaved town trees for some time. " Do you not think we might return to the Square ? "

Maggie could not find it in her heart to object, but took a hurried glance round the Square as they returned to it. Carriages stood at several of the doors now, waiting to take their owners out for their morning airings ; footmen hung about at the carriage doors to exchange a little gossip with the coachmen ; and everywhere the ubiquitous message boy was delivering parcels.

Maggie thought to put as brave a face upon it as possible, so, drawing up her fine figure, spreading out her rustling skirts, and holding her cushioned head very high, she sailed along the pavement.

They passed the first carriage and the second. A low snigger of laughter had followed them each time.

" How rude Englishmen are ! " Lucie remarked, innocent that it was herself alone who roused their mirth, and continuing her walk with great composure.

But as they reached rather a deserted corner of the Square, a man coming towards them stared so insolently at Lucie that she shrank back, and he, seeing her alarm, as he passed suddenly poked his head almost under the queer green silk bonnet, saying " Pretty or ugly, my dear ? "

Lucie started back with a scream, catching hold of Maggie's arm, and the man laughed loudly as he passed on.

" Don't look at the insolent brute," said Maggie, sweeping along the pavement, looking finer than ever in her hot indignation. " We shall come in darling ; see, we have only one half of the Square to go round now."

Lucie had some ado to reach home, however, for her knees

shook under her, and she was faint and sick with fear. She did not speak till they got safely indoors. Then she faced round on Maggie suddenly, " Tell me," she said, " am I so peculiar in appearance that people will insult me in the streets ? Was *that* why Mrs. Pelham did not wish me to go out, and why you wished me to stay in the gardens ? "

" Your—your dress *is* peculiar, Lucie," faltered Maggie, shaken out of her usual suave composure by the vexation of their adventure. She was almost ready to burst into tears through sympathy with her poor, queer little friend.

Lucie sat down with a curiously stricken look. She did not seem to find tears any relief.

" Why did I ever leave home, Maggie ? " she said, in a bitter dry voice. " I see it all now quite distinctly. It was *I* the people on Leith pier laughed at; and Lady Mary knew it, and that was why she wished me to wear her clothes ; and it was *I* these footmen laughed at—and that man—oh ! " She gave a little short scream like a dagger stab at the remembrance of it.

Maggie sat down beside her and tried some consolations. " It is only your dress, after all, Lucie dear," she said ; " and that will be put right in a few days. You must not think of this again."

But Lucie shook her head.

" Ah no, Maggie. I see my dress is peculiar, but I see more than that. I see I am altogether queer—unlike you— unlike Lady Mary—I suppose unlike every other girl. It could not be otherwise. We have lived so much alone— been so strangely brought up. I did not know it before, but I see it all now."

" Ah, dearest Lucie, do not speak like this ! It is quite a mistake. When you are dressed like other people you will be looked at only because you are so pretty," said Maggie in her cooing voice. " Come, let us go upstairs and tell mother about this. Things always appear in quite another light after she has heard them ; " and she drew Lucie's arm through hers, to lead her to Mrs. Pelham.

"You must tell her, then," said Lucie; "I cannot speak about it."

So Maggie told the story of their discomfiture with great eloquence.

Mrs. Pelham made very light of it. "My dear girls, anyone is liable to be rudely spoken to in the streets; 'tis annoying at the moment, but you should never give it another thought; why, I have been rudely addressed many a time myself, Lucie, and you do not suppose that I grieved over it," she said. But in her heart of hearts Mrs. Pelham was more annoyed than she could say. She had hoped to get Lucie properly dressed before she had awakened to any overwhelming sense of her own peculiarities—now it was too late; and to her morbid fear of strangers Lucie would add a dread of ridicule.

"You look quite pale, Lucie," she said. "You must go and lie down. I told you you were not strong enough to walk out yet."

Lucie made no objection to this proposal, and allowed Maggie to take her to her own room, and tuck her up in a quilt, without a dissenting word. But when the door had closed behind Maggie, Lucie gave herself up to despair. Sitting up in bed with clasped hands, she rocked herself backwards and forwards. "Oh, Harrie, Harrie dear, can you not come to me? Even though you are so far away, don't you know how miserable I am? Oh, why did I ever come to London; why did I ever leave you? I am not like other people; everyone laughs at me, and I am so frightened and bewildered. I want only you, Harrie, in all the world."

It was like a prayer, and Harrie her divinity.

Then, worn out with it all, Lucie lay down again, staring up at the ceiling with a pained, tired-out expression. "Why did I come?" she was asking herself over and over. Deep down in her heart the answer lay, but even to herself Lucie did not speak it. Then a thought came and tormented her like a stinging fly. "I must go out, whatever it costs me, for I may meet him anywhere; if I stay in the house, as long as I do, I may never see him. I cannot speak to the Pelhams of him."

She had that common delusion of country folk—that in a city which counts its inhabitants by millions there was a likelihood of her meeting among the throng the one man she desired to see in all London! So Lucie made a resolution, as she lay there, to conquer her fears and go out as usual, for there was a chance—a possibility—perhaps a probability,—and her breath came shorter and her pale face flushed at the thought.

When she came downstairs an hour later, Mrs. Pelham was delighted to see Lucie so composed again.

"I am going to take your advice, madam," she said, "and remain in the house till my new dresses are ready; and then I shall go out, and think as little as I can of what occurred to-day."

In the afternoon Dr. Cornelius came, which cheered Lucie further. She had persuaded Mrs. Pelham and Maggie to go out as usual, and was sitting alone in the drawing-room when he arrived.

"Ah, dear sir!" she cried, running across the room to meet him, with her little white hands held out in welcome, after a pretty way she had.

Dr. Cornelius sat down beside her, holding her hands still in his, and smiling.

"So you are still alive, Lucie, in spite of my desertion of you yesterday? And how are you, and how do you agree with your new friends?"

"Ah, sir, was it only yesterday? Yes, I believe it was. I seem already to have been a century in London, and have so much to tell you I do not know where to begin. The Pelhams are most kind. Maggie I feel sure I shall love dearly, and Mrs. Pelham is exactly like the mothers in books. Why, sir, she interests herself in Maggie's *clothes*! and they speak together of all manner of things which Harrie and I would never mention to our mother—is not that strange? And oh, sir, my clothes are quite peculiar. I can hardly tell you the vexation I have undergone. I am not to go out until I get new dresses and bonnets, and my hair is to be dressed on cushions to the height of nearly two feet, and I am to wear it *powdered white*, and high-heeled shoes on which I am confident I shall fall—and then I may go out.   And oh, sir, when can I hear from Harrie ? "

Lucie wound up her breathless torrent of words at last, and Dr. Cornelius leaned back against the sofa cushions, laughing heartily.

" My dear child, you must repeat that all over again more slowly, if you wish me to take in its meaning.   Your dress seems to bulk most largely in your mind's eye.   Pray what vexation did you undergo ? "

Then Lucie, almost in tears, told the story of her disastrous little walk in the Square ; and Dr. Cornelius listened gravely, and then laughed like Mrs. Pelham, and assured her it was a matter of no importance.

" But it has hurt me—hurt me at my heart, sir," said Lucie laying her hand over that organ expressively.   " I cannot tell you how miserable I was over it.   I feel that I am so different from other people.   That is what pains me."

" My dear Lucie, all women are sadly imitative, 'tis one of their worst qualities.   Before you have been here for three weeks, I doubt there will be no originality left in you."

" I—I trust not," said Lucie most devoutly.   " And you, sir, what have you done ?   I have forgotten to inquire after your affairs in my own preoccupation."

" Let me see.   I have called on some of my friends, and I have purchased new clothes,—like yourself,— and wished myself back in Eastermuir."

" Why, sir, I thought you loved town above everything," cried Lucie, with wide eyes.

" I am become too old, apparently.   I would give the whole of London for the muddiest road in the parish, and "—

" And what, sir ? "

" Can you not guess ?   Have you no idea of what my heart most desires ? "

" N—no," said Lucie, after having given the subject some consideration.   " I cannot imagine, unless it is Henrietta— but then you do not feel as I do to her."

Dr. Cornelius watched her face narrowly as she spoke, and read no hidden understanding of his thoughts there.

" Lucie," he said suddenly, " did Harrie tell you nothing ? did she never repeat to you what I said to her shortly before we left home ? "

" No, sir, she never said anything to me—anything . . . anything.   I do not understand what you are speaking about."

" She never told you that I asked her to marry me ?'

" To marry *you*, sir ?   *Harrie* !   You must surely be in jest, Dr. Hallijohn ? "

" Jest ! No, indeed, Lucie, most sober earnest.   But how did Harrie tell you nothing about this ?   I thought you had no secrets from each other ;? "

" No," said Lucie slowly ; " she must have had some reason for not telling me.   Perhaps you will tell me what Harrie said when you asked her to marry you ? "

" She said Yes."

" And she is going to do it ? "

" Yes."

" When, sir ? "

" Ah, there is our point of separation !   She cannot leave you, she says."

" Yes, I thought that was it," said Lucie slowly.   " Dear, dearest Harrie, she would not even let me grieve over it."

" But would you grieve, Lucie ?   This is why I have spoken to you about it.   My dear, I've known you both too long and too well not to know what you are to each other ; but tell me, would you wish Henrietta not to marry me, in case it should separate you ? "

" Nothing could separate us, sir."

" Then will you persuade her to do it ?   Ah, Lucie, I am young no longer ; and even if twenty years of life were left me yet, that would be too short a time to have with Harrie."

" But, sir, I thought you said that Harrie promised to do it ? "

" Yes, in the far future—the future we know nothing of. We have nothing in this unsatisfactory world but the day we are living, and yet she puts it off indefinitely ; that is where I wish your help, Lucie—persuade her not to delay our marriage."

"What is she waiting for, sir ? How would it be easier for us to be parted then than it would be now ? " asked Lucie ; but a flood of colour rushed over her pale face as she spoke.

Dr. Cornelius patted her hand kindly.

"Yes, yes, Lucie, many things might happen, of course. Your mother might even allow you to come and live with us— if you could not live half a mile apart ; but these arrangements are rather premature. When you write to Harrie, pray tell her also your own ideas on the subject. You are not jealous of me, Lucie ? "

"Jealous ! " laughed Lucie. "No, sir ; you are you, and I am I, to Harrie—the one does not take the other's place. I confess I am surprised—most exceedingly surprised, but not jealous."

"'Pon my soul, I wish you had more reason for jealousy, Lucie ! My one fault with Harrie, is that she thinks more of you than of me. I am jealous, if you like. 'Tis hard on a man, you must admit."

"Oh, sir ! oh, Dr. Hallijohn ! it is too laughable. Pardon me, but I have never heard you speak like this, and look like this—and for Harrie ! "

And Lucie went off into delightful little girlish ecstasies of laughter, which did not altogether please Dr. Cornelius. He rose and paced up and down the room rather impatiently.

"I hardly see the joke myself, Lucie," he said quite crossly.

But Lucie laughed on ; and a moment later Mrs. Pelham and Maggie came in, delighted to hear such mirthful sounds. Lucie could not explain the cause of her laughter, but Dr. Cornelius summoned up sufficient self-control to laugh also, and tell Mrs. Pelham that Lucie was laughing at him.

"She has never seen me in town before, madam," he said, "and she assures me I look most peculiar to-day ; perhaps my new lace ruffles are accountable for the change in my appearance. She is a sadly unmannnerly child, is she not, and wanting in all proper respect for her guardian ? "

"Well, he seems to have a good effect upon her spirits,

sir.   We were a little *triste* this morning, were we not, Lucie ?
but we have forgotten all that now over Dr. Hallijohn's
ruffles," said Mrs. Pelham ; and, sitting down, she entered
with zest upon a description of the various purchases she had
made for Lucie that afternoon.

" We are filling your pupil's head with vanity, sir," she
said to Dr. Cornelius ; " and when you come to see us next,
you will not recognise her in all her fine feathers.   You must
come to the play with us on Thursday evening, and have the
pleasure of escorting Lucie to it for the first time.   I think
her new dresses will be ready by that time.   Pray keep
yourself disengaged for that evening if you can, sir ; it will
add both to Lucie's and to our pleasure to have your company
there."

So Dr. Cornelius promised to come on Thursday and
escort Lucie to the play for the first time.   He smiled most
graciously in accepting the invitation ; but as he walked down
the Square a few minutes later :   " The play ! " he said to
himself ; " the play ! what can be duller than the play—when
you have the wrong woman sitting by you ? "

XXI

ON Thursday morning Maggie Pelham denied herself
to all visitors, and entered upon the arduous work of
dressing Lucie for the first time in fashionable garments.

Before anything else could be begun, Lucie's hair had to be
elaborately done after the prevailing mode.   This was a work
of both time and trouble, and involved the presence of a hair-
dresser for some two hours, who, following the recipe for
this style of erection, added " *false locks to supply deficiency of
native hair, pomatum in profusion, greasy wool to bolster up the
adopted locks, and grey powder to conceal dust,*" till a structure some
two feet in height was built up on poor Lucie's unaccustomed
head.

" Why, the weight of it is terrible, Maggie ! " she cried, as
she surveyed her image in the mirror, slowly turning her head
from side to side as she spoke.

" Oh, you will soon get accustomed to it. Why, that is a most moderate head-dress ! I would have had it some inches higher had I had my way, but mother considered that you should not be tried with too great weight at first, so I told the man to keep it low."

" *Low* ! " murmured Lucie, and Maggie laughed.

" Wait till you look round at the play to-night, and see if you believe me then ! Almeria Carpenter, I can assure you, would not be seen out of doors with her hair under three feet high—and plumes above that ! "

" 'Tis sadly uncomfortable," said Lucie ruefully ; but the glass gave back a distinctly pleasing reflection as she gazed into its depths, so she decided to suffer pain with pride's proverbial courage.

The next process was the donning of her hoop, and Maggie was soon speechless with laughter at Lucie's attempts to manage her ungainly new adjunct.

" My dear, *this* is how you sit down," she cried, recovering from her amusement to illustrate to Lucie that careful movement which was necessary in crinoline times when one sat down. " With the *greatest* circumspection, Lucie—to sit down hurriedly is fatal—slightly to one side, and keeping down the hoops with one hand as you subside into your chair —otherwise it jumps up round you most ungracefully. Cultivare slow movements, my dear I assure you they are necessary."

But the art of walking and sitting down in a hoop is no easy matter, and Lucie felt curiously ill at ease as she moved about. The hoop seemed to steer her, not she the hoop, and to sit down was a terror, when this mass of flounces had a way of springing up into her very face. Her tight and high-heeled shoes were an added discomfort ; but she certainly surveyed her pretty foot with great pleasure in spite of the trying pressure it was undergoing.

As the day wore on, Lucie became a little more sure of herself in the new clothes, and by four o'clock, when Dr. Cornelius arrived for dinner, she crossed the room to greet him with wonderful assurance.

" So my little bird has donned her fine feathers ? " he said.
" And do they feel very uncomfortable ? "

" I must confess, sir, to some uneasiness in my head," said
poor Lucie.   " The weight of all that I now carry on it is
considerable ; but I think in time I shall learn the management
of my skirts ; and already I am in love with my shoes ; " she
lifted her flounces elegantly to display the tips of her little
slippers as she spoke.

" I told you so—I told you so," laughed Dr. Cornelius ;
" women are all alike."

With what a thumping heart under her tight, long-waisted
bodice, did Lucie step into the coach that was to convey them
to Drury Lane that evening !

" You must not be frightened by the crowd at the theatre
door, Lucie," said Mrs. Pelham.   " Dr. Hallijohn, pray give
your arm to Lucie as we enter.   I am too old a play-goer to
need your protection."

Lucie sat looking out from the coach window into the blue
fog, but when they reached the more crowded thoroughfares,
the hurrying crowds and the lights seemed to press upon her
brain—she shrank back into the corner and covered her eyes
with her hands.

" It is fine, Lucie, the rush of life in the streets—you should
not shrink from it in that way," said Dr. Cornelius.   "When I
was young,—as once I was—it used to go to my head like
wine."

" It is terrible, sir !   Ah, must we really get out among this
crowd ?   Pray, madam, send me home in the coach and go to
the play without me ! " she begged of Mrs. Pelham as they
drew up before the theatre door.

" Come, Lucie," said Dr, Cornelius, standing at the step
and holding out his arms to lift her down.

She stood irresolute, half drawing back into the shadow
of the coach from the glare of the lights, a target for many
eyes, in her dainty dress, her powder, and her ribbons.

" If you are desirous of notice, Lucie, you are doing your
best to attract it," said Dr. Cornelius impatiently ; and

another reassuring word from Mrs. Pelham at last induced
Lucie to step out upon the pavement.

Dr. Cornelius drew her arm through his, and Mrs. Pelham
and Maggie following, they went up the theatre steps.   It was
a moment of absolute agony to Lucie—the crowd might as
well have been wild beasts as men, so great was her terror of
them.   When they entered the vestibule, her fear subsided a
little, and she turned round to look for Maggie.   Now
Maggie had hitherto appeared to Lucie only in the light of
home, and she hardly recognised this haughty-paced young
lady who was coming up the steps with such a fine air by
Mrs. Pelham's side.   All the men standing about the vestibule
were putting up their glasses to stare at her, and Lucie heard
one of them say, "There goes pretty Peggy," as Maggie
swept up the stair.

"Do you not mind, Maggie?" sld Lucie, as she joined
her.

"What, dear?" queried Maggie, with a would-be innocent
smile, and Dr. Cornelius laughed.

The house was full, the curtain just about to rise when
they came into the box.   Mrs. Pelham gave Lucie a seat at
one side, facing the stage, and Maggie and Dr. Cornelius sat
behind.

Lucie gave one peep over the edge of the box, down upon
the great throng below, another timid glance round the house
with its crowded tiers of seats, and then sank back behind the
curtain, covering her face with her hands.

"Oh, take me home, madam—pray, pray take me home!"
she cried.   "It is awful!   'Tis just like the judgment day we
used to read of in that book, the Bible, long ago—all these
crowds and crowds of waiting people!"

Mrs. Pelham laid her kind hand on Lucie's arm.

"There is nothing to alarm you, Lucie—see, we are shut
in by ourselves here, none of the crowd can reach us.   Try,
my dear, to look round you again."

Lucie ventured upon another look.

"Oh, it makes me giddy, madam! my head goes round
and round," she said helplessly.

" You will feel better when the lights are put down," said Mrs. Pelham reassuringly.   " Sit still for a little, my dear, and then try to look round you again ; by degrees you will be able to do it."

Maggie in the meantime, was taking a comprehensive survey of the house, and pointing out several notable people to Dr. Cornelius.

" There are few persons of distinction in town just now," she said, " but such as there are, are here to-night.   See, there is George Selwyn "—

" Yes, and old Queensberry too—ten years have not improved his appearance, truly."

" Most odious old man ! pray do not look at him, sir—he will kiss his hand across the house at me in another moment," said Maggie, turning her face resolutely in the other direction. " Ah, there is Almeria Carpenter ! Lucie, Lucie, I must insist upon you looking down at the stalls !—there is Almeria Carpenter, the most fashionable women in London.   See— she wears yards of tiffany on her head to-night ! "

But Lucie could not yet bring herself to look down again at that terible sea of men and women.   She leaned back behind the curtain, struggling for self-control, and listened to Maggie's lively comments on the crowd.

" See, sir, there is the Duchess of Devonshire—is she not most lovely ?—yes, to the right, with ostrich plumes in her hair ; and that is Sir Horace Walpole in the stalls—he looks ill, poor man, doubtless another attack of the gout—he suffers sadly from it, they say.   No, Royalty does not favour us to-night.   When is the curtain going up, I wonder ?   Tell me, sir, how long is it since you were at the play ? "

" Some ten years it must be, Miss Pelham.   At my time of life we think less of the vanities of this world.   I have devoted myself so exclusively to the duties of my calling of late years that I have been unable to come to town."

" Now, sir, you are jesting—but I declare I never know when you speak in earnest and when you jest," said Maggie. " For myself, I should not have imagined you so devoted to your calling."

" Maggie, Maggie, for shame ! " said Mrs. Pelham reprovingly. " The young ladies of the present day, sir, lose all
sense of propriety in conversation," she added, turning to
Dr. Cornelius, with an indulgent smile at her pretty daughter
even as she spoke.

Lucie had by this time had determined to venture on
another look at the crowd. She opened her eyes warily—
not daring to look down at first, but across at the mysterious
curtain as it flapped in the draught from behind the stage.
Then she gradually let her eyes fall to the orchestra, and thence
to the stalls and all the bewildering lights and colours there.

What a show it was ! So this was life ? Had all this
pomp and brilliancy really been going on always ?—it seemed
to her a sudden creation ; but when she considered the matter
she knew that of course it had always existed through the
dead years of her former life, and away back and back before
she had even lived. The great and noisy and moving world
had been rushing on while she and Henrietta had lived unaware
of it, buried as deep as if they were in their graves, at poor
sleepy old Balgowrie !

Maggie leaned forward and tapped her arm with her fan.
" How do you like it, Lucie ? " she asked, smiling.

" Oh, I think—I think that I have never been alive before ! "
said Lucie. Now that her first nervous fears were past, she
leaned her arms on the edge of the box and gazed down in a
fascinated way at the crowd below her. It was play enough.

A pitying contempt for her own lifeless life came over her.
" These people have all *lived*—they have been alive all their
lives—while I have been as good as dead ! " she thought.
" Why, each of these hundreds of men and women have a story
of their own—I had rather sit and look at them than at all the
acting in the world."

But the lights at that very moment went down, and the
great human spectacle was hidden from her eyes. The
curtain creaked up on its pulleys, sending a puff of air to fan her
ribbons, and with thunders of applause, David Garrick
stepped out upon the stage. Lucie started at the noise, and
Maggie leaned forward and whispered—

" Garrick—and there comes Mrs. Pope—ah, is she not charming ? "

And then little ripples of laughter broke out here and there from the darkness ; and then shouts of mirth.   Dr. Cornelius and Maggie were laughing till they wept, and Mrs. Pelham was smiling quietly behind her fan ; even Lucie at last forgot all her fears and agitations, and joined in the merriment. At the end of the first act her face was all smiles.   She turned with one of her quick, bird-like movements, laying her hand on Dr. Cornelius' sleeve.

" Ah, sir, I have but one regret, and you have it too, I feel sure—why, why is Harrie not here ? "

" And this is Thursday night," said he with an expressive little movement of the shoulders.   " I have been thinking of her this hour back."

" Thursday ? so it is—I lose count of time here.   How disagreeable of me to forget !   Yes, Maggie, poor Harrie will just be curtseying to the chairs at this moment, while we enjoy ourselves so much ! "

" Perhaps your mother will not insist upon these exercises when Henrietta is alone ? " suggested Mrs. Pelham.

" Ah, madam, you do not know my mother ! " cried Lucie, and Dr. Cornelius agreed that it would be very unlike Mrs. Marjorybanks' stringent habits to put off the reception on account of Lucie's absence.

" Never mind, Lucie, she will make up for it in days to come—what a bout of play-going she will have then ! " he said, with a smile that Lucie understood.

" But I am wasting my time in conversation," cried Lucie suddenly, turning with all the delicious animation that was hers when she lost her timidity, towards the front of the box. " Why, I have all this wonderful crowd to observe !   Now that I have got over the first feeling of alarm, it inspires me with nothing but interest.   Pray, Maggie, come beside me and point out those you know by sight ! "   As she spoke, Lucie was gazing anxiously round the house.   " Oh, it is most bewildering ! " she said in a hopeless tone.   " I do not think it would be possible to distinguish any one person among such a multitude.   Tell me, Maggie, can you do so ? "

" Why, yes, of course, and so would you, Lucie, with some practice."

" People look so strangely alike when you see them all together," said Lucie.   But to herself she added " No one is like Dan—I should see him among a thousand if he were there.   Ah, he cannot be here to-night ! "

And Dan Charteris, taking a masterly survey of the boxes and their occupants, remarked to the man beside him—

" Who's that with Peggy Pelham ?   I seem to know the face . . . By——, it's Lucie Marjorybanks ! " adding to himself, " Lucky I saw her !   I meant to pay my respects to Mistress Peggy to-morrow—now I shall be ' out of town.' "

XXII

LUCIE looked sadly white and weary when she came downstairs next morning.

" I fear that hot air and the late hours we kept last night do not agree with your country roses," said Mrs. Pelham, as she kissed the white cheek.   " I must take you for an airing this morning."

" Ah, madam, I am longing to be out ! " cried Lucie. " Only the thought of those crowded and terrible streets is so overpowering to me—I do not know how I shall summon courage to walk out in them."

" We shall drive, Lucie, through the crowded streets, and then you shall have a short walk in the Park with me, and drive back.   You will surely not feel any alarm in my company.   I am more of a protection than Maggie, am I not ? "

" I fear, madam, that I am stupid enough to feel alarm in any company," said Lucie, knowing too well the tremors that would overcome her.

But the day was bright, and as they drove along the brilliant morning streets, Lucie felt reassured.   Hyde Park Corner gave her pause indeed, and she held her breath for a moment at

sight of the crowd.   Then Mrs. Pelham bade her descend from
the coach, and she tremblingly obeyed; for all her sweetness
Mrs. Pelham had an air of great authority, and Lucie did not
dare to hesitate over her commands.   So they left the coach
and paced up and down the sweet greenness of the Park
together.

"My dear child," said Mrs. Pelham reprovingly, "you must
try to control your nervous fear of strangers.   You recoil
from each one you meet as though he were a murderer."

"I can only ask you to have patience with me, madam,"
said poor Lucie rather piteously; for in her heart of hearts she
had a hopeless fear that it was impossible for her to overcome
these feelings of nervous terror.   As they returned towards
Hyde Park Corner, she suddenly caught hold of Mrs. Pelham's
arm and pointed forward.

"Madam, madam, there is a crowd!—a real crowd!
Oh, what shall we do?   It is impossible to get through it to
the coach."

Mrs. Pelham walked calmly forward.

"'Tis nothing alarming, Lucie—a regiment crossing the
street merely—there is no great crowd, but the traffic is stopped
for a few minutes till they pass by."

Lucie drew in her breath and bit her lips.

I have never seen a regiment," she said softly.

"Then shall we go on and see it, my dear?" asked Mrs.
Pelham, a little surprised that Lucie should think of approaching the crowd.

"Y—e—s," said Lucy.   She had become very pale, and
gripped Mrs. Pelham's arm for protection.

On either side of the street the people stood in lanes, while
a long string of horsemen filed past with jingling bridles and
helmets that flashed in the morning sun.   The ground shook
with the tramp of the horses; the air vibrated with the quick
pulsing of the drums; and at that gallant sight Lucie forgot
her fears.

"Ah, how beautiful, madam!" she cried, with the quick
admiration of her sympathetic nature.   "And how that beating music goes to the heart!"

Then, looking up the advancing lines of riders, she suddenly held her breath, for Dan Charteris was among them.

On he came—looking rather intently before him, and at someone ahead; but just as he passed by where Lucie stood, he turned in his saddle to speak to the man who rode beside him, and she actually caught the echo of his words . . " At four o'clock, then " . . . as he rode past. But he never noticed Lucie's little figure among the crowd. He wore a laced coat.

" Why, that was Captain Charteris, Lucie ! " said Mrs. Pelham. " Did you recognise your former guest in all his military trappings ? "

Lucie could not reply for a moment. Then she spoke quietly—

" Yes, madam. I had seen his laced coat before."

" I must ask him to dine with us soon," said Mrs. Pelham. " Come, my dear, we can cross to the coach now—the last horseman has ridden by."

Lucie obeyed, scarcely knowing what she did, for she was straining her eyes to follow Dan's retreating figure for one more moment. As it vanished round the corner, she listened to catch the last strain of the music he rode to.

At first the gay marching tune floated high over the roll of traffic, then one by one its notes became indistinguishable, swallowed up in the city's roar, and only a distant throbbing of the drums, like the far-away beating of some giant heart, reached her ear.

" Lucie, Lucie ! are you dreaming, my dear ? " said Mrs. Pelham, laying her hand on Lucie's knee to attract her wandering attention.

She had climbed into the coach and seated herself in it quite mechanically, and though Mrs. Pelham had spoken twice, she had received no answer.

" I—I was thinking about home," stammered Lucie, with some, if not absolute, truthfulness.

The noisy streets had disappeared—she seemed to stand beside the low wall of the Balgowrie orchard on a wonderful spring night,—a night of strange enchantment,—and to feel on her lips again the kisses of his mouth—his who had ridden past her a moment before unknowingly.

"Ah, Lucie, you think too much of home ; we must make you forget it," said Mrs. Pelham, with an indulgent smile ; and Lucie, hardly following the drift of her words, cried out hastily—

"Forget it?—ah no, madam—never on this side the grave!"

"There is no doubt the poor child has been strangely brought up," thought Mrs. Pelham, quite mystified by the intensity of the reply.

"There is Apsley House, Lucie. 'Tis an important new building, erected only some six years ago by Lord Chancellor Apsley," she said, to divert the girl's attention from this strange brooding upon her home. "And there is the ' Pillars of Hercules '—a great dining place of the military men about town."

Lucie did not bestow much heed on Apsley House, but the " Pillars of Hercules " roused no little interest in her.

When they reached home, Maggie was entertaining company. Lucie had entered the room before she knew that strangers were in it, and the sight of their unknown faces made rhe stand still in dismay. There were several young women and two men, and together they contrived to make no little noise. Maggie glanced up at Lucie rather nervously, to see how she would meet all these strange eyes that were levelled at her, but she spoke in her usual gentle, cooing voice—

"Ah, Lucie, you are come in ! Have you had an agreeable airing ? Come and let me present you to my friend Lady Almeria Carpenter, and to Mr. Rigby and Mr. Savage."

Lucie came forward into the group with a heightened colour. Clasping her dear little hands together in nervous agitation, and glancing from one to the other of the party, she curtseyed low and tried to smile. But the colour suddenly deserted her cheeks, and crying out—

"Oh, Maggie, I cannot, I cannot ! " she turned and ran towards the door. Maggie rose quickly to follow her, then stopped and returned to visitors.

" My friend Miss Marjorybanks is not strong," she explained " I think she sometimes finds it difficult to meet strangers."

The fashionable Almeria smiled rather contemptuously, and one of the men made a stupid little joke, and they all laughed, and forgot Lucie—Lucie, who sat wringing her hands and weeping in her own room.

"I am a fool! I am unlike everyone here. I must go home to Harrie. Oh, I am so frightened! I cannot bear this town life, these strange people, and all the noise. I must—I must go home—and yet I cannot. Not half an hour ago I saw him —if I stay, I shall see him really—see him and speak with him again, and ask him why he has never written all these dreadful months; and he will explain, and I shall be happy again. I have almost forgotten what it is like to be happy now; and oh, how happy I was with him! but it seems so long ago."

Lucie was really hardly conscious how great was the strain upon her nerves of the sudden change from Balgowrie to London. The conventional retirement of her life there had, in fact, perfectly unfitted her for life in a town, and she was tried far more than she knew by it.

She sat, a bewildered, pathetic little figure in her unaccustomed trappings; a longing possessed her for " hame, hame," silent peaceful Balgowrie, far from noisy streets and strange faces, with only Harrie—dearest and most familiar.

Yet here she must stay—tied by her heart-strings to the great roaring city—there was no help for it. She dried her tears and tried to smile; then summoned up courage to go downstairs again.

The visitors had gone, and Maggie met her without any reference to what had passed. Only a little later she said gently—

"We are having some friends to dinner next week, Lucie; I hope you will not mind, dear."

"No, no," said Lucie hastily; and then she asked rather shyly who the guests were to be.

"Only Almeria and Mr. Rigby and Mr. Savage, and mother intends to invite Dr. Hallijohn and Captain Charteris, who are both friends of yours."

"I shall try not to be so stupid again, Maggie." said Lucie, with the tears in her voice, if not in her eyes. " You must have blushed for me this morning, I am sure, before all your friends."

Maggie, however, made light of the whole matter, and assured Lucie that her friends had thought nothing of it.

" We have asked them for Monday afternoon, and this is Friday," said Maggie. " You will have time to get quite accustomed to strange faces before Monday, Lucie. We are going to take you out every day—on Saturday you must walk in the Mall, and on Sunday you must go to church. Why, by Monday you will think nothing of two or three strangers ! "

" Do you really think so ? " asked Lucie ; and Maggie assured her that time would certainly prove a cure for all her fears.

XXIII

IT had taken little more than two weeks for all the events narrated above to befall Lucie. Of course, to her these weeks seemed like centuries, as is always the case when a great deal of incident is suddenly crammed into a hitherto eventless life ; but for Henrietta, time had been passing slowly enough. For, oh, the house was empty, empty !— and the garden deserted, and the village forsaken.

It was a gloomy lot for any young person to be thrown entirely upon Mrs. Marjorybanks for companionship. Every year the good lady's peculiarities increased : she preferred to be silent now when she and Henrietta walked out together, and would only walk upon what in the country phrase are termed the " back roads "—deep and muddy lanes leading inland, and used for little but the carting of field produce. Wrapped in her long black cloak, she would march along in the cart ruts with the stride of a grenadier, only occasionally looking over her shoulder to fling a word at Henrietta, trudging behind her through the puddles. The roads round Balgowrie were so unfrequented that they would sometimes walk for miles without meeting another human being—a strange-looking couple enough in their out-of-the-world garments.

It was well for Henrietta that she was gifted by nature with a singularly vivid imagination, so that on these lonely trudges she kept the blithest company, and sometimes would break into a little trill of laughter over her own imaginings ; then she would reprove herself for laughing aloud—remembering that Dr. Hallijohn had told her it was " a pity to be eccentric in one's habits."

At home there was only old Hester and Silence to talk to, but Henrietta found great relief in their society from the oppressive silence which her mother maintained sometimes for hours together.

She would call Hester upstairs at night to brush her hair, and together they would go over in imagination all Lucie's triumphs in London town.

The first week of her absence they had of course to follow Lucie in thought upon her journey.   And this was no light task ; for Henrietta had never left Eastermuir for ten years, and had come from another country village almost as remote; while Hester's travels had never extended beyond the Border. Yet from Henrietta's misty recollections of her one journey in a stage-coach, and Hester's confused version of a migration, conducted while in the service of another family, between Jedburgh and Edinburgh in a travelling carriage, they constructed some sort of theories upon Lucie's travels.   The journey by sea was baffling to both of them ; but Henrietta aided imagination by extracts from books of travel, and formed very alarming visions of billows running mountains high, while the ship tossed like a cockle-shell in the trough of the waves.   Hester, however, would not allow her young mistress to dwell on this dark picture, so when they knew that the boat must have arrived in London, they conjured up Lucie in more cheerful scenes—Lucie at the play, Lucie in the Park, Lucie in Westminster, Lucie at the Tower—the classic haunts so familiar to them by name, so unknown in experience.

" I am fancying Miss Lucie at the play to-night, Hester,"

Henrietta would say.   " How enchanted she will be ! how she
will be wishing that I were with her ! "

" I wish the same, Miss Harrie, indeed.   And what think
you will Miss Lucie wear to the play ? "

" Her bottle-green sacque surely, Hester ; or do you think
she will appear in the blue taffeta.? "

This was a point they could not agree upon, for Henrietta
held out for the green sacque, while Hester considered the
taffeta better suited to the occasion.   Twenty years ago, the
gay lady who travelled from Jedburgh to Edinburgh had been
in the habit of going to the play, and of wearing taffeta gowns
for it ; and, starting from the assumption that fashion is an
unchanging quantity, Hester maintained that taffeta was worn
by every gentle-woman at the play.   So they had just to agree
to differ on this point, and would wander off it into other
excursions of the fancy.

One day when Henrietta was feeling particularly ˙lonely,
she went down to the Manse to see Mrs. Allan.   The good
woman was getting old and frail now, but she would insist
upon taking her visitor all over the house, to see in what good
order it was kept in Dr. Hallijohn's absence.   Henrietta
followed her, smiling, through all these pleasant rooms that
were half home to her already, and would one day be home
indeed.   " It will be like the ' home ' in books," she thought,
—" a name to charm with."

On her return from this visit, Henrietta sat down to write to
Dr. Cornelius.   It was the first letter she had written to him
since his departure for town, and she felt that it was rather a
difficult one to write.

" Would Lucie see it ? " she thought ; " and is it going to
be what is called a love-letter ? "

The letter, when finished, certainly did not answer to the
generally received idea of a love-letter.

" MY DEAR SIR,"—it ran,—" I feel sure that Lucie has
shown you the letter which I wrote to her two days after she
left me, and which must by this time have reached her dear
hands.   But I feel equally sure that you will expect to receive
a letter to yourself, therefore I am sending you this, though,

as you are well aware, there is little of interest for me to relate
to you.

"I cannot express to you how long the days are now that
I am alone. I even find it a difficult matter to pursue my
studies steadily. I miss Lucie's presence in the room beside
me, and as I sit down to read, will often find my thoughts
away in London with her—and you.

"My mother has elected lately to walk in the East Loan,
and as the weather has beeen rainy and the road is much cut
up with the carts (they are carting the turnips from the high
fields at present), we walk daily over the ankles in mire. I try
to laugh at this discomfort, but find it hard work making
jokes alone.

"I went yesterday through a great slough of despond as I
trudged through the mire, and as I have little else to tell you
dear sir, I will tell you what I felt. I felt so cruelly hedged in
—do you know that I have never seen a town ? I have
never even entered a church door (but I think that I have
sometimes worshipped God). I have heard no music but
what Lucie can bring out of the spinnet and what the birds
make in the branches in the spring.

"Yet just beyond this life of mine is a great and wonderful
world where men and women *live* ; there is beauty that I cannot imagine—not if I strain my poor powers to cracking—
for does not Locke hold that the highest imagination is a
remembrance of something experienced ? I have experienced
so little that my imagination itself is stunted. I have been
starved in experience—the one thing in life worth living for.
What is study, and what is knowledge, and what is truth
itself (if we could find it ?). I wish to live, live, live—

"Oh, sir ! I passed some miserable hours. And, indeed,
discontent is a hateful sin. Then, all of a sudden, I remembered the words you said to me : ' *You shall see men and things
new and strange, and it will be like the entering a new life.*' And like
a cloud my discontent vanished, and I knew that you spoke
truly, and that some day I shall see all that I am fretting for
now. I looked down at such muddy boots, and thought
that instead of toiling along these back roads, I would one day

walk with you in all the places which are only names to me now—London—Paris, perhaps,—it might even be Rome— ' *the entering a new life* ' indeed !

" So that is enough of morbid thoughts.

" I went to-day to call upon Mrs. Allan. She would have me see over the house, that I might report to you in what good order she keeps it in your absence—as if you ever doubted that !

" I went into the study, which looked strange indeed all ' swept and garnished.' The dear books gave me welcome, it is true, but for the rest, it was bleak enough. Then she would have me go upstairs, that I might say that you required a new stair carpet. I daresay, sir, that it would give Mrs. Allan infinite pleasure did you purchase one—for myself, I would never have noticed that this one was worn out.

" She also desires fresh curtains in your room. I recommended a large-flowered chintz, as she would have me give an opinion, and I trust you will not find fault with my choice.

" And now, sir, it is I who must find fault most seriously with you—for I saw upon your writing table that new edition of the works of Spinoza which you told me you were getting. I brought it home with me to study, and on the title-page I read in your handwriting (which is terribly clear), ' *Henrietta and Cornelius Hallijohn*, Oct. 1775.' Now, Cornelius, I am not Henrietta Hallijohn yet, and it was extremely injudicious in you to write my name thus on your books and leave them for Mrs. Allan to examine. I do not imagine that the works of Spinoza would attract her beyond the title-page, but then that is the one page that it would be undesirable for her to peruse, and I do not doubt that she has already done so. My dear sir, when will you learn to be more judicious, and care a little for the opinion of the outside world ? Since ever I knew you,—and that is ten years now,—you have not cared a snap of your fingers for what is said of you—surely this is a great mistake ? Can anyone afford to do this ? I shall keep Spinoza till your return, and then you can erase my name from the title-page—or I can keep it till I have a right to it ! . . .

" I had meant to end here, but a letter from Lucie has just

reached me, written the day after her arrival in London—in the evening. She tells me of your visit to her, and of all that passed between you. I am glad—so glad—in one way, that there is now no longer any secret in my mind from Lucie ; but I trust she was not hurt about it. You made her understand everything ? You did not let her have the impression that I would ever leave her, even to come to you ? Pray, dear Cornelius, do not be annoyed with me for saying this. I do not know how it will be, but somehow I feel that it will all become plain, and that we shall not be parted : I mean Lucie and I.

"Expression sometimes seems to fail me ; but you will understand what I would say, as you always do.—And I am ever yours,

"HENRIETTA MARJORYBANKS.

"*P.S.*—I suppose you will show this to Lucie. I cannot write often enough to please her, so pray do so.

"H. M."

This document, which reached Dr. Cornelius' hands on the morning of the day on which he was to dine with the Pelhams, did not seem to give him much satisfaction.

"Show it to Lucie ! 'Pon my soul ! the first attempt at a love-letter that she sends me. Very likely. ' Pray do so,' forsooth ! " He folded up the letter and put it into the breast pocket of his coat with a half tender, half impatient movement. " And she is not in love with me as she should be," he continued. " She thinks of her marriage as a deliverance from the house of bondage merely—it isn't a personal matter with her yet. She must taste all the things she has been so long denied first, then perhaps she will be at leisure to fall in love with me. I have taught her all she knows —I must teach her how to fall in love too ! Well, if she learns it as well as her teacher . . . As I said to Lucie, I'd give all London just now for the ' back roads ' behind Balgowrie— if Harrie was there with me. And time was when I banished the thought of Eastermuir from me in town, dreading the very remembrance of its dulness ! " So he mused on as he took his way towards the Square—in the roaring Strand he heard Henrietta's voice, in the crowd of Piccadilly she was walking beside him like a shadow.   What a passion it was with him ! In his preoccupation he knocked up against people as he walked.

" Tush !   You are not fit to live among civilised men, with your thoughts four hundred miles away ! " he said to himself impatiently, as he apologised hurriedly for the second of these accidents.

XXIV

THE other guests had arrived at Mrs. Pelham's, and were getting through the *mauvais quart-d'heure* as best they might when Dr. Cornelius came into the room.   Mrs. Pelham, Maggie, Lucie, Lady Almeria Carpenter, Mr. Rigby, and Mr. Savage made up the party so far, and Dr. Cornelius, enumerating them mentally, perceived that another gentleman must still be coming.

" I feared I was late, madam " he said " but I fancy someone else is later still—am I right ? "

" I expected Captain Charteris," said Mrs. Pelham, with a shade of annoyance in her voice.   " But, strangely enough, he has never sent a reply to my invitation, so we shall not wait for him.   If he arrives, well and good ; if not, we can make shift without his company."

Dr. Cornelius looked curiously at Lucie, who stood by the fireplace talking—or, to be more exact, attempting to talk—with Mr. Rigby.   " If Charteris was the first, this is assuredly only the second man she has spoken to in her short life," thought Dr. Cornelius, wondering sympathetically how she was getting on with the unknown quantity.   He was a tall, vacant-looking man, wearing what in those days was termed a " quizzing-glass " in one eye, and as he spoke to Lucie, he stared her completely out of countenance.

" Have you been to the play since coming to town, Miss Marjorybanks ? " he was asking ; for Mr. Rigby was what might be called a persistent type—just as his representative of

1895 is ever to be heard with the query, "Been to the theatres?"
on his lips, so this gallant of 1775 was, in like manner,
"putting" Lucie " to the question ! "

" No—yes, yes—I mean no," stammered Lucie wringing
her little white fingers painfully.

" Which is it ? " he said, and laughed, and stared even
harder at poor Lucie.

She looked nervously round the room, and asked, in a
confused manner, " which is what ? " which certainly was
absolute nonsense.

Dr. Cornelius crossed the room to her assistance.

" Miss Marjorybanks was at the play with me on Thursday,"
he said. " Garrick. We all laughed until we cried. Next
time we shall go to see tragedy, and then we shall cry until
we laugh. I never find anything so amusing as a tragedy ! "

Rigby gazed at Dr. Cornelius through the quizzing-glass, as
if to ask who he might be ; then his eye fell before the steady,
amused expression of the older man. Lucie breathed a little
more freely, but Dr. Cornelius noticed that she was trembling
and shivering as if with an ague. His heart bled for her
pitiable nervousness.

" I am sorry that I am not to have the honour of taking you
down to dinner, Lucie," he said ; " for I have messages for
you from Henrietta."

He said this partly to prepare her for the ordeal of Rigby's
escort. Lucie cast an imploring look at him—a look of
absolute dsepair. But he could only smile to her as he
turned to offer his arm to Mrs. Pelham.

Lucie laid her trembling little fingers on Rigby's arm. Her
head went round, her whole body shook with fear. What
could she say to this man ? She must speak to him for the
next hour and half, and she had nothing whatever to say.
Moreover, he was laughing at her, she was sure ; he had seen
her run away from the room on Friday, and, no doubt, thought
her quite peculiar. Oh, why had Mrs. Pelham been cruel
enough to send her down with him ? In the extremity of
her nervous suffering, she almost forgot the disappointment
of not seeing Dan Charteris, as she had thought to do. As

they reached the dining-room she became aware that Rigby
had been saying something—indeed, it occurred to her that he
was repeating the same remark over and over again in slightly
different forms—

" Have you been in town before ? "

" Is this your first visit to London ? "

" I suppose you have been in town before ? "

" I suppose you have visited London before ? "

Lucie blushed fiercely at her own stupidity, and became
doubly stupid.

" I—no—I—I have never been in London before," she
managed to say, and sat down in the first seat she saw.   Then
she heard Rigby's voice remark icily—

" Pardon me, our seats are farther up the table, Miss
Marjorybanks."

She rose hurriedly, upsetting two wineglasses, and reached
her own chair at last.   " Now," she thought, giddy with
shyness,—" now I must make an effort to be like other people."
She glanced across at Maggie's pretty, tranquil face, and at
Almeria's expression of immovable ease ; then, with a terrible
attempt at calmness she did not feel, she turned to make a
remark to Mr. Rigby—

" I find London very "—she began ; but he faced round
upon her with an ironical expression, that a duller person than
Lucie would have easily interpreted—" Come away, country
cousin, with your comments on London," he seemed to say ;
and the words died on her lips.

Rigby was, in fact, in very bad temper, and wreaked it
unmercifully on Lucie.   He had expected to go down to
dinner with Lady Almeria, and instead found himself coupled
with a shy girl from the country, without a word to say for
herself, and, withal, a person of no importance.   Rigby had a
deep love for persons of importance.   He allowed a long
silence to fall, to impress Lucie thoroughly with the idea that
he had nothing whatever to say to her.   Then, as a sacrifice
to the goddess of civility he seemed to rack his brains for a
subject, produced it condescendingly, and gave Lucie another

chance to be amusing if she could. It was nothing very brilliant, only the invariable question—

"Did you enjoy Garrick on Friday?"

"Yes," said Lucie.

She was quite aware that he was behaving rudely. She would have liked to be rude to him in return, but instead she was only smitten with silence. She looked towards Dr. Cornelius with piteous eyes, but he was separated from her by the whole length of the table. There was another long pause.

"Do you prefer silence to conversation, Miss Marjorybanks?" asked Rigby; "or perhaps you disapprove of playgoing?"

"No," said Lucie; she could find nothing more to say.

"I am sure, now, that you find we Londoners most frivolous. You occupy yourselves more profitably in the country do you not?"

"Yes."

"Come! what do you principally find fault with here—is it our manners or our morals?"

"Neither, I mean to say"—gasped Lucie.

"That is enigmatical,   neither you mean to say.' Pray explain yourself, Miss Marjorybanks." said Rigby.

Poor Lucie became incoherent. She answered at random, and her confused replies only made Rigby more witty at her expense. At last, losing all self-control, she rose and ran from the room with a little gasping sob.

Rigby saw that he had gone too far, and was full of tardy repentance.

Mrs. Pelham, with her quiet suavity, desired Maggie to go and see how Lucie was, assuring the rest of the party that her young friend was subject to slight attacks of faintness, which need not cause anyone anxiety. But she added, *sotto voce*, to Dr. Cornelius, "Poor child, what can I do with her? I am at my wits' end."

"Patience, patience, and again patience, madam," he said. "You must remember that you have the habits of all her lifetime to combat."

When the ladies adjourned to the drawing-room, they

found Lucie there. She looked pale, and had evidently been weeping, but seemed quite composed, and joined in their conversation with the artless sweetness that she had at times. Even the fashionable Almeria unbent towards her, when she said with a shy smile, " I am so much alarmed by the presence of strangers, that I lose all self-control. Tell me, do you think it possible to conquer such fears ? "

Both Maggie and Lady Almeria laughed heartily at this and Lucie felt quite cheered by their mirth.

" I shall attempt a little more conversation with that terrible Mr. Rigby when he comes upstairs," she said bravely. " I can scarcely believe that neither of you two feel alarmed by him."

" If there is any question of alarm, 'tis on his side, I can assure you, Miss Marjorybanks," said Lady Almeria.

" Were you as afraid of Captain Charteris as all this, Lucie ? " asked Maggie innocently. " For if you were, his stay at Balgowrie cannot have been much of a pleasure to you."

Lucie blushed hotly. " Afraid of Captain Charteris ? Oh no ! I never felt in the least afraid of him," she said.

Both the girls looked at her curiously.

" Why not, Lucie ? " said Maggie. " I should have fancied him as quite as alarming a personage as poor stupid Rigby."

" I do not know, Maggie I fancy it was because I was at home, among everything that was familiar to me, and beside Henrietta—it was quite different there."

" I wonder if you would feel nervous in his company here?" said Maggie.

" I cannot understand his absence," said Mrs. Pelham. " Captain Charteris is generally ready enough to accept my invitations."

Almeria laughed, and Maggie frowned slightly; and as they were discussing the matter, a note was brought to Mrs. Pelham, who opened it, smiling.

" My young gentleman's excuses," she said, glancing over its contents. " ' Out of town '—' only returned an hour ago.' —Ahem ! Maggie my dear, ring the bell. Thomas, did you see Captain Charteris' man when you delivered my note on Friday ? "

" Yes, madam."

" Did he mention if his master was out of town ? "

" No, madam ; said as the Captain was playing a game of hazard with another gentleman, but 'e'd have the note immediate."

" That will do," said Mrs. Pelham, smiling again, and Almeria and Maggie laughed more than ever.

" I should not like to incur your displeasure, madam, by false excuses," said Almeria.

Mrs. Pelham rose and went across the room to her writing-desk.

" I shall let the young man feel the weight of my displeasure " she said.

" MY DEAR SIR,"—her note ran,—" When you would make excuses to such an old friend as I am, pray make them honestly. You passed within half a yard of me an hour before I sent my invitation to you, and I hear on reliable authority that it reached you as you were enjoying a game of hazard with ' another gentleman.' In future, be more careful how you invent your excuses.—I am, my dear Dan, yours, etc."

" I have not been too severe, as you see," she said, handing the note to Maggie to read.

" No, indeed, madam ! the young man is becoming intolerable," said Maggie.

So the note was despatched, and, the gentlemen coming up from their wine at the moment, no one remembered more of Captain Charteris and his false excuses, with the exception of Lucie, who sat and pondered the matter very gravely—" Why had he not come ?—why, why ? "

She was not tried by farther conversation with Mr. Rigby, for he had at once directed his attentions to Almeria ; while Mr. Savage, Maggie, and Mrs. Pelham were speaking together.

Dr. Cornelius came and sat beside Lucie. " I have a letter from Henrietta to-day," he said, " which she bids me show to you ; but I cannot obey her."

" Ah, sir, pray—pray let me see Harrie's letter ! " cried Lucie, her eyes brimming with tears. " I am so sad and unhappy to-day ! I would feel another creature if I saw it."

"Can you ask me, Lucie ?—the first love-letter Harrie has written me. No, it is mine, I am afraid—mine alone."

"But I know Harrie could write nothing, even to you, sir, that she would not like me to read," pleaded Lucie.

"Ah, I daresay not! But, even at the risk of being considered disagreeable, I cannot let you see it. You will be wishing to see mine to her next, Lucie."

"I am quite sure that if I were with her, Harrie would show them to me, sir," said Lucie, smiling a little mischievously.

"Happily you are not. Well, Harrie is well, but dull, walking on the back roads, poor darling, while we walk in Piccadilly. She treats me to various reflections."

"Oh, you need not try to *tell* me!" said Lucie impatiently. "I want Harrie's own words, and only them ; I do not care for it second-hand."

"Very well, cross-patch. But why did you run away from dinner, my child?" said Dr. Cornelius, changing his tone to one of gentle reproof.

"That—that terrible Mr. Rigby!" whispered Lucie, with a fearful glance towards her enemy.

"My dear, my dear! may you never meet greater lions in your path!" he said, laughing.

After their guests had gone, Maggie and Mrs. Pelham and Lucie stood chatting together by the fire, when Thomas came in with another note.

"Oh, may I see, madam?" cried Maggie, with her pretty head over her mother's shoulder even as she spoke. "I wonder if he gives the real reason this time."

Mrs. Pelham frowned slightly as she read.

"My dear Lucie," she said, "I did not think for a moment that there was any reason why you and Captain Charteris should find it painful to meet each other. Had you told me of it, you may be sure I would never have asked him to my house."

Lucie blushed, and stammered out something quite incoherent.

" You may read his note, as it concerns yourself," said Mrs. Pelham, handing it to her.

" Dear Madam,"—it ran,—" since truth, like murder, will out, I must acquaint you with the fact that I had something of a flirtation with your pretty little friend, Miss Marjorybanks, whom you so kindly asked me to meet. I thought 'twould be uncomfortable for us both meeting, and blundered into stupid excuses, which you, my kind friend, will pardon now that the truth is told you.—Yours, etc."

Lucie read the note over and over, staring down at the words, as if she did not take in their meaning. Then she handed back the note to Mrs. Pelham, saying gently, " Thank you, madam. I would not have felt it uncomfortable to meet Captain Charteris, but since he felt it, he was wise not to come."

" Ah, young men are foolish—they cannot stand a rebuff," said Mrs. Pelham.

Maggie looked mystified, and Lucie took up her work and sat down to sew as if her life depended on its being finished. The evening did not pass as pleasantly as usual ; and Mrs. Pelham sent Lucie to bed early, under the impression that she was over tired.

XXV

THAT was a night of wonderful moonlight. The cold, greenish light flooded in through the windows making the rooms almost as clear as day. It fell in a long streak across Maggie Pelham's bed, where she lay awake thinking over the events of the day. " That was very curious about Lucie and Dan Charteris," she thought ; " most curious. I wonder what it was ? I wonder if he asked her to marry him, and she refused ? Well, I thought he wished to marry me—I could have sworn he did "— She stopped short in her reflections and sat up on one elbow in a startled way.

" Oh dear me ! " she cried ; " what's that ? "

For a white figure was standing in the moonlit room— most ghostly to behold.

"Are you asleep, Maggie?" said Lucie's voice, dissipating her spectral fears.

"Oh, Lucie! Is there anything wrong? How you startled me!" said Maggie.

Lucie came up to the side of the bed and laid her hands on the pillow. She did not speak. Maggie sat up in earnest.

"My dear Lucie, what is wrong with you? You are as cold as ice. Come here beside me. Can you not sleep? Or have you had a bad dream? What is it?"

Lucie obeyed like a child, creeping under the blankets without a word. Then she suddenly buried her face in the pillow.

"Maggie, Maggie," she whispered, so low that Maggie scarcely caught the words, "I had to tell someone—oh, may I tell you? Oh, Harrie is not here, and I think my heart will break. He does not wish to see me—he does not love me—I have been deceiving myself all this time. Oh, it cannot be true that he does not care for me—tell me it is not true!"

The young are seldom good comforters—they have not suffered enough to be hopeful. When Maggie heard this revelation of Lucie's trouble, she thought there was no possible comfort she could offer her. "Why it must be all her world gone!" she thought. She took Lucie's hand in hers and kissed her gently.

"Tell me all about it, dear," she said. "Perhaps you will feel better if you tell me all about it."

So Lucie told her everything. All about Dan's coming to Balgowrie, and their walks and rides and talks—and the last night—how he kissed her, and how they were to meet again—how she mended his coat, and about the heart he cut on the west turret window, with 'United hearts death only parts' written round it—all the dear follies of first love that sound so pitiful in the telling and bulk so large in the heart.

Maggie listened with rising indignation. Her whole generous nature was hot with anger when Lucie had done.

"He is not worth the caring for!" she said angrily. "Oh, Lucie, darling, do not cry like that."

Lucie turned wearily on the pillow.

"It is not only that, Maggie—it is everything. I am not like other people. I am going home—going at once. I cannot stay any longer here—it is killing me."

There was a terrible lifeless sound in her voice.

"Going home? Lucie, you are talking nonsense. What do you mean?" cried Maggie.

"I have made up my mind—I am going home. All this time I have been finding out how different I am from other people. I only stayed because—because I had to—I could not go while there was a hope of seeing him. Now I do not even care to stay. You have all been so kind to me; but life is a torture to me among strangers—I should never become accustomed to it."

In vain Maggie argued and entreated—Lucie would only give the one reply— "I am going home."

"Oh, it will seem different when the morning sun comes in," said cheerful Maggie at last—she had never had a grief that seemed darker by contrast with day's radiance.

"I am afraid to face the morning," said Lucie.

"But we can tell mother about it," said Maggie simply. "She can always put things straight; she will assure you that your nervous feelings can be conquered, and that you are quite like other people, and—but perhaps you would not care that even mother should know about—about "—

Maggie did not mention names. You will notice that young people have in general a very delicate finger where affairs of the heart are concerned. An older woman would have mentioned her lover's name in full to Lucie at that moment, and made her wince sharply.

"Yes, you must not tell dear Mrs. Pelham. You must not think it is because I do not love her, Maggie; it is just that I could not bear a third person knowing. You—and Harrie when I get home—are enough."

"Yes, I understand," said Maggie quickly. "But you will tell mother about your feelings, will you not? I am sure she can make things appear in quite another light for you, and that you will remain with us."

"No one can make things different, Maggie. I have *got a*

sight of the truth—I saw myself through other people's eyes last night ; and I am going home."

" But what will Dr. Hallijohn say ? "

" I do not care."

" And Henrietta ? "

" She will understand when I tell her—almost before I tell her."

" And your mother ? "

" I have not got a mother."

" Oh, Lucie ! "

" When I see what Mrs. Pelham is to you, I see that I have never had a mother.   Why, she has spoiled all my life !   She has shut us up like nuns and made us peculiar ! oh, so peculiar ! and if I come home with all my happiness wrecked and done with, she will never know—because she does not care enough for us even to discern whether we are happy or unhappy.   She sits reading Votltaire and writing essays on education—we might die before her eyes and she would scarcely lay down her book or her pen ! "

All the pent-up bitterness of her loveless childhood found words, and Maggie listened in a sort of shocked sympathy.

" I think we would have been mad by this time if it had not been for Dr. Hallijohn," Lucie went on.   " He has been mother and father both to us all these years—he made all the happiness we ever had.   And we were happy in our own way, when we were children—before we understood.   I used to be so pleased with the world—with all the live things and flowers and sunshine—I love them still so dearly—till I came to see that we were shut in a prison that there was no escape from.   It was only this summer, after Captain Charteris was with us, that I saw it all, and then it seemed unbearable to me. Oh, Maggie, I have such capacities for happiness !   I have been so happy often over nothing at all.   But I shall never feel like that again, for *I have seen myself*, and how odd I am, and I have lost—oh, lost everything ! "

Maggie had nothing to say—she could only weep along with Lucie, tears of such sincere sympathy as seldom flow in this artificial world.   At last, when the night was far spent,

Lucie dropped into an unquiet sleep, and Maggie, tired out with her vigils, was fain to follow suit.

The next morning after breakfast Maggie told Mrs. Pelham of Lucie's desire to go home.

"I cannot hear of it for a moment—the poor child is barely come to us! 'Tis just a turn of home-sickness, Maggie. I will speak to her," said Mrs. Pelham decisively. But after a long conversation with Lucie, even Mrs. Pelham was rather daunted. For Lucie did not contradict her, nor was she hysterical or extreme in her expressions. She listened quietly to all that Mrs. Pelham had to say, and then said only, "I am going home, madam. You are most kind, but I cannot stay." Then would follow some more arguments—always listened to with the same attention, to be followed by the same reply— "I must beg you to excuse me, dear madam—I am going home." At last, completely baffled, Mrs. Pelham sent a messenger for Dr. Cornelius. He arrived in the afternoon, and was at once acquainted with Lucie's sudden determination to leave London.

"My dear Lucie," he said, "I must ask you not to behave like a fool."

Lucie winced : she had never had a harsh word from him before ; yet she only replied as before—"I am going home, sir,—I cannot stay."

"Well, you shall go alone then. Do you suppose that I am going to trundle back to Scotland before three weeks are gone?"

"I—I do not know," and Lucie's eyes brimmed up with tears. "I suppose I would reach alive even if did I travel alone."

"You can assuredly try," said Dr. Cornelius hotly.

Patience was not his distinguishing characteristic. He was irritated that Lucie, after coming to town against such opposition from her mother, should so quickly give in to what he could only suppose was a fit of home-sickness.

Lucie caught hold of his hand.

"Do not—pray do not be angry with me, sir! I cannot

stay—it will kill me outright.   Can you not see for yourself
how foolish I appear in society ?—I am quite unfitted for it."

" And how do you intend to fit yourself for it, Lucie ? or
have you decided to remain in Balgowrie for the rest of your
natural life, and speak only to the chairs ? "

Lucie considered gravely.

" Perhaps with Harrie I may some day leave Balgowrie
again—alone I never can.   If you knew a tenth part of what
I have suffered since leaving home, you would not wonder
that I wish to return," she said.

" At least, Lucie, do not be in a hurry about this—consent
to remain with your kind friends for a few weeks longer.
If at the end of that time you are still as miserable as you are
to-day, I will let you go."

" No," said Lucie ; " I cannot stay."

" Then you are going to travel alone ? "

" Yes."

" When do you start ? "

" To-morrow, sir, if I can manage to."

" My dear Lucie, I am out of all patience with you.   You
should not be so obstinate ; you should take the advice of
your elders.   You are merely homesick.   Wait for a few
days, and all these megrims will disappear."

" No, sir, I know they will not," said Lucie.

Dr. Cornelius rose impatiently.

" Well, take your own way.   Doubtless you can arrange
your own journey admirably.   I wish you good-bye.   I have
various engagements to-morrow.   If, as you say, you start
then, I fear it will not be possible for me to see you again."

He held out his hand in farewell.   Lucie bit her lips to
keep back the tears that were choking her.

" Good-bye, dear sir," she said softly.

Dr. Cornelius did not for a moment dream that Lucie
would think of starting for Scotland alone.   He reproached
himself a little for his hastiness, and decided to buy the child
a fine present as a peace-offering, and take it to her the next
day.   " Then I shall quiz her on the subject of her journey,
and we shall be good friends again," he said.

But Lucie was her mother's daughter. There was a ground-rock of determination in her character that did not appear often. When Dr. Cornelius had gone, she went upstairs and began to pack her things. Maggie came and stood helplessly looking on at these preparations for departure; and then Mrs. Pelham came and positively forbade her to continue them.

"I must keep you against your will, Lucie, if you will not stay with it, until I find a suitable escort for you. You cannot suppose that I would permit you to travel alone to Scotland?"

"Will you make inquiries, then, madam?" said Lucie.

She came up to Mrs. Pelham and placed her trembling little hands in hers, and looked up into her eyes with an expression that startled the older woman.

"Good heavens, child! how you resemble your father!" she said. "Yes, I shall find an escort for you, my dear, if you have a little patience."

"Now you will be good and sweet, Lucie," said Maggie in her cooing voice; "and let me remove those dresses from your trunk, and come downstairs, and we shall sing together, or sew, or what you please, so long as you are contented to stay with us a little longer."

"You do not think that it is *you* I wish to leave?" said Lucie. And they went downstairs together.

They had not been seated in the drawing-room for very long before a visitor was announced. It was Lady Mary Crichton, to wait upon Miss Marjorybanks.

The good-natured, loud-voiced girl came bouncing into the room, all smiles and exclamations.

"Why, is this you, Lucie? London has changed you amazingly. You seem six years older with the hair worn high! And how do you manage your hoop, my dear?—Miss Pelham? Ah, we have met before, I think, Miss Pelham, at some of the assemblies. You danced in a green brocade last year, did you not? Ah, yes, yes!"

She was quite breathless with all she had to say; her pleasure to see Lucie again—her excuses for not coming sooner—her desire to hear Lucie's impressions of London—all she had been doing herself, and inquiries as to how Lucie had employed her time. Maggie could not but smile to hear anyone ask so many questions without waiting to receive any answers to them.

"And I am in a special hurry to-day," she went on. "Indeed, I should be in James' Square at my packing, and not here, but I could not resist a glimpse of you in the passing. Is it not annoying? Really I feel more like weeping just now than talking" (it did not appear to her auditors). "For we have heard to-day from Scotland of the serious illness of my grandmother. The dear old lady was in such health when we left home. It seems a stroke of some kind, most sudden, and my father will be off to-morrow, and take me with him. At her age, he says, it may be fatal. I do not think so myself; indeed, I would think it more reasonable to wait for further news; but my father is determined, so we start to-morrow."

Maggie and Lucie exchanged glances.

"When are you going?" asked Lucie; "for I too, am going home."

"You are going home? You surprise me! Why, I thought you were to be the winter in town! I trust you have no bad news from home?"

"No, I thank you, I have no bad news." Lucie broke down, finding it impossible to explain the situation.

"What is it? Pray tell me what is the matter?" asked Lady Mary in great astonishment.

"London does not seem to agree with Lucie; we think she must go home, for really she has been far from well since coming here—so subject to fits of giddiness," said Maggie, rather lamely.

"But what a pity not to give yourself a little longer!" said Lady Mary. "No doubt you would soon begin to mend, and 'twill be most annoying to miss all the pleasures of a winter in town."

"You may be sure we have used every argument with dear Lucie," said Maggie. "She seems to feel that it is right for her to return to Scotland, so we were just going to try to find an escort for her."

"If to-morrow is not too soon"—began Lady Mary doubtfully.

Lucie started up.

"Ah, you will take care of me? You are most kind! To-morrow is none too soon. I can easily be ready to go with you, if you will really burden yourself with the care of me."

"Oh, it will be no burden, Lucie—my father is there to protect us both—I shall be glad of a companion; but the packet-boat sails at eight to-morrow—'tis an early start."

Lucie appealed to Maggie. Could she manage it?

"Well, dear, if you still insist on going, I think you will be wise to go in Lady Mary's company. It will be the same to us to send the coach to the docks at any hour."

"Will you ask Mrs. Pelham about it?" asked Lucie; and Maggie left the room to find her mother.

"Now," said Lady Mary, resolutely, facing round on Lucie,—"now, Goosie, what is this? Take my advice and stay; as surely as you sit there, Lucie Marjorybanks, you will repent it if you run home. Oh, I know, I know! You are just shy and home-sick, my dear. Stay and face it out, and in a month's time you will not know yourself for the same girl. I remember feeling shy myself when I first came out into society. No, no, you need not laugh; I swear I blushed whenever any one looked at me!"

"You are dear and kind," said Lucie, taking Lady Mary's large hand in hers; "but you can never know all I feel—no one can who has not had out strange upbringing. It is quite different for you."

"Pooh! not different in the least. Stay, Lucie—I entreat of you to stay."

"It is impossible; I must go home, and as soon as I can. The Pelhams have been more than kind to me, but I cannot stay; it is killing me."

Mrs. Pelham came in with Maggie at that moment.

"So I hear you are going to take Lucie away from us?" she said, as she shook hands with Lady Mary.

"Well, madam, I have been trying to persuade her to

remain with you, but she seems determined, so perhaps it is as well for her to travel with us."

"I suppose I must give my consent, Lucie," said Mrs. Pelham. "It seems such a sudden arrangement. I have no time to write to your mother."

"It will not occur to my mother to think it strange," said Lucie.

So Mrs. Pelham reluctantly made the necessary arrangements with Lady Mary, and the good-natured girl hurried away, shaking her head at Lucie, and assuring her "she was a sadly head-strong young woman," and that till she saw her on board the boat, she would hope that a night's reflection had changed her plans.

When Lady Mary was gone, Maggie followed Lucie upstairs to resume their interrupted packing. The wide new skirts were all to be folded up and crushed into Lucie's modest boxes.

"I think I shall take off my new things and travel in my old ones. I am going back to my old life," said Lucie; but Maggie would not hear of it, so the old garments were packed away. The evening was very sad, for they had come to love each other more than they knew in those two weeks. Mrs. Pelham said they would not work, but sit around the fire and talk for the last time. She made an effort to be cheerful, and put the best front upon Lucie's home-going.

"I wonder when we shall meet again, dear Lucie," she said. "This has not been a very happy time for you, I fear; but you must come again, bringing Henrietta with you, and then I do not think you will suffer from home-sickness."

Lucie sat looking into the fire. She did not reply for a minute, and then said slowly—

"I do not know, madam; looking into life, I seem to see nothing in the future. It may be a foolish thing to say, but I think it will stop when I go home."

"My dear Lucie, life does not stop, however monotonous it may be."

"No," said Lucie languidly; "perhaps it is only a feeling."

It was useless. They could not be cheerful. So Mrs. Pelham sent the girls to bed betimes, in preparation for their early start in the morning. She sat up late herself, reading over a bundle of letters written to her thirty years before by Lucie's father.

"Poor Henry! he was capable of such depths of feeling, and married without love after all—and that poor child is the end of it! She has all his feelings—Heaven send she has nothing else that he had!" she said to herself as she folded away the letters.

The morning sun was struggling out through the mists as Mrs. Pelham and Maggie stood on the landing-stage to see the last of Lucie. When the moment of parting came, Lucie flung herself upon Mrs. Pelham's neck in a burst of sobs, and then Maggie began to cry, and they all wept together.

"I shall never see you again—I know it, I know it!" said Lucie.

"The Lord bless you!" said Mrs. Pelham; not as the easy phrase goes, but as a prayer from the heart for one who was helpless and weary.

As the boat steered out into the river, Lucie still wept; but as one by one the towers of London town were swallowed up in the smoky mists, she stood dry-eyed on the deck to see the last of the city where her lover dwelt; she was saying those terrible, silent farewells of the heart that are not said with tears.

XXVI

UNDER the kind escort of Lady Mary and her father, Lucie reached Edinburgh in safety. There she had to bid farewell to her friends, and repair once more to Miss Hallijohn's house in Campbell's Close. The good lady was astonished indeed to see Lucie back again from London so soon. She did not need to be told that something was amiss, for Lucie's tremulous manner told that all too plainly; but, like a prudent woman. she asked no questions, and began to look about for someone to take care of Lucie on the journey down to Eastermuir. It would have been inadmissible in 1775 for any young woman to venture alone in a stage-coach, so Lucie had to restrain her impatience, and wait until a suitable travelling companion should appear. She had not long to wait, however. On the morning after her arrival Miss Hallijohn heard of "another gentlewoman" who journeyed in her direction, and under the severe eye of this elderly duenna, Lucie set off once again in the Eastermuir coach. She did not find much to say to her protectress, and answered the few questions put to her in such a far-away manner as made the older woman conclude that her young charge was slightly peculiar. All the way from Edinburgh—and a long, weary forty miles it is—Lucie sat gazing out at the landscape ; every now and then she would put her head out at the coach window to taste the country air, drinking it in as a thirsty man drinks wine, yet when her companion made any remark on the scenery, she scarcely replied. So they relapsed at last into total silence, and Lucie was left to her sad thoughts. As they came at last in sight of Eastermuir, she felt a curious stir at her heart. Ah ! there was the church, the inn, the handful of cottages, the Manse—and in the distance, over the tree-tops, one of the steep crow-step gables of Balgowrie.

"Ah, I have reached home at last !" she cried, as the coach drew up in the village street.

"You will be tired, no doubt. I have still ten miles between me and home," said her companion a little grimly, holding out her hand in farewell.

Lucie just pressed it for a moment and murmured some incoherent thanks ; she was in such a hurry to descend. Then she found herself standing like one awakened suddenly from dreams staring round her at the familiar sights of home. After the babel of London streets, the village seemed to be sleeping an enchanted sleep.

The girls had never been allowed to speak with the village people in a friendly way, yet the inn keeper had a word of welcome to Lucie none the less.

"Back, again, missie ? " he said, as he superintended the

hoisting down of her luggage, glancing curiously the while at her altered appearance.

" I am glad to be home again," said Lucie.   " Have you seen my sister passing to-day ? "

" No'for three days back.   Ye'll be for a machine up to Balgowrie ? "

" No, I thank you, I shall walk—I am tired with sitting so long in the coach ; but will you send up my boxes ? " said Lucie, and stepped away through the mud, holding up her wide skirts with some difficulty, and picking her steps across the cart tracks on her little high-heeled London shoes.

It was a very mild afternoon for the time of year—the mildness succeeding a night of wind and rain, which had left the roads if possible more miry than usual ; yet a reflection of the soft skies overhead smiled up at Lucie from the puddles, and in the calm air the gnats were dancing as if it had been a summer's day.   Just a month since she left home !   A week on the way—not quite a fortnight in town—and a week on the return journey.   Lucie stood still to look incredulously at a tree which still bore some tattered yellow leaves.   " The same leaves that were green on the branches when Dan was here," she thought.

But ah, how sweet the country air was, after the stale vapours of London !   And there was nothing and no one to fear.   She need not look round her here in terror.

Her feet could not carry her swiftly enough along the well-known road—for was not Henrietta at the end of it ?   Lucie arrived quite breathless at the front door, and had to pause for a moment on the topmost step.   Then she began to run up the old corkscrew stair.   The familiar fusty smell that hung about the walls of Balgowrie greeted her as she ascended, together with the swirling draught which always blew down that stair as if through a funnel.   The house was so silent that her racing footsteps echoed through it as she ran.   At the drawing-room door, which stood ajar, Lucie stopped again to regain breath and to look in, half expecting to see some alteration there—it seemed so long since she had stood on that threshold.   But there was no change.   The wood fire

was burning low, the hangings swayed in the draughts which
were a part of Balgowrie, through the west turret window a
shaft of sunshine came in and lay along the faded carpet ; and
in the window-seat at the far end of the room Henrietta sat
reading.

Lucie could not speak for a moment.   She wished only
to stand there and feast her eyes on the dear plain face bending
so intently over its studies.   But of a sudden Henrietta
looked up and let her book fall with an exclamation ; and
Lucie, forgetful of hoops and heels, ran towards her up the
great gaunt room, tripping over her skirts, and calling out
between tears and laughter, " I am come home, Harrie, I am
come home ! "

She flung her arms round Henrietta, and in that divine
moment of meeting it seemed that the former troubles were
forgotten, neither could come again to mind.   They clung
together as though years had parted them—or as lover
estranged who come again to their tenderness.

" Lucie, Lucie, why have you come back ?   Oh, I am dreaming, I think ! " cried Henrietta.

She rubbed her eyes and stared again, and fingered Lucie's
stiff skirts, and passed her hands over her cushioned head,
to try by one sense to verify the testimony of the other.

" Oh, do not doubt your eyes, Harrie.   'Tis me indeed,"
said Lucie.   " I think I am dreaming though ; as I came
picking my steps up from the village, I doubted if in reality
I had ever trodden London streets."

" Your own clothes might have convinced you, I think.
Why, Lucie, Lucie dear, I do not know you in these curious
fashions ! "

" Well, you will know me soon.   I am not going to
wear them here—Maggie would have me travel in them, but
this very night I must take them off ; above all, I must remove
the cushions from my poor head, which has borne them
these three weeks past."

" But tell me, dearest, why are you come back ? " persisted
Henrietta.

As she spoke she saw that the colour in Lucie's cheeks had

died down into a bright red spot in each of them, and that under her eyes there were transparent blue hollows.

"You are ill, Lucie," she cried. "That is why you have come home."

Lucie sat down and took Henrietta's hand in hers. "Oh no, Harrie, I am not ill," she said. "I shall tell you everything soon—I cannot just now—do you not understand? I should never have gone to London—that is all—'twas all a mistake. Oh, I am tired, tired, Harrie!" She leaned her head on Henrietta's shoulder and sat silent.

"You did right to come. Of course I understand. Did Dr. Hallijohn come too?"

"No. He was annoyed—angry with me. He wished me to stay; he did not know what was troubling me."

"And he allowed you to come by yourself?" asked Henrietta, with sudden jealous anger for Lucie's safety.

"Oh no; I had Lady Mary Crichton and her father with me—I was well protected. I shall tell you all about it—now I only wish to be still and with you. Where is mother?"

"She is in the library; had you not better come and see her now?"

"What will she say, Harrie?—she will ask me questions"—

"No, no, Lucie; do you not know our mother better? She will think it quite natural. Come, we shall go downstairs."

They went down to the library together hand in hand after their old childish fashion. Mrs. Marjorybanks sat at her writing-desk. She did not evince much surprise at the unexpected appearance of her younger daughter.

"So you are come home, Lucie?" she said. Then, with a glance at her altered garments, "I daresay you found yourself somewhat peculiar among other people?" For the widow had seen plenty of the world and its ways in her own day.

The angry colour leaped up into Lucie's pale face.

"I did indeed, madam," she said bitterly. "'Twas a shame and a cruelty sending me among strangers to suffer as I did."

"Such suffering is excellent discipline for young people. So you have returned? You have not made a long stay."

"How could I stay?" cried Lucie. "And such suffering is good for no one, it makes one only bitter and hard. You have been cruel to us madam—you have made us peculiar intentionally, when you might have saved us all such misery. You might have trained us like other girls, amd made us happy and able to face the world, and instead you have ruined all our lives."

Henrietta listened in horror: was this Lucie who was speaking?—this person grown suddenly older by years and years, and speaking so bitterly to her own mother. Mrs. Marjorybanks was less affected. She listened to Lucie's words with a slight smile.

"I am thankful if my daughters are not like the ninepin girls of society," she said at length. "But you seem to feel strongly on the subject, Lucie, and certainly express yourself somewhat unsuitably, considering whom you address."

"How can I do anything else after all I have suffered?" said Lucie.

The widow turned again to her writing, with a hard little smile on her lips.

"You had best marry, Lucie, and try your own theories on your own daughters, as I have done," she said, as she took up her pen.

Perhaps she did not intend this speech to be unkind, but to Lucie's ears it had all the effect of the most coldly premeditated cruelty. She turned and ran from the room with an expression of perfect horror on her face.

"How could she? how could she?" she cried when Henrietta came upstairs and sat down by her.

"She did not know, dearest," said Henrietta soothingly.

"Did not know!" echoed Lucie scornfully. Her whole gentle nature seemed to have been suddenly embittered, and Henrietta looked at her in wonder as she heard the cold and scornful sound of her voice.

"No, no, Lucie," she said, taking her hand. "She cannot know—she notices nothing that befalls us—she is wrapped up in her own theories, and scarcely cares if we live or die: it was quite unintentional."

" The whole of her system with us has not been unintentional, at least—she has wilfully made oddities of us. Oh, Harrie, you do not know yet, for you have never been out of this place or seen other people—you cannot realise how peculiar we are ; not only our dress, but all our habits and ideas are strange. Those things which seem as natural to the rest of the world as breathing, are unusual and difficult to us, and we would need to acquire painfully all the usages which are second nature to them. If you knew the torture of meeting strangers (other people like it !) and the terror of walking in streets, and the bewilderment of going to theatres or churches or other public places ! It would take us years to become accustomed to these things."

Henrietta listened gravely, with pained interest.

" I think you probably exaggerate our peculiarity, Lucie," she said. " I cannot imagine your being anything but pleasing in your manner or address ; and for the rest of it, these nervous fears would wear off sooner than you suppose."

" No, no, no, Harrie ! They increase, I assure you. How can one be at ease when one is different from everyone else ? And our mother has done it all. Oh, Harrie, if I had only been like other girls, how happy I might have been ! I am not ugly—'twas only that he saw me different in every way from those girls he was accustomed to be among. In the country—here where there was no one else—I seemed good enough ; but in town, others who had those ordinary advantages I have never had—others seemed better to him. I do not blame him, Harrie ; 'twas quite true—I could never have married him and gone about in the world with him. I only blame my mother. My heart is all hard and frozen, Harrie. It feels now like a stone."

They sat together in the dusk, and Lucie told all her pitiable little story—the ridicule she had been subjected to—the foolishness she had exhibited—her fears, her efforts at self-control, her failure, and her despair. And what could Henrietta do or say ? She sat and wept beside her and held her hand. Then the dusk deepened down to dark, and the room was only lighted by the fire that flickered away on the hearth, a quiet crackling accompaniment to their voices. Lucie dried her eyes and leaned back in her chair.

"Oh, Harrie," she said, "I have been speaking for an hour all about myself and my unhappiness, and I have never said one word about you."

Henrietta had not time to reply when the door opened and Hester came in with some wood for the fire. She advanced half-way up the long room, and then let the wood fall on the floor in her amazement.

"Miss Lucie!" she cried. "Preserve us all, am I seeing right?" The good old woman was frightened out of her senses.

"Yes, Hester dear; do not be alarmed," said Lucie, running to meet her. "I am not a ghost—I am here in reality." She dropped a kiss on her cheek as she spoke, and stooped to lift up some of the wood.

"Gude sakes! my dear bairn, to think on it! Miss Harrie, we little thought this morning to see her the night? Is it with the coach you came, Miss Lucie? Wait or I call Silence!"

She hurried from the room to summon him as she spoke— it was not often that such unlooked-for events fell out at Balgowrie. The hasty summons brought Silence, flushed from his afternoon nap before the kitchen fire, and, forgetful of appearances, in his shirt sleeves. He thought the drawing-room chimney, at the least, must have gone ablaze, to excite Hester in this manner. He dashed into the room with a handful of salt and an expression of interested excitement.

"Is't alow, Hester? Awa for the saut-crock, woman— I jist gruppit frae the cruet. It's no' been sweepit thae ten years back!"

But Hester in her genteeler southern speech rebuked his hasty conclusions.

"'Tis Miss Lucie come home, Silence. Lay by the salt, man," she said.

Silence was quite disappointed. He had almost hoped for a conflagration. He advanced towards the fire and surveyed Lucie with the freedom of old service.

"Losh me! an' wi' sic a heid!" he exclaimed.

Henrietta and Lucie laughed, with the relief of people who have been crying, and Lucie began to explain her own return.

" You see, London did not agree with me," she said, so I thought it better to return."

" Thae toons are awfu' for the health," said Silence, and Hester broke into exclamations upon Lucie's altered appearance —her thinness and her pallor.

Lucie rose with a look of weariness.

" Come, Hester," she said, " I shall want your help to take down my hair—I am weary with the weight of it."

Hester protested—it would be well to retain such a work of art upon her head ; and in the meantime she, Hester, might learn to dress Henrietta's locks after the same fashion.   But Lucie would not hear of it ; she carried Hester off upstairs to take down the pyramid of hair in spite of all her protestings, an operation, it proved, of time and difficulty.

That night, as Hester and Silence sat by the kitchen fire, they questioned shrewdly over the mystery of their young mistress's return.

" I jalouse there's mair in't nor a bit dwam," said Silence

Hester looked a great deal, but said nothing, and Silence resumed—

" When'll the Doctor be back, think ye ?   I'm fair scunnert wi' thae callants frae the toon that's preachin'.   No' that the Doctor's muckle o' a preacher himsel', but he's a wiselike man i' the poopit—thae toon bodies are sic shauchlin' trash.   But forby that, Hester, I'm aye easier i' the mind aboot oor young leddies when the Doctor's here.   Ay, it's time he was hame, I'm thinking."

Henrietta had come to the same conclusion in different words as she sat in the firelight after Lucie had gone to bed.   It was in their own room that Henrietta sat, and in the silence she heard Lucie's breathing as she slept.

Henrietta was troubled, not with Lucie's story alone, but with a cold fear that kept knocking at her heart.   Lucie was ill.   She had been ill all summer—she was worse since going to London ; it was not unhappiness that was stamping that curious look upon her face. Henrietta rose and walked softly to the side of the bed. Lucie was sleeping heavily tired out ; in the firelight her face looked startlingly thin, the hollows under her eyes seemed deeper than ever, and the little hand tossed out from under the covering was almost transparent. Henrietta knew nothing of illness, but as she stood looking down at Lucie she felt that the fear she had seen far off in summer-time was come several steps nearer now—it seemed to be standing at the very door. She turned quickly away and began to undress. Her fingers shook, and she could scarcely unfasten the buttons of her bodice. When she lay down beside Lucie, she was cold and trembling all over. Lucie stirred in her sleep and said something—she had always a trick of speaking in her sleep. Henrietta leaned nearer to catch the words.

"*United hearts death only parts!*" Lucie was saying.

The next morning broke with a blattering storm of autumn wind and rain that sent the faded beech leaves swirling, gathered them up into handfuls and flung them against the window panes, and then careered off round the gables of the house like some mad thing.

Henrietta and Lucie sat in the library in the morning, for Henrietta had all her books round her there, and Lucie liked to be near her.

"I suppose you are doing mathematics as usual ? " said Lucie, glancing round the room at the volumes piled everywhere, on the very floor, near the writing-table.

"Yes ; oh, Lucie, 'tis a perfect science—the beauty of it ! " cried Henrietta enthusiastically.

"I suppose so. I wish, Harrie, that I could love study as you do—I never feel that it is for any purpose. What use will it all be to you ? "

"I do not know enough yet. Some day—years hence—perhaps I may be able to do something with it," said Henrietta, her eyes lighting up in that eager way they had when any sudden thought inspired her.

Lucie walked to the window and stood looking out over the rain-drenched garden. Henrietta's heart was sore for her, but she said nothing, only began to turn over some of her mathematical notes on the table. After a long survey of the garden, Lucie turned back to the room ; then with a little half sigh, half sob, she huddled herself down in the corner of the sofa. Henrietta came quickly across to her, knelt down, and covered her face with kisses.

" Oh, Harrie, do you know how I feel : can you understand ? " asked Lucie pitifully.

" I know, I know, dearest : this life seems bare, bare—no reason for living it ! "

" Yes—oh, so bare—so bleak "—

" Lucie—dearest—now, if ever, you must call upon your soul and all that is within you to be stirred up. Love may have gone past you, but life is still here—wonderful life—life that is only the soul's probation, the food that the soul lives upon. Must it be here and now with you, Lucie ; can you not bear to have your joys withheld ? "

" If I had a life, Harrie—but this is hardly life, this existence between the four walls of this house. Perhaps if I had one duty, one bit of reality in my life, I could bear it—but what is there ? "

" There is reality enough of suffering, at least, Lucie—of denial of all that life properly holds."

Lucie turned her head wearily on the pillow.

" I do not know what it is, Harrie—I cannot express it—something seems to have stopped or broken here." she said, holding her hand quickly over her heart. " The something I lived by is run down—I do not think it can be mended."

" Oh, you are tired ; you are ill, Lucie. But tell me you will try to begin life again—begin it where it was interrupted—in May. Believe that there is interest and hope in everything still, even if you cannot feel it. For my sake. Lucie, tell me you will try."

Henrietta pled as a man might plead for his life. At first Lucie would only shake her head.

" I do not care about any of the things I used to do," she said. " I cannot pretend to"

But at last she rose from the sofa and walked once or twice up and down the room.

"Henrietta," she said, "this is over and done. I do not wish even you to speak of it again. I shall do all my usual work whether I care about it or not."

She left the room, and came back after a little while with a bundle of sewing in her hand.

"Stitches, stitches!" said Henrietta. "I have often wondered how such tiny things can hold a big garment together. It will be the same at the end of our lives, Lucie, I believe—we shall be surprised to see what we have fashioned out of all these trivial labours."

"Harrie, Harrie! you should have been a parson—you would have made a better one than Dr. Hallijohn any day. When you are married to him, I protest you will write all his sermons!"

"Shall we talk about that?" asked Henrietta, putting away every pretence of work.

She came and sat beside the fire, and you may be sure this topic lasted them some time.

XXVII

CHRISTMAS passed, and New Year, and yet Dr. Cornelius did not return to Eastermuir. Even that patient flock which he shepherded after such an indifferent manner began to complain. For three months there had been no possibility of marriages or christenings, and the funerals were conducted as best might be without benefit of clergy. Had they suspected how the minister's heart was turning day by day and hour by hour towards his home, they would have been still more at a loss to account for his absence. As it was, the general and rather disrespectful opinion ran, that the Doctor was "taking a long spree."

Dr. Cornelius had heard of Lucie's sudden flight from the Pelhams', when he called upon them on the day following her going. He was filled with self reproach that his last words with her had been impatient, and hastened off to write his apologies. Since then he had heard of Lucie's safe arrival from herself, and had also received letters every week from Henrietta. But these letters somehow seemed to ring false. What was wrong? Henrietta was not angry with him—of that he was confident—yet he read between the lines a note of constraint. The letters told of the usual walks and studies, of the Thursday receptions once more resumed by Lucie, of books, and of winter storms. Yet there seemed to be something behind it all. The lover pondered and frowned over them. " Perhaps Henrietta is piqued at my absence ; so much the better ; she will care for me more when I return," he said, and made arrangements for another fortnight's stay in town.

But one morning a very thin letter arrived, addressed in Henrietta's dear hand.

" She is angry," he said, smiling, as he cut it open.

Only a few words were scrawled across the page.

" *Oh, my dear heart,*" he read, " *when are you coming home ? I am in such trouble. Do not mention this when you come.—H.*"

He glanced at the date—a week old. Henrietta must be in sore trouble indeed to write thus, and another week must pass before he could reach her. He turned away from his untasted breakfast to prepare for the journey, cursing the miles that lay between him and Henrietta. Five days by sea with a favouring wind, and another half day in the coach between Edinburgh and Eastermuir. While by stage-coach —bah ! It took a fortnight at the least. By good luck a packet-boat sailed for Scotland the next morning ; but for twenty-four hours he must wait here in London town, while Henrietta sighed for him at Balgowrie.

After coming to this conclusion, Dr. Cornelius, being an elderly lover, returned to the breakfast-table, and made a wonderfully substantial meal. Then, being a lover as well as elderly, he went out and spent quite unjustifiable sums on presents for Henrietta—a ring first, and books to follow. This done, he whiled away the remainder of the day at White's, lost five guineas playing hazard with his thoughts three hundred

miles away, went to the play for a last sight of David Garrick
in *Macbeth*, and forgot to applaud his favourite actor ; finally,
went to bed and courted sleep with very indifferent success.

Then, at last, came the morning, and with it the longed-
for starting time.   The boat went rocking down the tide and
this impatient lover stood on deck and whistled for the wind.

A week later, Dr. Cornelius arrived at Eastermuir at three
o'clock of a January afternoon.   His unexpected arrival
made quite a commotion at the Manse.   Mrs. Allan bustled
about delightedly to prepare a dinner of her best cookery,
while James " put a light " to the ready laid fires, and poured
out a stream of parochial gossip as he knelt on the hearthrug
to watch the struggling flames.

" How are the ladies at Balgowrie ? " was of course the
first question that Dr. Cornelius asked.   To his great relief
James reported the ladies to be "just in their ordinar'."
Surely, then, this hasty summons had been something of a
fraud !

Dr. Cornelius would have liked to start there and then for
Balgowrie ; but prudence (which, at fifty, sometimes has the
upper hand) whispered that dinner and a toilet were a better
preparation for appearing at his best before the eyes of his
lady-love, than hunger and somewhat travel-tashed clothing.

So it was like another old-time lover, " barbered ten times
o'er," after an excellent dinner, and several glasses of excellent
wine, that Dr. Cornelius at length rode off in the gathering
dusk towards Balgowrie.

A great yellow moon came swinging up from behind the
bank of trees to the south, and the last rays of daylight were
mixed with its shining into a weird half-light.   Saul, fresh
from his long idleness, would not be held in, and broke into
a gallop along the quiet tree-bordered lane ; then, where the
road suddenly comes out from the shadow of the trees, he
began to shy at the moonlit puddles, and look askance at a
white milestone which stands there to tell weary travellers of
the forty miles which at this spot lie between them and the
capital of Scotland.

" And a weary forty miles it is in that damnable stage-coach," said Dr. Cornelius, recalling the eight hours of jolting with a shrug.

Then Balgowrie came in sight, tall and dark against the sky. A glimmer of light showed from one or two of the windows—firelight it seemed to be, from its flickering. The place was as quiet as the grave ; the only sound was a far-away " boom, boom " from the waves breaking along the great curve of bay to the west.

" What a living tomb it's been for the poor children ! " he thought, as he dismounted to lead Saul through the gateway and round to the stable. Silence appeared at the sound of his steps, with an air of studied unconcern.

" Ye've got hame, Doctor, at last ? " he said, with the intention that his remark should be cutting. But this careless shepherd did not pay much heed to the opinion of his flock. He merely laughed, and flung the reins to Silence, asking if the ladies were at home.

" Whaur wad they be ? " said Silence who was not accustomed to gadabout habits in his employers.

Dr. Cornelius did not wait for further parley, but strode up the stair. He opened the drawing-room door softly and looked in. The room was lighted only by the fire. Henrietta and Lucie sat beside it, their voices making a little murmur in that echoing, gaunt room, like the sound of falling water.

He tapped lightly on the panelling of the wall with the handle of his riding-whip, and both the girls sprang up at the sound, and ran forward to greet him.

" Ah, dear sir ! "

" Ah, Cornelius ! "

The sound of their voices, the sight of their dear faces, something in the childish way they ran to meet him, sent a choking throb of happiness through his heart. " Poor lambs ! I am all their help," he thought ; and, holding out his arms, he gathered them both up into a great, impartial, fatherly embrace.

" My dear children ! " he said. Their faces were indistinct in that half-light. So far as he could distinguish, Lucie seemed to be smiling ; yet for a moment he thought that Henrietta sobbed against his heart.

"Faith, that was a tender scene !" he said, laughing at his own show of feeling. "Come, let me have a look at you both"

He took the same old straight-backed chair beside the fire where one night long years before he had sat, and seen two little girls come shyly up the long room to curtsey to the stranger who was speaking to their mother. The little girls were changed indeed since these days ; but Henrietta came and stood beside his chair just as she had done then. She even took, his hand and began to twist the ring he wore round and round, a habit she had retained from her childish days. She used to do it as she repeated her Latin verbs.

She was asking him all manner of questions, scarcely waiting for his replies. Her cheeks were flushed and her great eyes flashed and glowed.

Dr. Cornelius looked up at her where she stood. "She loves me now," he said, and answered her questions almost at random. Then, turning to look at Lucie, who had taken a seat on the opposite side of the fire, Dr. Cornelius at first sight of her face knew what Henrietta's trouble was. For two months had worked a sorry change on Lucie. She sat there the chosen bride of Death.

"God help my poor Harrie !" he thought : even in this his thoughts went first to her.

Yet Henrietta wore no air of gloom. The first excitement of his coming over, she sat down and spoke just as usual. Dr. Cornelius inquired for Mrs. Marjorybanks, and Henrietta said she would soon be there ; she was writing downstairs as usual.

"Dear sir, we are so delighted to have you home," said Lucie. "And is Mrs. Allan not vastly pleased to see you ?"

"She expressed herself most prettily on the occasion. I protest it is worth while going from home to be so welcomed on one's return."

"And have you brought a new stair carpet ?" Henrietta inquired. "Mrs. Allan has had but one thought these three months past, and that thought 'stair carpet.'"

"I fear I forgot it, Harrie. I came off hurriedly at the end."

"And the Pelham's?" queried Lucie. "Have you seen them again?"

"But once, Lucie, since you left London. I waited upon Mrs. Pelham one day last week, but she was gone out; so I have no messages from them for you."

Their talk ran pleasantly till Mrs. Marjorybanks appeared. Her coming always seemed to cast a gloom, and Dr. Cornelius did not remain very long after she came. Mrs. Allan, he said, would never forgive him if he supped away from home that night.

Henrietta prepared to go down to the door with him.

"You are riding, I suppose?" she said. "'Twill be dark in the lanes to-night."

"Ah, we know our way, Harrie. Are you coming down-stairs with me?"

"I must call Silence to bring round Saul," said Henrietta, as they stumbled along the ill-lighted passages.

The twisting staircase was entirely dark; by contrast with its obscurity the night seemed clear when they reached the front door, though clouds had come across the moon. They stood together on the steps.

"What is it, Harrie?" said Dr. Cornelius, laying his hand on her shoulder.

She turned her face up to his; it showed in that dim light only as a white patch.

"Cornelius, do you not see? Lucie is dying," she said brokenly.

"My poor Harrie—my poor child!" he said. For the pity of it the tears welled up into his eyes.

"What can I do? Oh, tell me, is there nothing I can do?" cried Henrietta, catching hold of his arm with both her hands.

"Does she complain of illness?" he asked.

"No; I could bear it if she did; she says nothing. She goes about as usual, only every week she stops some one thing or other from want of strength. Some day she will just lie down and stop everything. When I ask her if she feels ill, she says, 'Only tired'; but she coughs terribly at times."

" I shall get a doctor, Harrie.   That at least we can do."

" My mother has a prejudice against them ; she will not have one into the house."

" She cannot prevent one coming to my house, though, and you must bring Lucie there to see him.   This is no time to hesitate at a little deception.   I shall send to Edinburgh to-night.   We'll have Gillies the surgeon down ; by to-morrow afternoon he will be here.   You must bring Lucie then.   Say I begged you to come to dine with me at four o'clock."

" Do you think he can do anything ? "

" Surely, Harrie !   My dear, your affection makes you over-anxious."

" Oh, it is good to have you here.   I feel better already," said Henrietta.

" Well, hasten Silence with my horse, child.   You will catch your death of cold in this draught, and I must get home to send the message to town.   James shall ride with it himself.   Harrie, you will kiss me before I go ? "

Henrietta raised her lips to his obediently ; then, as if thinking over his words—

" James ? " she said.   " Oh, go yourself, Cornelius, that you may make sure ! "

" James will do it perfectly, Harrie "—he began ; but she interrupted hastily—

" The doctor you wished might not be able to come, and he would know nothing about getting another.   Pray, pray go yourself ! "

Dr. Cornelius hesitated for half a breath,—a vision of home and supper and rest rising alluringly before him.

" The sooner the better, then, my love," he said.   " For it grows late already, and forty miles are not ridden in a hurry. Come, good-bye again, sweetheart, for I must be off."

" I shall send Silence round in a moment," said Henrietta, and flitted off into the dark house like a shadow.

" 'Tis no joke to be Henrietta's lover," said Dr. Cornelius, with a grimace, as he leapt into the saddle.   Five days have I tossed in that dammed packet-boat, eight hours to-day have

I jolted in that infernal coach, and at the end of it she starts me on a forty-mile ride at six o'clock of a January night!"

XXVIII

HENRIETTA was unaccustomed to interviewing doctors. She did not know anything about them, and felt an unnecessary dread of the serious-faced man who listened so intently to Lucie's breathing.

"I hope you do not find much wrong with my sister, sir?" she said anxiously, when the examination was over.

The doctor did not reply for a moment, then he bowed stiffly to Lucie, and said to Henrietta that he would give all the necessary directions if she would step with him into the next room.

She led the way into the study,—the dear study, hallowed to her by every happy memory of her childhood,—and stood rather nervously beside the fire.

"I hope you do not think my sister is very ill?" she repeated.

"My dear madam, is it possible that you are in ignorance of the grave nature of your sister's case?" said the doctor.

"You find her seriously ill, then?" cried Henrietta, with her funny stagey clasping of the hands. She turned her great eyes on him with a look he never forgot.

"I find her seriously ill, madam. I fear Miss Marjorybanks' lungs are incurably affected."

"Oh!" said Henrietta, drawing in her breath hard, and trying from her scanty knowledge of medical matters to imagine what this might mean.

"I fear we can do very little, madam. Had I seen your sister in an earlier stage of the disease something might have been done to arrest its encroaches; now I can only advise you to exercise the utmost care, and to guard her against over-fatigue or exposure of any kind."

"You mean that my sister is going to die, sir?" said Henrietta, looking him full in the face.

" My dear madam, it is inevitable," said the doctor sadly.

" Can nothing be done ? "

" Nothing."

" And how soon ? "—Henrietta could not speak the words.

" Your sister may live for six months ; more probably the end will come in three or four."

" Ah, sir, you have told me the truth !—I thank you for that, at least," said Henrietta, holding out her hand to him with one of her sudden frank impulses.

He offered her a chair, and sat down himself facing her, looking intently at her.

" If you can get your sister to go about as usual for a time, it would be as well, but do not persuade her to try anything she is disinclined for ; I fear her strength will not last very long." He paused and then added firmly, " After that, you should have someone else to share the fatigues of nursing with you."

" I shall nurse Lucie myself," said Henrietta.

" Madam, 'tis a false system to sacrifice the living for the dying." He looked at Henrietta sharply as he spoke.

" I could never allow a stranger to nurse her. I have plenty of strength for it myself," said Henrietta.

" I must be frank with you, madam," said the doctor, " and tell you that in families where there is a consumptive tendency, one member should not nurse the other. You must think of yourself as well as of your sister."

" Ah, sir, you need not be afraid for me," said Henrietta, with a sad little smile. " My life will be only too long now."

As she sat there in the familiar room, what desolation swept over her heart ! If Lucie left her, there could never be enough left in the world to live for. " And I was preaching to Lucie just the other day that no one should ever say that," she thought. " I said to her that there was always life— ' beautiful life '—left, whatever was taken away. I know better now. There is life, and there is Cornelius, and there is all I wish and hope to do and see in all this wonderful world, where as yet I have seen nothing ; and yet, if she goes, I care for none of these things. There will be just the *first* thing gone from my life, and what does anything matter then ? "

Then she realised that she was sittiing in silence, instead of speaking to the doctor.

" I shall follow all your directions, sir," she said, rising. " And now I wish you good-day. Dr. Hallijohn will be with you immediately. I must take my sister home now ; we live at some distance from here."

She shook hands with the doctor and left the room ; leaving with him an impression of her curiously individual personality, of her strange dress, her great, speaking eyes, and the scorching grief that was suddenly fallen upon her.

So, as the Scotch phrase goes, Henrietta had to " stand up to trouble."

She never did anything quite like other people, and her way of facing this was of course unusual. In the first place, she attempted no deceptions with Lucie, but told her plainly that she had probably only three or four months of life remaining to her.

Lucie received the news incredulously. " Harrie dear," she said, " I feel ill, and oh, so tired ! but surely I am not dying, for I cannot have been made only to be unmade again before I have lived at all ! "

Henrietta shook her head sadly. " I fear there is no mistake, Lucie. I am forced to believe it, and you must believe it, too ; it will be better for both of us not to be taken by surprise."

" But do you understand, Harrie ? "

" No, I am all bewildered ; but there is time for us to think about it—three months."

" It seems as if it were all a mistake, a blunder, that anyone should be created only to die. If I had even been very happy" —her blue eyes suddenly brimmed with tears.

" I see that terrible things are permitted in our lives," said Henrietta slowly, " but I do not think they are mistakes ; the whole world moves by order, and not by confusion— they are purposed, not accidental."

" But what am I to do these three months, Harrie ? Am I

just to sit and wait? I am so frightened!" shivered poor Lucie.

"I am with you, Lucie."

"But you cannot go with me."

" Ah, Lucie, you must not think about the pain and suffering! You must fix your thoughts on the tremendous something that must be waiting just beyond death. 'Twill make you forget the miserable present."

"I see nothing waiting. I love the world; and all that heaven that some people speak of could never make up to me for missing happiness here. Oh, Harrie, I have none of these wonderful thoughts and feelings that you have. I am afraid and reluctant to die. I do not wish to end—I wish to remain myself a little longer. One ends at death, does one not? We have always learned that from mother. I do not know what Dr. Hallijohn thinks; he never says."

"I do not care what either of them says; life must in reality be only beginning for you, Lucie. This life is not reason enough for our existence."

"'Do you think so, Harrie?'"

"Yes, I am sure of it; so sure of it that sometimes I am impatient to get done with this life and see into the next. I read a verse in one of David's Psalms once: ' *When shall I come and appear before God?* ' I have gone for days with that question sounding in my ears like bells—the thought of that appearance! I would not need to explain anything; to stand silent before God would be enough, while He reviewed all my life. If you get hold of that idea, Lucie, it will warm you through like the sun!"

Thus, day after day, and week after week, Henrietta supported the weaker nature that clung to her. She would speak of death only in one way—the entering a new life. She did not avoid the subject, but spoke of it often in the calmest, most cheerful manner. In another person it might have seemed almost an affectation, but Henrietta's nature was so direct that it did not surprise or shock Lucie in the least to hear her say—

"Dearest, are you going to try to finish the embroidery

you began? I am sure you could do so without fatiguing yourself. I shall send it to dear Mrs. Pelham after you are gone away." It seemed much more natural to both of them to act in this way.

They sat and sewed together, just as usual, in the afternoons, till the day came when Lucie's work dropped into her lap time and again from weariness. Then Henrietta rose and took it from her.

" I have been watching you, dearest; you are not fit to work now, you must not try. I shall finish it as well as I can. You must go to bed, Lucie; you are too tired now to stay up any longer."

" Yes, much too tired," consented Lucie.

" Will you come upstairs now? I will help you."

" Yes. But let me—let me " —Lucie's eyes filled up with tears as she spoke. " I should like to walk once up and down the room again, for I do not think I shall ever come downstairs again, I feel so weak. Strange to think it is for the last time ! "

She held out her dear, thin hands to Henrietta, who supported her as she rose from the sofa where she had been lying. They walked up the long room together slowly.

" Now take me into the west turret," said Lucie. She stood beside the little square window and traced on the pane the heart that was cut there. " This is false, dear Harrie," she said, turning upon her with a sudden flashing smile. " Even death can't part us. The other parting I had was sore enough, but *our* hearts will be ever together. Come, I am done with all this—done with love and done with life, Harrie."

She stood for a moment looking out through the little window, over the curve of the bay, where a long white line of breakers was coming in; then up at the sky, yellowing with the approach of evening.

" Come, Harrie," she said again gently; having taken her farewells.

Mrs. Marjorybanks protested against what she described as Lucie's " invalid ways." now that her poor child was unable to come downstairs any more. The widow, indeed, compelled her to make the attempt, and was scarcely convinced of her unfitness when she fainted at the foot of the staircase."

" 'Tis just vapourish nonsense," was her verdict.

Henrietta, stung at last to revolt, turned upon her mother with indignant, flashing eyes.

" 'Tis death, not nonsense," she said bitterly.

The widow laughed,—so little she knew or cared about her children in a practical way,—and walked off, leaving Henrietta and Hester to carry Lucie upstairs again. But after this she did not insist that Lucie should leave her room. She never visited her there, however; and to Henrietta, maintained that Lucie was suffering only from nervous illness. Her presence was not missed in the sickroom and the sisters lived a curious imprisoned existence there by themselves. Dr. Cornelius came every afternoon to visit Lucie, and to take Henrietta out for some exercise. Hester would sit with the invalid while they were out, and then Dr. Cornelius would stay for an hour, and they would talk together, if Lucie was not too tired.

"You conduct sick-nursing on new principles, Harrie," he said to her one day, actually laughing as he spoke, at the almost off-hand manner in which Henrietta mentioned her approaching death before Lucie. "You are your mother's daughter in some ways," he added.

"My dear sir," said Henrietta, "we all know about it— 'tis the thought uppermost in all our minds; surely it is best to speak about it? It would appear far more mysterious and frightful to us both if we never mentioned it."

Lucie looked up from her chair, where she lay propped by pillows.

"Tell me, sir, how do you visit those of your parishioners who are near death? Since I have become so ill myself, I am often wondering if there are many others in the same case, and though you are so delightfully kind to me, I am amused to see how foreign it is to your nature to come near what is melancholy."

" I am better suited for the house of feasting I fear, Lucie."

" But you do go to see those who are dying, do you not, sir ? Have you seen many people die of this illness of mine ? "

" Many a one, Lucie. There is a man dying of it at Eastriggs just now. What do I say ? 'Pon my soul, I often am in straits for words. I give the poor devils a crown now and then when I see it needed—and, when they ask it, I pray."

Henrietta laughed. " I fear you are but an indifferent parson, Cornelius. Do you remember Augustine's words : ' *Thou hast framed us out of a wonderful mixture of parts, and joined heaven and earth together in one man ?* ' There is a quantity of earth about you, sir."

" And little heaven, in truth, Harrie," he said. " I have warm affections ; they're my one link with heaven."

" You have been all our help, Cornelius," said Henrietta quickly, as if her words had been too severe. She laid her hands on his knee as she spoke. He took it in his own, and they sat hand in hand, while their talk flowed on.

" You see, sir," pursued Henrietta, who, in addressing him, vacillated between her old and her new style of address,— " You see, sir, my theory on death is this—it concerns the flesh, not the spirit. You see how our dear Lucie's body is suffering, and we cannot help it ; but we must turn all our attention and our powers to helping her mind, for it gets cast down by reason of the pain she has to bear."

" Yes," struck in Lucie. " And when at night I am worn out with pain and weariness, Harrie will begin with wonderful imaginings, till I nearly forget to think how ill I am."

" What sort of imaginings ? " asked Dr. Cornelius.

" Not all imaginings, sir," said Henrietta. " Some of them are, but others are taken from that curious book the Bible. 'Tis a most imaginative work ! Some of its words rouse one like a trumpet (not that I have ever heard a trumpet !) There is that part about ' the great white throne ' and the ' cloud of witnesses.' Who will the witnesses be ?—a cloud of them, pressing round one to get the latest tidings from the world they once lived on and loved in. And there is that expression ' the armies of heaven '—don't you see them ?—hosts on hosts, rank above rank of unconquered men—armies that have never known defeat, shining like the sun, and strong with a strength that cannot even remember what weariness was like !   And then the great light of Eternity when it breaks on us !   Have you ever lain awake with closed eyes, and the sun has come suddenly out ?   Even through the lids you feel it has flooded the world ; you are almost afraid to raise them in such brightness.   'Twill be just like that the moment before death—an almost unbearable heaven of light and peace shining through the flesh that covers our souls as the lids cover our eyes."

" Harrie, Harrie ! " said Dr. Cornelius almost roughly.

He rose as he spoke, and bent over Lucie to say good-bye.

" I am too earthly for these spiritual flights," he said.

As he walked slowly homewards, he frowned and shook his head, looked down at the dead leaves below his feet, and then up at the high March skies above him.

" Harrie my dear, you are uncanny," he said to himself. " 'Tis the unnatural life you have led.   When you have a husband and a home and children of your own, you will forget these unearthly fancies.   Ah, these are the big, vitalising draughts that have satisfied the thirst of the world since time began !   Give me to drink of these pleasures !   ' These all perish in the using,' say the saints.   What of it ?   One has had them—has had one's day.   Poor darling, she has had little enough of this world's joys.   Well, they are to come !— when she has passed through this Gethsemane, and a dark one it is for her."

When March and April had passed away, and May was come, Lucie was drawing very near to the gates of death.   Dr. Cornelius came every day to try to induce Henrietta to go out, for she was grown terribly thin and pale with the long nursing she had had ; but Henrietta would not go out now.

" The time is coming too near, Cornelius," she said, with her herioc smile.   " I cannot leave her now.   Why, I shall never be with her *here* again.   I have just a certain number of days and hours of *the Lucie I know* left me.   I do not know what she may be like when we meet again.   When I come out walking with you I feel that one of the hours is gone.   I cannot come."

So she never left Lucie now.   She sat beside her, holding her hand, and they spoke together over their short, uneventful life—" *All we have known of the world,*" as they said.

The last day that Lucie was able to sit up was one of those days of fervent heat which come in early spring.   The sun shone in through the deep-niched window, and a blackbird sang out suddenly in the blossoming orchard.

" Let me look out again," said Lucie.

Henrietta raised her from the chair, and she crossed the room slowly towards the window.   They stood there together listening to the great hum of life that rises in springtime from the growing world.

The tears fell slowly down Lucie's cheeks, and she suddenly stretched out her arms as if she would clasp something unseen.

" Oh, dear green earth, where I might have been so glad ! " she cried.   " I must leave you soon."

She turned away from the window then, and leaned her head on Henrietta's shoulder.

" I know the upper fields will be greener far," said Henrietta steadily.

After this Lucie never left her bed again.   And ah, how the poor child suffered and struggled !   Henrietta scarcely left the room even to eat ; certainly she never slept these last four days.   But when Dr. Cornelius came in the afternoons, she met him always with the same smile.   Then the last day came.

" We are suffering strange things in our poor body to-day," she said, indicating Lucie.   " My darling has not slept all night, and is sadly weary now."

Dr. Cornelius thought she was looking almost as weary herself ; her face seemed all eyes.   He took her place beside Lucie, supporting her through her paroxysms of coughing, and bade Henrietta sit down and rest.

" 'Tis new work for you, sir," whispered Lucie, looking up at him with her blue eyes that could still laugh, and then she patted his hand.   " So strong and soft ! " she said.

"Yes—idle hands, Lucie," he said. "Now that your cough seems better, perhaps you might sleep. We shall not speak—it is not good for you."

Henrietta had sat down in a chair by the fire, for very weariness her eyes closed. There was silence in the room, broken only by the singing of the birds in the orchard coming in through the open window.

"Just hear them," whispered Lucie, with a little touch on Dr. Cornelius' hand.

She lay back against his arm with closed eyes, listening to that ecstatic chorus. Henrietta dozed in her chair. Dr. Cornelius scarcely dared to breathe, for fear he should disturb either of them. The birds seemed to be singing them both to sleep, he thought at last, looking down at Lucie's face, where the look of terrible suffering had smoothed out, leaving it calm and sweet. She opened her eyes suddenly, and met his with a smile.

"Better," she said, drawing in her breath gently.

"Henrietta!" said Dr. Cornelius quickly.

She sprang up from her chair broad awake in a moment. He motioned to her to take his place, and she slipped her arm round Lucie, who, with a little nestling movement of contentment fell back against her breast. There she lay very still for a long time—only a flicker of breath came and went to show them that she still lived.

"Shall I go and bring your mother?" asked Dr. Cornelius, and Henrietta nodded. He rose and crossed towards the door.

"Ah! there she goes!" said Henrietta suddenly in a breathless whisper, just as though she had seen something pass out through Lucie's parted lips.

Dr. Cornelius started at the strange words, and came back to the side of the bed.

"What! is she really gone?" he asked, bending over Lucie. Henrietta smiled curiously.

"How could I be mistaken," she said, "when half my own life went with her?"

XXIXX

M RS. MARJORYBANKS found it impossible to deny that Lucie had really died; but she took the sad event as little to heart as anyone could have done.

"The way of all flesh," she said reflectively; an undeniable truism. Then she expected that Henrietta would resume all the routine of life which had been interrupted by Lucie's illness. But Henrietta had broken down at last; had given way to all her long pent-up misery, and, for weeks after Lucie's death, refused to return to life, such as it was, at Balgowrie. She shut herself up in her own room, or sat under the trees in the garden all day, doing nothing, sunk in a sadness that seemed as if it would never lift.

Dr. Cornelius came as usual every day to see her, and she received him with a far-away look, and seemed scarcely to care to speak with him. She would take his hand, saying—

"Now we shall sit quiet; I have nothing to say, Cornelius."

They were sitting thus silent in the orchard one lovely afternoon, when she looked up suddenly through the net-work of branches to that smiling summer heaven above them, saying—

"Ah, could you not come, even for a moment? I am so terribly sad! The orchard is most beautiful, and the sky so deeply blue! but they cannot please me without you. You could come down through that blue emptiness so quickly! It is not even as if it were a cloudy day; there is nothing but distance between us—empty blue distance. Come, come, Lucie! I am here!"

She rose, and stood with clasped hands, gazing up to the sky. Dr. Cornelius took her hands again in his.

"Henrietta," he said, speaking almost harshly, and at the sound of his voice she started, and seemed to come back to earth with an effort. "Come and sit down here. I wish to speak to you," he pursued. She took her place obediently beside him.

"Henrietta, you are a very clever woman; you can when you will, do almost anything which you attempt. I am going to speak very plainly to you, and you must give me your attention."

"Yes, sir," said Henrietta, as if she were back in the schoolroom again.

"You are aware of the great peculiarities of your mother, Henrietta. Are you also aware that, unless you make a most resolute effort, you will become equally peculiar yourself?"

"I probably am peculiar already, sir. Poor Lucie told me that I was quite unconscious of my own peculiarities."

"I was not speaking so much of outward things, Harrie, as of habits of mind. Do not call me cruel when I tell you that you must make a terrible effort of will now to separate yourself from the thought of the parting you have gone through, and to bring yourself back to this world. I am not speaking for myself, child : I could bear to be forgotten for a time ; but if you brood in this way on your trouble, you will positively unhinge your brain. Your life is far too quiet ; you are necessarily now thrown sadly in upon yourself, but if you choose to exert yourself, you can find something left yet in the world."

"I know, I know, Cornelius ; but just for a little—my grief is so new."

"This is July, Henrietta. Lucie died in May."

"What can I do, what can I do, Cornelius?" she cried, turning to bury her face on his shoulder in a burst of sobs.

Dr. Cornelius was thankful to see her tears. They, at least, were natural. He allowed her to weep on until she was tired, then he said gently—

"Henrietta, when are you going to marry me? Could you not do so soon? I have spoken to your mother about it, and she makes no objection, somewhat to my surprise. You are worn out and sad, my dear ; you need a change of scene and of ideas after the long nursing and sadness you went through in spring."

Henrietta shook her head. She would not speak, only sat silently holding his hand, her head resting on his shoulder. Every now and then she gave a little sob. At last, after a long silence, she spoke.

" You are quite right, Cornelius ; all you have said is true.
But I would rather not be married quite so soon.
Will you wait until October ?   I will marry you in October.
And now I shall take all your words to heart.   To-morrow I
shall begin all my usual occupations again.   I have been
morbid.   I have indeed been foolish."

" Not foolish, my love ; 'twas natural—most natural,"
he said.

Henrietta sat forward on the garden seat resolutely.

" I have been working ever since autumn—since—since—
since Lucie went to London—at a translation of Herodotus.
I had made but scant progress with it when—when the
interruption came ; but I shall begin upon it again.   Tell me,
sir, do you think it too ambitious for me ? "

" My dear Harrie, you have a hunger for overcoming
difficulties.   A translation of Herodotus ! "

" Indeed, Cornelius, I found great pleasure in it.   I worked
at it for five hours each day when—when I was alone.   Now
that I am alone again, I shall work as long," said poor Henrietta
choking back her tears.

" Till October, Harrie.   After that, you stop working for
a time.   I am going to take you away from here."

" To— ? " questioned Henrietta.

" To where you will, so long as you are happy."

" And your parishioners ?   Silence has told me they became
impatient this winter at your long absence."

" Parishioners, like children, should not be indulged—
parishioners be——"

" I remember the first time I heard you say that.   'Twas
about a parishioner too," said Henrietta, with a reminiscence
of her former self in her amused eyes.

" You have too good a memory, Harrie.   Let us pursue
our plans for the future.   We shall go—where ? "

" Not to London, I think, Cornelius ; it would be too sad
for me ; at every step I should be thinking how she was
there.   Will you take me to Paris ?   Ah, to see Paris at last ! "

" Paris be it, then, Harrie—and farther if you desire it.
Ah, life, life ! there are fine things in you ! "

Henrietta smiled rather a forlorn little smile but it was a step in the right direction.

"I wonder if you will make me as fond of the world as you are yourself," she said.

"Not in my way, Harrie. I love life for its own sake—always have and always will—for the taste of it and the fine heady feel of it. You will love it always as an experience, an intellectual thing to be thought over, not merely swallowed down at a draught."

Thus they talked on of the life that was to be.

The next day Henrietta went to work upon Herodotus, with something, too, of the old pleasure, as she fingered the musty volumes that had been her lifelong friends. She would take her books out to the orchard and study them there, with the tuneful birds keeping her company, the bee humming in the hives near at hand, and Lucie's pigeons sometimes fluttering down from the doocote to see if their mistress was not returned yet. Henrietta's eyes would fill suddenly with tears as they came wheeling down—a flurry of whiteness round her ; but she choked back her tears, and turned resolutely to the pages of Herodotus. Cornelius had wished her to work—he was all she had in the world now, and she would please him. The effort was bracing, and brought its reward in greater calmness and less painful brooding on the sad past. When Dr. Cornelius came, Henrietta would smile now, and speak of her work, and together they would speak of dear Lucie almost with cheerfulness.

But, with it all, Henrietta still looked thin and pale. As the summer went on, Dr. Cornelius often looked at her anxiously, and asked her if she felt ill. Henrietta replied that she was tired, and had never felt very well since Lucie "went away,"—that was all.

"My dear, it is time you had me to care for you," said her lover. "I fear Mrs. Marjorybanks is not very careful of your comfort and well-being."

Henrietta laughed.

"Poor mother ! her one care is fitting me for society. Do you know, Cornelius, that since Lucie left me, nothing has

tried me so much as thóse terrible Thursdays ? Why, the
Thursday after Lucie's funeral, I had to dress up in all my best
finery, (such as it is !) and go through the whole weariful
business. 'Tis a strange delusion ! One of the best things
about marrying will be to be done with these Thursdays ! "

" Well, you have not many of them now, Harrie—but
three or four."

" Yes ; this is September now. The end of October it is
to be, Cornelius, is it not ? "

" The beginning, if you will have it so, Harrie," he said
gallantly.

" Ah, no—the end, Cornelius. I am but now beginning to
prepare my mind for marriage. 'Tis a great step—I have
much to think of before entering upon it."

" You might have been thinking of it all summer, my dear,
had you had a mind."

" I was going to ask you, Cornelius, about another matter,"
said Henrietta, with some hesitation. " And this is it—I
spoke to my mother yesterday on the subject, but she would
not listen to me for a moment, and bade me ' give my thoughts
to less trifling matters.' I am not very frivolous, sir, and
at one time it would never have occurred to me that other
clothes than those I have were necessary. But now I know
that they are curious, and that I must be dressed like the rest
of the world before I enter it. How am I to manage this,
Cornelius, for my mother refuses to speak of it with me ? "

" My dear Harrie I know little more than yourself about
ladies' dress. I fear I can be of little assistance to you."

" I think," began Henrietta, actually blushing, an almost
unknown thing for her to do—" I think, Cornelius, that—that
if you will give me money to buy my dresses, I can procure
them."

Dr. Cornelius laughed for joy.

" Don't tell me, Harrie, that you thought twice of asking
me for money ! " he said. " Why, what a blockhead I was
not to see what you were driving at. Money, my dear ?—
as much as you will, and the more the better. And how will
you procure these garments ? "

"I thought of writing to Maggie Pelham," said Henrietta.

"And how long would that take ? Stay a moment, Harrie. My cousin Matilda will buy them for you in Edinburgh. 'Twill be a pleasure to the dear woman—she fell in love with Lucie at first sight, and will only be too pleased to do this for you."

"Ah, Lucie told me all about her—of the little room at the top of the house where she dreamed that we should come some day together ! "

"Dear Lucie ! I think I see her that night—sitting at Matilda's knee when I came in. She had been telling her all about you. You must write explicit directions to Matilda of all that you desire, and she will do for you."

"Explicit directions, Cornelius ! Can you fancy my explicit directions on fashion ? No, it must be Miss Hallijohn who sends me directions of how to assume the dresses when they arrive."

Dr. Cornelius laughed, and agreed with Henrietta that her ideas would doubtless be rather faulty.

"Cousin Matilda shall come down to Eastermuir for our wedding, Harrie. I can fancy her pleasure to deck you for the sacrifice with her own dainty old hands—she is a woman all over. I am going up to Edinburgh in ten days or so, and I shall bring her—and the dresses doubtless—back with me when I return."

"Ah, that is a beautiful arrangement ! I feel sure I shall love her. And what a comfort to me to have some one to speak to !—some woman, I mean. For poor mother hardly counts as a woman ; and dear old Hester knows no more than myself of this dangerous ' world ' that I am going to venture out into."

"I hope ' the world ' will not scare you as it scared poor Lucie," said Dr. Cornelius.

"Ah, no. I am really less sensitive than she was, sir. I am very indifferent to the opinion of any but those who are very dear to me."

"But my dear, you have never tried," he corrected with a laugh.

"I stand corrected," laughed Henrietta.

XXX

OCTOBER came. A cold month, and specially cold it seemed this year. When Dr. Cornelius came to bid Henrietta good-bye before starting for Edinburgh, he frowned at her pale face.

" What have you been doing with yourself, child ? " he asked.

Henrietta began to cough, and drew a little tippet she wore more closely round her.

" 'Tis this searching cold, Cornelius ; you have no idea of the cold of the house."

" I am marrying you none too soon," he said, looking at her uneasily. " Do you often cough like this, Harrie ? "

" In damp, cold weather. I have never been well since Lucie left me. I was tired—so tired with it all. I shall be better soon."

" Can you not heat the house or sit in the library while you cough so—that at least you might do."

" My dear Cornelius, to have known my mother so long, you have the most wonderful ignorance of her peculiarities ! If she fancies that I am self-indulgent in any way, she takes care to repress the tendency. When first I took this cough,—it has troubled me for nearly a year now,— 'twas in the bitter frost last January. The cold was frightful. In our room, where, even though Lucie was complaining of illness, we only had a fire when Hester lighted it by stealth— in our room, I say, the water in our bath used to be covered with ice in the morning. We used to lie awake and shiver with the cold—and ah, how my darling coughed ! Well, mother heard us complain, and after we were gone to bed one night she came into the room to see how many blankets were over us. Hester had only that night put on a third blanket, as she might not light our fire, and when mother saw this, she exclaimed in anger at our self-indulgence. ' You are the merest Sybarites,' she cried, and with that carried off the blanket, leaving us to shiver."

Dr. Cornelius shook his head despairingly.

" Well, you must take what care you can of yourself, Harrie. To-morrow is Thursday : what a night you will have of it with the chairs ! And bare shoulders in that barn of a room, too. Tell Hester as she loves me to light a fire in your bedroom. Should she get her dismissal from your mother, I shall pledge myself to take her into my own employ."

" I am accustomed to chills, Cornelius—do not be anxious. Enjoy yourself in town, dear sir. When next you are there, 'twill be hampered by a wife who is ignorant of all city ways," said Henrietta, with almost her old archness.

" Yes ; you can see me blushing for my boorish bride—instructing her when to curtsey, and directing her to keep the right hand of the passers-by in the streets, pre-vailing upon her to attempt a crossing through the traffic or using force to get her to enter a coach."

" See that your prophecies are not verified," laughed Henrietta. And they parted jesting.

Four days later, Dr. Cornelius received a note from Henri-etta, a scrawl so indistinct that it was with difficulty that he made out its contents.

" Pray come home, Cornelius," it ran. " I am so ill. On Thursday I was so cold, I ran upstairs to bed, coughing, and something broke in my chest."

Dr. Cornelius did not stop to consider the hours of the stage-coach's departure. His first thought was to reach Eastermuir at the utmost speed ; his second to bring a doctor with him. The profession were not so rife in Edinburgh in those days, but without much difficulty he procured the services of that physician who had seen Lucie in spring. Then they set off together in a post-chaise on that weary forty-mile drive. Dr. Cornelius, remembering Mrs. Marjorybanks' hatred of medical men, warned his companion that he must be prepared to gain an entrance to Balgowrie by artifice.

" I shall introduce you as my groomsman," he said.

" And under what pretence can I see the poor girl in her room ? " queried the physician.

" If madam is out, there will be no difficulty. If she is in, you must pay your respects to her for half an hour (damn her !), and when we go, I shall take you upstairs instead of down. I know the house well."

" As you think best.   I am entirely in your hands."

The long miles were gone over—more slowly, it seemed, to the anxious man who watched them, than ever before.

" On the way to funerals and meetings of Presbytery, I've seen the milestones seeming to flash past me," he said in exasperation.

The doctor tried to allay his anxiety.

" These hæmorrhages are often more alarming than serious, my dear Hallijohn," he said.   " There may be no return.   Much will depend on care in the future, and that you will be sure to give."

" Care !   The girl has been murdered, as her sister was before her ! "

It was late afternoon when they reached Balgowrie.   Dr. Cornelius strode upstairs without ceremony, followed by Dr. Gillies.   The drawing-room seemed empty at first sight ; then they saw that Henrietta sat in the corner by the fire. She was terribly pale, and sat propped up by pillows, her hands idle on her knees.   She gave a cry of welcome at sight of her lover.

" How are you, Harrie ? " he said, bending over her as a mother over her child.

" Ah, so ill, Cornelius !   I can scarcely speak," she said, turning her eyes questioningly on the other man.   Then, suddenly recognising him, she held out her hand.   " You have come again, sir ? " she said.

The words sent a thrill through Dr. Cornelius.

" Come, Harrie, surely you must be better to have come downstairs ; I expected to find you in bed," he said, affecting cheerfulness.

" My mother would have me rise.   I was in bed for three days, because it was impossible for me to leave it, but to-day I thought it better to try to get up—easier than bearing her displeasure."

" You will let Dr. Gillies examine you now, Harrie," said Dr. Cornelius.   " And tell him all about your illness."

" But mother—if she were to come in" objected Harrie.

" I have my lies ready.   I shall go to the end of the room and intercept her if she enters.   Go on, Gillies, as fast as may be while we are alone."

Henrietta's symptoms did not take long to relate.   Nor did it take long for a clever doctor to take in the possibilities of her case.

" With care, madam, you may avoid a return of the more serious symptoms—with the very greatest care.   If you will allow me to say it, I think that in your peculiar circumstances the sooner you can arrange for your wedding to take place the better."

" I shall make all possible speed," struck in Dr. Cornelius.

" And then I shall recommend a journey to the South—some considerable stay there indeed " pursued Dr. Gillies. " But Dr. Hallijohn tells me that you have already planned for this."

" I feel scarcely able "—began Henrietta.

" To be frank with you, madam, 'tis your best chance for speedy recovery.   These old houses are very cold, and Dr. Hallijohn tells me that Mrs. Marjorybanks approves rather more than is usual of the Spartan system.   You are not fit for it.   You will require the utmost care."

" I shall do just as you think best," said Henrietta.   " If you tell Dr. Hallijohn all about me, he will tell me afterwards, for, indeed, sir, your remaining here makes me most uneasy. You do not understand the peculiar prejudice which my mother has to gentlemen of your calling."

Dr. Gillies laughed.

" I'll be off, then, madam, for nothing can be worse than agitation for sick folk.   Yes, I shall tell Dr. Hallijohn all about your case, and I doubt not you will find him, before many weeks are gone, the best of nurses."

Henrietta smiled a little wanly.

" He was ever kind," she said.   " He does not need teaching in that."

The doctor rose and said good-bye, and Dr. Cornelius bent over Henrietta for a moment as he bade her good-night.

"Keep up your heart, dearest—before long you will be better. I shall be to see you early to-morrow," he said.

After the two men were gone, Henrietta leant back against her pillows and looked into the fire. She was not accustomed to illness, and the feeling of mental weakness it brings filled her with double melancholy. She rose and brought a book from the table, opened it, and tried to read. But the effort was fruitless, and the book was laid aside. Then her thoughts went on into life—life that was just beginning. And there they came to a sudden stop.

"*I am going to die—I shall never live—here,*" she said, speaking out aloud in that echoing room.

"*Here,*" repeated the echo faintly, and Henrietta shuddered, and looked round as if someone had spoken the word behind her.

"Tush! I am become nervous," she said, reproving herself, and taking up her book resolutely.

The next day, when Dr. Cornelius came, he found Henrietta much the same. She welcomed him tenderly.

"Ah, what joy to see you! I have had such fears and fancies all by myself," she said.

"I shall remove them all, Harrie. Come, let me send them scampering. I have arranged for our marriage to take place on Monday next,—that is not quite a week from now, this being Tuesday,—and must find some excellent reason for hastening it in this way to present to your mother. What shall it be, Harrie?"

"My mother never regarded a date in her life. 'Twill be all the same to her as if it had been the day we originally fixed."

"That was but ten days late, after all. So, shall I speak of this to her as a settled thing? Will she find no fault?"

"None, I think, Cornelius. She has become singularly indifferent to what goes on round her. She has just a few unchanging ideas—letter-writing, her daily walks, and our Thursday receptions;—for the rest of it, she scarcely notices anything."

"She will notice your leaving her, surely?"

"Scarcely. You see, she never misses dear Lucie. Since the day she died, she has never mentioned her."

"She will not be agreeable to the cleric who has to marry us, I fear. You know my cloth was condoned for curious reasons, Harrie! I fear I cannot assure her of the scepticism and lax morals of good old Dickson from Eastbarns and keep a clear conscience, for a better soul never breathed."

"I had not thought of that; but, after all, Cornelius, she was married herself by a churchman. So she need not object to my doing it."

"Well, it must be attempted," he said, smiling, and they sat silent for a minute or two.

"Cornelius, said Henrietta suddenly, "I think that I am going to die; I do not think that I shall ever be married to you."

"Good God, Harrie! why do you say that?" he cried.

"Because I feel it—I know it; and I am sure that Dr. Gillies knew it too. He is clever and hides his feelings, but he had a pitying sound in his voice that I heard quite distinctly through the reassuring things he said."

"You are grown fanciful, Harrie."

"No, I am not fanciful. I would not believe that I could get better if a dozen physicians said so. Ah, Cornelius, I must go—I feel it in me. I shall not be long here."

Her deep conviction stirred him with a horrible fear. He leaned forward with a passionate movement, taking her hands in his.

"Harrie, Harrie, stay with me! For the love of God, stay with me! You are my very soul!"

"I cannot stay, Cornelius. Why, I am halfway across already," she said sorrowfully.

"And all your powers—the talents I've seen growing and growing—all you might have done and been"—

"It is the Great Will," said Henrietta in her steady voice. "And you over-estimate me, Cornelius—you always did. The world will get on very well without me."

"And I?"—

"Ah, my dear, my dear!"

Dr. Cornelius rose, and paced up and down the room. Then he came back to where Henrietta sat.

" Now, Henrietta, we have had enough of heroics. You are fanciful, and you must not indulge your fancies. You are ill ; I can't disguise from you that you even might die, had you a return of your former illness. But at present there is no question of that, and if human care can prevent it, there will be no question of it after you're my wife. That's but five days now. For pity's sake, take care of yourself these five days ! Whatever your mother says, do not listen to her. You have me to obey now."

" I shall indeed do my best. And we shall go on with the arrangements for our wedding. My feelings may be mistaken, as you say. Do not suppose that I am frightened by these premonitions, Cornelius. I find them most curious indeed, but not alarming. I have no sort of dread of death. Too much that I love waits for me beyond it "—

" That is it, Harrie," said Dr. Cornelius, turning almost fiercely on her. " You care more to go than to stay. You stay with but half a heart down here with me."

" No," said Henrietta in her curious, meditative voice, as if weighing the matter while she spoke. " I would gladly stay with you. I am sorry—sorry beyond expression—to leave this strange world unexplored. I should have liked to see some of the wonderful works of men—what they have achieved ; but I am not sorry in another way, for oh, I weary to speak with her again ! "

" Do not take it for granted like this, Harrie," said Dr. Cornelius, but she went on, scarcely heeding him.

" Just to tell her every little thing again. If I went to-morrow, I would tell her how long the day appeared to-day, and the terrible evenings when I could not work, however hard I tried. And she would laugh and say, ' Stupid Harrie, always thinking about work.' For she will not have changed to me. We'll meet again just where we left off. Shall we sit hand in hand, I wonder ? Ah, we shall recall those dreadful hours before she left me ! I thought then it would be a life-

time till we were together again, and it is but five months—
though they have seemed so long."

"Harrie, I'll have no more of this," said Dr. Cornelius
sternly. "Your fancies have got the better of you—fancies
and nothing else."

"They seem strangely real to me, Cornelius. I have tried
to combat them, knowing that one is fanciful in illness, but
they return and return. I cannot help it."

"They will disappear as you gain strength; meantime,
you must disregard them, instead of giving them welcome."

"I shall try to. Let us speak of other things, sir. Pray
tell me, is Miss Hallijohn coming to our wedding, now that
it is to be hastened?"

"I have written to her, and doubtless she will come,
bringing your dresses with her. When I was in town (I had
forgotten to tell you this), she was immersed in finery, and
for ever asking my judgment upon it."

"She is most kind; I shall be most interested to see her,"
said Henrietta, driving away with a resolute effort all her
dark forebodings.

XXXI

"WE shall receive our friends as usual this evening at
seven o'clock, Henrietta," said Mrs. Marjorybanks,
as she rose from the dining-table on Thursday afternoon. Henrietta was a little better, and had made the effort
of coming into the dining-room that day, for the first time
since her illness began.

"My dear madam, I must ask you to excuse me this
evening," she said in dismay. "I am scarcely able for the
exertion of receiving company, and I fear my conversation
would be most wearisome."

"There is the more need that you should exert yourself to
make it entertaining; society, Henrietta, would soon come to
an end if its units allowed their conversational efforts to
depend upon their inclination."

" Madam, I am indeed annoyed to displease you, but I am quite unfit for the exertion," pleaded Henrietta.

"And you intend to celebrate your wedding upon Monday?" asked Mrs. Marjorybanks.

" I do, madam, and for that reason I am specially anxious to avoid any return of this illness."

" It is for the last time, Henrietta. I have tried to fulfil my duties as a parent in the past, to fit you for entering society, should it be your lot to do so ; and I shall not fail at the end. For six years—from your sixteenth year up to the present day— I have never omitted this social exercise, and it is not to be omitted now. I shall receive you at seven this evening as usual."

" I cannot, madam, I cannot," said Henrietta despairingly. She thought of the long hours of weariness implied by the " social exercise." of the cold room, and her own shoulders pitilessly exposed to the draughts which swirled through it, and remembered her promise to Dr. Cornlius to resist her mother's commands where they endangered her health.

" I cannot, madam," she repeated more firmly than before.

The widow was unaccustomed to contradiction. She took a quick turn up and down the room, and came back to where Henrietta stood, white and trembling, beside the table.

" I give you your choice, Henrietta," she said. " You obey me, or you are not married on Monday. If you are unable for the one exertion, you are certainly unfit for the other, so choose which you will have."

She cast a glance of positive triumph at her daughter, as though to say, " My will has conquered," and stood waiting for her eply

Henrietta knew her mother well, yet in desperation she made one more appeal.

" Pray, pray excuse me this once, dear madam ! " she cried, clasping her hands in the old stagey attitude of entreaty.

" This once, Henrietta ? This is for the last time. No ; I have said what my will in the matter is, and to it I shall stick."

Henrietta bowed her head silently. It was useless to resist

further. She went slowly into the drawing-room and lay back in her chair with closed eyes. The afternoon crept on. She rang for Hester, and asked her to bring her some writing materials.

" Mrs. Marjorybanks will have the reception as usual to-night, Hester," she said, raising her tired eyes to the old servant's kindly, anxkious face ; " and, indeed, I feel most unfit for it."

" Miss Harrie, 'twill be the death of you ! " cried Hester in dismay.

" Like enough, Hester—but I have said all that I can say. My mother says my marriage is not to go on unless I am fit for this."

Hester muttered incoherently—" The mistress, the mistress ! " she said.

And Henrietta, letting her voice fall to a whisper went on—

" You will stay with her, Hester, after I have gone ? I know the difficulties of serving my poor mother now. For my sake you will stay with her, will you not ? It is not as if I would be very far away either—I shall try to come often here to see her. I should be most uneasy did I leave her with any stranger."

" I will that, Miss Harrie, for your sake and the sake of her that's gone. And Silence the same. The kitchen lass will maybe give up her place, for the mistress is hard on her whiles, but you may trust to me, Miss Harrie."

" I wish I could take you with me to my new home, Hester. To tell you the truth, I have some misgivings of how I shall agree with good Mrs. Allan when I am her mistress. She has so long controlled Dr. Hallijohn's household, that she may find it difficult to take my way in everything."

" She'll be ill to please, Miss Harrie my dear, if that's her way. And if you'll take my advice, Miss Harrie, you'll lie down now an' rest before the hour for dressing."

" Yes, Hester ; but first I must write something—just a few lines. Give me my writing materials beside me ; and will you come and help me upstairs when the dressing-time comes?"

" I will, Miss Harrie, an' here are the things," said Hester.

" Thank you, that will do," said Henrietta.

She wished to think over something, to be quiet for a little. As she lay back in her chair, tears gathered in her eyes and flowed down her cheeks—they fell on the sheet of paper she wrote on, and blotted the words.

" I may be wrong," she said at last, as she finished writing ; " yet I cannot but feel that I am right."

When Hester came in again, however, Henrietta was quite calm. She spoke cheerfully with the old woman as she helped her to dress, recalling all the years that the curious rite had gone on since she and Lucie were children, and used to enjoy their Thursday evenings with the chairs.

" And then we began to weary of them, and then to hate them. And do you remember the evening that Captain Charteris arrived ? We were dressing here together,· Lucie and I, when we heard his knock upon the door. I remember our excitement. You met us in the hall, Hester, and told us a strange gentleman was come."

" Yes, yes, Miss Harrie. Well, well, to think ! A fine couple they'd have made if Miss Lucie had been spared."

" She was spared that," said Henrietta, with a sudden flash of bitterness. " He was a pitiful creature."

" Now, now, Miss Harrie, as the gentlemen go "— began Hester, who, though she had no great opinion of the other sex, would always try to uphold them where there was a possible marriage in the case ; but Henrietta cut her short.

" My shoes, Hester, and I am ready. Ah, how fatigued I am already ! "

" Come, Miss Harrie, lean on me down the stair," said Hester, and down they went.

Silence stood grimly at the back of the drawing-room door, as he had stood every Thursday night for the last six years.

" Miss Marjorybanks," he announced, for the last time, flinging the door wide ; and with faltering, slow steps, Henrietta went forward into the troom.

Mrs. Marjorybanks stood as usual at the far end, preparing her best curtsey of welcome. The chairs were grouped in easy conversational attitudes near at hand.

"For the last time," said Henrietta, to sustain herself, as she was waved to a seat and ceremoniously presented to her neighbour, the ottoman. A keen draught played upon her bare shoulders, and seemed to go through and through her.

"I hear that we are to have the pleasure of attending your nuptials upon Monday—may I venture to offer my congratulations to Miss Marjorybanks upon this auspicious event?" said the ottoman.

Henrietta bowed, as she had been instructed to do, and for lack of other matter of interest, continued to converse about her forthcoming marriage.

"'Twill be most strange to leave Balgowrie, the home of my childhood; I can scarcely realise it as possible," she said.

"This is a world of change," said the sententious ottoman.

Henrietta's conversation came to an end here. She was so cold that she could think of nothing else, and was overcome by a feeling of utter weakness.

"Ahem!" cried the ottoman.

Henrietta started, and began to cough violently. Then, making an effort to continue the conversation, she remarked upon the bitter weather. The ottoman considered that this was the season when the gentle exercise of the dance was especially agreeable, and begged Miss Marjorybanks to join him in the minuet. Henrietta politely signified her refusal, but an imperious gesture on the part of the ottoman—otherwise Mrs. Marjorybanks—constrained her to make the attempt. They paced it solemnly together in silence, and then returned to the pleasures of conversation. At ten o'clock refreshments of a chilly sort were partaken of, and towards eleven o'clock, Henrietta, after bidding a ceremonious good-night to her hostess, crept off upstairs, supported by Hester.

"'Tis for the last time, Hester," she said, and smiled.

XXXII

DR. CORNELIUS rode up to Balgowrie early the next morning. The day was beautifully bright, a touch of frost in the air, and a cloudless sky.

"Ah, this weather must do Harrie good!" he thought,

taking that view of frost which robust persons habitually lean
to.   The tingling air elated him like a draught of wine, and
sent misgivings flying.   " She grows dull about herself, poor
girl—naturally enough, after all she saw poor Lucie suffer.
When she has left Balgowrie, and come to me, and care, and
kindness, she will soon be better," he added.

As he rode up to the steps at Balgowrie, Mrs. Marjorybanks
appeared at the far end of the long walk which stretched away
from the front door.   She was pacing up and down the walk,
wrapped in her long cloak.   Dr. Cornelius dismounted and
went forward to meet her.   She stopped abruptly and held
out her hand.

" Henrietta is gone," she said, for greeting.

" Gone—where ? " he asked stupidly.

" Into darkness—she died last night," said the widow, and
resumed her pacing without another word.

Dr. Cornelius stood as if struck with a sudden palsy.   He
neither spoke nor moved.   The bridle slipped from between
his fingers, and Saul turned to nibble at a late autumn rose still
blooming in the borders.   Mrs. Marjorybanks, having walked
to the end of the path, returned to where Dr. Cornelius stood.

(" Your horse is eating the rose leaves,") she said paren-
thetically.   " I am left alone.   Hester will show you the
remains, if you care to see them ; " and with that she turned
away to resume her march up and down the path.

Dr. Cornelius turned towards the house.   He stumbled up
the stair with the horrid words ringing in his ears— " *the
remains* "—of all the world held for him.   What hope remained
now ?—only the remainder of a misspent life—the remains of
youth—the remains of life itself.   The word played through
his brain like a hideous tune.   At the head of the stair he met
old Hester.   She came forward with a burst of sobs.

" Ah, sir, sir !   I would have sent Silence—indeed, sir,
'twas no fault of mine—the mistress had some fault against it.
Indeed, as you may see, sir, her senses are near gone now, an'
I just must obey her whimsies as best I can."

" You can do no more, Hester.   Will you take me upstairs ? "
said Dr. Cornelius.

The stair, the room he knew so sadly well. How often he had climbed to it in the days of Lucie's illness ! A dark room—the window in one corner, and much grown over with creepers. But to-day the bright morning sunlight came in slantingly and fell just across the bed. Hester uncovered the face of the dead, and Dr. Cornelius stood staring down stupidly at the dear face on the pillow. He would have liked to send Hester away, but the words would not come to him. She talked on, sobbing and exclamatory—

" She went off that sudden in the end, sir ! Thursday night it was, as you know, sir, and the mistress would have her reception as usual. She's set in her ways, and Miss Harrie could get but the one word from her—she must do this, or the wedding was not to be. I dressed her with these old hands, sir, an' gave her an arm down the stair. The mistress kept her long at it—till near eleven, an' Miss Harrie was faint-like when I gave her my support up the stair again. But never a word of complaint, sir, an' she would have no great attention from me. Since ever she was ill, sir, I've slept on the floor beside her on a shakedown like—an' last night, what with grief and anxiety, I was wakeful. I heard her cough late on in the night, and rose up in a great haste. The blood came in a stream from her lips that very moment, an' I thought to see her die with never a word. I daren't leave to call the mistress, and she fell back like death into my arms. Her lips moved, an', begging your pardon, sir, these was the words she said : ' Tell my dear Cornelius,' says she, ' that he will see me again.' ' Harrie my dear,' says I (forgetting the Miss, sir, for she was like my own), ' if I can leave you, dearie, for a minute, I'll send Silence for Dr. Hallijohn.' But she said, ' No ; too late, Hester,' an' closed her eyes. She spoke but the once again. She said, ' *New and strange, the entering a new life,*' and then, suddenlike, stretched out her arms with such a smile ! 'Tis on her lips yet, sir. I looked over my shoulder to see who was come in, but the room was empty as you see it, an' with that she fell back on my arm."

Hester paused, expecting some comment, some word of expression of grief from her listener. But he gave none, only stood gazing down stonily at the dead body of the woman he loved. Hester began again : " You see, sir "—

" Go away, Hester," said Dr. Cornelius, finding words at last ; and with a dim sense of the profundity of his grief, Hester tiptoed across the creaking floor, and left him alone with the dead.

Dr. Cornelius had ridden up quickly to Balgowrie, and, as he stood there, could feel the warm blood pulsing through his heart. Ah, the cruel contrast ! He laid his strong glowing hand on Henrietta's, as if trying to waken her from that stupid, impassive sleep, to chase away from her lips that smile that was not for him. Then, falling on his knees beside the bed, he cried out in his despairing grief.

" Harrie, Harrie, come back ! It cannot be you've left me without a word ! "

The great, unanswering silence fell. He rose to his feet again with a gesture almost of anger.

" Fifty years I've lived in a dying world," he said bitterly, " and at the end of it I try to waken the dead ! " Bending down, he kissed Henrietta's smiling lips : " Good-bye, good-bye, and good-bye," he said. " I might have known."

XXXIII

MRS. MARJORYBANKS did not long delay poor Henrietta's obsequies.

" Pray arrange the matter as swiftly as may be," she said to Dr. Cornelius. " These remains of frail humanity are best consigned to the dust." She also signified to him her wish that he should dispose as he thought best of all Henrietta's small possessions. " You are as good as her husband," she added, " so do what you will with her goods, as you could not have her person."

Hester sobbingly fell heir to all her young mistress's wardrobe—those strangely-fashioned garments. The more personal possessions—books and papers, all the paraphernalia of a studious life—Dr, Cornelius took down to the Manse.

In Henrietta's writing-case he had found a letter addressed to himself, written on the Thursday afternoon before her death.

"DEAREST CORNELIUS,—Something makes me write this. If I am happily married to you on Monday, I shall tear it up ; if not, it will come to your hands. I should like Hester to have my dear Lucie's work-box—because I think it is more natural and cheerful to use things which belonged at one time to those who are gone than simply to lay them by. You would have no use for it, so pray give it to Hester. There is a book of Lucie's pencil drawings, on which she bestowed great pains, will you take it ?—also you will find the bit of embroid-ery which was her last work. I could not part from it. 'Tis in my bureau drawer. Pray have the goodness to send it to Mrs. Pelham when you write to her, which you will do soon I feel sure. Along with the embroidery, return to her the bundle of letters written to me during many years by dear Maggie Pelham, whom I never saw in this world, but whom I hope to hold converse with in the unknown Splendour where Time is forgot. You, my dear Cornelius,—almost my dear husband,—will take all my own books—the books which, since my childhood, you have yourself given to me at intervals. My name is written in them all. Also all my papers—the ridiculous translation of Herodotus, which runs to some 100 pages of MS., and the verses on various subjects, which may interest you. That is all. Ah, I had almost forgot ! Will you take dear Lucie's lark,—the one she had so long,—or do you think it had better be given its liberty ? As you think best. Her pigeons, I fear, would not leave the doo-cote, or I would have asked you also to care for them. Silence is not careful of them. He says ' many a good hen's meat ' is wasted on them ! Perhaps he will be more tender of them now.

"You will sometimes visit my poor mother, will you not, Cornelius ?

"And yourself—I can't write—I could never say all the love I have towards you—dear father and lover in one—so I shall not try. Ah, comfort yourself ! And do not use too much bad language at ' cruel Fate.' I never liked the habit. I must be done.   You see I am become flippant, because after all it strikes me I may tear this up on Monday.—My dear heart, farewell: ever yours,   HENRIETTA."

This simple disposition of Henrietta's affairs was easily carried out.   It took Dr. Cornelius only an hour's work to gather together the few possessions mentioned, and consign each to the person Henrietta had indicated.   He did this the day before the funeral, for, in spite of Henrietta's request that he should sometimes visit her mother, he felt that it would be almost impossible for him to do so.   Mrs. Marjorybanks had virtually murdered Henrietta : that was a fact he could never forget.   In his excelling wrath and bitterness towards her, he could scarcely bring himself to address her, even on the arrangements necessary for the funeral.   Even the poor woman's manifest irresponsibility could not soften the hard indignation he felt.   When all was over, he said, when Henrietta's last behests were fulfilled, then he would turn his back on Balgowrie and its mistress for ever.   She might die alone as she had chosen to live, unloved and forgotten ; reaping what she had sowed.

Henrietta's writing-case was filled with fragmentary compositions—translations from Latin and from Greek, essays on philosophical subjects, poems, ideas jotted down for future use—all the first-fruits of a growing mind jumbled together without design.   The poems were dated, and began many years previously.   The last, bearing date of 17th October, seemed strangely significant to Dr. Cornelius as he read it—

"HER GRAVE.

"O grave ! O grave !—when next the spring comes here,
    Thy turf shall waken as the blue days pass
    To buds and bells and blades of springing grass,
Whose life is from the earth that now is sere.
But the sweet haste of the revolving year
    Brings not my love to me—with buds and grass.
    The form that held the soul I loved, alas !
Is dust in dust—and will not reappear.
O faithless heart ! dumb witnesses they tell
Of the great certainty that satisfies !
Life cannot end—so love knows no farewell.

At last—one day—that comes like spring's surprise
To winter earth—the soul above the swell
Of death's dismay shall rise, shall rise, shall rise ! "

He folded up the paper and laid it away with a groan.

The funeral was most elemental in its simplicity, resolving itself into what, after all, a funeral really is, however much ceremony attends it,—the burying of a dead body. This was Mrs. Marjorybanks' idea of what funerals should be : she would permit of no empty forms in her house. In arranging matters with Dr. Cornelius, she merely said, " You will come at any hour you think fit to-morrow to remove Henrietta's body." Nor did she notice or understand the involuntary shudder he gave at the words.

A very small company assembled in the churchyard the next day. Dr. Cornelius, Silence, James, and the sexton lowered the coffin into the grave, and Hester and Mrs. Allan stood sobbing beside it. Mrs. Marjorybanks had not expressed any desire to be present and Dr. Cornelius had not urged her to come. There had been no prayer at Balgowrie, and the little company of mourners waited for the minister to give it at the grave. The formula of his funeral prayer was well known. The sexton, in the pause that followed the lowering of the coffin, had almost prompted Dr. Cornelius with the familiar words. He coughed slightly instead, and fidgeted, to signify that the time was come.

" O Almighty God "—began Dr. Cornelius ; and there the often-repeated form of words deserted him, and he stood dumbly looking from one to another of the little group standing round the grave. They were all sorrowing with him, and this knowledge broke through conventions.

" I cannot pray," he said simply. " You know that I have lost my all," He signed to them to fill in the grave, and turned away.

The men worked quickly and silently, with only an expressive glance and grunt to each other over their work. Hester and Mrs. Allan moved slowly away, and as the afternoon shadows began to gather, Dr. Cornelius was left alone. He came back to stand beside the grave which had closed over his hope. And from behind a sullen wall of cloud that had covered the sky all day, the sun came out for a moment just before it set, a great scarlet world of flaming, triumphing glory. It blazed across the autumn land in a flood of red light, and smote with its level beams across the eyes of the man standing alone beside the newly-made grave.

"Great God," he cried, raising his face towards the sky, "it's a splendid world! And we're crushed down like worms into its dust as surely as we aspire to a little hope or a moments joy."

Then, pointing down at the grave as if calling it to witness, "And shall the dust praise Thee? look at the souls Thou hast made, and tortured, and brought down to the dust again!"

He turned away and took his heavy way homewards. The sun sank behind the clouds as suddenly as it had appeared, and dusk fell over the world like a mantle.

Dr. Cornelius did not look to the right hand or to the left. He walked in at his own gate without closing it behind him, and through the hall into the study. The room seemed full of the absent presence. He flung himself down into the arm-chair by the fire and rang the bell.

"Bring me a bottle of brandy, James," he said.

The order was soon obeyed. He poured out a glass with a bitter smile on his lips.

"I'll drink myself drunk. I'll sleep like a hog, and waken and drink again. I've a cellarful of good French brandy, and I'll play the deuce with it before the year is out. I'll drink myself mad, and then I'll forget for a time. I'll drink myself into my grave, and then I'll forget for ever. Oh, I'll die a jolly death—that's in my own hand—no fate can rob me of that. I'm damned if I'll be sober once for the next six weeks. We'll see what that will do for me!"

He raised the glass to his lips, half drained it, then lay back in his chair with closed eyes, to feel the hot tickle of the liquor as it stole through him.

There came to him then, out of the shadows at the far end of the room, a well-remembered figure in a quaint, childish gown. This little visitor stood still, saying in a trembling voice, "'Tis very dark, sir"—and "Dark it is, Harrie—the darkness that cannot lift," he said, answering her out of the gloom that covered him. Then by that mysterious process which goes on in dreams (or visions, or whatever they are), the child, as she advanced towards him, grew and grew—first into Harrie—("Dear Harrie!" he cried, stretching out arms of love to her)—then into someone white and wonderful; the dead Harrie he had kissed, but alive, radiant—a soul whose conflicts were past. She stood beside him and spoke the words he had spoken in bitterness over her grave—

"*The dust shall praise Him, Cornelius—the grave and pain and loss shall praise Him. All I could never do . . . all you have left undone—my work and your own, and the time is short.*"

She seemed to pass beside him, just letting her hand rest for a moment on his grey head at the last words. He turned in his chair to clasp her hand, and wakened to the silent, empty room, the blazing fire, and the half-drained glass of brandy.

The impulse of all sane men is to laugh at dreams. Perhaps Dr. Cornelius was hardly sane at the moment,—grief and sleepless nights may have wrought upon his usually steady brain, for he rose to his feet with a great oath.

"By Hell and Judgment, and the love I bore this woman, I'll never touch it again!" he cried.

Some memory of long ago stirred in him. He caught up the wine-glass and cast it down on to the hearthstone, just as Henrietta, an impulsive child, had broken his Dutch bottle there years before. Dr. Cornelius had spoken and acted half-dreamingly, now at the splintering of the glass he started broad awake.

"Harrie, Harrie, you're gone!" he exclaimed, gazing round the empty, firelit room, where only a moment before, clear as day, Henrietta had passed by him. In the intolerable silence that followed his words, her voice seemed still to speak.

"*My work and your own, and the time is short,*" it repeated again, and yet again. He sat down and listened to that insistent whisper, telling him to live and work in a world where love was no more. It spoke in Henrietta's tones, and breathed the spirit of her whole life—strenuous—aspiring —at war with circumstance that hedged her in on every hand, but fighting forward, hopeful and heroic.

The fire died to ashes, the slow hours passed, and Dr. Cornelius still sat on. He reviewed the wasted past, the lonely present, the dark future—a sorry company. And then of a sudden he cried out with a loud voice, "It's God! it's God!"

He had caught sight of the purpose of this heavy stroke that was fallen upon him—had felt the touch of that mighty Hand which moulds each man to his destined shape by processes of terribly individual pressure. And at the sight Shame and Humility and Hope came rushing into his heart— a crowd of gentle guests.

"No other thing would have done it. I doubt if I'm worth it. Yet . . . O God, save my soul!"

XXXIV

ON a beautiful June day, thirty years—yes, fully thirty years—after Henrietta's death, Dr. Cornelius sat in his garden reading. A very old man now with, snow-white hair and stooping gait.

He had just laid down his book, and was looking round the sweet, blooming, bee-haunted garden, when he saw the gate open, and a man and woman advanced to where he sat. The woman came forward, smiling and holding out her hand.

"I must recall myself to your remembrance, sir, I fear," she said; but paused, as if to give Dr. Cornelius time to recognise her.

She was an elderly woman, with the remains of great beauty, and carrying herself as only women who have been much admired can do.

"My dear lady," said Dr. Cornelius, rising slowly, "I

fear I am grown both blind and dull with the creeping years. May I ask ? " —

" Do you remember Maggie Pelham ? " she asked, with just that winning smile she used to bear.

" Ah ! ah ! " said Dr. Cornelius, drawing in his breath as if a remembrance stabbed him.   He held out both hands to Maggie, gazing into her face.

" I have brought my husband to see you," said Maggie. " I had never been in Scotland before, but I was resolved to see you when I came, and to see the place I have so often heard about from Henrietta and Lucie Marjorybanks."

Thirty years of life and experience had not changed Maggie Pelham's warm heart.   As she spoke their names, her kind eyes filled with tears.   She grasped Dr. Cornelius by the hand, and stood gazing round the garden and up at the house, and then back again at the old man beside her.

" So this is the place, and they are gone, and you are still here ? " she said at last.   " It seems to me like a dream that I should come here to see it all ! "

" Sit down, madam—sit down," said Dr. Cornelius, offering her a seat beside his own.

There was a moment's silence, and he passed his hand over his eyes before he spoke again.

" Yes, I am still here," he said slowly.   " I have lived long after man's allotted time on earth."

" Are you pleased to live so long ? " asked Maggie's husband.

He was an elderly man, of rather eccentric address.   His very bright eyes seemed to be always on the alert for observation.

Maggie smiled indulgently, and turned to Dr. Cornelius.

" You must pardon my husband, sir ; he is for ever asking questions."

" 'Tis the best way to come at conclusions, madam.   And now I must ask your pardon for a moment before I answer this question, for I have clean forgot your married name ! "

" Oh, our name is Balderstone, sir," said Maggie, laughing.

"I remember writing to tell you of our marriage very long ago—'tis no wonder our name has escaped you."

"Ah, I remember!   Now, sir, I shall answer your question I would willingly have done with life now; but there seems still so much for me to accomplish and fulfil in it, that I do not complain of this 'long disease of living.'"

"So, so," said Balderstone interestedly.   "I had feared that life lost its grip in extreme old age."

"Come, John, I will not listen further to your disserta- tions on life," said Maggie.   "I am come here to speak about human beings.   Go away and philosophise by yourself, if you will, while I talk of old times with Dr. Hallijohn."

"Ah, you wish to be alone, Maggie? you find me in the way," he said, rising laughingly.   "Well, I'll walk round the garden while you talk."

Maggie and Dr. Cornelius watched his figure disappear down the hedge-bordered path before they spoke.

"Happy, my dear?" he asked, wasting no time on subjects of indifferent interest.

"Ah, dear Dr. Hallijohn! happier than I have words for! We are so unlike, we have always been so unlike! And when first we married we were so delightfully poor, for I would not take money from mother, and he had none.   Now, alas! I have all of hers since she has left me.   But perhaps it is well to have money when we are elderly—it is not like one's young days.   And the children—I have three sons and one daughter.   Ah, my sons are great grown men by this time—the eldest is five-and-twenty this year.   They have filled my heart with happiness till it can hold no more."

"I have often thought of you, and wondered how life went with you," said Dr. Cornelius.

"I fear I am one of the people who get all the good things of this world," said Maggie, in a sober tone.   "I often think I have too much."

"It is not every one who needs trial; there are souls that live always in the light," said Dr. Cornelius.

"But here I am speaking only of myself, sir.   Ah, I have so much to speak of with you!   Tell me, how did Mrs.

Marjorybanks die ?   You sent my mother an intimation of
her death, but did not write of it to her."

"That is an old story.   Twenty years ago she died—ten
years after Henrietta.   She became more and more peculiar,
and died most suddenly, in some sort of attack from the brain.
I never saw her again after the day of my poor Harrie's funeral.
Madam, I did wrongly ; but to this day, had I it in my power
again, I should do the same !   For she killed Henrietta.   I
could not forgive her."

"Ah, it was sad—sad !   Do you know, sir, though I never
saw Henrietta, I loved her so strangely ?   I have every letter
she ever wrote to me.   I read some of them over again but
the other day.   Such clever letters !   She used to just write
out her soul in them, and her life into them.   The world
felt empty to me for a while after she left it."

"She was by herself," said Dr. Cornelius musingly.

"And Lucie—dear Lucie !   I knew and loved her.   I
shall never forget the morning we parted at the docks.   I
knew in my heart somehow that we would never see her again.
Ah, the dear, pretty, quaint-mannered child that she was in
these far-away days ! "

"Can you tell me what became of that fellow Charteris ? "
asked Dr. Cornelius, sitting forward eagerly, with a reminiscence of youthfulness in his voice.

Maggie laughed.   "Yes, sir, indeed I can.   This is what
I know of Dan Charteris," said Maggie, in a tone of the
deepest satisfaction.   "Perhaps you remember, sir, that I
was good-looking in my youth ?   Ah, well, Dan Charteris
knew it, and so did I.   When I heard of Lucie's death, I took
my resolution.   There is much in woman's feeble hand
sometimes.   I led that man on, sir, with my every art, and I
had many in these days, till he was mad with love.   I had him
tied to my apron-strings for months.   One day he offered me
his fine hand, and finer heart.   I made him my best curtsey.
' You have not much to offer me, sir,' I said ; ' but had you all
the riches of this world, I would not have you.'   He was mad
with love for me.   He swore and prayed by turns, and told
me I had been false, and had played fast and loose with him.

At that I gave him one more curtsey. 'I thought you had played fast and loose with too many people yourself, sir, to imagine that I was in earnest,' I said, and then held out my hand to him, saying, ' Come, Dan, we are old friends ; let us remain such, with no more of these high words. Come, let us change the subject. Did my mother inform you of the sad news we had from Scotland of the death of my friend Henrietta Marjorybanks ? She has not been very long of following her dear sister. 'Twas Lucie was your special friend, was it not ? " Well, I never saw Dan Charteris enter our door again, and did not regret the fact ? He married next year. I never see him now."

" I fear revenge is a horrid passion, madam, but you did well—you did well ! " said Dr. Cornelius.

" And what came of ' Hester ' and ' Silence ' ?—such familiar names to me ! " asked Maggie.

" Silence left the place at Mrs. Marjorybanks' death ; Hester came to my service, and lived some years here before her death. She was the last link with Balgowrie. I felt more alone after good Hester died. The sadness of old age, madam, lies in this, that we so often survive all those persons who were part of life when we were young."

" I should like, sir, to see Balgowrie beyond everything. It is shut up, is it not ? Would it be possible for me to go through it ? " asked Maggie.

Dr. Cornelius rose with sudden energy.

" Ah, my dear madam. Ah, what a pleasure to speak with someone to whom their memory is dear ! I cannot walk so far now, but we shall drive to Balgowrie. Will you come indoors till my carriage is ready ? You will perhaps find it interesting to see the house you have heard of so often."

The study had changed very little in thirty years. Maggie stood beside the fire and looked round the room with brimming eyes.

" I feel as if I knew every book here, as if I had often stood here before," she said. " My dear sir, are you not lonely now, in your old age, with no one to care for you but servants ? "

The old man smiled. " No, no, I am not lonely. I am

not alone so much as you suppose, madam. I have the care of all this parish on these old hands. Ah, you are smiling! Yes, I remember the days when I used to take it lightly enough. Now I have doubly to work, remembering these 'years that the locust hath eaten.' But shall I send for your husband to come with us to Balgowrie?" he said, turning the conversation hastily away from his own affairs.

"Yes, indeed, if you can find him," said Maggie.

An hour later they all stood together on the Balgowrie steps. Dr. Cornelius had sent for the woman who had ostensible charge of the house. She stood on the threshold jingling her rusty keys.

"Are you coming in, sir?" asked Maggie gently.

Dr. Cornelius hesitated for a moment, then shook his head.

"I cannot," he said, and turned away.

When Maggie came down to the door again, after her journey through the old house, Dr. Cornelius was standing on the steps. He did not seem to notice her approach. He stood with his face turned up to the fair summer sky, and spoke to one unseen. Said he—

"The sooner the better, my love, for it grows late."

THE END